A KILLER'S
MIND

OTHER TITLES BY MIKE OMER

GLENMORE PARK MYSTERIES

Spider's Web
Deadly Web
Web of Fear

A KILLER'S
MIND

MIKE OMER

THOMAS & MERCER

Text copyright © 2018 by Michael Omer

Published by Thomas & Mercer, Seattle
www.apub.com

Amazon, the Amazon logo, and Thomas & Mercer are trademarks of Amazon.com, Inc., or its affiliates.

ISBN-13: 9781503901902 (hardcover)
ISBN-10: 1503901904 (hardcover)
ISBN-13: 9781503900745 (paperback)
ISBN-10: 1503900746 (paperback)

Cover design by PEPE *nymi*

Printed in the United States of America

First edition

To Liora, for understanding that serial killers are a valid discussion for our anniversary vacation

CHAPTER 1

Chicago, Illinois, Sunday, July 10, 2016

The sharp scent of formaldehyde filled the room as he poured the liquid into the mixture. He had hated the smell at first. But he'd learned to appreciate it, knowing what it represented: eternity. The embalming fluid kept things from deteriorating. "Till death do us part" was an unambitious concept at best. True love should ascend beyond that point.

He added more salt than the last time, hoping for better results. It was a delicate balance; he'd learned that the hard way. The embalming fluid promised eternity, but the saline solution added flexibility.

A good relationship had to be flexible.

There was a creak beyond the locked door. The noises—a series of irregular squeaking and scraping sounds, intermingled with the girl's labored groans—grated on his nerves. She was trying to untie herself again. Always moving, always trying to get away from him—they were all the same at first. But she'd change; he would make sure of that. There would be no more incessant movement, no muffled begging, no hoarse screams.

She would be quiet and still. And then they would learn to love each other.

A sudden crash broke his concentration. Irritated, he put down the salt and went over to the barred door. He unlocked it and pushed it open. Light spilled into the dark room beyond.

She was lying on the floor, squirming. She had tipped the wooden chair onto its side, and it had broken. Somehow she'd managed to get her feet loose and was pushing herself across the floor on her bare back, trying to . . . what? Leave? There was no leaving. Her naked body was wiggling in a way that made him feel uncomfortable. That, along with her muffled grunts, made her seem more animal than human. This had to stop.

He walked in, grabbed her by the arm, and pulled her to her feet, ignoring her scream. She started thrashing and wriggling.

"Stop that," he said harshly.

She didn't. He nearly hit her then but instead forced himself to breathe deeply several times, unclenching his rigid fist. A bruise wouldn't fade easily from a dead body, and he wanted her reasonably unblemished.

Ideally, he wanted to postpone this moment. With the previous girl, he'd actually had a romantic candlelit dinner just before the transformation. It had been nice.

But not necessary.

He could leave her in the room, but she might hurt herself, scrape her perfect milky skin, and he didn't want that to happen.

Instead, he shoved her into his workshop and sat her down in his own chair. She squirmed, her left foot striking his shin. The foot was bare, the kick painless, but it annoyed him. He grabbed the scalpel from the table and placed the sharp blade on her left breast, just under her nipple.

"If you don't stop moving, I'll cut," he said, his voice cold.

She slumped immediately, trembling in fear. Her submissiveness excited him, a sweet moment of foreplay, and his heart raced faster. He was already falling in love.

He gently picked up the noose he had prepared beforehand from the table. He was happy with the rope's texture. Previously, he had used a regular cotton rope and had hated the mark it left. The friction had marred the perfect skin. This time he would use a synthetic all-purpose rope. The texture was smooth, pleasant. He thought she might like its touch.

He placed it around her throat. As she sensed the silky rope tightening on her neck, she began thrashing again, but it was too late for any of that.

The noose was a simple slipknot with one tiny change. He had wedged a slim metal bar inside the knot. Now he slid the knot until the noose was tight around her throat—tight enough that it wouldn't move around. He wanted only one mark, not more. Then, grasping the metal bar, he turned it clockwise. One twist, two twists, three twists—the noose gripped her neck tighter and tighter. Her thrashing became even wilder, and one of her feet hit the table violently, leaving a bruise for sure. One final twist . . . it was enough.

As her thrashing weakened, he considered the mark the noose would leave. Initially, he had wished there would be no mark at all. But he now thought of it as his first gift, a beautiful necklace to signify their bond. Regular people used a ring around a finger. No wonder the divorce rate was so high.

When the squirming stopped, he trembled with excitement. He really should start working on her. The faster he got the embalming mixture into her body, the fresher she would be.

But he was overcome by desire.

He decided he could have a bit of fun first.

CHAPTER 2

Dale City, Virginia, Thursday, July 14, 2016

Zoe Bentley sat up in the darkness, a scream wedged in her throat, her fingers clutching the bedsheet. Her body shook slightly, and her heart thrummed in her chest. Her relief at realizing she was in her bedroom was palpable. *Just another nightmare.* She had known it would come when she'd gone to sleep. The nightmares always came back when she got the brown envelopes in the mail.

She hated herself for being so easily manipulated, so weak.

She picked up her phone from the nightstand and checked the time. The bright light of the screen made her blink, spots dancing in her vision. Twenty-one minutes past four. *Damn it.* It was just early enough to start the day rather than having a chance to coax herself back to sleep. It would be a seven-cups-of-coffee kind of day. No way she could manage with her usual five.

She got up and untangled herself from the blanket. She had managed to twist it several times around her waist during the night. She turned on the light, blinking. Through the window, she watched the building opposite hers, still shrouded in the night's darkness. All its windows were dark. She was one of the first on the street to wake up—an undesirable achievement. She looked at the messy bed, the clothes on the floor, the scattered books on her nightstand. Chaos, in her mind and out of it.

Zoe, open the door. Can't stay in there forever, Zoe. And then that giggle, the sound of a man consumed by need.

She shuddered and shook her head. She was thirty-three years old, damn it. She wasn't a child anymore. When would her memories release their hold on her?

Probably never. The past had a way of sinking its roots deep inside. She, of all people, should know that. How many of her subjects had been permanently scarred and changed by their own pasts?

She plodded into the bathroom, discarding her shirt and underwear on the floor behind her. The water of the shower cleared her head, helped her to shake loose the last threads of sleep. The shampoo bottle was empty. She filled it with some water to get the dregs and came up with nothing. She had used this trick yesterday—and three days ago. If she wanted shampoo, she'd have to buy some. She let the water caress her skin a bit more. Refreshed, she walked out of the shower, thinking, *Add shampoo to shopping list. Add shampoo to shopping list.* She rummaged through the clothes on the floor, finding nothing she wanted to wear. Opening the closet, she located a blue button-down shirt and black pants and put them on. *Add shampoo to shopping list.* She combed her auburn hair impatiently, stopping once the worst tangles were gone. *Add shampoo to shopping list.*

She plodded to the kitchen and switched on the light. Her eyes immediately focused on the king of the kitchen: the coffee machine. She walked over and picked up the jar of Colombian ground coffee that stood next to it. She never ran out of coffee, not since the debacle back in the summer of 2011. Two filters went in the machine to make it stronger. She needed an aggressive caffeine jolt to get her going in the morning. She put a small mountain of coffee inside the filters, then added a bit more. She poured the water on top and turned the machine on, watching the beautiful sight of coffee trickling into the pot.

While she waited for the liquid of life to brew, she walked to the shopping list on the fridge door and stared at it. There was something she had to add. Finally, she wrote down *toilet paper*. It was a safe bet; she was always running out of toilet paper. She returned to the machine and poured the coffee into her favorite, albeit chipped, white mug, ignoring the row of unused mugs on the shelf. They had been exiled from use for being too small or too large or having a thick lip or an uncomfortable grip. The coffee mug hall of shame.

She sipped the brew, inhaling as she did. She stood next to the machine, just drinking and enjoying the feeling of coffee spreading through her body, until the mug was empty.

One. Six more to go.

The brown envelope lay on the wooden kitchen table, the gray strip of cloth protruding from it. She had discarded it there the night before, as if trying to prove to herself that she didn't care, that it didn't matter anymore.

Now, in the darkness of early morning, it seemed like a stupid thing to have done. She picked up the envelope and walked over to her home office, where her desk was. She gathered her courage and opened the desk's bottom drawer, the one that she almost always kept closed.

A small stack of similar envelopes lay inside. She shoved the newest envelope onto the pile, crumpled it, and slammed the drawer shut. She felt better. She walked back into the kitchen, her steps a bit lighter.

As the clutches of the nightmare faded, she realized she was starving. Here was the one good thing about waking up early: she had ample time to make herself some breakfast. She cracked two eggs into the frying pan, let them sizzle, put a piece of bread in the toaster. She decided she deserved a dollop of cream cheese on her plate as well. She smiled as she slid the eggs out of the frying pan and laid them gently on the plate. Both yolks remained unbroken. A win for Zoe Bentley. She cut the toast into triangles, then carefully dipped one of them in the round yellow yolk and bit into it.

Exquisite. How could a simple egg taste so good? And the thing to really go with this breakfast was a cup of coffee. She poured herself another one.

Two.

She glanced at her phone again. Five thirty. Still too early to go to work. But the thought of staying in this silent apartment, with the envelope lurking in the drawer, was unpleasant.

If I need to break this door, you'll regret it, Zoe.

The hell with it. She could do some paperwork. Chief Mancuso would be happy.

She went downstairs and slid into her cherry-colored Ford Fiesta. She switched the engine on and put on Taylor Swift's *Red*, fast-forwarding to "All Too Well." Taylor's voice and guitar filled the car's small interior, soothing Zoe's frayed nerves. She could always count on Taylor to make it all better.

The streets of Dale City were nearly empty. The sky was still dark, and a shade of dark blue signified the approaching sunrise. Zoe enjoyed the silence as she drove down Dale Boulevard. Maybe she should start waking up every day at four in the morning. She had the world to herself. Just her and the bastard trucker who cut in ahead of her, forcing her to slow down. Taylor's song was now mixed with the torrent of curses that Zoe hurled into the open air, honking furiously. The trucker sped on.

She got on I-95 and drove south as Taylor switched to "22." Zoe pressed the gas pedal, relishing the acceleration. She cranked up the volume and sang along, her head rocking slightly with the song's cheerful beat. Life was pretty good after all. She'd make herself a third cup of coffee when she got to work, she decided. Those three cups should carry her until lunchtime. She got off on Fuller Road, the road signs to Quantico leading the way.

She parked her car in the nearly empty parking lot, a small smattering of other cars dotting her surroundings. A short walk, an ID card flipped at the entrance, two flights of stairs, and she was in her office. The silence of the entire floor was a bit disconcerting. The FBI's Behavioral Analysis Unit was hardly a noisy place even in the middle of the day, but she could usually hear agents talking in the corridor or the occasional hurried footsteps passing by her doorway. Today, it was all quiet except for the hum of the air-conditioning. She sat down in front of her computer, preparing herself mentally for the weekly report she knew Mancuso would demand as soon as she arrived. Zoe was required to turn in a weekly report every Monday, summarizing her previous week's work. She typically handed it over on the following Friday, by which time Mancuso would have threatened to send her back to Boston. But today would be different. For once, she'd have the report ready on Thursday, only three days late, freeing her from this bureau-cratic nightmare until next week. Zoe smiled as she started typing it in.

The phone on her desk jolted her awake. She gazed in confusion at her monitor, where the words *Weekly Report July 4–8, 2016* remained orphaned, with no report following. She must have fallen asleep trying to think of how to start. The time on the bottom right of the monitor was 9:12 a.m. So much for getting an early start. She answered her phone, rotating her head in an attempt to relieve the pain in her neck. "BAU, this is Bentley."

"Zoe," Mancuso's voice said. "Good morning. Can you drop by my office? There's something I want you to have a look at."

"Sure. On my way."

The unit chief's office was four doors down the corridor. The bronze plaque on the door read **UNIT CHIEF CHRISTINE MANCUSO**. Zoe knocked on the door, and Mancuso immediately called her in.

Zoe sat down in the visitor's chair across from the desk. Mancuso sat on the other side of the desk, her chair turned sideways. She was staring in deep concentration at the aquarium that stood against the rear wall. She was an impressive-looking woman, her tawny skin smooth and hardly touched by age, her black hair pulled back, silvery-white strands intermingled in it. She faced sideways, and the beauty mark by her lips pointed directly at Zoe.

Zoe looked at the object of the chief's fascination. The aquarium's interior changed often, matching Mancuso's whims. It was currently designed to look like a lush forest, clusters of aquatic plants coloring the water green and turquoise. Swarms of yellow, orange, and purple fish swam lazily this way and that.

"Something up with the fish?" Zoe asked.

"Belinda is depressed today," Mancuso muttered. "I think she's upset Timothy is swimming with Rebecca and Jasmine."

"Well . . . maybe Timothy just needed some time off," Zoe suggested.

"Timothy's a bastard."

"Right . . . uh, you wanted to see me?"

Mancuso turned her chair and faced Zoe. "You know Lionel Goodwin, the analyst?"

"He's the one who always complains everyone is stealing his food."

"He's a part of the Highway Serial Killings Initiative."

Zoe took a moment to remember what that was. A disturbing pattern of women's bodies discarded along interstate highways had emerged over the past ten years. Analysts in the FBI had found some common ground for the murders. The victims were mostly prostitutes or drug users; the suspects were predominantly long-haul truck drivers. To try to match specific patterns to suspects, the FBI had launched the Highway Serial Killings Initiative. They would search for similar crimes on ViCAP, the FBI's database of violent crimes, then try to match them to routes and timelines of the suspects.

"Okay," Zoe said, nodding.

"He thinks he's found a pattern, and he's matched it to a group of possible suspects."

"That's great," Zoe said. "What do you need me to—"

"The group consists of two hundred seventeen truckers."

"Ah."

Mancuso opened a drawer, took out a thick folder, and slammed it on the table.

"Are these the suspects?" Zoe asked.

"Oh, no," Mancuso said. "Those are just the crime files from the various police departments involved." She took out two additional folders and put them on top of the first one. "These are the suspects."

"You want me to narrow it down?" Zoe asked.

"Yes, please." Mancuso smiled. "If you can give me a group of ten suspects by the end of next week, that would be great."

Zoe nodded, excitement rising within her. It was the first real-time profiling she'd been asked to do since she'd joined the Behavioral Analysis Unit. Narrowing a group of 217 suspects down to 10 in a *month* would be a difficult job. Could she do it in a week?

She could. This was what she did best.

"Oh, and the weekly report . . . do you have it ready?" Mancuso asked, her voice growing thorns. "You should have submitted it on—"

"Almost done," Zoe said. "I just need to add a few last notes."

"Send it to me by lunchtime."

Zoe nodded and got up. She picked up the three folders and left Mancuso's office. Walking back toward her own office, she was already flipping the top folder open. The first page was a crime report describing the body of a nineteen-year-old girl found in a ditch in Missouri, along I-70. She was naked and bruised in multiple places, with bite marks on her neck. Zoe was trying to flip to the next page when she ran into a man. Her folder rammed his stomach, and he emitted a surprised *ooof*.

He was tall, with wide shoulders and a mane of jet-black hair. His eyes were brown and deep, hidden under thick dark eyebrows. He looked like an older version of a smug college boy on a football scholarship. He placed his palm on his stomach, a half smile on his face. Zoe was instantly irritated with him, as if it were his fault she'd crashed into him.

"Sorry," she said, bending to pick up the folders that had dropped on the floor.

"Don't worry about it," he said and crouched to help her.

She snatched the last folder from the floor before he could touch it. "I've got it—thanks."

"I see that," he said, his grin widening as he stood up. "I don't think we've met. I'm Tatum Gray."

"Okay," Zoe said distractedly, trying to organize the folders in her hands.

"Do you have a name, or do I need a higher security clearance to know it?" Tatum asked.

"I'm Zoe," she said. "Zoe Bentley."

CHAPTER 3

Tatum gave Zoe a cursory look. At first, he only noticed her angular nose and the way she wrinkled it in irritation when he asked what her name was. But then she raised her face and looked straight at him, and he almost took a step back. Her eyes were light green and intense. He felt like she could look into his brain and pick at his thoughts as if browsing a bookstore. The nose and eyes together almost gave the impression of a bird of prey, but the effect was broken by a sweet, delicate mouth. Her hair was cut just above her shoulders, and a few strands were in her face, the result of their collision. She tossed her head back in a careless manner he found quite charming, removed the offending hairs from her eyes, and smiled thinly at him.

"Well, it was nice meeting you, Tatum," she said and turned to leave.

"Hang on," he said. "Can you tell me where Chief"—it took him a moment to recall the name—"Mancuso's office is?"

She glanced down the corridor. "Three doors down," she said.

"Are you a part of the BAU?" he asked.

"I'm a consultant," she said, and he could almost hear the defensiveness in her tone. Her eyes narrowed, as if she expected a snide remark.

"Oh, right." He recalled someone telling him about her. "You're the psychologist from Boston."

"That's me," she said. "And you're the agent from LA."

"Yeah," he said, surprised. "You know about me?"

"There was an email yesterday," Zoe said. "Please welcome Agent Tatum Gray, assigned to us from the field office in LA, and so on and so forth."

"Oh, right," Tatum said again and smiled. This woman made him feel distinctly uncomfortable. "Well . . . see you around, Zoe."

She strode on, carrying her heavy-looking folders. Tatum stared after her, momentarily entranced. Then he realized he was standing in the corridor, essentially watching a woman's ass as she walked away from him. He quickly turned around, went to Chief Mancuso's door, and knocked on it.

"Yeah?"

He opened the door. Christine Mancuso, the new unit chief, sat behind her desk, framed by a huge aquarium in the back of the room. He had asked around about Mancuso. She had quite a record in the Boston field office. After managing the task force on a very public kidnapping case, she had been promoted to unit chief in the BAU. There was a lot of resentment about this. The assistant section chief had wanted to promote someone from within the unit but had apparently been ordered to assign Mancuso instead, and she'd immediately begun changing protocols and assignments. Even worse, she'd brought in a civilian as a consultant.

"Chief Mancuso?" he said. "I'm Tatum Gray."

"Come in," she said and gestured at the chair in front of her. Tatum closed the door and sat down. He found his eyes were repeatedly drawn to the beauty mark by the chief's lips.

"So . . ." she said, opening a folder on her desk. "Special Agent Gray, from the Los Angeles field office."

"That's me," he said, smiling.

"Recently promoted after the *successful* conclusion of a yearlong pedophile ring case." The way she emphasized the word "successful" made it sound less than successful—almost unsuccessful, in fact, which Tatum resented.

"Just doing my job."

"Did you? Your chief didn't see it in the exact same light. And I see there's a possible pending internal affairs investigation . . ." She flipped a page and appeared to read it, though Tatum guessed she knew it well. He felt a sliver of rage growing in his gut.

She put down the folder. "Let's lay our cards on the table. You were promoted because this was a high-profile case."

"Must sound familiar."

She tensed up.

Nice work, Tatum. Less than five minutes, and your superior already hates you.

"But it wasn't really a promotion," Mancuso continued, her voice steely. "They just wanted you out of there, somewhere you can't do much harm. Behind a desk in the BAU, looking at pictures of crime scenes."

Tatum said nothing. Mancuso was right. This was essentially what they'd told him behind closed doors when they'd "promoted" him.

"And you were assigned to me," she continued, "because I'm the new unit chief, and it's fun to mess with me."

He shrugged. He didn't bother with upper-management politics and couldn't care less where Mancuso stood in the pecking order.

"I'm not going to let you sit behind a desk and look at crime scenes," Mancuso said. "That would be a waste."

Tatum said nothing, unsure of where this was going.

Mancuso pushed another folder toward him. He leaned forward, picked it up, and opened it. The top image was of a girl standing on a wooden bridge above a stream, staring at the water, her eyes vacant. Her skin seemed strange, pallid.

"This is Monique Silva, a prostitute from Chicago," Mancuso said. "She was found dead in Humboldt Park a week ago. As you can see, she's posed as if she's staring at the water."

"Dead?" Tatum frowned and looked at the image. The girl looked very lifelike. "How—"

"She was embalmed," Mancuso said. "The medical examiner says she'd been dead for five to seven days before her body was found. She went missing two weeks ago, according to her pimp. She's the second victim to turn up that way. Because of the public places these girls are left in and the way they're posed, this has become a very public case. The Chicago PD is under a lot of pressure to find the killer. Enough to ask for our help."

"What's the Chicago field office saying?"

"The bureau's field agents in Chicago have their hands full at the moment. A large arrest of Latin Kings members is about to take place soon."

Tatum nodded. The Latin Kings was a huge street gang with bases of operations across the country. The top brass of the Latin Kings were located in Chicago.

"While the Chicago field office would be interested to help in the matter of this killer, it has been decided that their resources were better allocated elsewhere."

Tatum's bullshit decoder decrypted the sentence to "Someone on top decided that they should keep their nose out of this. They are shitting themselves in rage."

He sighed, looking up at her. "What do you want me to do?"

"I want you to go there tomorrow. Talk to the lead police detective, see exactly where the investigation is going, and report to me. Then we'll decide how to move forward."

"Do I report to the Chicago field office as well or . . ."

"It would be best if you let me handle that."

"Okay," Tatum said. He would be happy to leave *that* political tiptoe dance to someone more capable. This assignment would mean a weekend in Chicago, but he didn't mind. He'd never been to Chicago before.

"Agent Gray, the FBI is there to *consult*. I don't want to hear that you took over the case or in any way behaved as if you were in charge. We're working hard to get the police to trust us enough to ask for our assistance in future cases. Got that?"

He nodded. "Got it, Chief."

"Anything else?"

"No," he said and got up. "Nice fish."

"Yeah, you want one?"

He looked at her, confused. "You want to give me a fish?"

"I can spare one for your new home," Mancuso said, glancing at her aquarium. "But I'm warning you—he's a bastard."

CHAPTER 4

Zoe unlocked the door to her apartment automatically, her thoughts far away, sifting through crime scene data. She had spent the entire day reading and rereading the cases of the eight murders Mancuso had given her, the two folders of suspects untouched. She should have been faster, she knew, worked harder. But something jarred her, preventing her from carrying on. Some of the details didn't mesh, and she had pored over the evidence trying to home in on them, figure out the problem.

The case had hounded her on her way home, and she had nearly missed her exit off I-95. It was a constant buzz in her head, and she already knew she'd have a hard time falling asleep.

She stepped into the apartment and immediately tensed at a sound from the kitchen.

"Zoe, is that you?" a voice asked.

She relaxed and dropped her shoulder bag by the door. "Hey, Andrea," she called.

Her sister's smiling head popped out of the kitchen's doorway. "Hey," she said. "Are you hungry?"

"Starving."

"I made pasta, so I hope you feel like Italian," Andrea said and disappeared back into the kitchen.

Zoe wanted to say something funny, something about the kind of Italian she wanted. She tried to frame her witty repartee: *Sure, if it's an*

Italian man with a sexy body. But it didn't sound funny at all, not even in her mind. Like most of Zoe's jokes, this one died an early death in her head. Wit was something that happened to other people, and if it happened to Zoe at all, it was usually three hours too late. "Yeah, pasta sounds great," she finally said.

"Awesome," Andrea said happily.

Zoe stepped into the kitchen, then paused. "Holy crap, this is amazing."

Andrea had placed two plates on the checkered tablecloth that hid the ugly square table. Each one was layered with green basil leaves on which a serving of yellowish-white spaghetti was placed. On top of the mouth-watering pasta lay a small slice of salmon with a garlic-spotted light-brown crust.

"I don't deserve this magical meal," Zoe said weakly.

"Sure you do. Come on—dig in. I brought a couple of beers as well."

Zoe sat down and took a bite of the salmon. The crust was paper thin and crispy, and the fish practically melted in her mouth. She closed her eyes and inhaled. It was the first time all day that her mind had emptied completely, and she savored the pure physical joy of eating a wonderful meal.

Andrea placed a bottle of beer in front of her, the glass perspiring, a slice of lemon on top.

"This is like eating in a restaurant," Zoe said.

"I suppose you meant that as a compliment." Andrea smiled at her and swirled her spaghetti around her fork. "So . . . how was work?"

The eight dead girls flooded back into Zoe's mind.

"That bad?" Andrea asked, watching Zoe's face.

"No, no," Zoe said quickly. "It was actually very good. Very interesting. Just . . . intense."

She managed to hook three strands of spaghetti, twirling them around the fork. She topped them with a basil leaf, then sliced a piece of salmon and put the well-crafted bite into her mouth. Sublime. "I'm just looking at some murder cases. Eight girls were discarded in ditches in several states, and we think they may be connected. They all have bite marks on them. All eight were raped vaginally; four were raped anally; two had some teeth missing. But the weird thing is—" She paused.

Andrea took a drink of her beer, her fork discarded on the plate. She looked quite pale.

"Are you okay?" Zoe asked.

"So . . . when I ask you, 'How was work?' I want more stories about how your boss was bitchy or how the printer stopped working. And fewer stories about, uh . . . anal rape and missing teeth."

"I'm sorry," Zoe said. "I just—I was looking through those cases all day, and I didn't think . . ." She cursed herself. She had always been careful to avoid talking about her work with Andrea. She didn't want her sister exposed to this, not again.

"I just don't understand how you can look at these things every day," Andrea said, staring at the table. "Especially considering what happened in Maynard."

Zoe said nothing. It would have been easy to tell her sister that it was her coping mechanism. That "this was how she made sure what happened in Maynard wouldn't happen again" or some other piece of drama. But it would be a lie. She liked what she did. She was good at it. She was very much aware that her past had shaped her, but she wanted to believe that she was over that.

It was better not to discuss her work at all. Protect her sister from that part of her life. As she had always done. As she had done that night long ago.

Don't worry, Ray-Ray. He can't hurt us.

"It's okay." Andrea shook her head. "I mean, this is your job."

Zoe nodded. "Yeah, sorry for mentioning that, Ray-Ray."

There was a moment of silence.

"You haven't called me that in years," Andrea said, raising an eyebrow.

Zoe grinned at her sheepishly. "I guess that this dinner you cooked is making me sentimental."

Andrea snorted and pushed her plate away. "Whatever. I think I'll eat the rest a bit later. I stuffed myself with salmon before you even got home."

"Okay," Zoe said, taking another bite. "Did you season this with lemon?"

"Just a bit," Andrea said, standing up.

"I can taste it," Zoe said happily. "It really adds a lot. I think—"

The puzzle pieces suddenly clicked.

All bodies had been found naked, their clothes discarded nearby, but in three of the murders, the underwear and the shoes had been missing. This wasn't in the crime reports; the reports only listed the evidence found. None mentioned the things that were unaccounted for. The missing underwear and shoes were trophies taken by the killer. But in the other five cases, no trophies were taken. Two different signatures. It was possible there were two killers, not one.

"Everything okay?" she heard her sister say. "You're just staring at your plate."

"I just figured something out," Zoe said.

"Yeah? What is it?"

She hesitated, then shook her head. "Nothing," she said. "Just work."

CHAPTER 5

Dale City, Virginia, Friday, July 15, 2016

The loud thumping woke Tatum up with a start. His vision snapped into focus only to see a pair of large, menacing green eyes staring at him, mere inches from his face. His hand shot down to pull his Glock from its holster, but he was in his underwear, no gun in reach. Reflexes took hold, and he pushed himself backward, away from his attacker. He tumbled to the floor, scrambling for any sort of protection. His attacker disappeared from sight as Tatum bounded to his feet, his heart racing. He turned on the light and blinked.

His ugly orange tomcat stared at him with disdain.

"Damn it, Freckle!" Tatum yelled at him. "I told you not to get on the bed."

Freckle blinked and yawned, clearly bored. Tatum looked for the water pistol, Freckle's nemesis, but it was nowhere in sight. In all likelihood, the cat had destroyed the thing when Tatum wasn't around, like he'd done to the three previous ones.

There was another thump. Someone was knocking on the door; that was what had woken him, not his sociopathic cat. He put on a pair of shorts and a T-shirt, grabbed his Glock from the night table, and walked over to the front door. He'd gotten used to the new apartment in Dale City, but he was groggy from sleep, and in the dark, the hallway felt almost unfamiliar. He missed his previous apartment in LA, even though this one was much more spacious, in a better neighborhood.

"Who is it?" he asked.

"Police," a sharp, formal voice declared.

Tatum flattened his body against the wall and unlocked the door, then opened it slightly and peered out. A cop in uniform stood outside, an old, confused-looking man next to him. Tatum sighed, put the Glock on the small stand nearby, and opened the door.

"Good evening, sir," the cop said. "Do you know this man?" He glanced at the befuddled gray-haired man beside him.

"Yeah." Tatum sighed. "He's my grandfather. His name's Marvin."

"We found him wandering around Logan Park," the cop said.

"Where is Molly?" Marvin asked in a frail voice.

"He keeps asking for her," the cop said.

"Molly was my grandmother. She passed away," Tatum said. "We just moved here . . . I think he's having a hard time adjusting."

"I'm very sorry," the cop said. "He was with some young men who ran once they spotted us. I think they were about to rob him."

"I see," Tatum said. "Thank you, Officer."

The cop glanced at the table where the Glock rested.

Tatum cleared his throat. "I'm a federal agent," he said. "My badge is in the bedroom, if you want to—"

"That's okay." The cop nodded. "You should make sure he stays indoors, sir," he said. "He shouldn't be walking around at two a.m. It's dangerous."

"You're right, Officer. Thank you. You heard that, Grandpa?"

"Is Molly asleep?" Marvin asked, his voice trembling.

"You have a good night, sir," the officer said and walked away as Tatum closed the door.

Tatum and his grandfather looked at each other silently as the cop's footsteps faded.

"Goddamn it, Marvin." Tatum exploded once he knew the cop would be out of earshot. "What the hell?"

"Well, what did you want me to do?" Marvin asked, straightening, the confusion fading from his face. "I don't run as fast as those youngsters. Would you rather I called to say I'd been arrested for buying drugs?"

"I would rather that you weren't buying drugs at all," Tatum said. "What the hell are you buying drugs for, anyway? You're eighty-seven years old."

"They're not for me. They're for Jenna," Marvin said, striding into the apartment.

"Who's Jenna?"

"A woman I know, Tatum."

"Where did you meet this woman?"

"Bingo night."

Tatum shut his eyes and breathed deeply. "How old is Jenna?"

"She's eighty-two," Marvin yelled from the kitchen. "But she's very feisty."

"I'm sure she is," Tatum muttered, walking after his grandfather. "Well, if Jenna's eighty-two, she shouldn't be doing cocaine either."

"Tatum, at our age, we can do whatever we want," Marvin said. "I'm making a cup of tea. Do you want one?"

"I want to go back to sleep."

"You have a flight in a couple of hours anyway," Marvin said.

"Yeah, listen—about that. Don't get arrested while I'm gone. I need you to take care of Freckle."

"No way."

"It's just for a few days."

"Why don't you take the cat to a shelter? Or, I don't know, dump it on the highway."

"I should take *you* to the shelter," Tatum grumbled as Marvin handed him a mug. He took a sip. "Listen, just make sure he has food and that he doesn't destroy the house. We just moved in. And make sure he doesn't eat the fish."

"What fish?"

"The one in the bowl in the living room. I need you to get an aquarium for it. I'll leave you some money."

"We have a fish?"

"Yeah. His name is Timothy, and apparently, he's a bastard. You two should get along great. Just keep Freckle away from him."

"That beast hates me."

"He hates everyone," Tatum said. "But maybe if you stopped throwing your shoes at him—"

"If he'd stop pouncing at me, I might stop throwing shoes at him."

Freckle prowled into the kitchen, glanced at Marvin, and hissed menacingly.

"Cut that out," Tatum told the cat. "I need you two to behave when I'm gone."

The cat and the old man both looked at Tatum, their eyes round and innocent.

Tatum sighed. "And feed the damn fish," he said.

When Tatum saw Lieutenant Samuel Martinez from the Chicago PD, he was quite taken with the man's mustache. He shook his hand, wondering how the mustache would look on his own face. It was well groomed and thick, with a Tom Selleck-ish style, giving Martinez's mouth an aura of importance. The thick-rimmed glasses framing the man's eyes further elevated the seriousness he conveyed. Tatum suspected that if he tried the same face décor, he'd look like a pervy literature teacher who slept with his students. Some mustaches belonged on other people's faces. So far Tatum had failed to find one that belonged on his own.

"Agent Gray, I'm glad you could come," the lieutenant said. They stood in the entrance of the Chicago Police Department headquarters, where the Central Investigation Division was housed. It teemed with people, both cops and civilians, and the air carried the faint buzz of several conversations merged together. Martinez's voice penetrated the hubbub easily, his words clipped and measured. "Please follow me."

They took the elevator up two floors and then walked down a corridor into what appeared to be a meeting room. Half a dozen people sat around a large white table in the center. Several whiteboards hung on the walls, on which various images were tacked and timelines drawn. A large map of Chicago was taped to the wall to Tatum's left, marked with circles drawn with a red Sharpie in two spots.

"This is the situation room for the Strangling Undertaker cases," Martinez explained. "Please, come in."

"The Strangling Undertaker?" Tatum raised an eyebrow.

"That's what the newspapers started calling him," Martinez said. "A reporter came up with the nickname a few days ago, and it's caught on."

"I can't imagine why," Tatum muttered.

Martinez introduced Tatum to the people in the room. Five were detectives. The sixth, a much older man with frizzed hair and numerous liver spots, was introduced as Dr. Ruben Bernstein.

"Bernstein joined the task force three days ago, soon after we found the second body," Martinez said. "He's an experienced profiler, and he's already been a tremendous help."

"That's good to hear." Tatum nodded and shook Bernstein's hand. The old man's handshake was limp, making Tatum feel as if he were handling a dead fish. "I take it there's been some progress? When my chief filled me in, she described the situation as quite dire."

"Well, it's definitely bleak," Martinez said, his face grim. "People are scared. These bodies showed up in very public places and were seen by families with kids. But Dr. Bernstein's narrowed the pool of suspects significantly, so we're finally making some headway."

"Good," Tatum said. "I'm glad to hear you're moving in the right direction. Do you want to fill me in?"

"Have you read the case files?" Martinez asked.

"I did," Tatum said. "And I'm only here to consult, but I'd be glad for a short summary and an up-to-date assessment of the situation."

"Absolutely. Have a seat," Martinez said.

Tatum glanced at the table. The five detectives all sat on one end, Dr. Bernstein at the other, with several empty chairs on either side. He sat down next to the old profiler.

"This is Susan Warner," Martinez said, pointing to an image on one of the whiteboards. It depicted a woman lying on the grass, her entire body rigid, her mouth agape. She was dressed in a black evening dress, one of its sleeves torn, the bottom scrunched up to her thighs. Her legs were bare. Her body seemed to be in almost perfect condition, her skin pink except for her left foot, which was black and green and slightly bloated.

"Victim is twenty-two years old. She was found on April twelfth of this year on the shore of Foster Beach. The body was embalmed except for the left foot, which was already in an advanced state of decomposition. Warner was an art student living alone in Pilsen. She was reported missing by one of her friends four days before her body was found. Time of death was hard to estimate because her body was embalmed, but according to the state of the foot, the medical examiner estimated she'd been dead for at least five days. The cause of death was strangulation. We found traces of embalming fluid and blood in the shower at her apartment. There were indications that the body was sexually assaulted postmortem."

Tatum listened carefully. He had read all that twice already, but he wanted to know what the lieutenant would focus on.

"The second victim"—Martinez pointed at another image—"was Monique Silva."

Tatum looked at the picture he had first seen in Chief Mancuso's office. Monique Silva's body stood on a wooden bridge above a stream, leaning on the railing, as if staring at the water. Her eyes were open, her mouth shut. She was dressed in a skirt, stockings, and a long-sleeved T-shirt. Her skin was completely gray.

"Silva was aged twenty-one, a prostitute working Logan Square. She was found a week ago, on July seventh. A man who identified himself as her cousin but is a known pimp reported her missing only a day before her body was found, but he said she had been missing for at least a week before that. Cause of death was, again, strangulation. There were bruises indicating she had been tied up before being killed. Again, the body was sexually assaulted postmortem. We checked with eyewitnesses—"

"Hang on," Tatum said. "Was there embalming fluid found in her home as well?"

"No, but she wasn't living alone," Martinez said. "We believe she was snatched off the street and taken somewhere else."

"Okay." Tatum nodded. "Do you know why the body's skin color is gray? The first body's skin looks much better." This hadn't been mentioned in the case file.

"According to the ME, the killer probably used a different mixture of embalming fluid," Martinez said. "The lifelike colors in the first body are because of a red dye in the embalming fluid."

"I see," Tatum said. "What are your leads?"

"The killer was careful," Martinez said. "Hardly any traces of DNA on Susan Warner's body. There was a reasonable amount of semen found on Monique Silva, but she was a prostitute, so that wasn't entirely surprising. No matches on CODIS to the samples."

Tatum nodded.

"Absolutely no witnesses for the first murder," Martinez said. "The second victim was probably taken from the street, and we've interrogated some of her associates. We have several descriptions of male customers who approached the victim the last evening she was seen on the street, but they're very general. We found a bunch of fingerprints in Susan Warner's apartment, at least seven different people, and tracing those fingerprints led us nowhere."

"So you have nothing substantial so far," Tatum said.

He could sense the atmosphere in the room tensing. He got dirty looks from two of the detectives, and Martinez's mouth pursed. Tatum made a mental note to be careful with anything that might sound like a criticism. "I mean, the killer covered his tracks very well."

"On the contrary," the throaty voice of Dr. Bernstein interrupted. "I'd say the killer has left us a very clear path."

Tatum folded his arms and looked toward the doctor. "I take it you have a lead?"

"Well, I have a description," Bernstein said. "And using that description, the detectives can find the killer."

"All right," Tatum said. "Let's hear it."

The doctor stood up and walked over to the whiteboard. Martinez sat down, giving the doctor his full attention.

"The killer is male, white, in his late twenties or early thirties," the doctor said. "He—"

"How do you know?" Tatum interrupted him.

"What?"

"How do you know he's a white male in his late twenties or early thirties?"

"Well, I don't really *know* anything. But the probability is very high, and we need to narrow the pool of suspects."

"Okay. What makes you think he's *likely* to be a white male of that age?"

"Well . . ." The doctor seemed to be warming up. "He's male because—"

"I know why you think he's male. Fine. Why white?"

"Almost all serial killers are white," the doctor said. "And the sexual assault of white women is very indicative."

Tatum's face remained fixed, but his heart sank. "I see," he said. "Why early thirties or—"

"This murder couldn't have just popped into the killer's mind overnight," the doctor answered patiently. "It's the result of a very intricate fantasy. It has likely taken years to reach the point where the killer had to act it out, so he can't be too young. And if he were older, we would have seen other similar murders."

"Okay," Tatum said, feeling tired. "Go on."

"He's leaving the bodies in very public places, clearly demonstrating his superiority over the police and enjoying his moment in the spotlight. It is likely he either talked to the police, pretending to be a witness, or has involved himself somehow in the cases—by approaching the families of the victims, coming to their funerals, and so on. He is intelligent, with a high school and even possibly a college education. He owns a car. He is clearly well acquainted with embalming practices, which leads me to assume he has worked in a funeral home or perhaps still does. He plans everything meticulously, choosing his victims in advance. The fact that he keeps the bodies for longer periods each time displays an impressive amount of patience. He is single, though he might be dating quite often, and may be quite charming and manipulative."

"That's a very detailed profile," Tatum said.

"It has been my experience that this kind of murder—"

"What experience?"

"Excuse me?" The doctor looked insulted.

"You said it has been your experience. Where did that experience come from?"

The doctor's face flushed in anger. "Young man," he said, "I've spent years studying the practices of serial killers. I've been an expert consultant on the matter for more than a decade. I—"

"I'm sorry." Tatum raised his hands. "Like you, it's my job to be a consultant to the police. I tend to doubt everything I'm told. It comes with the job. I didn't mean to imply that I question your impressive credentials."

The doctor frowned, clearly suspecting he was the butt of a joke, but Tatum had already turned to face Martinez and the rest of the detectives.

"So what are you all doing now?" he asked.

"According to the psychological profile, the suspect is likely to have worked in a funeral home," Martinez said. "We've begun searching through the records of funeral homes in the areas where the killer has struck, looking for someone who matches the profile."

"Okay." Tatum massaged the bridge of his nose. "What about staking out the crime scenes where the bodies were dropped?"

Martinez shrugged. "These are very public places," he said. "Thousands of people go there every day."

"But they're empty at night, right?" Tatum said. "I assume that's how the killer managed to drop the bodies."

"Well . . . yes. But why would he . . . ?"

"Serial killers sometimes return to the scene of the crime," Tatum said and added, "I'm sure Dr. Bernstein can tell us why."

"Of course," the doctor said. "It's a very common phenomenon. Serial killers often subconsciously want to get caught—partly out of guilt and partly to receive the fame they desire."

Tatum sighed. "Lieutenant, thank you for filling me in," he said. "Is there somewhere I can sit down, go over your recent case notes? I need to write up a report. You know how the bureau is."

Martinez smiled. "Of course. There's an available desk in our task force room. Let me show you the way." He turned to the rest of the detectives. "Dana, can you split today's locations between you? I want to get some progress on those funeral homes."

"Sure, Lieutenant," a serious-looking woman said.

Martinez led Tatum out and down the corridor. Once they were far enough out of earshot, Tatum stopped.

"Listen," he said. "Your profiler is useless. Fire him."

"I'm sorry?" Martinez asked, tensing.

"I doubt he has any real experience. He—"

"Dr. Bernstein is well known in this area, Agent," Martinez said coldly. "He's the number one media expert on serial killers in Chicago."

A media expert. Of course. Tatum shook his head. "Listen, maybe he's good enough for the media, but—"

"Are you a profiler, Agent Gray?"

"All FBI agents are trained as profilers," Tatum said.

"But do you have actual experience as a profiler?"

"No, but—"

"Dr. Bernstein does. He's personally interviewed John Wayne Gacy and written a book about it. He's frequently hired as an expert witness on sexual murders. Trust me—he knows more than you or I ever will about serial killers."

"Serial killers don't go back to the crime scene because of guilt or desire for fame, Lieutenant, no matter what your profiler thinks," Tatum said, irritated. "They go back to recall the crime and masturbate. Your killer might go back to one of the crime scenes this very night to relieve himself, and if you'd only stake out the—"

"We don't have the manpower to stake out the crime scenes," Martinez said. "No offense, but this is exactly why I was hesitant in involving the bureau. You storm in here, take over the investigation with your patronizing manner and offensive tone—what next? Will you tell the media how inept we are?"

"I'm sorry," Tatum said, apologizing yet again. "I've had a long night. I've hardly slept. You're right, of course; I was out of line. I assure you the FBI wants these coordinated efforts to work well."

"Maybe they shouldn't have sent *you* then," Martinez said.

Tatum wholeheartedly agreed.

Tatum leaned back in his chair and sighed. He felt cramped and slightly claustrophobic. The special task force headed by Lieutenant Martinez had been created specifically for the current serial killings, and the team was cobbled together from detectives from various units in the Chicago PD Bureau of Detectives. The room they'd been assigned felt as if it had been similarly cobbled. It was a decent size for a living room but quite small when it came to housing six detectives and a desk for Dr. Bernstein. Now they had to create extra space for Tatum as well, and they managed it, but not in a way that was particularly welcoming. His desk was positioned in the room's corner, a file cabinet behind him and the room's watercooler just to his right. When he moved the chair slightly backward, he inevitably collided with the cabinet, emitting a loud clang.

As the day went by, the detectives around him talked and joked with each other, went to lunch together, and pointedly ignored him.

He suddenly yearned to be one of them. How had he gotten here? A job in an agency that didn't appreciate him, in a department he didn't want to be a part of, with no friends and a superior who distrusted him.

And a bunch of self-pity to boot. Disgusting. People would give their left kidney to be an FBI agent and their right one to be in the Behavioral Analysis Unit. Except that would be counterproductive. Having at least one functioning kidney was a requirement for all FBI agents, he was pretty sure of it.

He saved the report he was working on. He had spent the entire day going over the autopsies of the two victims, talking to the medical examiner, and discussing the case with the detectives assigned to it. The task force was actually on the right track—or had been, up until three days ago. The first thing he had to do was to help them get back on course. He had a vague idea how to do it. He took out his phone, about to call the chief, when he saw the notification of four unread messages. He opened them—all four were from Marvin.

> Where is the cat food?
> Never mind found it.
> That wasn't the cat food but he likes it.
> I think the cat is ill, he vomited in the living room. The fish is fine.

Tatum groaned and wrote back that the cat food was in the leftmost cupboard in the kitchen. He wondered what Marvin had been feeding Freckle and decided that any answer to that would only make him feel worse. Scrolling down his contacts, he located the contact *Christine Mancuso* and pressed the call button.

She answered after a few seconds. "Hello?"

"It's Tatum." He looked around him. The room was currently empty; all the detectives were either somewhere else or had gone home.

"I know."

"Right. Okay, listen. The guys here are fine. The lieutenant in charge is pretty sharp, they have a decent task force working on those murders, and they were doing well until recently."

"And then what happened?"

"They hired a profiler."

"Ah."

"This guy is spouting serial killer clichés at an alarming rate. He seems to be the media expert on serial killers in Chicago, and his face is familiar enough that the detectives are happy to follow his lead. He's wasting the time and resources of the investigation, and they're paying him to do so."

"Did you tell them that?" Mancuso asked.

"Yes," Tatum said, doodling with a pen on the paper pad in front of him. "I told the lieutenant, and I got the cold shoulder. They're very sensitive about the bureau meddling in their business."

There was a moment of silence. "How do you want to proceed?"

Tatum drew a sad face, then tapped the pen, peppering the paper with random spots. "You know that civilian you brought in? She has an impressive record, right?"

"Zoe Bentley? She worked on the Jovan Stokes case," Mancuso said. "So that earned her some recent media fame. She also has a PhD in clinical psychology and a JD from Harvard."

He lowered his voice, even though he was the only one in the room. "I think she should fly here, dazzle the detectives with her credentials, and convince them to kick this quack out. Then she can help me nudge this investigation back on the right course."

"How would she help?" Mancuso sounded mildly amused.

"Use her profiler buzzwords and charm. I have some really good ideas on how this investigation should progress."

"So you want her to come over and back you up."

"They won't really listen to anything I have to say, because I'm just a fed. But she's a civilian profiler, so her words might carry more weight."

"Okay," Mancuso said. "I'll send her over."

"Awesome."

"Good night, Agent Gray." She hung up.

Surprised by the abrupt end to their conversation, Tatum put the phone back in his pocket. Then he looked at the sad face he had drawn and, after a moment of thought, added a pair of glasses and three hairs.

CHAPTER 6

Chicago, Illinois, Sunday, July 17, 2016

It wasn't working out. He'd hoped she would be the one, but he could already feel the magic fading, the boredom taking hold. When he woke up next to her, he no longer felt the thrill of lust and excitement. All he could feel was disappointment.

Part of it, he knew, was the embalming fluid.

He hadn't gotten it right. Her body was too rigid, the color of her skin imperfect. He should, perhaps, have added more dye to compensate for the saline solution. But he didn't know how much, and the online material he'd found about it was hazy in the details.

Two nights ago, frustrated, he'd slapped her, and she had fallen off the chair, slumping to the floor, her body still bent in a sitting position. Furious, he'd left the house, slamming the door behind him, driving around the city, knowing that if an opportunity were to present itself, he would kill. But all the women he'd seen were in pairs or groups, and when he had approached a whore on the street, she'd said she was done for the day, her eyes betraying fear. What had she seen in his face that made her so scared? Horrified, he had hurried back to his car and examined his face in the mirror, but it looked the same as always. He had driven home and relieved himself in the bathroom.

The next one would be better. He would figure out a way to make her more lifelike. Perhaps glass eyes would help. He should look into that.

But first he had to break up with this one.

He lifted her from the floor, placing her back in the chair. She stared at the table, no doubt feeling the tension in their relationship.

He put his hand on her arm, caressing it gently.

"We've had some good times, haven't we?" He smiled at her.

He let the silence between them linger. How should she react? He tried to think of all he knew, the movies he had seen, the books he had read.

She would cry.

He took her left arm and bent it at the elbow. He wanted to get it just right, and it was tricky, but finally he managed to place her palm on her face. Taking her right arm, he did the same so that it looked as if she had buried her face in her hands while sobbing.

She was beautiful. He almost changed his mind then and there, almost told her that maybe they should give it another chance, but he knew it would only hurt them both, eventually. It was best to remain silent.

He poured them both a glass of wine, for old times' sake. She didn't touch hers, so he drank that as well. Then he helped her stand up and dragged her to the car. He placed her in the passenger's seat, her face still in her hands, still crying.

It was difficult for them both.

He sat by her side for a moment, trying to think where she would go to mourn their relationship.

He had the perfect place.

CHAPTER 7

Maynard, Massachusetts, Saturday, September 27, 1997

Zoe's parents were talking with each other, their voices low, almost inaudible. Her mother's voice could usually be heard for miles, so it was easy to notice when she spoke in a hushed tone. As soon as Zoe realized this wasn't a conversation she was supposed to hear, she froze, intent on catching every syllable. She stood in the hallway, out of sight. The light from the kitchen spilled onto the hallway floor. A shadow moved across it—her father, perhaps, always pacing when he was agitated.

"Do they have any suspects?" her mother asked.

"Arl told me that the police chief said they did," her father answered. He was also speaking quietly, but Zoe's father always had a soft tone, so he didn't have to try very hard. "But he wouldn't say who, of course."

"Her poor mother," Zoe's mom said, her voice breaking. "Can you imagine? Hearing that . . ."

"I try not to."

"Was she . . . I mean, did he . . . rape her?"

Zoe had never heard her mother utter that word, and the sound of it, from her mother's lips, chilled her. Her father didn't answer. Was he just thinking? Was he nodding? Shaking his head? She had to know. She crept toward the doorway, catching a glimpse of her parents' faces. They were both standing close to each other, her mother leaning on the counter. She could only see her mother's profile but nevertheless could see that she was distraught, her mouth curved in a way that hinted at a hidden sob.

"We'll need to talk to Zoe," her father said. "She should know—"

"Absolutely not," her mother hissed. "She's only fourteen."

"She'll find out, and it's better if she learns about it from us."

Her mother was about to answer when Zoe's sister zinged past her into the kitchen, a blur of flailing limbs, a mass of hair and noise.

"Are we making pancakes?" she shouted. Even at the age of five, Andrea took after their mother, having only two volume settings: shouting and asleep.

Her mother cleared her throat. "Is your sister awake?"

Zoe tensed.

"Yeah, she's standing in the—"

"Good morning," Zoe said, quickly walking into the kitchen herself. The kitchen's tiled floor was cold, and her bare feet nearly froze. Her mother leaned on the counter, and her father stood in the middle of the room beside the table. There was a disconcerting lack of breakfast on it. Zoe's mother always had breakfast ready when they woke up on weekends, but apparently this wasn't any regular weekend. Zoe stretched and gave a wide, completely fake yawn. "Want me to help with breakfast?"

"I want you to get dressed," her mother said, looking at her over her crooked nose. Zoe had her mother's nose, or as she called it in her darker moments, the beak. At least she had her father's eyes. Her mother sniffed and added, "You'll freeze to death."

Zoe was still wearing the loose T-shirt and thin pants she had worn to bed. "Okay," she said. She had been on her way to the bathroom when she'd heard her parents talking. Her bladder was a second away from bursting, and the cold floor wasn't helping. She fidgeted uncomfortably. "Anything going on?"

"No," her mother said, perhaps a bit too quickly. "Just getting the Saturday breakfast going. Your sister wants pancakes. Do you want some as well?"

"Sure," Zoe said. "I'm going over to Heather's later, and—"

"You're staying home," her mother interrupted her.

Zoe frowned. "But we need to work on our chemistry assignment. It's due on Monday."

"I'll drive you," her father said.

"I prefer taking my bike. It's a nice day, and—"

"I'll drive you." His eyes focused on her intently, and there was no arguing with his tone. "And I want you to call when you need to come home. I'll pick you up."

"Mommy, I want pancakes," Andrea whined.

"What's going on?" Zoe asked.

Her parents were both silent.

Her father finally said, "There was—"

"Nothing is going on," her mother interrupted him, looking down at Andrea, who still whined for pancakes. "We just don't want you to walk around by yourself."

"They found a dead body," Heather told her once they were in the privacy of her bedroom. "By the White Pond Road Bridge."

"How do you know that?" Zoe asked.

"I heard my dad and the neighbor talking about it this morning. The neighbor said it was a girl and that she was naked."

A shiver ran up Zoe's neck. They were both lying on Heather's bed, the sheets scrunched around them, Heather's clothes scattered everywhere. Her room always looked as if a tornado had hit her closet. Heather nibbled on a sliced apple her mother had cut for them. Their chemistry project lay untouched on the desk, as it would probably stay for the rest of the day.

"Did he say who she was? Is she from Maynard?" Zoe asked.

"No," Heather whispered. She scooted closer to Zoe, her arm touching Zoe's shoulder. Heather smelled faintly of shampoo and soap, and Zoe regretted not taking a shower herself that morning. She felt uncomfortable lying on the clean sheets, the soles of her feet probably dirty from walking barefoot at home. Heather never seemed to mind, though. They always ate on her bed, and she'd often dump her laundry basket there, fishing for some article of clothing. Well, if Zoe's mother changed Zoe's bedsheets every three days, like Heather's mom did for her, perhaps she wouldn't mind it when they got dirty either.

Heather tensed slightly. "Oh my God, Zoe, what if it's someone we know?"

An image instantly popped into Zoe's mind. The dead, naked body of Carrie from school, lying at the side of the bridge, water lapping at her feet. The picture was so vivid in her mind she nearly burst into tears. Why had she thought of Carrie? Why would she even imagine such a thing? What was wrong with her? She shut her eyes, trying to banish the image from her mind.

"I think everyone is freaking out," Heather said. "The neighbor told my dad he won't let his kids out of the house. I bet my mom is going to do the same. She'll keep me inside all the time. Mom can be so hysterical sometimes."

"My parents wouldn't let me come over by myself," Zoe said. "They drove me over." She gazed outside through Heather's window. From her position on the bed, she could only see the blue sky and the foliage of a nearby tree. It seemed so peaceful.

Heather shook her head. "I hope this blows over fast," she said. "I don't want my parents looking over my shoulder at everything I'm doing."

Zoe nodded distractedly, but she had a feeling it wouldn't blow over anytime soon.

Her bicycle wheel whined in complaint as she pressed the handbrake. She stopped on the side of White Pond Road Bridge, lungs burning from exertion. The only reason her mother had let her ride her bike to school that morning was because she had been late for work, and Zoe had promised she would ride with Heather and then straight back home after school. And she had meant to do just that.

But she hadn't.

Every time she'd seen Carrie in the hallway at school, there was a lump in her throat, guilt and shame flooding her. She felt as if Carrie could tell Zoe had pictured her naked and dead by the water. When Carrie had smiled at her during gym class, Zoe's face had flushed, and she'd quickly looked away, trembling. The image had lingered at the back of her mind, threatening to return at any given moment. Finally, Zoe had decided that if she went to the bridge to look at the place, she could clear the horrid picture from her thoughts.

She got off the bike and paced down the grassy edge of the Assabet River, just up to the calm water. Green algae floated on the river surface, rising and falling on small, almost imperceptible waves. Was this where they had found the body?

She knew the body had been slightly submerged in the water—or at least that was what everyone at school said. Other rumors were whispered endlessly. Someone told Zoe that the girl had been raped before she died. Someone else said she had been tortured, that her face was bruised and swollen. Her hands were bound behind her back. She had been sliced with a knife. Each rumor made Zoe feel weak, scared, helpless.

She knew who the victim was now. Her name was Beth Hartley. She had been a secretary for a local accountant, twenty-one years old. Zoe had seen a photo of her in the newspaper that morning. The face seemed familiar. Had Zoe ever seen her walking down the street? Having her hair cut? Grabbing a pizza? She probably had. Maynard was a small town. The paper didn't give any other details but mentioned that an investigation was underway.

Now that she was here, the sun reflecting on the water, fragments of light making the surface shine, it seemed almost impossible. Zoe couldn't imagine the body in the water anymore, not even when she tried. It was so bizarre, so alien.

Still, the fear wouldn't let go . . . and amid the fear, something else. Agitation. Thrill.

Something rustled in the leaves behind her, and she whirled around, her pulse racing. There was nothing there. A bird, perhaps? She shivered, even though it was a relatively warm day.

Trying to break the spell, she picked up a rock from the ground and hurled it into the water. It hit the surface, creating circular eddies that widened and faded, the green algae moving away from the spot the rock had hit. She got back on her bicycle and rode home.

Rod Glover, their neighbor, was in his front yard, tending the garden, his white shirt soaked in sweat. As she got off the bicycle, he stood up and waved at her, shears in hand. They were her mother's shears, which Rod always borrowed.

"Hey, Zoe." He smiled and wiped his forehead. His brownish-red skater haircut was a bit messy, but his bright, cheerful smile and happy eyes made up for it. Although he was about ten years older than her, he was easygoing and fun to talk to. He had a goofy sense of humor and a knack for imitating celebrities and people around town.

"Hey." She smiled back. "How are you?"

"Can't complain. Coming home from school?"

"Yeah . . ." She hesitated, feeling the need to talk to someone. "I went by White Pond Road Bridge."

"Not exactly on the way, is it?" he said, leaning against the fence.

"I just wanted . . . that's where they found the girl, you know?"

He nodded. "Yup, I heard."

"It's terrible, what happened to her," Zoe said.

Rod nodded. "It is," he said. "So . . . looking forward to tonight?"

She looked at him, perplexed. "What's tonight?"

"Uh . . . hello? It's *Buffy* night, remember?"

Buffy the Vampire Slayer. Rod and Zoe both loved the show; they'd talk about it after every new episode ran. But the shift in discussion was jarring, and Zoe remained silent.

He changed his posture to mimic Giles, one of the series characters. His words developed Giles's English accent. "Really, Zoe, it's the second season; you can't afford to be distracted. This episode is of the utmost importance."

"I have to go," Zoe said apologetically. She was uncomfortable with his attempt to make her laugh, considering the circumstances. No one joked these days. "See you later."

"See ya," Rod said.

She turned toward the door. Just before she walked inside, she glanced back. Rod grinned at her and then acted as if he were removing his imaginary glasses and cleaning them, another Giles-like move.

CHAPTER 8

Monday, July 18, 2016

The airplane's steady hum vibrated in Zoe's ear as she flipped through the thin folder in her hand. She wasn't able to ignore the constant noise, and it made her feel irritable. She suspected that the problem wasn't really with the engine. She hated to be yanked from what she was doing. There was a certain joy in starting a project and seeing it to completion. She was fascinated with the highway serial killer case. It kept jumping into her thoughts even at home, and she searched for patterns within the crimes, trying to find not one but two profiles for the murderers.

And then Mancuso had called on Saturday night to tell her she had been reassigned. There was a serial killer in Chicago, and the agent in the field wanted her help. While the details they had about the case were intriguing, Zoe had pointed out that the murder rate and the victim count of the highway killings were much higher. Mancuso had agreed with her and then said again that Zoe was going to Chicago.

Mancuso had sent the case file over, and Zoe had left it untouched on her nightstand, intent on getting a bit of rest before her flight. But a nightmare had woken her up after only three hours, and she hadn't managed to fall back to sleep.

She read the autopsy report of the first victim, Susan Warner. The thing that kept drawing her attention was the decomposing left foot.

She had already made some definite assumptions based on that fact. And there was the interesting detail about the mouth . . .

"Working on the plane, huh?" a friendly voice asked.

Zoe shut the folder and looked at her neighbor. He was a middle-aged man with thinning blond hair, a tan that seemed fake, and a you-gotta-love-me smile. He held a small glass of whiskey in his hand, swirling it to melt the one cube of ice. Zoe sighed inwardly, preparing for the arduous task of the small-talk ceremony.

"Yes," she said. "It's a good way to save time."

"I'm Earl Havisham."

"Zoe."

"I try not to work while traveling," he said. "It's a good time to focus on myself, you know?"

Zoe nodded, somehow managing not to comment that he wasn't focusing on himself right now. "Well, I like to work while traveling," she said and opened her folder, hoping they were done.

The time of death had been several days before the body was found, but the location it was found in was a public place. What had the killer done with the body during that time span? There was the torn dress that—

"I have a slight fear of flying," Earl said.

He glanced at her folder's contents, the top page clearly marked "Autopsy Report." Annoyed, she shut the folder again.

"That's why I drink," Earl continued.

"Okay," Zoe said. She was done being polite.

"I'm a technical writer for a start-up company in Silicon Valley."

"Sounds exciting."

"Well . . . not as much as you'd think."

He sounded completely serious. Was it a subtle display of sarcasm? Didn't feel like it.

"What do you do?"

"I'm a forensic psychologist."

"Oh, wow." His eyes shifted just a bit, his body tensing.

It was a typical reaction to her profession. Some people were cautious with psychologists, feeling they might be analyzed at any moment. And almost everyone was weirded out by the word *forensic* because it made them think of dead bodies. The combination of the two brought many conversations to a screeching halt—which would be great in this instance.

When people *did* ask her what that meant, she'd explain that what she mostly did was analyze crimes to try to come up with a profile of the criminal. This helped the investigators narrow their suspect pool from "all the people in the world" down to a tight, manageable group. It was a very careful explanation that avoided the terms *serial killers*, *sex crimes*, *victim profiles*, *crime scenes*, and other phrases that tended to make people shift uncomfortably in their seats.

"Do you like it?" he finally asked.

"It has its moments." Her tone was curt and unpleasant, and she gave him a narrow-eyed stare. She had been told several times she had intense eyes. She hoped they would shut him up.

She opened her folder for the third time and thumbed to the second victim. The victim's mouth had been sewn shut with a black thread. Did that have any significance? Perhaps he'd killed them to—

"So where are you headed once we land?" He leaned toward her, his voice lower.

Zoe shut her folder, her jaw clenched tight.

He kept leaning closer. "I need to go to my company's branch at the Gogo Building. But I'm not expected there until ten, so—"

"Then maybe you should use that time to find a woman who is interested in hearing about all the times your mother was disappointed in you," Zoe said. "If you get lucky, she might not notice that wedding ring outline in your pocket . . . nice tan on your finger, by the way. It's a good thing you remembered to take the ring off before they sprayed you. And then maybe you'll have sex, and your self-confidence will be bolstered enough for that business meeting you're clearly so worried about."

Some of it was just guesswork. Everyone's mother was disappointed in them at one point or another. It was nothing more than a psychological parlor trick. But from the outrage in his eyes, it seemed she was right on every mark—even his business meeting. She was beginning to enjoy their conversation.

"Bitch," he muttered, turning away.

"Oh, Earl." She smiled at him. "That's really no way to talk to someone who works for the FBI."

CHAPTER 9

Chicago, Illinois, Monday, July 18, 2016

Tatum had almost decided to let Zoe get to the police headquarters on her own, but he decided at the last moment to pick her up, talk to her a bit before she met Lieutenant Martinez and his fake profiler. It was best to make sure they were on the same page. While he waited for her, he called Marvin to make sure the old man was fine.

"Of course I'm not fine, Tatum. You left me to take care of your beastly creature. It already scratched me twice."

"I meant how are you aside from Freckle. Are you feeling well? Did you remember to take your pills?"

"I've been taking those pills for nine years, Tatum. You think just because you went to Chicago, I'll suddenly decide to stop? Of course I remember the pills."

"Good. And what about—"

"I stopped taking the blue one; I told you that. It made my throat itch."

"What? When?"

"Last week. I told you that, Tatum. Don't you remember?"

"You didn't tell me anything about that." Tatum felt his gut sinking. "Did you ask Dr. Nassar about it?"

"No, there's no need. I talked to Jenna about it."

It took Tatum a moment to place the name Jenna as his grandfather's girlfriend with the cocaine habit. "Is she a doctor?"

"No, but she had the same problem a year ago. Her doctor prescribed her something else. She had some extra, so I'm taking those instead."

"Marvin, you can't do that. Talk to Dr. Nassar—"

"Nassar is a busy man, Tatum. And these green ones are great, no side effects—"

"What green ones?"

"The ones Jenna gave me."

"Do any of these pills have a name? What are you taking?"

"I don't remember, Tatum, but it's fine. Jenna told me. She had exactly the same side effects and—"

Tatum noticed Zoe amid the hundreds of people heading out of the terminal. She was striding quickly toward the exit, her gray suitcase dragging behind her.

"Listen, I have to go. Take your damn pills, even the blue one with the itchy throat. And don't take the ones from Jenna. And call Dr. Nassar. He will give you what you need."

"I have what I need."

"If you don't call Dr. Nassar, I will."

"You're a pain in the ass, Tatum."

"Take your pills. And remember to feed the fish. Bye." He hung up and hurried after Zoe. He caught up with her and tapped her shoulder.

"Dr. Bentley." He smiled, trying to temporarily set aside Marvin and the green pills.

"Agent Gray. I thought we'd meet at the police station."

"Yeah, but I figured I could pick you up. I rented a car yesterday, so no need to take a cab."

"Thank you. That's very thoughtful."

She seemed to be in a cheerful mood. Perhaps she was glad to get out of the office for a bit. It made Tatum feel better about asking for her.

"Want to grab some breakfast first?" he asked. "There's a place called Hillary's Pancake House not far from here, and it has some nice reviews on Yelp."

"Sure," she said, her eyes lighting up. "I'd kill for some coffee."

"Let's go, then," he said. "Want me to get your suitcase?"

"I'm fine."

The drive to Hillary's Pancake House was quick. It was still just a bit before rush hour, and Chicago was still waking up. The pancake house itself seemed a bit of a letdown, a dirty-looking structure with dark windows and a sign with the place's name alongside the image of a woman holding a shining plate of pancakes, a murderous grin on her face. Once inside, though, it looked distinctly better. The interior was mostly wooden, radiating a homely atmosphere. The smell of sizzling oil and coffee intermingled in Tatum's nose, cuing his stomach to rumble hungrily. The place was half-full, mostly with men and women dressed for their nine-to-five office work and a couple of sleepy-looking cops who were probably at the end of their midnight shift.

"Good morning," their waitress chirped as soon as they sat, dropping menus in front of them. She was young and blonde, her hair in a ponytail, and Tatum did his best to focus on her eyes and to avoid glancing at her chest in her tight uniform. His eyes kept gliding downward anyway, so he ended up looking at her nose most of the time.

"Would you like me to give you a few moments to—"

"Coffee, please," Tatum said, before their waitress could make her escape. "And the . . ." He glanced at the menu, choosing the first option that sounded good. "Apple and spice pancakes."

"That dish has nuts; is that okay?"

"Absolutely."

"Bacon and eggs for me, please," Zoe said. "The eggs sunny-side up and the bacon extra crispy."

"Okay. And coffee for you as well?"

"Yes. Very strong. And seriously, you can't make that bacon too crispy as far as I'm concerned."

The waitress gave them a final toothy smile and then turned away.

"Did you have a nice flight?" he asked Zoe.

"The guy who sat next to me tried to hit on me and got quite unpleasant when I turned him down," Zoe said. "But other than that it was fine."

"I'm sorry to drag you to Chicago like this, but I could really use your help."

"No problem. The case sounds fascinating."

"Well," Tatum said, feeling uncomfortable with her choice of words, "it's definitely unusual."

"I mean, what I find so interesting is the reasoning. This guy obviously has necrophiliac tendencies, and the embalming must make the sexual act much more complicated because—"

"Perhaps we should talk about this later, in a more private place," Tatum said hurriedly, noticing that Zoe's voice became louder when she was animated. The woman sitting at the table next to them put her fork down noisily and gave them a disgusted look.

"Okay." Zoe nodded, then became silent. She was less talkative when serial killers weren't the topic of conversation.

"I found a nice clean motel not far from the police station," Tatum said. "I took the liberty of booking you a room there for tonight. Is that okay, or do you want to look for a different motel, or—"

"That's great, thanks," Zoe said.

He nodded, and she nodded back. He added a strained smile, which she returned. They were the essence of awkward silence.

"So I understand you're also new to the BAU," Tatum said. "I heard you were in Boston until recently?"

Zoe nodded. "I worked there as a consultant for the FBI for several years. But Mancuso was determined to get me into the BAU, and quite frankly, it's every forensic psychologist's dream, so I couldn't really refuse."

"I totally get that," Tatum said. "Do you have family in Boston?"

"My sister used to live there," Zoe said. "But she moved to Dale City with me."

"Really?" Tatum raised an eyebrow. "You two close?"

"Yeah," Zoe said. "And she said she needed a change. She hated Boston. She left a bad relationship back there."

She looked uncomfortable discussing it, and Tatum nodded non-committally, deciding not to push the subject.

She cleared her throat. "What about you? How did you get from the field office in LA to the BAU?"

"Oh . . ." Tatum mumbled. "I don't really know. It was a promotion of sorts, I guess."

The waitress returned, putting their plates and coffee mugs in front of them. Tatum was glad to stuff some pancake into his mouth and have a reason to stop talking about his "promotion." While chewing, he looked at Zoe handling her meal. She picked up a piece of toast, carefully broke off a piece of bacon, and speared them both with her fork. Then she dipped the happy couple into her egg carefully and lifted the fork, inspecting it as if it were a rare specimen. Finally, she put it in her mouth, chewed a bit, and shut her eyes, inhaling deeply through her nose.

"So . . . it's good?" he said.

Zoe kept chewing and finally swallowed. "It's good," she said. "I like my bacon a bit crunchier."

She sliced a piece of the egg white, placed another bacon chip on it, and carefully lifted it to her mouth. Zoe was not a fast eater. They would be here for a while. Tatum tried to slow down. He'd already eaten a third of his plate, while she'd taken just two bites.

"So about the case," he said, deciding to broach the safer topic, their job. "The guys investigating it have hired a local profiler. A Dr. Bernstein?"

Zoe twisted her nose in disgust, as if he'd just mentioned a malignant skin disease. "Oh," she said.

"You know him?"

"I've seen him on TV a few times."

"I don't think he's very good," Tatum said. "I have some ideas about the case, and the investigators aren't very receptive because of this guy."

"Okay."

"I figure you go in there and wow them with your credentials. I think they'll be a bit nicer, since you're a civilian. And then back me up a bit, so we can get some headway with the investigation."

"Oh," Zoe said. "You really planned this carefully. So you have an idea."

"Several," Tatum said.

"And you asked for me to help you get rid of the competition."

"Well . . ." Tatum hesitated. "And hear your opinion, of course."

"Of course."

Somewhere, he had taken a misstep. He tried to correct the situation. "I hear you did a really good job on the Stokes case," he said.

"Really?" Zoe said disinterestedly, creating another bacon, egg, and toast sculpture. "I'm glad. Who knows? I might even be as good as a real FBI agent one day."

Tatum sighed. He just couldn't catch a break with people lately.

CHAPTER 10

Dan Finley was not enjoying his time on the beach as much as he wanted to. For one, a snotty-nosed toddler next to him was excavating a large hole, throwing scoops of sand over his shoulder in complete disregard for the people around him. Two scoops had already landed on Dan's beach towel. He would have said something, but he didn't think it was his job to discipline other people's kids or to teach parents how to be parents. These days, people gave birth to kids without taking responsibility for them. Instead, they lobbed their children onto society and then complained when crime rose or unemployment got worse.

He shook his head sadly and turned over onto his stomach, letting the sun tan his back. If he wasn't going to enjoy this trip to the beach, the very least he could ask for was a nice uniform tan. He only hoped his sunscreen was good enough to filter out the cancer-y bits from the sun, leaving only the wholesome tan-y bits. These days, sunscreen companies cut costs without even thinking about the consequences. It was probably cheaper to get good lawyers and evade medical lawsuits than to make high-quality sunscreen.

The thought of cancer made him nervous. When he had woken up that morning, the sun had seemed inviting, alluring. Now it felt a bit more like a scorching ball of doom, peppering his skin with tumors.

Feeling anxious, he sat up and put his shirt on. Was it worth it? Dying of cancer before the age of forty just to have nice tan skin?

It was not. These days, people focused on the now, ignoring the future. His health was the most important thing he had.

The woman to his left still sat there, sobbing. She had been there for the past hour, and he had done his best to give her the privacy she deserved. He had noticed she was crying only after he had sat down, or he would have chosen a different spot on the beach. Sitting next to a crying person was an absolute downer. Of course he wasn't enjoying himself, with this chick crying her eyes out ten feet from him.

Perhaps she wasn't crying at all. She was sitting on the sand, her face buried in her hands. It totally looked as if she were crying. But maybe she had just fallen asleep. Come to think of it, she hadn't moved much since he'd sat down.

Maybe it was just a cry for help. Was she sobbing on the beach, hoping someone would ask her what was wrong? Of course, no one would. These days you could climb a building and threaten to jump, and all the passersby would just film you for their YouTube channels. No empathy. He was outraged.

Slowly, he got up and walked over to the woman. She seemed sickly somehow, her skin pale, almost gray. Maybe she had a skin condition. She shouldn't be in the sun like that. Had she put sunscreen on? She had no bag with her, not even a towel. She just sat on the beach, dressed in a long-sleeved yellow shirt and a skirt.

"Excuse me, uh . . . miss? Are you okay?" he asked.

She didn't move. Didn't answer. He almost turned away. She didn't want to be bothered. But something seemed . . . *off* with her. She needed help; he was sure of it.

"Miss? Are you okay? Do you want a drink?" He crouched next to her. "Miss?"

He put a hand on her shoulder.

Her shoulder was rock hard, rigid, and cold. He suddenly realized her neck had a very clear, dark bruise around it, that her skin was gray, that she wasn't moving at all. Not even breathing.

"Shit!" he screamed, falling back.

This girl was dead.

CHAPTER 11

Tatum tried to rectify his mistake—Zoe had to give him that—but she was furious and far from a conciliatory mood. She had been doing something important at Quantico, and he had yanked her away from it to essentially be his wingman. She was icy for the remainder of their meal and their drive to the police headquarters, where Tatum quickly led her to the special task office and introduced her to Lieutenant Martinez.

"Nice to meet you," the lieutenant said, shaking her hand. "I didn't know the FBI would send any more agents. We really don't have anywhere you can sit. This wasn't my intention when I asked for the bureau's assistance—"

"I'm not a federal agent," she said quickly, sliding into her intended role. "I'm a forensic psychologist. And I'm here just for a short visit; I don't need anywhere to sit down. I'm just interested in what Dr. Bernstein has to say about this case. I find this murderer intriguing."

"Do you?" Martinez said, his eyes looking from her to Tatum in suspicion. "Are you familiar with Dr. Bernstein?"

"Most people in my profession are." She smiled sweetly at Martinez. "He's very well known. And I'm sure he's probably heard of me, so it would be an interesting discussion. We might have some new conclusions when we're done."

"I'll ask him," Martinez said.

Zoe waited as the man made a phone call. He clearly suspected Tatum had brought her to shoot down their profiler. It was a cheap trick, incredibly transparent. But she might as well do her job if she was there.

"Okay, great. See you there," the lieutenant said and put down his phone. He turned to Zoe and smiled at her. "You're right. Dr. Bernstein has heard of you and was excited at the prospect of discussing this with you. He just walked in the building. Let's meet him in the meeting room. I'll call the other detectives—"

"No need to waste their time yet," Zoe hurriedly said. "I think just the four of us should do, at least to kick things off. Maybe later we can have a larger, formal meeting."

"Well, they might be out in the field later." Martinez frowned. "Okay, let's head to the meeting room and see what the doctor thinks."

She followed the two men as they led her to a room down the hall. Dr. Bernstein already sat inside at a long table, reviewing his notes. Zoe was familiar with the man, had seen him several times on TV. He seemed to pop up whenever a serial killer was in the media's focus. He wasn't the only one. There was a group of so-called experts who were always overjoyed to be interviewed and to show off their extensive knowledge of the subject. These people weren't harmless. They spread misconceptions and hysteria in the general population and often changed the course of investigations, just like this case.

"Dr. Bernstein." Zoe smiled, her eyes widening in fake admiration. "It's an honor to finally meet you."

"Thank you," the man said, standing up to shake her hand. His handshake was limp, passive.

Zoe kept her smile, sitting down. "So I'm interested in what you have to say about this . . . Strangling Undertaker."

"Wouldn't you prefer we start discussing it from scratch?" The doctor sat down as well. "It might prevent your own opinions from being influenced by mine."

Zoe was amused by the idea of Bernstein affecting her opinions. She glanced at Tatum and Martinez, who sat down at the table. "I don't want to waste time. You've clearly put a lot of effort into it, so let's start with what we already have."

"Very well." Dr. Bernstein stood up again. "Well, the subject is male, probably white, in his late twenties or thirties—"

"I definitely agree," Zoe said, nodding.

Bernstein smiled modestly and sent a victorious glance over to Tatum, whose face was blank, his jaw clenched.

"In fact," Zoe continued, "I'd say there's a sixty-three percent chance he's white and only a twelve percent chance he's black and a sixteen percent chance he's Hispanic or Latino."

The doctor blinked in confusion.

"That sounds very specific," Lieutenant Martinez said. "How can you tell—"

"That's the division of the population in the United States," Zoe explained. "So if you choose any man at random, it would match these probabilities. I assume that's what the doctor meant, since there's no other way to know he's white. Serial killers are spread pretty evenly through all races."

"That's not entirely what I meant," the doctor said, pursing his lips. "As I've said in two of my books—"

"I'm sorry," Zoe said, her tone apologetic. "I haven't read any of your books."

There was a moment of silence.

The doctor finally cleared his throat, turning away from her, speaking to Martinez. "Well, if Dr. Bentley here had my experience, she'd agree he targets white victims, and that indicates—"

"We have two victims," Zoe said. "We don't know what he targets yet. And there have been white killers who killed black women and vice versa." She felt impatient. His jab about her experience rubbed at her.

"It's very easy to speak of those things as an academic," Bernstein said. "After all, you've only recently graduated. How long have you been practicing forensic psychology as an agent . . . I'm sorry, I meant as a *consultant*?"

She flushed and smiled, baring her teeth. "A few years. How many cases did you help profile? Aside from your media interviews, I mean."

"Do you agree with the doctor's assessment of his age?" Martinez asked, raising his voice slightly.

"It's probably a good estimate." Zoe shrugged. "But I wouldn't treat it as fact. Monte Rissel began to rape women when he was fourteen. He moved on to killing them soon after. By the way, he's a good example of a serial killer who murdered both white and black women. Right, Doctor?"

"Well, yes . . . uh . . ." He seemed at a momentary loss.

"I really think we're making progress," Zoe said. "Please go on."

"Well . . . he leaves the bodies in public spots, demonstrating his superiority over the law enforcement agencies and enjoying his fame. He—"

"Has he written any letters to the newspapers or the police?" Zoe asked.

"No," Martinez said.

"Then how do you know he isn't just doing it as part of his fantasy, getting off on danger? Or maybe those locations hold some significance for him. I see no demonstration in these murders of any search for fame or a game of cat and mouse. The spots he chose are public, that's true, but they're also guaranteed to be quite empty at night and have no security cameras in them. And posing the body seems to have a meaning for him. The chosen spot could have something to do with this meaning."

"That's *your* interpretation," the doctor said. "But—"

"Well, if we have two contradictory interpretations, we can't really assume one of them is probable until we've agreed that the other is not likely," Zoe said firmly.

"Okay," Martinez said, raising his hands as if trying to control the heated discussion. "Perhaps we should start with the points we've definitely agreed upon. Dr. Bernstein said that since the man is acquainted with embalming practices, he's likely worked in a funeral home before. I definitely agree, and—"

"Why?" Zoe asked.

"Why?" Martinez looked at her, annoyed. "What do you mean?"

"Why do you agree? Did you look for suspects in funeral homes before Dr. Bernstein did his profile?"

"Well, no, but it sounds quite logical that—"

"It does," Zoe said, deciding she'd had enough. "Everything sounds logical when spoken by a man with the cultivated appearance of knowledge. Definitely when he is elderly and has white hair and tends to appear on TV with the tagline *serial killer expert*. But if our killer is so experienced in embalming, why was the foot of the first victim decomposing when she was found? Let me tell you why. It was decomposing because he hadn't embalmed many times before, and he was still learning the process. The second victim was completely embalmed. Our killer is learning. Also, Agent Gray told me the second victim was embalmed with a different mixture of embalming fluid. He's experimenting because he's new at this. I'd say that if you want to exclude a portion of the population, I'd exclude all people who have worked more than a few weeks in a funeral home. They already know their job."

The room was silent, and Zoe realized she was practically yelling. Andrea often complained that she raised her voice when she was excited or agitated. She took a deep breath, then turned toward Martinez.

"There is a well-known phenomenon that always follows serial killers. I'm talking about pseudoexperts who talk on TV about serial killers. They mislead the public, contribute to mass hysteria, and taint jury pools. They cause immeasurable damage. They have a name. In my profession, we call them *talking heads*."

She looked at the doctor, who was crimson by that point. Was he about to have a heart attack? She rehearsed her first aid training in her mind as she said, "Dr. Bernstein is a talking head. You can keep listening to his so-called profiling opinions, but you won't find your killer that way."

The doctor blinked and his jaw clenched, and then he stood up and grabbed his briefcase. For a moment he seemed about to say something; then he simply turned and left, slamming the door behind him. There was a moment of silence. Tatum looked at her, his eyes wide. Zoe met his stare calmly. He'd brought her to deal with the profiler, hadn't he? Had he expected it to go nicely?

"That was unnecessary," Martinez said curtly.

"I have to disagree," Zoe said. "I'm sorry things got a bit heated, but this man has given you some bad advice, and it could potentially lead to a waste of valuable time."

"Now what?" Martinez asked. "You tell me your friend was right? That we should stake out the current crime scenes in case the killer returns?"

Zoe and Tatum's eyes met. "Not this killer," Zoe said.

"I'm sorry?" Tatum said, his voice tense.

"It's true. Serial killers often return to the scene of the crime, mostly to recall the act and masturbate. But these crimes were not committed where you found the bodies. The first victim was killed in her own apartment, and I doubt he'll go back there. The second victim disappeared from the street, and there's an indication she'd been tied up. This leads me to assume she was taken somewhere and killed there—otherwise why tie her? The locations where you found the bodies won't fulfill the killer's fantasies; he'd be drawn to the actual places where he killed the women. There's no point in staking them out. It would be a waste of manpower."

Another tense silence settled upon the room as Zoe sent a challenging glance toward Tatum. His face darkened, but he said nothing.

Martinez cleared his throat. "So what do you think—"

The door opened, and a man stood in the entrance, his eyes wide. "Lieutenant," he said. "We have another one."

CHAPTER 12

There was a crowd of spectators alongside the lake beach on Ohio Street, standing as close as they could to the yellow crime scene tape. Some of them, inevitably, were taking pictures with their phones. Tatum could spot two news crews, the reporters talking animatedly to the cameras. He followed Lieutenant Martinez to one of the cops on the scene, who was trying to get the spectators to stand back. He was holding a small notebook.

"Lieutenant Martinez." The lieutenant flipped his badge. "These two are with me."

They identified themselves to the cop, who dutifully scribbled their names in the crime scene log, the wind flipping the pages as he did so. One of the media crews ran in their direction, spouting questions. Tatum turned his back to the camera and marched onto the beach, Zoe by his side. He did his best to ignore her. He was furious at her for undermining his influence with the lieutenant and was already thinking of ways to tell Mancuso she had to call the woman back to Quantico.

His black shoes sank into the sand, leaving deep footprints behind him. He knew he would have a mound of sand in each shoe when he left, as well as in his socks. He was definitely not dressed for the beach.

They walked toward a group of people who shuffled around a woman sitting on the sand. If Tatum hadn't known the woman was dead beforehand, he would have assumed she was just enjoying the sunny day. When he got closer, he saw that the body was posed as if she had buried her face in her hands.

Zoe paused five yards from the body.

"Are you okay?" Tatum asked, despite himself. "You don't have to be here."

"I'm fine," Zoe said shortly.

"It's one thing to see pictures of dead bodies, Bentley. It's another thing to actually be in—"

"I've been at dozens of crime scenes and have seen plenty of dead bodies," Zoe said, not looking at him. "I'm just trying to get the big picture, and frankly, Agent Gray, you're disturbing my concentration."

The profiler was insufferable. Tatum gritted his teeth and kept walking. As he got closer, he scanned the people around the body. One man, clearly in shock—probably the one who had discovered the body—was talking to a Chicago PD uniformed cop. Another man circled the body, taking pictures. To the body's left, a woman, her black hair swept back into a ponytail, carefully picked something up from the sand and placed it in a paper bag. Those two were probably from the Forensic Services Division called for the scene. Another man, who Tatum guessed was the medical examiner, was inspecting one of the body's feet.

Tatum crouched next to the woman with the ponytail. There was a box of latex gloves at her feet.

"Hi," he said. "Agent Gray, FBI. Mind if I borrow a pair of gloves?"

She turned to face him, her dark-brown eyes looking at him closely. For a moment he almost blurted, "Tina?" Her face was nearly identical to his high school sweetheart's. But she wasn't Tina, and his lips moved weirdly as he tried to get them under control.

"Audrey Jones," she said, raising an eyebrow as he gaped like a fish. "Sure, take a pair. Make sure to give your associates some as well."

He nodded and put on the gloves. They were small, perfect for Audrey's delicate hands, but his clumsy paws felt as if the latex were slowly squeezing the blood out of them. He told himself not to clench his fists, an action that would surely tear the gloves in half.

"When did you get here?" he asked.

"About half an hour ago," she said. "The body was discovered at half past nine."

Tatum looked around him. "Was the beach empty? Why did it take so long to discover the body?"

"I gather people just didn't notice her," Audrey said, slowly folding the paper bag she held. She took a pen from her pocket and scribbled something on it. "They thought she was sleeping or something."

Tatum shook his head in disbelief. A woman dead in the middle of a public beach on a sunny day, and it took people two, maybe three hours to notice her. "Find anything?"

"There were some footprints," Audrey said. "But this entire scene was trampled, so I doubt any of them are relevant. We took some photos anyway. I found a couple of cigarette butts and a used condom almost completely buried in the sand."

Tatum suspected that if Audrey were to search any other part of the beach, she'd find a similar collection of items.

"Thanks, Audrey," he said, standing up.

"No problem," she said, smiling and glancing at him, her head quirked sideways. Even her body language was like Tina's. He wondered if Audrey was bioengineered to mess with his head.

Zoe approached them, and Tatum wordlessly handed her a pair of gloves. She slipped them on and looked at the body, her eyes intent. Tatum followed suit, trying to see what she was looking at.

The victim's hands covered her face in a perfect imitation of a person sobbing. If it weren't for her unnatural stillness and the slight grayish hue of her skin, it would have been impossible to guess she wasn't alive. She wore a long-sleeved yellow shirt and a brown skirt, which was bunched around her thighs. Her feet were bare. There was a bruise circling her throat and bruises around her wrists and ankles. Tatum didn't need the ME to tell him she had probably been bound. Had she been tied when she was killed? Had her death been painful? Had she screamed, begged her captor to let her go? He looked away and stared at the waves, feeling angry.

It was a windy day, and Lake Michigan's small waves broke against each other randomly, creating eddies of white foam. *A bad day for surfing*, he thought automatically, even though he hadn't surfed for over fifteen years. Once he had begun surfing, he could never look at the waves without trying to assess if they were good enough.

It was a nice beach, the water on one side, the high buildings of the Chicago shoreline on the other, their windows mostly tinted blue, as if mirroring the water. There was a small green park to the south. The residents must love coming here, walking or running alongside the beach, maybe going for a swim. How long before they began doing that again? Would the beach be full tomorrow, even though a dead woman had been left there not long before?

"Can you estimate the time of death?" he heard Zoe ask. He turned to her and the body again. She was talking to the ME.

"Maybe later, when I do the autopsy, but I'm not sure. If she's embalmed, like the ones before, it'll be tricky."

"Are you the ME who checked the previous two?" Zoe asked.

"Yeah," he said.

"I'd be happy to talk to you later, compare your findings for the three victims."

Happy. Zoe sure could pick her words. *Happy* to talk about women who were strangled to death and embalmed. Overjoyed. Tra-la-la.

The ME nodded, then grabbed one of the victim's hands carefully while holding the upper arm firmly with his other hand. He pulled, and the hand moved away from the face.

"She's more flexible than the other two," he told Zoe.

"Her eyes are closed," Zoe said, looking closely.

"And her mouth," the ME said. "The first victim's mouth wasn't shut." He slid a paper bag over the palm and fastened it there with a rubber band.

"She has a ring," Zoe said, pointing at the other hand.

"Yeah. They'll remove it in the morgue," the ME said, pulling the second hand down, uncovering the face completely. Both of the victim's eyes were shut, her face a mask of calmness.

"Can I?" Zoe asked, motioning at the palm.

"I'd really prefer that you—"

"I'll be careful," Zoe said. She grabbed the palm carefully and slid the ring aside. She looked carefully at the finger, then at Tatum. "No tan line," she said.

"Maybe she has no tan," Tatum suggested.

Zoe shook her head impatiently and gently shifted the shirt's collar. A slight difference in the skin tone was clearly visible. "She had a tan line here," Zoe said. "A different type of shirt, one that exposed more skin." She pulled the collar downward, exposing the same tan line near the body's chest. "More cleavage," she added.

"So?" the ME asked as he put a paper bag on the second hand.

"She was used to being in the sun in shirts that exposed her body." Zoe chewed her lip. "There's a good chance she was a prostitute."

"Or a bike delivery girl," Tatum said. "Or a Cubs cheerleader. Or an unemployed girl who liked to walk in the morning in a spaghetti strap shirt. You can't deduce—"

"I'm not deducing anything," Zoe said sharply. "But one of the previous victims was a prostitute. High-risk victims are the main targets of serial killers. I think it's probable."

Irritated, Tatum turned and walked away. He approached the civilian who stood with Lieutenant Martinez. The man had blond hair and an almost invisible mustache. The contrast to Martinez's facial hair was very noticeable.

"Is this the guy who found the body?" Tatum asked.

"Yup." Martinez nodded. "Dan Finley."

"And I really need to go," Dan said, his voice high. "I have business to attend to and—"

"What kind of business?" Tatum asked.

"I'm a quinoa supplier. I have stores and restaurants that depend on me. These days, if you're late on one shipment, people move on to a different supplier. There's no loyalty, no partnership. It's every man for—"

"What time did you get to the beach?" Tatum asked.

"I went through this twice already. How many times do you expect me to answer the same questions?"

"It's a murder investigation, Mr. Finley," Martinez said. "We don't want to make any mistakes. I'm sure you understand that."

"Like I told the others, I got to the beach around eight."

"And you didn't report the body until nine thirty?" Tatum asked.

"I didn't know she was dead. I thought she was crying."

"There was a woman crying on the beach for an hour and a half before you checked it out?"

"No one else approached her either. I didn't want to intrude," Dan said, his mouth twisted in bitterness. "These days you can't go to the beach without something like this happening."

"You can't go to the beach without finding a dead body?" Tatum looked at the man, incredulous.

Dan pursed his lips and said nothing. Tatum shook his head and walked away. Martinez joined him a minute later.

"Third victim," Tatum told Martinez.

Martinez nodded. "And only eleven days after the last one."

Tatum folded his arms, looking at the lake. He was frustrated and worried. He hoped they'd manage to get the killer before a fourth dead woman showed up.

CHAPTER 13

Zoe stared at her chicken salad with disinterest. Aside from the parking spot they had found nearby, the place they had stopped for lunch didn't have a lot going for it. The waitress—a curt, unpleasant woman with a rash on her neck—had recommended the chicken salad. She said it was her favorite dish. Zoe doubted that. The chicken was dry and spiced with an unidentifiable green herb, and the vegetables had been frozen and defrosted so many times they had the texture of a napkin.

The company didn't help her appetite either. Tatum was surly and silent, stewing in his rage. He ate a hamburger, taking huge bites and swallowing them without chewing more than a couple of times. Clearly, he wanted to get this lunch over with.

Finally, he put down his half-eaten burger and said, "You could have backed me up. Staking out the crime scenes is a solid approach, and now Martinez won't do it."

"It wouldn't have done any good," Zoe said, trying her best to stay patient. Back at the most recent crime scene, Tatum had made her question her own deductions, and she'd said nothing to Martinez about her theory that the victim had been a prostitute. She regretted that now. "The killer won't return there."

"You don't know that. You're only guessing."

"I am not guessing," Zoe said sharply. "I am deducing from previous cases and from the available evidence. That's what I do. That's my job."

"Speaking of your job, couldn't you have been a bit subtler with Bernstein? I brought you here to shake their trust in him, not to decimate him."

"You're not the one who brought me here. Mancuso sent me. And she sent me to consult with the Chicago police. Which is what I did and what I'm still doing."

"Consult? You're like Dr. Bernstein. The two of you are no better than psychics. Inventing stories for the detectives, messing with the investigation, just to justify your paycheck."

Her face heated up, her heart racing. She felt like grabbing the chicken salad and chucking it in his face. "Fuck you. You know what, Tatum? I don't know what your damn problem is with me. The reason I didn't back you up was because your suggestion was dumb. Anyone with a shred of experience with serial killers could have seen that. But of course, you don't *have* any experience. You got to the BAU because they didn't want you anywhere else. So get over the size of your penis or your bed-wetting issue or whatever it is you're compensating for, and man up. If you want me to back you up, you'll have to keep up with me. And I move fast."

She stood up and stormed out of the restaurant. He could damn well pay for the tasteless chicken salad.

She stomped down the street, feeling like she was fourteen again, that cop looking at her with a patronizing face.

Listen, honey, leave the policing to the grown-ups, okay?

Damn Tatum, and damn that cop from nineteen years ago whose name she had intentionally forgotten. Damn all the FBI agents who resented her for taking a "real agent's" job. Damn the condescension that kept following her despite all her achievements. Would there ever be a point where she'd get the appreciation she deserved?

There were tears of anger in her eyes, and she quickly wiped them away with the back of her hand, swallowing hard, forcing herself to calm down. She stood still and focused on her breathing. A deep breath emerged with a tiny hiccup; the next one was completely smooth and steady. Her heart slowed down. The anger was there, but she was back in control.

Tatum called her name behind her. Damn it. She started walking away again.

"Zoe! For God's sake, wait up."

"Leave me alone."

"Sure, whatever," he said coldly behind her. "But I thought you might like to know they've identified the girl. There was a match with a missing person report. Her name is Krista Barker, and she was a working girl."

A working girl. That was Tatum's way of saying she was a prostitute without using the word *prostitute.* Without admitting she'd been right. She should have told Martinez when she'd thought of it. It would have made him more receptive to see she got things right.

"They're on their way to talk to her roommate, a girl named Crystal. Martinez asked if we want to join him. Should I tell him you're not interested?"

She whirled around, furious. Tatum looked at her, his face blank and cold.

"No," she said coolly. In complete control. "I want to hear what the *prostitute* has to say."

CHAPTER 14

Crystal fidgeted on the bed, occasionally glancing at the strangers who had come to see her. Agent Gray had said he was from the FBI, and Martinez was from the Chicago PD. The woman hadn't said where she was from. Was she the FBI agent's girlfriend? It sure looked that way. The way they were pointedly avoiding each other's eyes was a dead giveaway. And the way they both nodded when the detective talked but actively ignored each other. Yeah, those two were banging each other, no doubt about it.

She wished they'd go away. She'd just had a morning client, which only happened, like, every third day. Men usually preferred the cover of darkness when paying for sex. A twenty-dollar bill sat in her pocket, and once the cops left, she could go downstairs to R. T., buy a rock from him, and smoke it—start the day on the right foot.

Her stomach rumbled. She could also get something to eat. When had she eaten last?

No, first a rock, then she'd try to get another morning client. Who knew? She might get lucky. Then she'd definitely buy some breakfast.

She wasn't listening again, and the detective, Martinez, looked frustrated.

"Sorry, what?" she asked.

"When did you see Krista last?"

Krista. She missed Krista so much. Her friend had been what made life bearable. Krista could really make her smile, sometimes. They were always a pair, Krista and Crystal. People would laugh when they introduced themselves, like it was some sort of hilarious joke. Look at the two crackheads, Krista and Crystal. R. T. used to say they should start using meth instead of crack. Then they could say Krista and Crystal were doing crystal. Har-har, ain't life just a barrel of jokes.

"I don't know," she said. "A week ago, I guess? Maybe more?"

"You reported her missing four days ago," Martinez said.

"Yeah, then I guess maybe it was more than that. Because she was missing for, like, four or five days before I reported it."

"Why did you wait so long?" Agent Gray asked.

She could feel the ants crawling under her neck. She always did after a day without crack. The day before had been crap. Only one customer, just wanted a BJ, and he had stiffed her, given her only ten bucks when he was done. R. T. had said he'd chase the guy, get the missing money, but he never did. What was the point of having a pimp if he didn't stick up for you when it mattered?

"I don't know." She shrugged. "She's been gone before. Krista was always disappearing. She had clients who'd pick her up for a day or two. Krista always got the classy clients."

Because Krista was good looking, unlike her. Her teeth were still good, and she wasn't as skinny.

"Do you know who those clients were?" the woman asked. What was her name? Zoe. She had freaky eyes. They burrowed into Crystal, digging up all her secrets. She looked away. God, she needed a rock.

"No," she said.

"Who does?"

"No one." R. T. probably did, but he'd kill her if she gave them his name. "Any progress? On the case? Do you think you'll find her?"

Crystal knew the score. Girls like them, if they disappeared, they didn't come back. Only Julia Roberts could disappear for a week and come back with a new wardrobe and a billionaire for a lover. A girl like Crystal, if she disappeared, you could be sure she was lying in a ditch somewhere.

But not Krista. Crystal always assumed her friend wouldn't go that way. Krista was almost like Julia Roberts, in a way. She had this glow, this . . . aura. Like she was meant for something else.

"I'm afraid I have some bad news," Martinez said. "Krista is dead."

The first thought that went through Crystal's mind was the eighty dollars Krista had hidden from R. T. The eighty dollars Crystal had sworn she would never touch. It was the money Krista had saved to get out of Chicago for good. Her emergency fund. And it was Crystal's now, and she could use it to buy four rocks . . . no, three rocks and a good breakfast and . . .

At that point she burst into tears. The three strangers probably thought she was crying for her dead friend, but she wasn't. She was crying for herself.

The agent and the detective became restless. The hell with them both. But the woman, Zoe, crouched to look into Crystal's eyes. Her intense gaze mesmerized Crystal, whose sobbing slowly faded into a whimper.

"I'm sorry for your friend," Zoe said. "It was a man who did it."

Crystal nodded. Of course it was.

"We're looking for him," Zoe said. "We want to catch him before he hurts anyone else, and we could really use your help. But I need you to focus. Can you focus, Crystal?"

Maybe the woman was from social services. She definitely reminded Crystal of a social worker she'd met once. She had the same look in her eyes, like she wanted to help but also knew there was no help for someone like Crystal. There was no pity there, no sadness or disgust. There was understanding.

"Sure." Crystal sniffed.

"Was Krista doing crack too?" Zoe asked.

Bam. The woman didn't beat around the bush. Crystal didn't ask her how she knew. Crack left its marks—though it wasn't always obvious. Some were better at hiding it, but Crystal sure wasn't.

"Sometimes," she said. "Not as much as I do."

"What was Krista like?"

"She was . . . kind. Some of the whores on the street, they can get real mean, you know? But Krista was never like that. And she got along with almost everyone. Even most of the mean ones."

And R. T. didn't beat her as much as he beats me.

"Did Krista have a ring?"

"A what?" Crystal asked.

"A silver ring. With a small ruby. It might have been fake."

Crystal snorted. "She would have pawned it a long time ago if she did. Or someone would have taken it."

"She probably got it very recently."

"No ring," Crystal said.

"How did Krista usually dress?" Zoe asked.

"You ask the weirdest questions, lady. She dressed like a crack whore."

"Did she own a long-sleeved yellow shirt or a brown skirt?"

"She would never wear a yellow shirt," Crystal said. "She always said yellow wasn't her color. And she didn't own a brown skirt."

"Okay." Zoe nodded. "Lieutenant Martinez? Do you want to ask any additional questions? Or maybe you, *Agent?*" She said *agent* like people usually said *asshole.* What was up with these two?

"Yes," Martinez said. "Who sells you the crack?"

"I want to help, but I'm not telling you that."

"Even if it was the same man who killed her?"

"It wasn't."

"Can you tell us about the last time you saw her?" Agent Gray said.

"We were working in the street, and I went into the alley with a john," Crystal said. "When I came back, she was gone."

"Did anyone see who she went with?"

"No."

"Did you see any suspicious people that night?"

She snorted. "The places I work in, everybody's suspicious."

"Anyone that stood out?"

"Yeah," she suddenly recalled. "There was this really creepy dude in a banged-up car. Tried to get a bunch of us to go with him, but no one would."

"How did he look?" Tatum asked.

"Tats all over him. Face, arms, neck," Crystal said, thinking back to that night. "And he talked funny. Like, a real high voice."

"Do you know the type of car?" Martinez asked.

"I don't know. But it was blue. The color was peeling off."

"Did he try to get Krista to come with him?" Agent Gray asked.

"Yeah, but she'd never get into a ride like that."

"Where were you working that night?" the agent continued.

"Next to Brighton Park. We have a street corner there."

"Can you show me where it is exactly?" Martinez asked.

Crystal hesitated. That corner was her prime spot—she got the best customers there. If she showed it to him, he'd know where to send vice.

As if it were some big secret. Everyone knew where the whores of Brighton Park worked.

"Sure," she said. "I'll show you."

CHAPTER 15

His house felt . . . empty.

This breakup had been the toughest for him so far. He knew it had been the right thing to do, but he hadn't been prepared for the loneliness that followed. There was something wholesome about waking up in bed with the woman you loved, watching her lie there—her eyes closed, her face innocent, her body warm . . .

Well, maybe not warm.

It had been reassuring, leaving home and knowing that when he returned, she'd be waiting there for him. Always there, right where he left her. Completely predictable. She had been someone he could trust.

But frankly, if the spark was gone, there was no point in postponing the inevitable, right?

The next woman would be the real thing. He would be wary, choose more carefully. Though the last one had been charming and full of life, there had been a certain . . . trashiness in her. Their relationship had saved her from a slippery slope of drug abuse; he had no doubt about it. He'd always know it, and she'd always know it. Perhaps *that* had been the real problem that had led to their breaking up. That and the mediocre job he had done when embalming her, of course.

No, the next time would be better. He would choose better, and he would do a better job with her. She'd be perfect.

Should he look for one tonight? The relationship had only ended the night before. And he was exhausted after his sleepless night, driving her to the beach and carrying her to where she wanted to be.

For a moment that night, he had thought it might all end.

There was another couple there, snuggling on the beach. He hadn't noticed them in the darkness, or he would have kept going, taken her to a different location. He was dragging her, her heels occasionally touching the sandy ground. He breathed hard, cursing himself for not parking closer. Once or twice he almost decided that he was far enough. But deep inside, he knew she'd want to be close to the water, watching the lake's small waves lapping at the shore. He had almost reached his destination when the couple stood up, apparently deciding it was time to go home.

He spotted their double silhouette against the background of the moonlit water, less than twenty feet away and walking in his direction. He had only seconds. His hand slid to the knife in his pocket, heart beating hard.

He quickly devised a plan. He'd slit the man's throat first. The woman would be easier to deal with. Maybe he could take her home and . . .

But it was too risky, and he didn't want to drop his girl. Instead, he straightened her, put his arm around her waist, leaned his head against hers. She stood, her face buried in her hands. The couple would see what they truly were: a man consoling a heartbroken woman.

The couple went by, not sparing him a second glance, entranced with each other. He knew how it felt. It was a wonderful thing to be in love.

He dragged her on, helped her down to the sand. He was sorry he hadn't brought her a small towel to sit on. He carefully adjusted the skirt that had slightly twisted itself on the way.

Finally satisfied, he bid her farewell, not wanting to drag this out too much, and left.

And now he missed her. Or at least he missed her presence in his home.

He needed to fill the void. Next time would be different. He would find the right one.

He would start searching tomorrow.

CHAPTER 16

Maynard, Massachusetts, Thursday, October 23, 1997

Zoe's parents were whispering to each other again. This happened almost every day now. They had always been a family that was too loud, but now they had turned into a family of hushed conversations, of strained silences, of silent weeping.

Her mother had known the second girl who had been killed five days ago. Jackie Teller had been the daughter of a woman in her book club. Zoe's mom had gone to Jackie's sixteenth birthday, two years before. And now she had also gone to her funeral.

Zoe's dad tried to act like things were normal, but it was nearly impossible. Her mom would lapse into long, trancelike stares, not hearing a word anyone said to her. She insisted the girls be driven back and forth from school. Zoe had to be home before it got dark, which meant five in the afternoon. The day before, Andrea had opened the door and run outside with her ball, and their mother had chased her, screeching at her hysterically to come inside. Andrea had burst into tears, terrified. When her mother had dragged her into the house, Zoe had hugged her, whispering reassurances in her ear.

Halloween was next week, and pretty much everyone knew there would be no trick-or-treating this year.

And now, in the living room, her parents whispered but stopped instantly when Zoe walked into the room.

"Hey, Dad. You didn't throw away the paper, right?" she said.

"No." He smiled at her. "It's on the kitchen table."

"Great, thanks," she said and quickly turned away.

"What does she need the paper for?" she heard her mother ask.

"Some sort of school project," her dad said. "She needs to keep the weather forecast page or something; I don't know."

She took the paper, went to her room, and closed the door. Then, heart pounding, she read the headline on the second page: "Police Report Progress in Hartley Murder."

She glanced momentarily at Beth Hartley's familiar portrait. They always used the same picture: Beth smiling, looking a bit goofy as she stared sideways at the camera. Would Beth have approved of this picture being plastered in the newspaper over and over again? Zoe doubted it. But Beth was dead. And after what she'd suffered, Zoe didn't think Beth would have cared much about a bad picture, anyway.

Her eyes scanned the article quickly. Like most of the articles about the two murders, it was frustratingly lacking in detail. What progress had been made? Did they have a suspect or suspects in custody? Did they know why Beth had been killed?

The police just said they had made progress. When asked if they thought Jackie Teller had been killed by the same person, the cops said they were still investigating all possibilities.

Jackie Teller had been found dead in Durant Pond. She had gone walking with her dog in the evening, and when she hadn't returned an hour later, her mother had gone out to look for her and afterward called the police. The dog had come home a few hours later, its leash still attached. Jackie had been found by a search party that same night. She had been naked, her body lying in the shallow water of the pond, her hands tied behind her back. Zoe knew all this because Roy, Heather's nineteen-year-old brother, had been part of the search party. He had come back home, shaken to the core, and blurted the entire story before their parents could whisk Heather out of earshot.

Two young women found naked, dead. Everyone was terrified. It was a small town's worst nightmare. Zoe's dad had driven to the supermarket the evening before, and he said the streets had been completely empty. Maynard had become a ghost town at night, its residents hiding in their homes.

Thoughts of the killer still roaming free in the streets chilled Zoe's heart, but it fascinated her too. She had always loved reading thrillers and mysteries, and this was a thriller that had come to life just next door. She couldn't stop thinking about it, trying to piece it all together from the meager facts she knew and the rumors she'd heard.

She took out the scrapbook from under the bed and opened it to the next free page. Then she carefully cut the article from the paper. She leaned her back against the door, prepared to shove the paper and scrapbook under the bed if her parents suddenly barged in. She taped the article into the scrapbook and read it again.

Progress. What could that mean? Were they about to arrest the killer? The man who grabbed women at night, stripping them and killing them? The *monster*?

That was the papers' favorite word when mentioning the killer. A monster on the loose. A monster preying on helpless women. A monster hiding in Maynard.

But Zoe realized the horrifying truth. This wasn't a monster. This wasn't some sort of alien or a scaly creature rising from the sewers. Much worse. It was a man. A guy walking Maynard's streets, probably living there. Maybe he had even gone to Zoe's school when he was younger. Maybe she'd seen him yesterday on her way to school. Maybe her dad had met him in the supermarket. He might have been at Jackie Teller's funeral, by her mother's side, the killing of the girl still fresh in his mind.

Every stranger she met on the street brought the same question. *Could it be him?* She found herself staring at people intently, trying to see the flicker of guilt in their eyes. Two days before, she'd noticed the school janitor had a scratch on his throat—a scratch he could have gotten from a young woman, desperately fighting for her life. Trembling, she had gone to the bathroom and stayed there for almost ten minutes, trying to calm down.

She flipped through her scrapbook, pausing here and there, and then turned to the end, where she had taped a small map of Maynard. She had marked two locations on the map: Durant Pond and the White Pond Road Bridge.

Would there be a third?

For some reason, the streetlights weren't working. Zoe paced quickly down the street, regretting her decision not to call her dad to pick her up from Heather's. The night's darkness surrounded her, chilling, suffocating. The wind blew through the trees, leaves rustling around her the only sound except for the fast tapping of her footsteps. She hugged herself, shivering. It was cold, and the icy air crawled into her collar, the ground freezing her soles. She couldn't wait to get home.

One of her shoelaces was loose, but she didn't want to stop in the dark street and tie it again. She hastened her pace a bit more. It wasn't far now. Why weren't the lights working? She shivered, the black shadow of a tree blocking what little moonlight there was.

She could hear something behind her. Footsteps. Another pair of feet, walking briskly down the street. Getting closer. The hard, labored breathing of a man intermingled with the sound of rapid pacing. She was almost home. If she screamed, people would come to help. It was probably nothing, just a man out for a brisk stroll.

He was getting closer, and she found herself hurrying, then running, panicking, sucking in large gulps of icy-cold air that chilled her lungs. Someone whimpered in fright. It was her. Behind her, the man was running as well. He didn't shout at her to stop, didn't call her name—he simply ran, his breathing heavier than before, almost like a growl, a snarl.

How many footsteps to her home? Thirty? Fifty? Tears of fear ran down her cheeks, and she glanced backward, saw his shadow—wide, tall, dark—his eyes predatory, narrowing, gleaming in the blackness of the night.

There was nothing to do but scream. "Help! Someone!" Her voice sounded strained, broken, not as loud as she'd wanted. No doors opened, no windows. No one came out of their houses to help her, and the man who chased her was upon her, grabbing her by the shirt. The collar choked her as she struggled onward, and he pulled her back, dragging her to a clump of bushes, throwing her to the ground, out of sight, helpless. A knife in his hand, he tore at her clothes, his eyes full of wildness and lust and hate . . .

Her hand jolted, trying to stop her attacker, and she woke up, a scream lodged in her throat. She lay in the darkness, breathing hard, her heart pounding, feeling constricted in her chest. Slowly, recognition seeped in. She was in her bedroom, just one door away from her parents' room. The night was cold, and she had thrown the blanket off at some point. She picked it up from the floor, trembling, not sure whether from the chill or the nightmare. She fumbled at her light switch and turned it on, squinting in the sudden glare.

Andrea was asleep on the bedroom floor, and the light made her sister shift in her sleep. Zoe quickly turned it off. It was the second night she'd found Andrea asleep in her room. Supposedly, her kid sister knew nothing about what was going on, but she could feel everyone's fear, and she knew she couldn't go outside to play anymore. She could obviously sense something was wrong.

Zoe curled up in her blanket, afraid to go back to sleep. The dream still lingered in her mind. It felt so vivid. Was that how Jackie Teller felt before she died? Or Beth?

No. For them, it had probably been worse. And there had been no waking up afterward.

"Zoe?" Her sister's sleepy voice broke the silence in the room.

"Yeah?" Zoe tried to keep her voice steady.

"Was Jackie old?"

"What?"

"Jackie. The woman that Mom knew. Was she very old?"

Zoe wondered what Andrea had overheard and how much of it she understood. She was only five.

"No," she said. "She wasn't old."

"But Mommy told Daddy Jackie died. And only old people die, right? Really old people."

Zoe lay on her back, staring at the ceiling, remaining silent.

"Was Jackie old?" her sister persisted. This wasn't going to go away.

"No, but . . . this wasn't supposed to happen."

"But she died, right?"

"Yes. She died."

"Do you think I might die? I don't want to die." A frightened sob. "Mommy said only really old people die. Older than Grandma."

"Yeah, don't worry, Ray-Ray," Zoe heard herself say. "Only old people die."

"Older than Grandma?"

"Yeah, older than Grandma."

"So I won't die?"

"Only when you're really old, Ray-Ray."

"And will you die?"

"Yeah, but only when I'm really old. Go to sleep, Ray-Ray."

"Can I sleep in your bed?"

"Sure," Zoe said, partly relieved. "Come on."

Her sister leaped into the bed, nearly killing Zoe with a knee to the stomach. Andrea snuggled against Zoe as she tried to catch her breath.

It seemed to take only seconds before her sister's gentle breathing steadied. Zoe stayed awake, feeling as if she would never sleep again.

Her math teacher was sick Friday morning, and Zoe suddenly had two free blocks until the next class. Heather suggested they cut school and get some hot chocolate. Zoe was happy with the idea at first, but then a different, haunting thought popped into her mind.

She could go to Durant Pond.

There was no real danger. It was morning; there would probably be joggers there or people walking their dogs. She just wanted to have a look. And her parents would never know.

She didn't have her bicycle with her. Dad had driven her to school that morning, but her house wasn't far away. She could sneak out, get her bicycle, and ride to the pond. Take a quick look and then go back home, leave the bicycle, and get back to school on time for the next class.

She knew it was a strange thing to do, but the more the idea blossomed in her mind, the more she *had* to do it. She didn't know why, but she just couldn't let it go. She remembered how reassuring it had been to go to the White Pond Road Bridge. Maybe if she finally saw Durant Pond, she could stop thinking about Jackie Teller naked, hands tied behind her back, struggling for her life.

Zoe and Heather left the school premises, walking briskly toward Main Street. Though they had two hours, the nearest café was almost a mile away, and they had to hurry. A couple of seniors stood on the other side of the street. When they spotted the girls, they began catcalling Heather, whistling and jeering. Heather hugged her chest, embarrassed. She was always self-conscious about the way her breasts looked when she was walking fast.

"Idiots," Zoe muttered as they walked out of earshot.

Heather was beet red. "Yeah."

They reached Main Street, but when they got to the café, Zoe paused.

"Listen, I . . ." She hesitated. "I have to go do something."

"What are you talking about?" Heather asked.

Through the café's window, Zoe spotted a few girls from their math class and nearly changed her mind. It was a cold day, and some hot chocolate sounded great.

"I forgot my English notebook at home," she lied. "I'll just run and get it."

"Get it later. We have more than an hour."

"I'll do it real quick. Go on—I'll join you."

Heather shrugged. "Sure, whatever," she said and walked into the café. The smell of baked goods filled Zoe's nose as the door closed behind her friend, and she felt like a moron.

Just a quick visit to the pond, get it out of her system, and she'd still have time to join Heather.

She half walked, half ran to her home and grabbed her bicycle. From there, it was just a fifteen-minute ride to the Durant Pond trail. She pedaled furiously, the cold wind whipping her face. She quickly got to Summer Street, breathing hard, fighting the gentle slope upward.

A woman glanced at her as she whizzed past, and Zoe had a moment of panic. Did that woman recognize her? Would she tell her mom? She convinced herself that she hadn't been recognized, that it was just a stranger. But Summer Street was one of the busiest streets in Maynard. If she stayed on it, someone would spot her.

She swerved right on Brooks Street and followed the small streets and avenues that took her to the Durant Pond trail, hidden from prying eyes. Heart beating from exertion and nervousness, she got on the trail.

The trees around the pond were mostly bare, the ground carpeted with brown leaves that crinkled as her bicycle wheels ran over them. Her heart was beating hard with the effort and the thrill, knowing that her parents would be horrified if they knew where she was.

Jackie Teller had walked this trail only a few days before, holding a leash. What had happened then? Had she heard a noise? Had someone approached her—perhaps even someone she knew? Had he attacked her immediately, or had he talked to her first? Asked her about her dog, mentioned the weather?

She reached the pond and cycled alongside it for a minute. Then she stopped and gazed at the water. The pond was completely calm, mirroring the view on the opposite shore: a line of trees, a clear sky. Many of their leaves had dropped onto the water, dotting the green surface with brown and yellow. A group of ducks swam in the center of the pond. The entire setting was tranquil.

Both bodies had been found in shallow water. Was that significant somehow? Did the killer stalk near water sources? She got off her bicycle and walked until her shoes sank in the muddy shore. She imagined this place at night, the search party walking along the trail, their flashlights illuminating the ground, and someone suddenly noticing a pale, lifeless form floating in the water. A dead body, her hands tied behind her back.

Heather had said she heard her brother crying behind his closed door every night. Her parents were seeking therapy for him.

The silence around her was disconcerting. She had expected to see a jogger or two, maybe a mother taking a baby for a stroll. There was no one.

Why would anyone walk in a park where a girl was murdered less than a week ago?

She didn't want to be there anymore. She regretted not going to the café. She quickly walked back to the bicycle. She began cycling back, but then she spotted a figure between the trees. A man. He stood with his back to the trail, and she couldn't see his face or his hands. Was he just taking a leak? She didn't want to find out. Was it her imagination, or was he breathing heavily?

She began cycling away when she ran over a dry branch. It snapped noisily. Panicking, she glanced back.

"Zoe?"

She stopped her bicycle, exhaling. It was Rod Glover, their neighbor, and suddenly she realized how relieved she was that she wasn't there alone anymore, that a responsible grown-up was there with her.

"Hey," she said, smiling.

"What are you doing here?" he asked, walking toward her, hands in his pockets.

She shrugged. "I had some time off at school, so I thought I'd go for a ride." She frowned. "Don't tell my parents. My mom would have a fit."

He reached her and grinned. "Your secret is safe with me."

She nodded, feeling that she could trust him. He didn't strike her as someone who'd blab. "What are you doing here?" she asked. "Shouldn't you be at work?"

"Crazy thing," he said. "There was a fire in the office today. Some sort of electricity malfunction."

"Really? Is everyone okay?"

"Yeah." He nodded. "Our secretary almost got caught in the flames, but I got her out in time. I had to carry her because she inhaled a lot of smoke and couldn't stand."

"Holy crap. Did they put the fire out?" A pang of worry flashed in her mind. Her dad's office was two buildings down from the telemarketing office where Rod worked.

"Yeah, totally, but they sent us all home. The boss made sure to clarify that tomorrow is just as any other day." He furrowed his brow and stuck out his lower lip, a face he always made when imitating his boss. "Eight thirty, all of you—we have phone calls to make and people to bother."

Zoe grinned at him. "I'm glad you're okay."

He smiled back. "You shouldn't really be walking around here alone. I'll walk you out."

The idea bothered her. When she was a few years younger, she'd enjoyed Rod's company and even hung out with him a couple of times. It was thrilling, talking and spending time with an adult who spoke to her at eye level. But now it suddenly felt strange. The idea of him walking with her in this park made her squirm uncomfortably. Their ten-year age difference seemed a bit creepy instead of cool.

"It's okay," she said. "I'm just leaving. My bike will get me out in three minutes."

He frowned. "Okay," he said. "See ya."

As she cycled away, she began to feel sorry for blowing him off like that. He'd only been looking out for her. They were neighbors, after all, and he was a nice guy. She'd have to remember to thank him next time they met and explain that she had been late to school.

What was Rod doing there, anyway? Did he want to see the pond where Jackie had died, like her? The thought reassured her. Maybe she wasn't such a weirdo after all. People got curious. It was only natural.

CHAPTER 17

Chicago, Illinois, Tuesday, July 19, 2016

Abramson Funeral Home was just a few blocks away from the police station. Zoe patiently sat in the waiting room, its decoration equal parts expensive and tasteless. A large chandelier lit the room in a somber yellow light that gave the gray wall-to-wall carpet a sickly hue. The couch she sat on had rose-patterned upholstery that probably cost much more than it deserved. Several other leather chairs and couches lined the wall, but she was the only one waiting. Were there days when the seats filled up? Was there a good season for funeral homes?

She rubbed her eyes tiredly. She had slept terribly the night before, as she usually did when sleeping away from home. It was the fifth night she hadn't slept much, and she could feel the agitation and irritability that always followed sleep deprivation. She wasn't even sure what she was still doing in Chicago. Agent Gray clearly didn't want her there anymore, and she mostly wanted to get back to the highway murders she had been working on. But instead of getting on the first plane to Washington, she'd told the girl at the motel's reception desk she would probably be staying there for a few more days.

"I'm sorry to keep you waiting," a man said as he approached her. He had thick-rimmed glasses and a soft smile that seemed to radiate sadness. It looked like a smile cultivated to project reassurance and sympathy. Here was a person who understood your pain and was ready to take charge.

"It's quite all right," Zoe said, standing up and shaking his hand. "I didn't schedule beforehand."

"Very understandable," he said. "I could hardly expect that in your moment of grief—"

"I'm not grieving," she quickly interrupted him. Then, realizing that might sound a bit cold, she clarified, "No one in my family has died."

She flipped her employee badge quickly. It had the initials FBI on it, which she hoped would be enough. "I'm with the FBI. I was hoping for a moment of your time."

"Oh." He seemed taken aback. "I don't quite know how I can help the FBI."

"I'm actually more interested in talking to your embalmer," Zoe said. "This is about the murderer the press is calling the Strangling Undertaker."

"Oh, right," he said and twisted his mouth in distaste. "I find that name quite offensive."

"I'm sure you do. So do I. It's very clear the murderer is not an undertaker and doesn't work in a funeral home."

The man's face softened as she said that. That was an aspect of these killings she hadn't yet considered, the hurt feelings of funeral directors.

She pressed on. "I wanted a bit of help understanding the killer's embalming techniques. I found your funeral home online, and there was a lot of praise, specifically about your preservation service." She didn't add that there was also a litany of complaints about the cost of coffins at the Abramson Funeral Home. That was hardly relevant.

"I see." He smiled, an authentic smile this time, full of pride. "Well, I'm Vernon Abramson, and I'm both the owner of this funeral home and the main embalmer. I have two other embalmers working for me, but I tend to take the difficult jobs. I'd be happy to help in any way I can."

"Good." Zoe nodded, satisfied. "Is now a good time?"

He took her down a clean, sterile staircase, lit with a single bulb. The transformation from the fancy waiting room to the sparse staircase was strange but not surprising. She assumed most customers would never see the downstairs. A door opened to a small room, its floor white linoleum, the walls cream colored. A counter stood in front of them, holding various containers, with a line of white cupboards above it, all closed. There was a closed roller shutter opposite the entrance, probably used when bodies were delivered for embalming. In the center of the room stood a flat metal bed. Zoe entered the room and looked at the bed in fascination.

"How long does it take to embalm a body?"

"It really depends on the body. Some are more decayed than others. On average, it takes about two hours."

Zoe nodded thoughtfully.

"I assume you have specific questions? About the killings?"

"Right. Can I show you some pictures? Of the victims?"

"Of course."

She took the folder from her shoulder bag, opened it, and pulled out the photos. Hesitating, she almost spread them on the metal bed, where the room's light was focused, but it felt completely wrong. She spread them on the counter instead. Vernon approached and looked at the pictures with interest. Zoe examined his face. It was strange, showing the pictures to a civilian who wasn't shocked or disgusted. Vernon moved his eyes from one picture to the next, his stare completely cold and emotionless. This was a man very familiar with death.

"I agree with your assessment," he finally said. "Whoever did the embalming wasn't a professional. At least not in the first two cases."

"What makes you say that?" Zoe asked. She had some basic ideas, but she was sure the funeral home director would have a lot more to say.

"Well, for one, no self-respecting professional would mess up the embalming process in the leg like that. The body must have stunk to high heaven when it got to this point."

"Why would the leg decompose? Didn't he get the embalming fluid in?"

"When you insert the embalming fluid into the body, you have to massage the limbs to get the fluid to flow in and replace the blood," the director said. "I assume he didn't do that, or he did but was impatient. Either way, something, maybe a clot, prevented the embalming fluid from flowing freely into the left leg. And your killer didn't notice."

"That's what I thought."

"Also," Vernon said, "the mouth is a dead giveaway."

"The mouth?"

"See the way the mouth is closed with those two victims? It's been sewn shut. But with the first victim, it wasn't, and it's open."

"Right," Zoe said. "I figured the killer was making a statement. Like he was shutting them up, or—"

"You don't understand," Vernon said. "You're *supposed* to sew the mouth shut. Otherwise it remains open, and it doesn't look good. You can see the first body's face. She doesn't look peaceful. She looks surprised—or horrified."

Zoe looked at the photos, seeing it for the first time. He was right. The sewn mouths made the latest victims look serene.

"I see. So you think he figured it out later on?"

"Oh, I'm certain. You can see how he did those two. He clearly learned how to do it right. I mean, I've seen better. But for an amateur, this is very good work."

"How would he learn to do it? Would he have to get someone to teach him?"

"I think you can find stuff online, if you try. Of course, if you learn that way, you make mistakes. Like the mouth on this victim." He gestured at a picture of Monique Silva, the second victim. It was a close-up of her face. "See the side of her mouth? This blackening here?" he pointed at a discolored spot. "That's decay. He didn't disinfect the mouth. The nose, mouth, and eyes have to be disinfected before anything else."

"The third body doesn't have decay," Zoe said, examining the image of Krista. The sunlit face of the dead woman seemed unblemished, though the skin was a bit gray.

"Could be that he's learning," Vernon said, looking at it. "She's definitely embalmed better, though he used less dye than the first victim, which gives the body the gray appearance."

"Why would he use less dye?" Zoe asked.

"No idea. Maybe he's experimenting? Trying to achieve a better solution? Or maybe he just ran out?"

A better solution? Zoe considered the bodies. The first one had been found lying on the grass, straight as a plank; the second one, standing on a bridge, her hands on the rail. The third had been found sitting on the beach, face buried in her hands, her knees bent—just like a living person would do.

"An embalmed body," she said. "How flexible is it?"

"It isn't, at least not the ones embalmed in the standard method," Vernon said. "They're completely rigid."

"What if you change the concentration of the . . . whatever it is you put in it?"

"The formaldehyde?" Vernon asked, his tone amused. "Then the body could be more flexible. But it would decay faster."

"How much faster?"

"In weeks or months, instead of years. Could even take days. Depends on the concentration."

"Could he be fiddling with the concentrations? To get the bodies more flexible?"

"Sure, but what for?"

"I'm not sure yet," Zoe said, half to herself. "I'm not sure at all."

CHAPTER 18

Dr. Bernstein didn't show up that day and didn't answer his phone. Martinez temporarily gave Bernstein's spot in the special task force room to Zoe. The desk was a flimsy old thing that kept wobbling, even with the endless pieces of paper Zoe stuck under its legs. Despite the constant wobbling and the fact that the desk's surface was scratched and spotted, there was something reassuring in knowing she had somewhere to sit, at least for now. She sat at the desk and stared at the page of her notebook in front of her. She used pen and paper to jot down her initial thoughts when profiling. So far she had written down, *The killer is a man; the murder is premeditated, with indications that he is a lust serial killer.* She frowned, frustrated. Maybe a bubble diagram was in order. She drew a bubble and wrote *Fantasy* inside.

The fantasy was always the foundation stone of lust serial killers. Lust serial killers typically daydreamed and fantasized about sexual assault. This fantasy became more intricate and violent as time progressed. As the fantasy became more detailed, the man was more likely to act upon it, trying to fulfill it.

She drew a line from the bubble, creating another bubble, and then wrote in it, *Power or Anger?*

Old-school profilers often stated that lust serial murderers were split into two typologies. Power killer fantasies revolved around the sexual assault, and the murder was a byproduct of the assault. Anger killers were motivated by hatred and sadism.

She stared at the two typologies. Neither really applied. The murder was obviously a very integral part of the fantasy, which seemed to indicate anger typology, but the motivation clearly had to do with power. She crossed both of them off, obliterating both words with multiple angry strokes. This was much more complex.

She drew a different line from the central bubble and tried to think of something different. Then she added a couple more lines. It looked like a sun. She drew a cloud and two birds.

She was supposed to be profiling a killer, and instead, she was doodling inane scribbles.

She stood up and looked around. Behind her, Agent Gray sat at his own desk, reading the autopsy report for Krista Barker.

"Agent Gray," she said, her voice as formal as she could make it. "Would you mind sitting down with me for a bit? I need to talk about the killer."

He whirled his chair around and frowned at her. Finally, he said, "Okay. I'll ask Martinez if he wants to join us."

She already regretted approaching Tatum instead of Martinez. She didn't need the agent to listen to her theories and then detail all the ways she could be wrong. It wouldn't do any good. But it was too late to change her mind.

Martinez said he had half an hour before he had a meeting with his captain. The three of them walked to the task force's meeting room and sat down. Someone had filled one of the several whiteboards in the room with the crime scene pictures of Krista Barker's body, and a timeline was drawn underneath. She hoped they wouldn't find themselves running out of whiteboards. A red circle on the map now marked Ohio Street Beach, and there was a red *X* in the Brighton Park neighborhood where Krista Barker had worked the street the last night she had been seen. The marks on the map made it very clear that the killer wasn't focusing on a certain area of Chicago.

"I think we can start narrowing the suspect pool down," she said, looking at Martinez. The lieutenant and Agent Gray sat next to each other on one side of the table. She sat on the other side.

Martinez nodded. "Sounds good to me."

"We know the subject is a male. I talked to an embalmer this morning, and he verified what I already assumed. The killer is not someone who works in a funeral home, or if he is, he's started very recently."

She bit her lip. Now for the tricky part. Every detail she added to the profile would narrow down the suspect pool, but if she added the wrong detail, the police might completely overlook the killer, searching for someone who fit the profile better.

"The killer is very intelligent," she said. "He seems to have learned the embalming process very quickly, but he almost certainly did so by himself, by learning from his own mistakes. The first victim shows a lot of amateur mistakes, the second victim a bit less, and the third was embalmed well enough to meet the approval of the embalmer I talked to this morning. That indicates he has high technical skills. He also has unusual self-discipline."

"Why self-discipline?" Martinez asked.

"Learning such a complex skill alone and persevering requires a level of self-discipline most people don't have."

Martinez was leaning forward, jotting in his notebook. Tatum sat back, his face a mask of boredom, arms folded.

"Stating something that's probably obvious, he has both an apartment or house and a car. He would need the car to pick up the prostitutes and drop off their bodies, and the victims were found in wide-ranging areas. Both Monique and Krista were embalmed outside their homes, which means he did it somewhere he felt safe. This also indicates he's living alone."

"Or he has a workshop," Tatum said.

Zoe nodded. "That's definitely a possibility as well. The killer was strong enough to drag the embalmed bodies of Krista Barker and Monique Silva to the locations where he posed them," she continued. "So I'd say we're looking for a strong man, but his appearance won't be very intimidating."

"Why?"

"Because both Monique and Krista agreed to ride with him," Zoe said. "Crystal told us Krista had refused to go with another man who seemed suspicious. She was more careful than most working girls. If it was someone intimidating, she would have talked to her pimp first and made sure he was watching her back, or she would have told him no. This also leads me to believe that he drives a nice-looking car or at least a well-maintained one."

"You don't think it was the guy Crystal described? The one with the tattoos?" Martinez asked.

"I really doubt it. If it was someone that suspicious looking, people would have noticed. I read in the case report that you had several generic descriptions of Monique Silva's last client. If it was someone like that, you'd get a very detailed description. And again, I doubt she'd enter willingly into his car."

"Okay, that's reasonable."

"Now . . . the first victim was an art student. He attacked her in her home and then stayed there to embalm her. But the second and third victims were prostitutes. He probably paid them to come with him and then killed them in a safe place."

"Maybe he killed them on the street or in an alley," Martinez said.

"Then why tie them up?" Tatum asked. "They were still alive when he tied them, and it would be difficult to do that in the street. He could easily get them to come with him."

Martinez nodded reluctantly.

"The second and third victims are classic targets for serial killers," Zoe said. "High-risk occupations and vulnerable. But what about Susan Warner, the art student? And if he already targeted her, why stay at her place? Wasn't he worried that a roommate or a boyfriend would show up?"

"He knew they wouldn't," Tatum said. "He knew her."

Zoe nodded, feeling an inkling of appreciation she was careful not to display.

"Now, the thing that motivates a sexual serial killer to strike is a fantasy. At a certain point, the fantasy becomes too much, and he has to fulfill it. But reality never quite manages to live up to the fantasy, so he wants to try again. Do it better next time. Our killer was acquainted somehow with Susan Warner and probably fantasized about her murder. He knew she lived alone and was vulnerable. And then one night he struck. But things didn't go as expected. The embalming didn't work out so well, and he wanted to do it again, to do it better."

"But he didn't know any single women except for her," Tatum said.

"That's right." Zoe nodded. "That's why he began to target prostitutes."

Tatum didn't look bored anymore. His eyes had a spark that Zoe knew well—the spark of a predator catching the scent of his prey.

"Okay," Martinez said, scanning his notebook page. "So let's talk about the elephant in the room. Why is he embalming them?"

"He's not only embalming them," Zoe said. "He's posing them and dressing them. The first body had an evening dress on with one of the sleeves torn. I'm guessing it tore when he dressed her because her arms were rigid and hard to maneuver. Krista Barker was wearing clothing that her friend said didn't belong to her. She had a ring on her finger that wasn't hers."

"Okay," Martinez said. "Why?"

"It could be some sort of power fantasy," Zoe said slowly, feeling the doubt gnawing at her. "Playing with these dead women like dolls." It didn't feel right. Why embalm them? He had sex with the bodies after killing the women. There was clearly a necrophilia angle on this case. But after embalming them, she doubted he could repeat it. That meant a *loss* of power. It didn't fit. "But I don't think so. I don't know why he's embalming them. Not yet."

"Right," Martinez said. "Anything else?"

Zoe said, "I'd look for reports about stray animals found embalmed and discarded in the streets. Even considering the mistakes in Susan Warner's embalming, it was a decent job for his first attempt. I'm willing to bet the killer did some practicing."

CHAPTER 19

He slowed down when he spotted her on the corner. She stood with a group of others, but he hardly gave them a second glance. They were crass, boring, ugly. Unremarkable in every conceivable way.

But *she* was something else. Her entire being radiated an innocence rarely seen in her profession. The way she looked around, her eyes half-searching, half-terrified of what she might find. Her clothing was more modest, showed less skin, leaving everything to the imagination. And his imagination went wild.

This was the one. He could *feel* it in his bones. This was a woman who made him feel alive again, who would fill every day with excitement and joy.

This time, it would be different.

When his car stopped near them, one of the prostitutes immediately jumped forward, grinning, bending down, giving him a view of her cleavage. She wore no bra, and she wiggled a bit, grinning at him. But behind the grin, her eyes were tired. The moves were mechanical, calculated, something she had done hundreds of times before. He opened the passenger's window.

"Looking for some fun?" she asked, and he could almost hear how vacant her soul was in her tone. "You look like you're in a hurry. Twenty dollars for a quick blow job? Or are you looking for something else?"

He ignored her, turning his eyes to the innocent one. It was probably her first day on the street. He'd save her before she even began.

"What about you?" he said. "Want to join me for a ride?"

She turned to face him, her eyes widening in alarm.

"Me? Uh . . . I mean . . . you want me to come with you? Wouldn't you rather just go upstairs with me?" she gestured at the motel behind her, its glass-paned door dirty with grime and worse. "I have a room. I just got it—I moved there just a few days ago. It's really nice."

He knew it. She didn't belong here. He smiled at her warmly. "I prefer my own bed," he said. "I'll make it worth your while."

Something flickered in her eyes. Wariness. She might be new, but she wasn't as innocent as he had thought. She knew to take care of herself.

"Do you live far?" she asked.

"Twenty-minute drive from here," he said. It was more like thirty. She took a small step back. He was losing her. But unlike her, he knew this game well, and he had a trick up his sleeve.

"But, uh, I have a special request," he said.

"Oh?" she said, taking another step back. "What sort of request?"

"Would you mind if we buy you some clothes? I want to dress you like my ex-girlfriend. It's kind of weird, I know, and you don't have to if you don't want to. But it would mean a lot to me, and you can keep the clothes afterward." He smiled apologetically. He could see her relax. That was the thing with these girls—living on the streets, they learned to listen to warning signs. They could see something was off about him, even if they didn't know what. All he had to do was tell them they were right, he was a bit strange, but wearing another woman's outfits . . . that wasn't dangerous.

"Okay," she said. "But it'll cost you extra."

"Sure." He smiled.

"Two hundred fifty," she said. "It's a long ride, and I'll need some money for the cab back to the motel."

He nodded. "You got it."

She leaned forward, opened the passenger's door, and climbed inside. The car filled with her perfume, an innocent, sweet fragrance, something a schoolgirl would wear.

He was in love.

CHAPTER 20

Lily watched the client as he drove. He was a nice-looking man, clean, nice clothes. His teeth were a bit crooked and could do with some cleaning, but whose weren't? Bad breath was far from the worst thing this job could inflict. Occasionally, he would glance at her and smile sheepishly. She took care to always look a bit apprehensive.

They always went for the virgin whore.

It was her third year on the street, and she was doing just fine, thank you very much. Always got the best customers, was always tipped. Occasionally, she'd land someone who would tip her an extra hundred or two to "clean up and get off the streets." All she had to do was cultivate the look of a good girl in the wrong place. That was her, an innocent child falling in with a bad crowd, trying to get out of an impossible situation.

Nate, her boyfriend, said she was a prodigy. A real genius, the hooker version of Einstein. And seriously, there were no drawbacks. She always wore warmer clothing; the whole point was to act shy. She never needed to try hard. She'd just face sideways when a customer showed up, looking afraid, as if she secretly hoped he'd pick someone else. If it was a real nice car, she'd tremble slightly or shed a frightened tear.

Men were so easily manipulated.

By this point she hardly needed to pick up new clients. She had three clients who saw her regularly to "keep her off the streets." They all assumed they were her sole customer. She gave them her second phone number, the one she kept for work, and when that phone rang, she knew it would be an easy, lucrative night.

Lily looked around her in the clean car. She inhaled deeply. The car's interior smelled a bit funny, sterile.

"What's that smell?" she asked.

"Formaldehyde," the client said. "Nasty smell, right? But you get used to it."

She wasn't sure what that was. "Are you, like, a doctor or something?"

"Something like that." He nodded. "Are you okay? You seem cold."

She wasn't. But she shivered slightly anyway. "No, I'm fine," she said. She considered telling him it was her first time, then decided not to. Sometimes it worked really well, and the guy would be turned on. But other times they'd feel guilty and drive her to the bus station, offering to buy her a ticket back to her hometown.

"So, uh . . . is your place a lot further?"

"No, not far. We'll just stop to buy you the clothes and then go straight there, okay?"

"Yeah, okay. Uh . . . but if we'll be long, I'll need to explain it to the guy I live with. He gets angry if I take too long and don't charge extra. I don't want him to be angry." A subtle tone of dread, leaving the rest for the client's imagination.

"Don't worry. We won't be too long. And I'll pay you an extra fifty. I don't want you to get in trouble."

"Thanks, mister." She laid a grateful hand on his wrist. Her dumb knight in shining armor, saving her from her monstrous and imaginary pimp.

"You're a really sweet girl," he said. "What are you doing on the street?"

She shrugged. A look of sorrow. The weight of life on her young shoulders, and so on and so forth. "I just had some bad luck."

"Yeah," he said, nodding. "I thought so."

She could hear it in his voice. He was falling for her.

She permitted herself a small smile. He had completely entangled himself in her web.

CHAPTER 21

Zoe's motel room had two beds. One was covered with all her case notes and pictures, divided into three groups, one for each victim. She was lying on the other, staring at the ceiling, hoping the couple in the room next door wouldn't have the stamina to keep the noise up much longer. On online reviews, people usually talked about the cleanliness of a motel or the service or the price. They never spoke about the thin walls and the distinct feeling that the couple in room 13 were orgasming into the ear of the person in room 12.

She always found it hard to concentrate in adverse situations, and this was absolutely ridiculous. It was their second time that evening, which at least meant they were both still alive. The woman had screamed so loudly the first time Zoe had thought she was being murdered.

Finally, she heard the sound she was embarrassingly happy to hear: a male groan. The bed in room 13 squeaked a bit longer—probably inertia—and the deed was done.

Zoe got up and returned to the case notes.

It was always about fantasy. What was this killer's fantasy? She looked at the images: a corpse lying on the grass, another standing on a bridge, the third sitting on a beach crying. She had visited the first two crime scenes earlier, trying to get a feel for what had gone through his mind as he positioned the bodies. It was part of her process. She always visited the crime scenes, even if no shred of evidence remained.

It helped her picture the crime better, and with that came a better understanding of the killer.

She shifted the picture of Susan Warner aside. She was important, even crucial, since the killer had probably known her, but the way her body had been discarded spoke only of failure. The killer hadn't gotten it right. The dress had torn when he'd tried to put it on the body, the limbs had been too rigid to move, and the position hadn't been lifelike, the mouth open. One big failure as far as the killer was concerned. She was sure of it.

She had been found on April 12. Then nearly three months went by. What was the killer doing in that time?

Learning. Experimenting. Trying to figure out how to get a body to have some flexibility even after embalming. Learning how to sew the mouth shut.

And then Monique Silva. Taken from the street, found a week or so later. What had he done with the body during all that time?

She read the autopsy report again, even though she knew it by heart. She'd visited the morgue and gone over the autopsy reports with the medical examiner after spending time at the crime scenes. Ligature marks on the body's throat indicated a thin, strong, smooth rope of some kind had been used to strangle the woman. There was a round bruise on the back of her neck, and the medical examiner said it was probably because the rope was fitted around her throat and then twisted from behind, constricting the noose. Lacerations on her wrists and ankles indicated she had been bound and that she had struggled against the ropes.

The body had been sexually violated postmortem. However, according to the medical examiner, the embalming would have made future intercourse almost impossible due to the body's rigidity. He'd seemed distinctly creeped out when she had asked him about it.

She had managed to creep out a man who performed autopsies for a living. *Achievement unlocked.*

She picked up Monique Silva's picture from the bed. What had he been doing with her all that time?

Her phone blipped. She picked it up and glanced at the display. It was a message from Andrea:

Miss U. What R U doing?

She typed, Reading an autopsy report.

The reply was instant. U know how to have fun.

Then came the emoticon barrage: a sad face, a dead-looking face, two skulls, a ghost, and a thumbs-down. Messaging with Andrea made Zoe feel like an archaeologist, perplexed by ancient Egyptian hiero-glyphics. I'll be here for a few days, she wrote.

The response was a GIF of Fozzie Bear screaming into the air. Zoe sighed and put down the phone. She was about to get back to her papers when a sound came from room 13.

It was the woman. She was asking who was a dirty little boy.

Zoe prayed that she was simply wondering about a dirty boy she was watching on TV.

But no, the response came quickly. The man was, apparently, the dirty little boy. Zoe considered thumping the wall and suggesting a shower to rectify the situation.

There was laughter. A whoop.

The bed began squeaking again.

Zoe collected all the papers from her bed and left the room, slam-ming the door behind her.

CHAPTER 22

Tatum had the distinct suspicion that Marvin was having a party at their house.

"Marvin, what's all that noise?" he yelled into the phone. The music emanating from the phone's speaker forced Tatum to hold the device away from his ear.

"What? I can't hear you!"

"The noise, Marvin, what is it?"

"Hang on."

There was the sound of a door slamming, and the volume of the music diminished slightly. "Sorry," Marvin said. "I couldn't hear you because of the music."

"What is that?"

"I invited a couple of friends over," Marvin explained.

"The neighbors will call the police," Tatum said. "The noise is ear shattering."

"I invited the neighbors, Tatum," Marvin said. "They're enjoying themselves."

Tatum sighed. "Everything okay there?"

"I think your cat is angry that you left him alone with me."

"Why do you think that?"

"You know that pair of brown shoes you left in your bedroom?"

"Yeah," Tatum said, his heart sinking.

"He shat in the shoes, Tatum."

"Damn it. Did you throw them away?"

"I'm not touching them. I closed the door so the smell won't get out. It also masks the pee smell."

Tatum sat down. His life was being dismantled. "What pee smell?"

"Your cat peed in the bed. And then he shredded the blanket."

"Maybe you should take him to a shelter until I get home," Tatum said with a heavy heart.

"Yeah, I already tried that, Tatum. He nearly scratched my eye out. My hands look like I've been mauled by a tiny lion."

"Right."

"Frankly, Tatum, this cat is a menace. I've started going to sleep with a loaded gun by my bed."

"You don't have a gun."

"I do now."

Tatum tried to control himself. Yelling at his grandfather over the phone wouldn't do any good.

"Listen, Freckle just needs a little love. Pet him a bit, let him sit in your lap—"

"That fiend is not getting anywhere near my lap. You know what's in my lap? Some very important stuff."

"Yes, I get the picture, but—"

"My penis, Tatum. My penis is in my lap," Marvin clarified. "I'm not letting that thing near my penis. You get your serial killer and come back here, because this cat is getting out of hand."

"Working on it. Did you talk to Dr. Nassar about the pills?"

"Not yet, Tatum. He's a very busy man."

"Call him first thing tomorrow morning, or I swear to God, I—"

There was a sound of a door banging open, and the music volume intensified.

"Marvin, are you coming?" Tatum heard a woman shout over the music. "The booze is here!"

There was a sudden crash in the background and a feminine cry of dismay.

"Marvin," Tatum said. "Don't ruin my house."

"It's the cat, Tatum. Everything is the cat's fault. I gotta go." The line went dead.

Tatum's hand went slack, the phone nearly dropping to the floor. Next time he would hire someone to babysit Marvin and Freckle. The ongoing destruction of his home was only half of his worries. Marvin, despite his behavior, was not seventeen years old. What if the old man had a heart attack? God knew that with the amount of alcohol he drank and the weed he smoked, it wasn't a far-fetched idea. He needed someone around to watch over him.

Tatum needed a drink. There was a nice-looking pub just on the other side of the road, a place called Kyle's.

He shoved his wallet into his pocket and holstered his gun on his hip. Then he left the motel and crossed the street to Kyle's. On his way, he looked around him, soaking in the atmosphere. Damn, he missed the feeling of a real city. LA had been his home for the past ten years. At first, having grown up in Wickenburg, Arizona, a town where you knew almost everyone by sight, he had found LA to be loud and oppressive. His senses were constantly under attack—too many lights, too many people, too many smells, and way too many sounds. But slowly the place had grown on him. He had begun to enjoy the feeling of the constant vibrating life around him. And then, due to one small misunderstanding between him and his superiors, followed by about fifty similar misunderstandings, he found himself living in Dale City, Virginia. Hardly a place of endless thrills.

Chicago was not LA, but it was a place where he could once again feel the excitement of being in a place where things happened. A group of women passed him by, laughing hysterically as one of them blew him a kiss. Three men went past him, all looking at their phones in concentration. A taxi driver stopped, asking if he needed a ride. Movement. Life.

He reached Kyle's and opened the door, welcomed by a Leonard Cohen song, which instantly made him like the place.

"Hey." The hostess smiled at him, a cute redhead, looking fresh out of high school. "Joining a table?"

"Uh . . . no. I'm on my own."

"Well, we're quite full tonight," she said apologetically. "We have a few spots on the bar, but—"

"The bar's fine," he said.

Hesitantly, she led him to the bar, and he was immediately struck by something strange. The place was packed, but there were four empty stools on the bar, two on each side of a woman sitting with her back to him.

"I'm sorry," the hostess said. "We'll tell her to clear the photos again. She's making everyone uncomfortable."

"It's okay." Tatum grinned at the hostess. "I can handle it."

He sat on a barstool and glanced at the woman. Zoe, of course. She stared intently at a row of photographs she had spread on the bar top. The images were from the three crime scenes, as well as close-up images taken during the autopsy. No wonder the people around her had fled. The barman approached him.

"A pint of Honker's Ale, please," Tatum said.

The barman nodded. "If you can get her to put those away, the beer's on the house," he said.

"I don't think I can get her to do anything," Tatum answered truthfully.

The barman poured him a pint and walked away, trying to avoid looking at the pictures.

"You're making everyone uncomfortable," Tatum said.

"Can't be helped. I can't concentrate in my own room. There's a couple screwing next door."

"They're bound to stop eventually," Tatum said.

"You'd think so, right?"

Tatum sipped from his mug, relishing the taste. Sometimes nothing was as good as beer. "Any thoughts about the case?"

Zoe shook her head, frustrated. "I don't get what he's doing," she said, pointing emphatically at the pictures. "If I didn't know better, I'd say he's playing with them like a child plays with dolls. Dress them up, pose them, move them from place to place . . ."

"And that's impossible? This isn't a normal person."

"No, he isn't," Zoe said. "But he isn't completely delusional, either. This is him living out his fantasy. But I doubt his fantasy is to play with human-sized dolls."

"How do you know he doesn't hear voices telling him to do it?"

"Whoever did this is cold, calculated, calm. Anyone under delusions such as you describe would be prone to impulsiveness, acting out his delusions at the spur of the moment. He isn't impulsive . . . well, mostly not impulsive, at least."

"Mostly?" Tatum asked.

"The bodies have signs of sexual intercourse postmortem," Zoe said. "That happened before the embalming. I think this was just him acting out an impulse craving. I don't think any of those sexual acts were planned beforehand."

"What makes you say that?"

"The bodies have almost no bruising, despite the fact that they'd been strangled to death and some of them bound before," she said. "It makes sense. Any bruise wouldn't heal after embalming. But the sexual intercourse is rough, violent. He lost control when it happened."

Tatum took another sip. It wasn't as enjoyable as the first. Zoe had managed to ruin beer.

"Listen," he said. "You're in a pub. Put those things away, okay? I'll buy you any kind of drink you want."

She pursed her lips.

"I'll talk with you about the case tomorrow morning. We'll think about it together."

"You mean you'll come up with a theory, then discount mine and tell me I'm just inventing it to get a paycheck?"

"It was a rotten thing to say. I'm sorry."

"You said I'm like Bernstein."

"You said I have bed-wetting issues."

A glimmer of a smile. Slowly and carefully, she collected all the images, put them back into the folder, and put it in her bag. The barman sent him a grateful look.

"Give her another . . . whatever it is she's having."

Zoe shook her head, pushing her empty glass away. "That was soda. I'll have a pint of beer now, please. Do you have Guinness?"

The barman nodded and turned to the beer taps.

Tatum raised his mug to his lips, enjoying his small victory. He used to be really good with people once, before . . . well, before Paige had left him bitter and confused. It was nice to see he could still make a woman smile.

"So," he said. "Where do you live? I mean back in Virginia."

"Dale City."

"Really? I just moved there."

She nodded. She didn't seem to be blown away by the coincidence.

"Do you have anyone waiting for you in Dale City?" Tatum asked.

"Why do you care?"

"Just making conversation." Tatum shrugged. "You don't have to play along. We can sit here and drink in silence."

Zoe seemed to be weighing the options. "My sister," she finally said.

"You told me about her. I mean besides her."

"Oh, like a boyfriend? No."

The barman put a tall glass full of foamy brown beer in front of Zoe, and she took a healthy swig from it.

"How about you?" she asked.

"Just my grandfather and my cat. Oh, and my fish. I completely forgot I have a fish now."

"But no wife or girlfriend?"

"Not anymore."

She sipped from her beer, looking at him.

He exhaled loudly. "There was a girl. Back in LA. We nearly got married."

"What happened?"

"She left. Halfway through planning the wedding, she packed up and left."

"I'm sorry."

"Thanks."

"Your grandfather moved with you when you transferred to Quantico?"

"Yeah." Tatum tried to figure out how to explain Marvin. "My grandma died last year, and he took it pretty hard, so he moved in with me back in LA. Just a week after Paige left me. Then when I told him I was going to Dale City, he informed me that he was doing the same."

"Sounds nice to have a grandfather you're so close with."

"That's one way to put it," Tatum said. "He's difficult to handle."

"Yeah, aging people often are," Zoe said, nodding. "They're often entrenched in their own routine, so any diversion from it is very challenging for them."

Tatum blinked, trying to think how well Marvin matched that depiction. Aside from the word *challenging*, probably not too much.

"Yeah, well, he and my grandma raised me as a child, so the least I can do is help him with his . . ."—Tatum cleared his throat—"routine."

The background music changed, Nick Cave's voice filling the bar. Tatum was really happy with this place.

CHAPTER 23

Tears rolled down the woman's cheeks as he took a step back to look at his handiwork. He had tied her hands behind her back and then to a hook he had drilled into the wall. No more chairs that could be knocked over and broken. She sat on a thick blanket; he didn't want her to scrape her skin on the rough cement floor. Her body shivered, probably a mix of fear and cold. She had taken off her shirt and skirt just before he had put the knife against her throat. He wondered if he should get her something to wear, then decided she'd be fine. It wasn't chilly enough to give her actual frostbite, and the cold would probably make her weaker and more lethargic, which would only help when he had everything prepared.

He had discarded her handbag and clothing on the floor. Once he was done with her, he would burn them, as he always did. He now picked up her handbag and rummaged in it, until his fingers brushed against her phone. He took it out and turned it off. In one of the previous attempts, the woman's phone had rung just as he had been about to start the embalming process. It had scared him half to death. He slid her turned-off phone into his pocket and tossed the handbag on the floor by the clothing.

He walked away and shut the door behind him, ignoring her muffled protests. He had work to do, and the sooner he was done, the sooner she'd be quiet.

He felt giddy with excitement. She was absolutely perfect. A dream girl, one he'd never thought he'd be able to find on the streets. It almost felt like fate.

This made him hesitate before mixing the embalming fluid. He had very little formaldehyde left after the last one. It was enough for what he had originally intended . . . but was it enough for her?

It was a delicate balance. Too much formaldehyde and her body would become rigid, impossible to handle. But too little and she'd begin to decay in a few years.

He wanted to spend the rest of his days with her. Could he really afford to skimp on formaldehyde? Wouldn't a little rigidity be worth ten more years in her company?

He smiled to himself, imagining getting old with her by his side. Spending the cold winters cuddled on the couch, covered in a blanket, watching TV together. Lying in bed, her head leaning against his chest, a book in her hand as he hugged her waist. Sitting by the dinner table, telling her about his day as she listened with adoring affection. He was surprised to realize that he had a tear in his eye. He was so happy.

He definitely needed to get some more formaldehyde.

He glanced at his watch. Too late to do it this evening. He would have to get some tomorrow.

A twinge of impatience nearly made him change his mind. He glanced at the noose on the table, imagined it tightening around her throat. The final spasm as life fled her body. He felt the tightening in his pants as he thought of her inert body, at his mercy. He turned back to the formaldehyde bottle. Surely it was enough. He picked up the bottle, his hand trembling with excitement.

No. He would spend the next few decades with this woman. He could wait another day. He put the bottle down, taking a deep breath. Tomorrow. He would do it tomorrow.

He thought of opening the door and apologizing for the delay, but he doubted she'd be very understanding. None of them were, before the procedure.

Instead, he left the workshop, locking the door behind him. He was glad to notice that her faint screams couldn't be heard at all beyond the walls.

CHAPTER 24

Maynard, Massachusetts, Sunday, December 14, 1997

Zoe stared at the open coffin, trying to feel what she was probably supposed to. Grief, horror, fear.

All she felt was emptiness and regret for not going to the bathroom earlier.

When the principal had walked into class two days before, informing them that Nora's big sister, Clara, had been killed, Zoe heard the kids around her sobbing, screaming, whispering in shock. She could only gaze at the principal's red eyes, thinking she had never seen him cry before.

Nora was her age, was in most of her classes. Zoe had been to her house three times when she was much younger. They had been friends when they were six years old. She had hazy memories of Clara, then a beautiful ten-year-old girl whom Nora had idolized.

Zoe was worried about her own reaction. She had been borrowing books about serial killers lately and reading a lot about psychopaths. People who had no empathy for other human beings. There were a surprising number of psychopaths. One percent of the general population. Was she a psychopath? Was that why she couldn't feel anything for Clara? Was that why she hadn't shed a tear for Nora's suffering? Her mother cried by her side, and she didn't know Nora or Clara as well as Zoe did. The chapel was full of people crying, their sobs echoing in the spacious hall. Zoe tried to make herself cry, tried to think how Nora felt right then. Clara, her only sister, taken by the Maynard serial killer. Raped and killed, discarded like trash in the Assabet River.

Nothing.

The school counselor had told them that all reactions were normal, that people experienced grief in different ways. But surely she didn't mean not having any reaction at all. That was not normal. And obsessing about a murderer, collecting all the articles that mentioned him—that wasn't normal either; she was certain of it.

When it was time, she made herself approach the coffin, look at Clara's face. Only four years older than her, killed brutally.

Clara didn't look like someone who had been killed brutally. She looked as if she were asleep.

Zoe turned away, facing a crowd of teary eyes, searching for anyone who, like her, felt absolutely nothing. Some small kids seemed quite calm. They couldn't understand what was going on. But every adult face Zoe glanced at was full of tears or seemed as if it were on the brink.

She started heading outside. Her mother followed her, stroking her hair.

A small hand grabbed her own. She looked down at Andrea, who walked by her side, her face serious. Did Andrea know what was going on? She was sleeping in Zoe's bed every night now. She knew something was very wrong.

The world was white, snow carpeting the chapel's yard, covering the trees, the grass, a thin layer of snow on the low wall that stood between the yard and the street. She followed her parents to the car, everyone completely silent. Got into the car. Heard the engine start, its sound strangely muffled. She felt lightheaded, almost somewhere else.

No tears in her. No empathy. Just like the killer.

Andrea laid her head against Zoe's arm as they rode home. She played with Zoe's fingers, like she sometimes did at night, caressing Zoe's thumb over and over. Zoe said nothing, even though it tickled.

The car ride was quick, like every ride inside the tiny town. When they reached home and got out, Zoe couldn't figure out why the world kept tilting.

And then she was kneeling on the ground, throwing up her breakfast, her heart beating fast. Her mother pulled back her hair, talking, but she couldn't understand the words. They seemed to blend into each other, and she was coughing and spitting, looking at the lumpy yellow sludge spattered on the snow, trembling violently.

Zoe checked the time again. It was seventeen past two in the morning, and she suspected sleep would not come, ever. Andrea was curled by her side, the blanket covering her up to her neck, a loose strand of hair dangling on her cheek. Zoe had gotten used to sleeping on half a bed. She hardly minded it anymore.

She had cried. Couldn't stop, in fact. She'd shivered and cried for over an hour, her mom hugging her and caressing her and trying to find the words that would make it stop. Finally, Zoe had stumbled into her room and crashed on the bed, staring at the ceiling, trying to empty her mind of the horrific images that kept assaulting her. The rest of the day had been a haze. She wouldn't talk to anyone, just wanted to be alone. Except for Andrea. She hadn't said anything when Andrea had walked into her room and plopped on the floor. It had been a slight relief.

And now she just wished she could finally sleep. She was exhausted.

Finally, she sighed, turning on the night-light. Andrea tensed and then rolled over, facing away from the light. Zoe picked up the book she had hidden under the bed, the one she had borrowed from the library. *Whoever Fights Monsters*, by Robert K. Ressler. It was the fifth book she had borrowed about serial killers, but it was the first one written by an FBI profiler. She hadn't even known the profession existed.

The more she read, the more things began falling into place. Maynard was far from the only place struck by a serial killer. And these killers, as monstrous as they were, could be explained. Ressler kept stressing that the thing propelling most serial killers to act was a fantasy. It would grow, becoming more powerful and detailed, taking over the killer's thoughts until he tried to fulfill it. That fulfillment would satisfy the killer for a certain period of time, until he felt the need to kill again.

The detailed profiles Ressler came up with astounded her. What would Ressler say about the Maynard serial killer?

She wished the Maynard chief of police would ask for the help of an FBI profiler.

She'd just begun reading about Ressler's interview with David Berkowitz, who had been nicknamed the "Son of Sam." Berkowitz had shot multiple men and women, though he targeted women. Zoe was reading the interview summary with morbid fascination when she reached a paragraph that gave her chills. Berkowitz told Ressler that on nights he couldn't find a victim, he'd go to one of his earlier crime scenes to look at them and masturbate. Ressler pointed out in the book that this was the first time they had actual proof that killers returned to the scene of the crime, as well as an explanation for it.

She read the paragraph several times, feeling something niggling at her. It was itching in her mind, a sickening feeling that she didn't want to pinpoint. Instead, she shut the book, shoved it under the bed, and tried to sleep again.

She might as well have tried to fly. Sleep visited other beds in Maynard that night.

Her mind kept conjuring that day a month and a half ago.

What had Rod Glover been doing at Durant Pond? She had asked him that question and never received a straight answer. Instead, he had told her about a fire and how he had saved the life of their secretary. A strange story.

It occurred to her she hadn't heard about this fire from anyone else. Maynard was a small town. If someone had a flat tire, half the town would know about it by the end of the day.

A fire in an office? A woman rescued heroically by her coworker? Even with the murders going on, it would have been mentioned and discussed endlessly.

And then she thought of other strange stories he had told her about. Hadn't he once told her he'd been an extra in one of the first episodes of *Buffy the Vampire Slayer*, but they'd cut his sequence out because he had an argument with the producer? And he claimed that he used to be a CIA informant, though he couldn't tell her anything about it.

Zoe was not naive. She always assumed he was yanking her chain or stretching the facts a bit. But now, as she thought about those stories, they seemed less like humorous anecdotes and more like lies, serving no purpose.

She got her notebook and flipped through it until she found what she was looking for. She had photocopied a section from an article about psychopaths, describing the Hare Psychopathy Checklist. This list detailed traits that correlated with psychopathy. Zoe, loving bullet-point lists, had taped the list in her notebook. Third in the list: pathological lying.

She looked at the rest of the list. Superficial charm—check. He always smiled when he talked to her, often touching her arm in a friendly manner. His endless imitations and corny humor, trying to make her laugh. And it worked, she was embarrassed to admit to herself. She liked him. That was all it took to get on her good side.

Lack of empathy. She tried to think what that meant. Understanding what other people felt, right? But Rod understood feelings. He would listen to her when she complained about her parents or school, nodding sympathetically. And she could see the care in his eyes. She tried to imagine the eyes of someone who didn't care. Empty, dead.

She put the list aside. Rod was a good guy. And of course he understood other people's feelings; he—

He had shown zero interest when she spoke of the first murder, immediately trying to make her laugh. She compared that to other people whom she talked about the murder with. Her friends, the sadness and fear on their faces. Mrs. Hernandez, crying as she spoke to the class about it. Teary red faces in the hallways.

And Rod, making an impression of a *Buffy* character.

Psychopaths weren't zombies. Their eyes still worked. She got out of bed and looked at her reflection in the mirror. How hard would it be to feign caring? She crinkled her eyebrows a bit, looking in the mirror. Her reflection gazed sadly at her. Full of "empathy."

How hard would it be to feign caring? Not hard at all, apparently. The look in someone's eyes meant nothing.

She slid back into bed, careful not to wake Andrea up. She picked up the list again and scanned it.

Parasitic lifestyle. She suddenly remembered the dozens of times Rod had dropped by to borrow gardening tools. Or small things like milk or sugar or beer. Often showing up during dinner, commenting about how tasty everything looked, receiving a belated invitation to join them from her parents. She had heard her mother muttering about it more than once, had always assumed she was just petty and cheap.

Slowly, she began to spot other connections, moments in the past aligning themselves with the list. It was far from a perfect fit. She had no idea if he'd had early behavioral problems or juvenile delinquency. In fact, she didn't know anything about him beyond the fact that he had moved to Maynard three years before. Moved from where? Why? Did he have a family somewhere? The little things he had told her or her parents all revolved around implausible stories. Suddenly, his past seemed very foggy.

Still, what she knew began to click.

Was Rod Glover a psychopath?

Maybe. But that hardly made him a serial killer. One in every hundred people was a psychopath. A lot of them were mostly harmless.

She tried to imagine him crouching, waiting for Clara to come closer. With his big toothy smile and his ridiculous acts. His messy hair. Would a serial killer have such messy hair? It felt wrong.

What had he been doing at Durant Pond that day? Had he come because it was a nice place to stroll or because he was revisiting the scene of the crime? What had he been doing when she'd seen him there?

She had thought he was peeing.

She shivered, her fingers clenching into fists. She thought of his fast breathing. She felt bile in her throat. This couldn't be true. It couldn't be.

Except she knew it could. She would have to tell someone.

CHAPTER 25

Chicago, Illinois, Wednesday, July 20, 2016

Zoe sat at her temporary desk, reading the morning news on her laptop, her mouth twisted in distaste. The media was hyping up the serial killer. The involvement of the FBI was mentioned. There was a picture, the fuzzy faces of her and Tatum with Martinez at the crime scene enlarged for the reader's enjoyment. According to "sources within the police department," the murderer was probably a white male working in a funeral home.

She wanted to kill Bernstein. That sack of bloated self-importance had probably called every journalist and blogger in the city. He was probably appearing daily on several news shows, charging them a tidy sum for his "expertise." She was willing to bet he wouldn't turn up at the police station again. He had a better-paying, less ego-bruising gig with the media.

A stack of papers landed on her desk. She raised her eyes to meet Martinez's face.

"What's that?" she asked.

"A list of reports from the Department of Animal Care and Control," he said. "Starting July 2014 and ending March 2016. A total of twenty-seven cases. Guess what they all are."

"Animal embalming?"

"Well, the first six were taxidermies. But all twenty-seven cases are from West Pullman. That's a neighborhood in the southern part of Chicago."

"That was probably his initial plan," Zoe said, leafing through the reports. "To taxidermy his victims."

"Why did he change his mind?"

"I don't know. I'm not a big expert on the difference between taxidermy and embalming," Zoe said. "It doesn't say any of those animals were embalmed, though."

"Dead cats and dogs usually don't undergo an autopsy. But you can see varying descriptions of rigidity and unnatural poses, which I am guessing is what happens when you embalm an animal."

"Yeah," Zoe muttered, reading through the report of a dog found lying on its side, dead and rigid as stone. "Were all these animals taken from the same neighborhood?"

"All the ones whose owners were located."

"Did any of them see who took their pets?"

"Not in the reports, but Scott and Mel went to start interviewing them all and verify it. You think he lives in West Pullman?"

"Or used to," Zoe said. "He was a lot more careless about discarding his animal carcasses than he was about his human victims."

"He must have assumed, and rightly so, that Chicago PD wouldn't start a major hunt for a pet serial killer," Martinez said.

Zoe didn't answer, flipping through the reports. Martinez walked away.

She opened the browser and did a quick search about taxidermy. She clicked WikiHow, her favorite guide site for dummies. She mostly loved it because of the illustrations, which were sometimes comical and absurd. The "How to Do Taxidermy" page wasn't as funny as others, though. She quickly learned that taxidermy was vastly different from embalming.

According to the reports, he had taxidermied six cats and dogs before abandoning the idea. Probably reached the conclusion that it wouldn't work well with humans. She scribbled the word *Methodic* on a half sheet of paper on her desk. Then she underscored the phrases *Self-tutored* and *Fast learner* she had written on the top of the page two days before.

She chewed her pen. Did he really abandon the idea? Or did he try it?

She got up and walked to Martinez. "Say, Lieutenant, did you find a taxidermied body of a young woman sometime between 2014 and 2015?"

"Uh . . . no."

Maybe he tried and failed. "Perhaps just a body of a young woman, missing some large swathes of skin? As if someone had skinned her?"

Martinez looked ill. "No. I think I would have remembered if that had happened anywhere in Chicago last year."

"All right. That's probably good news."

"Yes. I'd definitely file it in the good news section."

Zoe returned to her seat and began reordering the reports according to their date. The first few reports were sporadic. Two in July 2014, one in August, two in September, one in October, then the next report was in March, but Zoe guessed there were other animals that had been taken in the interim. There were probably no complaints because people just assumed they had frozen to death when they found them.

But then in 2015, two pets in April, one in May, two in July . . . one or two pets every month, occasionally skipping one. But there had been five embalmed cats and dogs found in West Pullman in March 2016. He had gotten reckless and desperate. Propelled by a growing need.

He was anxious to do the real thing.

According to the estimated time of death, he had killed Susan Warner on April 5, give or take a day. Just a week after the last embalmed pet had been found. Monique Silva had been murdered around the first of July. And Krista Barker had been murdered on July 10 or 11.

Was he accelerating? She couldn't be sure; there wasn't enough data. But if she had to guess . . . she'd say he probably was. Just nine days between the last two murders.

How long did they have this time? A week? Five days?

Were they already too late?

She got up and walked over to Martinez's desk again. "Listen," she said. "He might kill again soon. Very soon."

Martinez swiveled his chair and looked up at her. "How soon?" he asked.

"A few days at most."

"You think he'll target prostitutes?"

"I think they're the highest-risk group, yes."

"We can stake out a few likely areas," Martinez said after a moment of consideration. "But we frankly have no idea what to look for."

"Strong guy, not too intimidating, reasonably good-looking car . . ." Zoe's voice faded. It was a very weak profile.

Martinez smiled sadly. "You just described most of the men in the department," he said.

Zoe raised an eyebrow. "I wouldn't ignore the possibility that it's a law enforcement officer of some kind," she said. "But we still don't have enough to tighten the suspect list further."

"Still, you think he might strike again soon . . . I'll call vice. I know the lieutenant there. She'll help—she gets things done. Maybe we can make some inquiries, see if anyone went missing. Tell them to keep their eyes open. Any particular area we should focus on?"

Zoe hesitated. She hadn't done a thorough geographic profiling of the case yet, but from what she saw, this killer didn't match the standard patterns. He struck all over Chicago, didn't focus on a certain area. "I have no idea," she finally admitted.

CHAPTER 26

Tatum rubbed his face and sighed. His head pounded, and when he shut his eyes, he could still see the glare of his monitor etched in his field of vision. He had been reading reports for the past three hours, and he needed some fresh air.

He was going over burglary reports in West Pullman. Serial killers often started on their path with "fetish burglaries." They would break into homes of women and steal lingerie, clothes, or other items that sparked their fantasies. It was likely this serial killer had started the same way. With a bit of luck, they would find some fetish burglaries in the crime reports that could shed some light on the identity of the murderer.

Well . . . more than a bit of luck. West Pullman was a huge neighborhood, sprawling over two beats in district five. Burglaries were a frequent occurrence there, and Tatum got tired of reading about stolen laptops and jewelry. He managed to mark three suspicious reports, two because the list of stolen items included lingerie and one because it was reported by a widower whose dead wife's jewelry had been stolen. Tatum reasoned that if the killer was turned on by death, stealing a dead woman's jewelry could be in his list of earlier transgressions.

They would add these reports to the mounting pile of possible leads. They might find a connection there. Or just background noise.

He was beginning to suspect they were chasing their own tails. He wanted a break.

He backed his chair up a bit, its wheels squeaking on the tiled floor. He looked around the room. Only Zoe and Martinez were sitting at their desks; the rest of the room was empty. Was there a party they hadn't been invited to? He looked at the faces of the other unpopular kids of the team. Zoe's face showed no emotion as she stared at her monitor, occasionally hitting a button with one finger. Martinez muttered to himself as he wrote down something on a pad of paper. Tatum assessed the distance between his own desk and Martinez's. It was about fifteen feet, with no obstacles in the way. He grabbed his desk and, pulling hard, shot his chair across the room in a straight line toward Martinez.

Wheeeeeeeeee.

He misjudged his aim a bit and nearly crashed into the neighboring desk, knocking down a wastebasket. Sheepishly, he bent to pick up the discarded papers as Martinez looked at him, one of his serious eyebrows raised.

"Hey," Tatum said, straightening up.

"Everything okay, Agent Gray?" Martinez asked in a tone usually reserved for a principal approaching an unruly student in the schoolyard.

"Yeah. Didn't find anything so far. Just some weak leads, nothing concrete," Tatum said. "What about you? Any news from your detectives?"

Martinez double-clicked an icon on his desktop, opening a document with a list of names and assignments.

"Let's see," he said. "Scott is talking to people whose animals were embalmed or taxidermied. Dana and Brooks are looking into Susan Warner's friends and family, following up on our assumption that the killer knew her. Mel is down in Organized Crime, talking to people from vice. Tommy is checking out some security cam feeds of streets near the Ohio Street Beach crime scene, trying to see if he can find a likely candidate for our killer's car. So far I have no news."

"What contacts do you have for Susan Warner?"

"Her parents, of course. An uncle who lives nearby. One ex-boyfriend, a few friends from art school."

"I can go talk to some of them," Tatum said hopefully.

Martinez raised an eyebrow. "I think my detectives can handle these interviews, Agent. No need for—"

"I'm not trying to barge in on the investigation, Martinez." Tatum raised his hands. "I need to clear my mind a bit, and I'm going insane reading burglary reports."

"Okay," Martinez said, his lip quirking in what could be interpreted as a smile. "You can talk to . . ." He glanced at the screen. "Daniella Ortiz. Another art student, Susan Warner's friend."

"You're a good man."

"I just want you out of my task force room." The lieutenant grinned.

Tatum rolled his chair back to his desk and headed for the exit. Then he paused and turned around, approaching Zoe. He glanced at her monitor. She was reading burglary reports as well and showed no signs of boredom or tiredness. She was probably a robot; it would explain everything.

"I'm going to talk to one of Susan Warner's friends," Tatum said. "Want to join me?"

"Aren't the detectives doing it?"

"I'm giving them a helping hand."

"We need to go over these reports."

"Fine." He shrugged. "I'll go alone." He turned to leave.

"Wait." Zoe grabbed her bag and stood up quickly.

"You were dying to join me—you just wanted to play hard to get," Tatum said accusingly.

"That's not true," Zoe said, marching out of the room. "I'm driving."

CHAPTER 27

Harry Barry watched the plume of smoke rising from his cigarette. It spread slowly as it intermingled with the general pollution that lingered over Chicago.

He was leaning against a soot-covered brick wall, wondering if he should smoke two cigarettes or settle on one and go back to work. He was leaning toward a second cigarette.

Up until a few years before, Harry's boss, the owner of the *Chicago Daily Gazette*, had been content to let the smokers that worked for him smoke leaning out of the window, as if they were contemplating suicide in a half-assed manner. But after a litany of complaints by people citing the Chicago Clean Indoor Air Act, Harry's boss had caved. Harry and his three smoking comrades were told politely to keep their stench far away from the office.

They had all relocated to a small, dirty alley down the street, quickly dubbed "Lung Cancer Alley." Ironically, ever since their exile, Harry's tobacco consumption had nearly doubled, following the reasoning of, "Well, if I've already walked all this way . . ." The Chicago Clean Indoor Air Act was destroying Harry's lungs.

He dropped the stub, stepping on it, and put a fresh cigarette in his mouth. He lit it, brooding about the article he'd read that morning in his paper about the Strangling Undertaker.

Harry was a capable reporter even though his name was a constant obstacle. He made sure to sign his articles as H. Barry. It gave him an air of a respectable American citizen, as opposed to a man whose name was a Seussian rhyme. Despite his struggles, he didn't change either of his names, because he liked being a Harry, and he liked belonging to the Barry family. As he often said to his friends, if life gave you lemons, you made lemonade. You didn't go trading the lemons for papayas.

He thought the article was shit. He had sent an email to his editor, the subject of which was "This Is Shit," and the content of the email was the link to the article. It was not, perhaps, the most political thing to do, but he was in a rotten mood, and besides, if people didn't want to hear about shit, perhaps they shouldn't publish it.

Someone walked into Lung Cancer Alley. It was his editor, Daniel McGrath. Harry quickly deduced that Daniel, not being one of the smokers, was there looking for him.

"You got a problem?" Daniel asked. No pleasantries.

Harry sucked on his cigarette, thinking the question over. "You let an amateur write the article about the hottest crime this city has seen since the killer clown."

"What's it to you? I thought the article was good. It had some sordid details. It had several quotes from the police. It had an expert. It had—"

"Our readers don't care what the experts have to say. He sounds as dry as pencil shavings. Our readers don't want to hear what our so-called police source had to say either. Especially when all the police say is 'We're looking into it.'"

"Really? And whose opinion would our readers like to hear?"

"Oprah."

Daniel blinked. "Oprah Winfrey?"

"It's her city. What does *she* think about a creepy man sculpting women into statues?"

"That's not what he does . . . and Oprah lives in California. And she isn't exactly an expert in crime. Or serial killings."

Harry dropped the half-smoked cigarette on the ground and stomped it angrily. "No one wants her to be an expert; she's Oprah. And she owns an apartment in Chicago, which makes her one of us. Hell, we could do a whole article about the Chicago celebrities and what they think of the monster roaming their beloved city. Kanye West, Tina Fey, Harrison Ford—"

"None of them live here."

Harry brushed it away. "They used to. This is *their* city, and this deranged undertaker is threatening the safety of *their* people."

"That's ridiculous."

"Fine. Not Oprah, then. You know who you should ask what they think? People on the beach."

"The beach?"

"Yeah. Women, mostly. One hot guy. Preferably put their pictures in the article, in their swimsuits. Ask them how they would react if they came across one of the Strangling Undertaker's works of art."

"He's an artist now?"

"Sure. Why not? It's a good angle. Our readers would love that. My point is this is sexy."

Daniel gave him a supposedly piercing stare, but Harry prided himself on being immune to those.

"Harry, you're good at writing human interest stories. You're the master of sex scandals."

Harry nodded in appreciation of his dubious title.

"But this is a story about a monster. And what our readers want is the story about the hunt. The attempts of the police to grab the elusive killer as he kills yet another innocent woman. They want to read about the violence, the fear, and the death. This is what excites people about serial killers."

"It's the wrong way to go about it, Daniel. That's what *everyone* is doing."

"That's precisely why we should do the same."

They both stood facing each other and for a second let the sounds of Chicago's traffic fill the air.

"Let me do it," Harry finally said. "I can nail this thing."

"I don't want an article about what Oprah thinks about this killer," his editor said, his tone sharp and final. "This isn't your story. You can't write about crime. Go do your job."

"Why don't you do *your* job for once?" Harry asked.

The change in Daniel's face made Harry think that perhaps this hadn't been the most prudent thing to say.

"You know." Daniel folded his arms. "I have a really important article I need you to write."

CHAPTER 28

Daniella Ortiz lived in a tiny two-bedroom apartment in Pilsen, a neighborhood on the west side of Chicago. It was a neighborhood well known for its thriving art, and art students in Chicago, like Daniella and the late Susan Warner, tended to flock there.

The small living room was not much different than Zoe's own living room back in Dale City. But while Zoe kept her walls bare except for two tiny paintings Andrea had bought for her, Daniella's walls were covered with framed photographs. The cluttered decoration made the room seem much smaller, almost claustrophobic.

"Please come in," Daniella said. "Can I get you anything to drink?"

Her fashion sense matched her interior design tastes. It looked like she was striving to wear all the colors at once. She had a red bandanna, a yellow blouse over a green shirt, blue jeans, and orange-and-pink sneakers. She had several beaded bracelets on her right wrist, their dominant colors purple, brown, and black. *She should be accompanied by a warning for people with epilepsy.* Zoe was pleased with her own wit. She would have to remember to tell Andrea about it later.

"Nothing, thanks," Zoe said, just as Tatum asked if there was any coffee.

"Sure," Daniella said and smiled at Zoe. "Are you sure you don't want any?"

"Uh . . . yeah. If Agent Gray is drinking a cup, I'd love some as well, thanks."

Daniella went to the kitchen, and Zoe approached the wall, looking at the pictures. They seemed to be a collection of enlarged close-ups. A large photograph of a dewdrop on a leaf. A series of icicles on a branch. A winged insect, photographed from above, its wings translucent and intricate. Some pictures on the far wall were urban pictures of streets that felt European. All the pictures were beautiful, but as a whole they bombarded the room with colors and shapes. It made Zoe uncomfortable.

Daniella came back, holding two cups of coffee. "You like them?"

"Uh . . . yeah, they're very beautiful."

"The close-ups are mine. My boyfriend did the streets of Venice. He was an exchange student there a year ago."

"You're both art students?"

"Well . . . I still am. Ryan's working at an auto repair shop now. But we met in college when he was a student as well."

"That's nice," Zoe said. She had only met two guys at college, and both had turned out to be crappy boyfriends.

"Have a seat, please," Daniella said, nodding at the one couch in the room. Zoe and Tatum sat, and she set their cups of coffee on a low round table that stood next to the couch. For a moment, Zoe thought Daniella would sit on the couch between them, an awkward arrangement for questioning, even more so since the couch was a two-seater. But to her relief, Daniella walked back into the kitchen and returned with a small chair on which she sat, facing them both.

"I saw in the news that they found another victim," she said. "That's so scary. I don't dare leave home after dark now, and I check that the door is locked at least four times a day. Are you any closer to catching this guy?"

"We're making progress," Tatum said. "Can we ask a few questions about Susan?"

"Sure. Whatever I can do to help. Hang on; maybe my boyfriend can answer some questions too. He met Susan a couple of times."

"Sure," Tatum said.

"Ryan!" Daniella shouted, and Zoe's teeth gritted at the piercing sound. "Can you come here a sec?"

A tall, wide-shouldered man with rich black hair came from the bedroom. "Yeah? Oh, hello," he said, noticing Zoe and Tatum. "Sorry, I was wearing my headphones. Didn't hear you come in."

"Ryan, these are Special Agents Gray and Bentley. They're here to ask some questions about Susan. Want to join us?"

"Sure," Ryan said. "Anything to help." He looked around, searching for a place to sit down. Eventually he grabbed another chair from the kitchen and sat down with them.

Zoe sipped from her coffee cup, the taste jolting her. Seemed like Daniella loved *everything* strong and intense. She watched Tatum as he began questioning Susan's friend.

"How long did you know Susan?"

"I met her about a year before she was killed. Maybe a bit more," Daniella said. "But Ryan only met her after we started dating. So he only knew her for a couple of months."

"Right," Ryan said. "She was nice."

"Were you two good friends?"

"Yes," Daniella said, her voice softening. "She was my best friend. And I think I was hers too. She didn't have many friends."

"Why not?"

"Oh, she was a quiet type, you know? Always preferred to stay home and study or paint. She didn't go out much."

"So she didn't ordinarily invite many people to her place."

"No, not at all. And her apartment was even smaller than mine. She couldn't really have large gatherings there, you know?"

"Did she date?"

"A bit. She went through a big breakup two years before she . . . died. Never got over him, really."

"Did she date anyone just before she died?"

"No. I don't think she had any dates in the six months before she died. At least, nothing she talked about."

"Did she seem worried about anything or anyone? Can you think of any man who knew her and might have . . . bothered her?"

"No. I don't think she even had any male friends."

"Any male relatives? A cousin? A brother?"

"Maybe. I don't know."

"Didn't she have an uncle living nearby?" Ryan said. "I'm pretty sure she mentioned him once or twice."

"Oh, yeah."

Zoe nodded. Susan did have an uncle in Chicago. He was seventy and in a wheelchair. But he was on the list, and someone was bound to talk to him soon.

"Did she mention any of her neighbors?" Tatum continued.

"No."

A plethora of negatives. Zoe sighed and intervened. "When was the last time you saw her?"

"Uh, a week before . . . before she disappeared. I went over to visit her."

"What did you talk about?"

"Just the usual. Studies. Art. Guys. She said she wanted to move out."

"Did she say why?"

"Oh, yeah. Tons of reasons. The apartment was crap. The insulation was terrible; the place was freezing cold in the winter. I remember she mentioned that. What else?"

"There was a real problem with moisture and mold on the walls," Ryan said. "It was really serious."

Daniella nodded. "Right. It even ruined some of her paintings once. Oh, and the sewage kept backing up. One time it actually flooded the apartment. We had to go there with Ryan's van and get her furniture to a storage facility until the place dried up."

"Yeah. We just threw away the carpet," Ryan added. "Also, the landlord was an asshole—"

"An asshole how?" Tatum asked.

"He kept dodging her when she needed stuff," Daniella said. "She had to pay for the sewage thing herself once. And a real bastard when he needed the rent. Kept threatening to raise it too."

"Do you know his name?"

"No."

Zoe and Tatum exchanged looks. It was likely that the detectives had already checked the landlord, but Zoe made a mental note to make sure.

"Anything else you can think of?" Tatum asked.

Daniella shook her head. "I wish I could help more," she said. A tear materialized in her eye. "I really miss her."

CHAPTER 29

By the time Zoe and Tatum returned to the police station, a steady rain was pattering on the car. Zoe stared at a drop trickling down the windowpane as it merged with another drop, accelerating. Her eyes followed the trickle until it reached the bottom of the glass. She thought of Daniella's description of Susan, trying to create a profile for the victim. A young art student, living alone, spending most of her time by herself in her apartment.

The perfect victim. The killer had chosen well. He had been careful.

But now his caution was slowly slipping. He preyed on random prostitutes. Though he probably had certain criteria, he no longer targeted lone women. Krista had lived with a friend and had been described as someone who got along with everyone. She had had a pimp.

Was the killer getting cocky, or was the urge to kill increasing, making him careless? Either way, he was moving faster. He would make more mistakes, which meant they had a better chance of catching him . . . but the price would be high.

She was frustrated by her inability to give Martinez a stronger profile. Specifically, it irked her that the killer was careful enough to strike all over the city, obviously driving for hours just to get far enough from his home. Geographic profiling was a great way of narrowing the group of suspects, and her inability to use it was crippling.

Tatum killed the engine, and Zoe was startled out of her thoughts. They were back at the station.

Neither of them had an umbrella, and Zoe ran half-crouched to the entrance of the department. Once under the cover of the lobby's ceiling, she turned around, her hand brushing her hair, and watched Tatum as he walked casually in the rain as if it didn't bother him. His mouth was quirked in a slight smile as if her hunchbacked trot had amused him. She was satisfied to see that by the time he got to her, his hair was dripping wet, and his shirt was visibly soggy. Who was laughing now?

Zoe, that's who.

They went up to the task force room, which was mostly empty. Martinez sat hunched above some papers on his desk, his hand on his forehead. He looked exhausted. Across from him, Mel was talking on her phone, cradling it between her cheek and her shoulder as she typed on her keyboard.

Martinez glanced at them. "Anything interesting from the art student?"

Zoe shrugged. "A general description of the victim's habits. Nothing more."

"Okay. Which of you types up the report?"

"What report?" Tatum asked weakly.

"You talked to a witness, right? Here in the police we have something we call a 'case file.' Witness accounts go inside it. In a report."

"Right." Tatum cleared his throat. "I think that Zoe—"

"It was your idea to help out," Zoe said sweetly. "Don't you want to help out anymore?"

"I'll send you the template for the report," Martinez grunted, turning to his computer.

Mel slammed her phone in its cradle and cursed loudly. She then clearly realized that the agents and the lieutenant were staring at her.

"Sorry," she muttered. "It's been a long day, and this list is endless."

"List?" Zoe asked.

"I sat down with the lieutenant from vice today," Mel said. "We called all the districts and composed a list of all the reports of missing women from the last seventy-two hours. I'm now trying to follow up on them. But it's taking ages."

Zoe walked over and asked to see the list. She leafed through the stapled pages. There were four pages, each containing a short list. Altogether there were twenty-nine names. Each name came with a list of phone numbers and addresses, both of the missing woman and her acquaintances. There was also a description of the missing woman and a short line detailing the circumstances of the disappearance. Seven of the names were crossed out, and one was circled.

"What's the one you circled?" Zoe asked.

"It was the only one I followed up on who's still missing. The ones I crossed out have been located. Well, actually, five of them just returned home."

Zoe flipped through the pages again and frowned. "Did you order those according to the date?"

"Yeah. I thought I'd start with the ones that have been missing the longest, since they are most likely to have returned. And if they didn't, it's more—"

"That's a bad way to prioritize."

Mel stared at Zoe, gritting her teeth.

"You should focus on the past thirty-six hours, at least a day after we found the body of Krista Barker. Call the women aged nineteen to twenty-five first. There are five names here that mention recent bruising on the face or arms. You can leave them for last. Bruises don't heal after death, and our killer likes his corpses in good condition—"

"These women are adept at hiding their bruises with makeup," Mel said.

"He would be very alert to that. This man is careful. My guess is that he avoids prostitutes with heavy makeup precisely because of that reason. Probably tattoos and piercing as well. We'll push down any of the women that have a visible tattoo or piercing. Also, we should start with women gone missing in the evening and night." Zoe grabbed a pen from Mel's desk and began marking names. "This one. And this. And this one here."

She marked four more. Then, scanning the names she marked, she numbered them, one to seven. "Start with those, in this order. And meanwhile, I'll prioritize the rest."

Mel stared at her for a long moment and then grabbed the phone and began punching the numbers in fast, furious movements.

Satisfied, Zoe turned back to the list.

CHAPTER 30

Lily's younger brother had been afraid of the dark when they were children. She'd mock him about it, call him a baby and a scaredy-cat. When their mother yelled at them to turn off the goddamn light and go to sleep, Lily would switch off the light and then start to hiss and growl like a monster until her brother would leap screaming out of the bed, only to be punished by their irate mom.

She wished she could go back in time and tell him that she understood now. That she finally realized the dark really was scary. Because when it was dark, really dark, you were left with only your imagination.

She moved her feet, trying to spot the movement, any movement at all, but she couldn't. She wanted to wave her hands in front of her eyes—surely she would be able to see that. But her hands were twisted behind her back, the metal bite of handcuffs on her wrists. She trembled in the cold, terrible thoughts flooding her about what might happen to her soon. That guy . . . when she rode in his car, he had seemed so normal. So much better than most of her clients. At first, when he put the knife to her throat, she had almost believed it was a joke. A bad joke, sure, but still, a nice guy like that . . .

She'd heard stories, of course. Working on the streets, you couldn't avoid them. Girls who disappeared completely or were found dead in an alley. But somehow, she assumed the girls had been careless, that they'd gone with the wrong customer, that they hadn't paid attention to the warning signs.

Now, a bit late, she discovered some guys gave no warning signs. With those men, the first warning sign was the knife against your throat.

He had left the radio on in the other room. She suspected it was mostly to mask her screams. Not that she could scream so loudly anymore. The cold, hunger, and fear had sapped all her strength. The best she could do was moan and sob. The radio played some music, but it was mostly talk shows, the voices of the callers and the host muffled through the door. There were moments when she got confused, suddenly certain those were real people talking outside the door, and she screamed for help through the rag in her mouth, only to recall a second later that it was nothing but the disembodied voice of a person traveling on radio waves to drive her mad.

Something hummed, the sudden sound jolting her. She opened her eyes, realizing she had nodded off. There was a small buzz somewhere inside the room. A strange faded light glimmered, not far from her eyes.

By the time she understood what was happening, the humming had stopped, and the light had faded away, the room sinking back to blackness. It was her phone. Her *other* phone. She had seen him take her work phone from her handbag, but he must have left her personal phone in it. It was set on vibrate. Customers didn't like it when her phone interrupted, so she always set it to vibrate when she was working. And the buzzing had been a call.

The handbag was discarded by her clothing. Far from where she sat. Too far. For a moment she struggled against the handcuffs that forced her hands behind her back. The handcuffs themselves were chained to the wall, preventing her from reaching her handbag. She pulled her hand, trying to escape the metal cuff around her wrist, feeling her skin rip painfully, tears springing to her eyes. Her shoulders slumped. It was impossible. The handcuffs were too tight.

The hum began again, the faint light of the device's screen filling the room with a soft digital light. She could clearly see both her body and her handbag, discarded on the floor. Frantic, she stretched, trying to get her foot to touch the handbag. Perhaps she could pull it over somehow . . .

The hum stopped. Darkness. Toying with her, teasing, a hint of freedom inches away from her bare feet. There and then gone.

A thought suddenly struck her. How much battery did she have left? She had charged the phone before leaving. But she had been in this place for what felt like more than a day. What if her battery ran out? Her last glimmer of hope gone?

She began stretching in the darkness again, groaning. Her shoulder was about to pop out of its socket as she forced herself further, inch after inch, fumbling for the handbag with her toes, screaming with frustration and pain.

The hum began again, and in the light from the phone, she could see that she was almost there. Almost. Screaming into the rag, she pulled against the handcuffs, her skin tearing, shoulders burning, sweat drenching her body . . .

She managed to grab one of the straps of the bag with her toe, and she pulled.

The handbag fell aside, spilling its contents on the floor, her phone, by some divine intervention, facing up. Her eyes were immediately drawn to the battery mark on the screen.

Six percent.

The call stopped, the phone darkened, and Lily whimpered. She fumbled at the phone with her foot but couldn't get a good grip. Breathing hard through her nose, she tried again. Her foot was barely touching the device. She kicked the phone a bit farther by accident and groaned fearfully. Had she kicked it too far?

The screen turned on again; the hum resumed. The battery indicator was at 5 percent. The phone was still within reach.

She slid her foot against the screen, cursing the design that required her to slide to answer the call rather than tap the screen. Over and over she tried to slide her toe across the screen, managing nothing, screaming herself hoarse.

CHAPTER 31

Zoe was almost finished prioritizing the list when Mel suddenly hissed, "Shit."

Zoe raised her eyes to the detective. She gripped the phone hard, her eyes scanning the room and its three other inhabitants.

"Lieutenant," Mel said sharply, "get over here."

The tense tone got Martinez moving, and he stood up quickly and began crossing the room. Mel hit the speaker button on her phone.

Zoe frowned. All she could hear was the muffled sound of two people talking in the background. She couldn't figure out what had prompted Mel's reaction.

Mel hit the volume button, several times, increasing it to its maximum, and then said, "Hello?"

Nothing. Just the faded background noise of a faraway conversation.

"Hello? Lily? This is Detective Mel Parks with the Chicago PD. I just wanted to make sure that—"

Another sound. High pitched, tense, and unclear. A car wheel squealing? No, it kept going, rising and falling. And then, her heart sinking like a stone, Zoe understood what she was listening to.

Muffled screams.

Martinez reached the desk and listened. After a second, Mel said, "Lily? I need you to calm down and try to answer me. Is your mouth gagged?"

A moment of silence. Then a muffled response. It sounded like a woman trying to say, "Uh-huh."

"Is there some way you can remove the gag from your mouth?"

"Uh-uh." An almost imperceptible shift in tone, but clearly the answer was no.

"Do you know where you are?" Mel asked.

"Uh-huh."

Zoe glanced at the list. Lily Ramos. Aged twenty, working as a prostitute, reported missing by her friend, who was supposed to meet her when the night ended. She'd been missing for a day, last seen trying to pick up a customer in the evening. She had been described as Caucasian, with almost no makeup, wearing a skirt and a long-sleeved blouse—relatively modest for her profession. She had only one tattoo, not visible when she was clothed—a black cat on her lower back. Zoe had marked her as number three on the list.

"Can you describe the man who took you?"

A muffled, frustrated grunt.

Martinez took control. Picking up the phone, he said loudly, "Lily, this is Lieutenant Martinez. Do you know the address you're at?"

Since he had picked up the phone, the woman's voice could no longer be heard, but after a second he nodded. "Okay. We'll do this letter by letter. When I get to the right letter, I want you to stop me, okay? We'll get you out of there. Here we go. A . . . B . . . C . . ."

In the background, Tatum was talking rapidly on the phone. He was trying to get someone in the FBI to trace the call. He turned to Zoe and mouthed, *Phone number.*

Martinez's voice droned on. "D . . . E . . . F . . ."

Zoe grabbed the list and rushed to Tatum, handing it to him, pointing emphatically at Lily's phone number. Tatum gave her a curt nod, his face grave. He began reading the phone number to the man on the other side of the line.

Her fists were clenched. Her heart pounded, its rhythm aligning with the letters as Martinez spoke them.

"G . . . H . . . I . . . is it I? Is it H? Okay, good. Again. A . . . B . . ."

Zoe turned to Martinez and waved her hand at him frantically. He glanced at her, frowning.

"Vowels," she said. If the first letter was H, the next one would be a vowel.

He paused, then nodded. He cleared his throat. "E . . . I . . ."

Mel was tapping on her keyboard furiously, the sounds merging with the voices of Martinez and Tatum.

"O . . . U . . ."

Zoe glanced over Mel's shoulder on the screen. There was a list of names there. Street names. All starting with H.

"Is it U? Okay, good. Okay. Third letter. A . . . B . . . C . . ."

Mel hit the letter *U*, and the list shifted, displaying only the street names starting with *HU*. She frantically sent it to the printer, then dashed across the room to where the printer was located. Zoe clenched her fists, focused and alert as she listened to the one-sided conversation, a macabre version of the ABCs.

Mel grabbed two pages as they slid out, then jostled past Zoe and slapped the pages in front of Martinez. He stared at them, then nodded.

"Okay, Lily? Are you there? Good. Listen, I have a list of Chicago streets here starting with *HU*. I am going to read you their names, and you stop me once I get to the right one, okay?"

Zoe could imagine the woman grunting as she understood what Martinez said.

"Hubbard . . . Hubbs . . . Huber . . ."

Tatum stopped talking, and Zoe turned to him as he slammed the phone in its cradle. He strode to his own computer, tapping. A map of Chicago appeared on the screen. Did he have a location? She walked over to him, wiping a bead of sweat from her brow. He was looking at a Chicago neighborhood, but the scale was small. The location was far from accurate. She felt sick. She couldn't imagine what Lily was going through right now.

CHAPTER 32

Lily listened to the man drone the street names. Too slow. Much too slow. Her eyes didn't budge from the battery indicator. Two percent.

"Huck . . . Hudson . . . Huguelet . . ."

She wanted to shout at him to hurry up; the call would be disconnected *any second*. But she couldn't stop him. Could only grunt.

"Hull . . . Humboldt . . . Hunt . . ."

He was nearly there. And then they'd have to get to the house number. Was it 3202? Or 3204? She wasn't sure. Either way, it was a large number. How would she be able to convey the number to him? Her throat constricted in despair.

They'd have to do it digit by digit, she realized. Four digits. It could be done. The cop sounded intelligent; he'd figure it out. And then she'd have to give him the apartment number. Though probably once they had a house number, they could send some squad cars . . . she began to feel hopeful.

The battery indicator changed. One percent.

"Hunter . . . Hunting . . ."

She tensed. Almost there. She had to be alert. If she missed the street name, they'd never find her.

It was then that she realized she could no longer hear the radio outside her door. Instead, she heard footsteps approaching the door.

"Huntington . . . Hurlbut . . . Huron . . . Hussum . . ."

The door flung open, flooding the room with light, the silhouette of a man in the doorway. She barely noticed that Martinez had said the correct street name and gone right on, intoning street names in a calm, steady voice. She started screaming hysterically into her gag.

"Is it Hussum Street? Hello? Lily? Is it Hussum Street?"

The man walked forward, picked up the phone from the floor, and disconnected the call. He looked at her, trembling. He crouched down, and his hands shot forward, grabbing her throat.

His fingers squeezed. Hands tied behind her back, she could do nothing but squirm, trying to breathe.

CHAPTER 33

"Damn it!" Martinez shouted. "The call disconnected." He hit redial, and after a second the prerecorded voice of a woman informed him that the number was not available.

"I have an approximate location from the cell towers," Tatum called. "I have the map over here."

Martinez rushed to Tatum's computer, joining Zoe.

"It's within one mile of 805 North Trumbull Avenue," Tatum said, pointing at the map.

"Any streets there starting with *HU*?" Martinez asked, scanning the map. "There. Huron Street."

He turned around and barked at Mel, "Get dispatch to send squad cars to Huron Street, now. We'll try to get you a more accurate address."

Mel was on her phone, already talking by the time he finished his sentence.

"Any way we can get more specific?" he asked Tatum.

"One mile from that address pretty much encompasses all of this part of Huron Street," Tatum said, pointing at the screen. "I'll talk to the cell company, try to get a better estimate."

"He'll make a run for it," Zoe said, looking at the map. "And he'll take her with him."

"Why?"

"He's not done with her yet. The women he takes mean a lot to him. He keeps each one for a week or more after killing them. He won't give her up easily."

"Tell dispatch to alert all squads," Martinez shouted at Mel. "The suspect might be on the move. Stop any man walking alongside a woman or carrying sizable luggage. Stop all the cars on the street. We can't let this guy get away."

"He might manage to leave the area by the time they get there," Tatum said.

"He'd have to be damn fast," Martinez growled.

"He will be," Zoe said. "And he'll have the cover of darkness and the rain working for him."

Martinez was nodding as he held his phone to his ear. "Sir," he said to someone on the other side. "We know his approximate location, and he's making a run for it. His victim might still be with him. Yes, sir. I need a helicopter and—"

There was a pause, and then Martinez said, "Yes, sir." He hung up and hollered, "Get a helicopter up above that neighborhood. And I want roadblocks. Stop any car driving north from Huron Street to Chicago Avenue and any car going south from Huron to West Ferdinand Street."

"He might go west, via Kostner Avenue," Tatum said, scrolling the map.

"And a roadblock on the crossroad of Kostner and Pulaski," Martinez called to Mel, who was rattling the instructions to dispatch. "We'll get him."

CHAPTER 34

He teared up as he dragged her body to the embalming table. That was what happened. That was precisely why so many couples broke up. Spouses cheating on each other, backstabbing each other, calling the police. Before he changed them, there could be no trust, no reliance. No real love.

He didn't have much time, he knew, but he had to do this before they left, or their relationship would never last. The neighbors would complain about the smell again.

No, if he really loved her, he had to risk it all and do this. He made the incision, his fingers trembling. His hands worked fast, frantic, mixing the embalming fluid. No time to be accurate; he would just have to hope he got it right. How soon would they find him? How had he screwed this up? Why the hell hadn't he checked if she had another phone? It was love. Love had made him careless.

He put in the tube and started pumping the liquid in. After a few seconds, he realized in frustration that he'd forgotten to make an incision for the drainage. He reached for the jugular vein, cutting hurriedly, and a spurt of liquid drenched him. Blood.

Damn, damn, damn. That damn woman and her phone call—look at what she'd done to him.

He looked at her body, his heart broken. Her neck was a mess, a large rip where he had cut. Her wrists were completely mangled; she had hurt them badly when she'd struggled to get to her damn phone. She had bruises and scratches on her feet . . .

She had been so beautiful. And so innocent. Or at least that's what he had thought.

The hell with the embalming. He would take her like she was. They could have a few wonderful days together, before she would have to leave. He removed the tube from her neck, another spurt of blood drenching his fingers and her delicate skin. Her entire chest was a mess. Frantic, he began dressing her up, struggling to put a shirt over her head. Was that the sound of sirens?

Damn it!

He picked her up. No time for her pants. Carrying her over his shoulder, he got into the garage. If he hadn't had a garage available, he would have given up on her. No way he could walk out the door with the woman's body on his shoulder, with the police out in the street.

He hesitated. Should he put her in the back or in the front seat? The cops might be less suspicious about a man driving with his wife in the passenger's seat. But if they looked closely . . .

He opened the back, dumped her inside. Looked at himself in the side mirror.

He was covered in blood. He walked back to the workshop, washed his face and hands. There was a huge stain on his blue shirt, but perhaps in the dark it would be harder to see. He could hear more sirens. Time to go. Now.

He entered the van and opened the garage door. It rose slowly as he gritted his teeth. Come on . . . come on . . .

Finally, the door was open. He drove outside, headlights off. Closed the garage door behind him.

First things first. Get off the street. He quickly turned right on North Ridgeway Avenue, switching on his headlights as he did so. Just another man on the road, driving his van somewhere unimportant. No need for the police to check too close.

Above him, he heard a helicopter. The street flooded with bright white light behind him. He forced his foot to remain steady on the gas pedal. If he started speeding now, he'd be pulled over in no time. He had to stay calm. He would just drive up to Chicago Avenue, turn left, and drive home. There was no reason for the police to . . .

There was a roadblock up ahead. A cop signaled the vehicles to stop, checking each one closely. He stopped the van, frantically looking around. Saw the alley.

There really was only one course of action.

CHAPTER 35

The rain spattered on Officer Mikey Calhoun's yellow raincoat, trickling down his neck onto his back. By that point, the raincoat was a sham, a nylon wrapping just as effective at trapping water inside as it was at keeping it out. When he had left for work that morning, rain had seemed unlikely, and anyway, he was supposed to be in a car. The future had seemed reasonably dry. But here he was. He had water in places he couldn't even speak about in public. They were getting intimate, the rain and him. Much more intimate than Mikey and his current girlfriend were lately.

The cars were honking incessantly. He got it. People didn't like to be held up. They didn't like traffic jams, and they definitely didn't like roadblocks. He didn't either, okay? When he took his daughter to school, he wasn't happy if he suddenly ran into road construction or a holdup because of an accident. But he knew this was part of living in a big city—not just the job opportunities and the bars and the well-maintained roads. You sometimes got roadblocks. And if you did, the best thing you could do was be a good sport about it and stop that damn honking. Let's consider for a moment that the interior of a car was dry, right? Much drier than Officer Mikey Calhoun, thank you very much. They even had wipers for their windows, didn't they? All Mikey had was a hand, as wet as the rest of him, with which he could occasionally wipe his face.

He motioned for the next vehicle to come forward. The traffic moved at the pace of an undernourished snail. The vehicle inched slowly forward, stopping next to him. A dark Nissan van. One driver, no passengers. That meant, according to the instructions Mikey had been given, that this was someone he had to check carefully.

"Hello, sir," he said. "Where are you going?"

"Driving home, Officer," the man said. He gave a civilized smile, which Mikey interpreted as understanding. This guy realized Mikey was just doing his job. Maybe he was even sympathetic to Mikey's predicament, standing outside in this weather.

"Yeah?" Mikey ran his flashlight over the floor of the van. It was spotlessly clean. Mikey avoided turning his light on the man. If people gave him some lip or were impolite, Mikey would aim the beam at their eyes. Sure, it was a bit petty, but at times, pettiness was all Mikey had.

"Would you mind opening the back of the van for me?"

"Why?" the man asked.

"Because I want to look inside."

"Don't you need a warrant for that?"

He did. Unless he had probable cause to believe this man had committed a crime. Which he didn't. Mikey contemplated turning the light on the man. Was he giving him lip? But he just sounded matter-of-fact. A man concerned about his own privacy.

"I need to check your car, sir."

"The thing is, my van is a bit of a mess."

"Open the back, please, sir."

If he wouldn't, Mikey would tell him to step out of the car. He didn't really want to do that. It would just hold up traffic even more. And the honking would get louder. But this was his job. He took pride in it.

The man hesitated for another second, and Mikey began to wonder if he had a reason to hesitate. Was this the man they were looking for? His flashlight turned toward the man, the beam of light illuminating his clothes. His shirt was stained with barbecue sauce or something. Mikey moved the light upward to the man's face . . .

"Okay, Officer, it's open. I'm really sorry for the mess."

Mikey went over to the back, keeping an eye on the driver, who sat, both hands on the wheel, like he should. Mikey pulled the door open and cast the flashlight's beam on the cargo area. It wasn't that messy. Just a couple of plastic containers. One of them was on its side, and it seemed to have spilled on the cargo area's bottom, leaving a large dark stain. Mikey shut the door and went over to the man.

"Thank you, sir."

"Say, what's this all about?"

"Just routine, sir."

"Routine? You have the entire neighborhood blocked off. My girl-friend lives back there. Should I be concerned?"

Mikey sighed. The car behind this one honked. He felt very wet. "I'd tell her to stay inside tonight, sir. There's a dangerous person on the loose. Now, please drive—you're holding up traffic."

The car drove off, and Mikey shook his head at the honking car behind them. That one looked angry and agitated. He would get the "light on face" treatment for sure.

CHAPTER 36

Just before midnight, Martinez answered a phone call. As he spoke, mostly in monosyllables, Zoe perceived his shoulder slumping, the hand holding the phone loosening, the color slowly draining from his face. Finally, he turned around, the phone still held in his hand, not bothering to return it to its cradle.

"The body of Lily Ramos was just found in an alley south of Chicago Avenue," he said listlessly. "The ME is on the scene, and he hasn't said anything definite yet, but her throat was slashed, and the body is drenched in blood, so I'd say that sounds like a cause of death."

There was a long silence as the task force digested the information. The rest of the detectives had been summoned back and were all in the room.

"Are we sure it's Lily?" Scott asked.

Zoe noticed how he asked if it was Lily. Not Lily Ramos. Not Ramos. In the past few hours, as they all did their best to find her and save her, the investigators in the task force and Lily had become close.

"She fits the description we have. Specifically, she has a tattoo of a black cat on her lower back just like Lily did."

A tattoo. But hidden from sight. It still matched her assumptions. Zoe felt no sense of victory, only emptiness.

"Is she embalmed?" she asked.

"I don't know," Martinez said shortly. "I'm going to the crime scene right now. Mel, I want you to come with me. Agent Gray, Dr. Bentley, if you want, you can ride with us too. Scott, I want you here talking to dispatch. I'll get approval from the captain to keep the roadblocks and the helicopter up for half an hour more, so I want you to be our man in the situation room. I want the rest of you following in separate vehicles. This murder is fresh, meaning that the leads are fresh. We will probably split after reviewing the crime scene and start working those new leads."

New leads. Fresh scene. On paper, the case had just received a considerable windfall. They'd have additional data to analyze. They knew the exact street where the killer had held . . . and probably killed the victim. The killer would be spooked, would be prone to make mistakes.

But just hours ago they had the victim alive, on the phone. Had been closing in on her location. If they had been faster, smarter, better, she would have survived. Perhaps they would have even had the killer behind bars.

They were one step closer to catching the killer. But the cost was too terrible.

The mood in the car was grim. Martinez and Mel sat in front, Tatum and Zoe in the backseat. Zoe thought about Lily. She had heard what were probably Lily's last sounds. Trying desperately to save herself. Zoe knew very well how it felt to fear for your own life, to have a predator in the next room.

To know that help might be on its way . . . but probably not.

Zoe, open the door. Can't stay in there forever, Zoe.

She shivered.

"Are you okay?" Tatum asked. There was something soft in his eyes she hadn't seen before. Or maybe she was just looking for something she needed.

"Yeah," she said. "Just some unpleasant memories."

CHAPTER 37

Maynard, Massachusetts, Monday, December 15, 1997

The sound of her alarm clock buzzing made Zoe jump in her bed. Her heart beat wildly, and she looked around her in confusion, getting her bearings. She had given up on falling asleep altogether the night before, but apparently, just before dawn, sleep had finally caught up with her.

Andrea was already gone, which was strange. Andrea usually didn't get out of bed on school mornings before their mother physically pulled her out. But mom hadn't woken Zoe up. Why?

She got up and waited for a moment as a spell of dizziness hit her. She had slept no more than an hour the night before. Once she felt steady enough, she plodded to the kitchen, where Andrea was prattling, an untouched cereal bowl in front of her. Their mother was at the counter, staring at two slices of dry toast that had popped out of the toaster.

"Mom? Why didn't you wake me up?" Zoe asked.

"She said you need to sleep," Andrea squeaked. "And I wanted to sleep too, but she said that *I* have to wake up, which isn't fair because I'm also tired—"

Her mother turned around, and Zoe saw the exhaustion on her face. She hadn't slept well either, it seemed. "Andrea, eat your cereal already. We're going to be late. Zoe, I thought you might like to stay home today," she said, trying to insert a fake cheerful tone to her voice.

Zoe thought of her meltdown the day before. "Okay, yeah," she said hesitantly. "Mom, there's something I need to talk to you about."

"What is it?" Her mother began smearing cream cheese on the toast in angry, sharp strokes.

"Uh . . . can we talk somewhere else?" She glanced pointedly at Andrea.

Her mom glanced at her watch. "I have to go, Zoe. And I think you really should get back to bed. I heard you moving around in your room all night. Let's talk in the evening."

"Mom, it's important." She lowered her voice. "It's about the girls who were—"

Her mother's eyes widened, and she gripped Zoe's arm tightly. She dragged her out of the kitchen.

"Where are you going?" Andrea piped.

"I'll be back in a minute, sweetie," their mother said. "Eat your cereal."

"I don't want to be alone."

"Andrea, I'll be right back. And you're not alone. We're in the next room."

Once they were reasonably out of earshot, her mother hissed, "I asked you not to talk about it in front of Andrea."

"That's why I said we should talk somewhere private," Zoe answered, exasperated. "Listen, I had some thoughts last night. About the killings."

"Honey, it's perfectly natural to—"

"Mom, listen for a second."

Her mother became silent. Zoe tried to organize her speech, the thoughts jumbled in her head. Everything had seemed so sharp during the night, but now it just felt like a hazy clutter of half-formed ideas.

"I think I know who the killer might be," she said in a shaking voice.

Her mother's eyes widened, but she said nothing.

"A few weeks ago, after Jackie . . . died, I went to Durant Pond."

"What?" Her mother's voice came out sharp, furious. "Why did you go there? Did you go with friends? I told you—"

"I went alone, Mom, on my bike. For just a few minutes."

"Why? Do you want to die like . . . like . . ." Her mother's lips quivered.

"Mom, listen. I saw Rod Glover there."

And then she realized that to fully explain to her mother what she was talking about, she'd have to tell her about serial killers masturbating at the crime scene. No. There was no way.

"He was. I mean . . . did you know that serial killers sometimes return to the scene of the crime?" she asked helplessly.

"You think that Rod Glover is the killer?" Her mother stared at her. "Because you saw him at the pond? Zoe, hundreds of people—"

"There's more," Zoe hurriedly said. "There's a checklist for psychopathy. I learned about it . . . in school. And Rod matches some of those traits."

Her mom straightened. Zoe knew she was losing her. "Like what?"

"Like . . . superficial charm and . . ." She tried to remember the list, but her mind was fuzzy, and she felt panic rising. "He's weird. I heard you say that to Dad once. You know that he's weird, right? And he was at the pond. He was . . . he was . . . he told me about a fire, and I think he was lying and—"

"Who are you talking about?" Andrea asked from the kitchen's doorway.

"No one," her mother said quickly, her voice strained. "Did you finish your cereal?"

"Not all of it. Some of it is squishy."

"Okay, go brush your teeth. We need to go."

Andrea bounced to the bathroom, and their mother turned back to Zoe.

"Listen," she said quietly. "I understand. Your friend's sister died, and you're hurt. We'll find someone for you to talk to—"

"Mom. It's not that. She wasn't even really my friend."

"But until then"—her mom raised her voice, ignoring the interruption—"I want you to rest, and don't you *dare* go anywhere alone. There's a killer out there, Zoe. Do you understand? He kills young girls like you, and he . . . he . . . *rapes* them first. I know you think that it can never happen to you, but it *can*. You can *never* go anywhere alone until they catch him. Do you get that?"

"But . . . will you tell anyone about Rod Glover?"

"Honey, Rod Glover is a nice man. He's a bit strange, that's true, but that doesn't turn him into a monster."

"The killer isn't a monster, Mom. He's a—"

"Yes, he is," her mother whispered ferociously. "He's a *monster*."

The spare key to Mr. Glover's front door turned in the lock smoothly. Her parents and Glover had exchanged keys a year before, in case of an emergency. At the time, it had seemed like a smart move. Glover could drop by and check if her mother left the stove on, a concern that had driven her to return home early on more than one occasion. But now the thought of Rod Glover having a key to her home gave her chills.

She locked the door behind her, shoving the key into her pocket. Glover was at work—it was a Monday morning—but it made her feel slightly better.

She had been to his house once, on an errand from her mother to retrieve a long-borrowed blender, so she knew the kitchen and the living room. She decided in advance she would ignore those rooms and focus on his bedroom. The bedroom door was closed, and for a moment, she hesitated. What if he was sick and had stayed home?

But no, she hadn't seen his car parked out front. She twisted the door handle and pushed the door open.

His bedroom was dark and had a sweaty, unpleasant smell to it. The window was covered with a purple cloth, not really a drape, more like something he'd just hung on top of it. She switched on the light and looked at the door, hesitating. Should she close it? She wouldn't be able to hear if he came in. She decided to leave it open.

It was a small bedroom, the double bed taking up most of the space. It was a mess, bedsheets crumpled, the pillow on the floor next to it. A nightstand stood beside the bed, and a wooden dresser was against the wall. There were a few books and magazines in a pile on the nightstand.

She stood in the entrance, wondering what had driven her here. What did she expect to find? Something to convince her mother? Or perhaps something to make her realize that her suspicions were unfounded? She bit her lip and approached the nightstand, her hand touching the top book in the pile. It was a Batman comic book. She moved it aside to uncover an issue of *Hustler*. Uncomfortable, she shifted it aside. There was another issue. Then two more superhero comics and a book by John Grisham.

She piled the magazines and the book as they had been before. Not the most wholesome reading material, but probably not so different from what other men had in their homes.

She opened the top dresser drawer, finding shirts and pants thrown together in disarray. She looked through them carefully but could see nothing interesting. The second drawer contained underpants and socks.

The third drawer was a different story.

Her first impression was that it was just brimming with porn. There were numerous issues of *Hustler* but also other magazines she wasn't familiar with. Some of them displayed women tied up in various poses, half-dressed or nude. Zoe had seen porn before, both in magazines and on TV. She and Heather had once found a videotape that her dad kept in the garage and had watched it for ten minutes, giggling hysterically. But this was more than she had ever seen, and the images depicted made her sick. There were several videocassettes as well, the handwritten labels

173

in large, uneven letters with annotations like "Tied Up" or "Flogging and Whips." Did Glover buy these somehow? Had he recorded them, and if so, when and where?

Aside from the porn, there were at least ten ties in the drawer. Just bland gray ties that Glover probably wore for his job. Why didn't he keep the ties in the drawer with his socks and underwear? There was plenty of room there. Did he enjoy looking at his porn hoard every morning when he put his tie on?

Part of the drawer was empty, and there was a square-shaped vacancy in the thin layer of dust that had accumulated in the drawer's bottom. Something was missing. Perhaps the magazines on the night-stand? But they weren't quite the right shape. She shut the drawer.

Where else could she look? She glanced under the bed. There were some clothes discarded there. Apparently that was where Glover kept his dirty laundry. She was about to stand up when something caught her eye: a smear of something brownish gray on a pair of pants. Hesitant, she pulled the pants from under the bed.

They were a pair of blue jeans, and the bottoms of the pant legs were slightly muddy. She thought about the location where they had found Clara. Another spot on the Assabet River. Clara, like the previous victims, had been half-submerged in water.

How did these jeans get mud on them?

She began pulling out more clothes from under the bed. Some shirts, another pair of pants, none of them muddy. And then her fingers touched something that felt crusty with mud. She pulled it out. A sock, stiff with dry muck.

What else was there? She reached, grabbed a handful of other clothes, and pulled them out. Another shirt, a pair of underpants, and a pair of feminine underwear.

She held up the underwear. They could be explained, of course. Rod Glover occasionally had a woman over.

But there was a smudge of mud on the yellow cloth.

She stared at it for long seconds, her heart pounding. It dropped from her fingers.

She was becoming convinced she was standing in the bedroom of the Maynard serial killer. She had to get out of there. She bent to push all the clothing back under the bed, when something else grabbed her attention. A rectangular black shape under the bed. A shoebox. With trembling fingers, she pulled it out and lifted the lid.

There was a clicking sound, and it took a second to register. The lock on the front door.

She dropped the lid on the box, her mind in turmoil, and pounced at the bedroom door. She quickly shut it, taking care not to let it slam, just as she heard the front door opening. Had he seen? She leaned against the door, listening, hearing only the thumping of her own heart.

And then, a cupboard opened. He was in the kitchen. She let out a shaking breath and looked around her. Quickly, she shoved all the clothing and the shoebox under the bed, her mind still processing what she had seen in it. A few pieces of crumpled female lingerie. A bracelet.

She pushed the thoughts away. She couldn't be distracted right now; she had to get out. Get out and call the police. They would handle it all.

Moving slowly, she managed to get to the bedroom window. She removed the cloth that covered it. Would Glover realize someone had been in the room? Or would he assume it had just fallen? It didn't matter. Just get out and call the cops.

Carefully, she twisted the window handle. It was a bit stuck, and she had to push hard. She could hear Glover walking around the house and prayed he wouldn't come into the bedroom right now. Just a few more seconds . . .

She pushed the window, and it squeaked. Glover's footsteps paused.

She grabbed the window ledge and lifted herself out, tumbling, her foot hitting the pane, thumping. She quickly stood up and shut the window, the frame cracking as she did so. There was no way he didn't hear it.

She turned around and hurriedly walked away, crossing his yard toward her home and safety . . .

"Zoe?"

She froze, knowing she should just bolt, not able to move, her legs frozen in place. She turned around.

"Hey," she said, her voice shaking.

He looked at her with confusion, his eyes narrowing. "What are you doing here?" he asked. "Why aren't you at school?"

"M . . . my mom said I could stay home today. She sent me over. She wanted to know if you had some sugar. But then I remembered that you must be at work."

"Right," Glover said. His face was blank. His usual goofy grin was gone.

His eyes flickered to something behind her. Zoe glanced over her shoulder. Mrs. Ambrose was outside, shoveling the snow from her doorway.

"Hi, Mrs. Ambrose," Zoe called, trying to sound nonchalant, her voice high pitched and hysterical.

The neighbor raised her eyes and gave her a grudging nod. Zoe turned around and realized Glover was now much closer. He had crossed the space between them in less than a second. His jaw was locked tight.

"I have some sugar," he said. "How much do you need? A cup?"

Zoe nodded hesitantly.

"Come in," he said. "Let me get it for you."

"You know what? I just remembered that I can't . . . I can't eat sugar. I might be diabetic. I . . . thanks."

She turned and strode away, her steps fast, wondering if Glover would grab her, pull her into his home, rape her, and kill her.

"Zoe. Hey, Zoe," he called after her.

She kept walking, rigid with fear.

CHAPTER 38

Chicago, Illinois, Thursday, July 21, 2016

The alley was lit by flickering red and blue lights shimmering on the brick walls that enclosed it. The body of Lily Ramos had been discarded on the ground. It was a tight space, and Tatum and the detectives pushed their way ahead of Zoe, who made no effort to get there first. She could see glimpses of the victim between the people who huddled around the body. A palm, facing the sky, fingers outstretched. The woman's face, her eyes wide open and vacant, mouth parted. Her hair, disheveled, spread on the ground.

"Do you have an estimate for the time of death?" Martinez asked.

Someone answered, but Zoe couldn't see past the wall of people in her way.

"Time of death is between nine thirty and ten thirty."

Zoe assumed it was the medical examiner. She sighed and walked closer, shoving her way forward a bit until she could see the man crouching by the body.

This body was not posed, and there was no mistaking it for a living woman. Her arms sprawled on the ground, her left leg bent at the knee, the other straight. She wore a shirt and underwear, no pants. There was a dark-crimson gash on her throat. The entire neck was covered in dried blood as well as some on the body's chin. The blood had also trickled under her collar.

"She was still alive at nine thirty," Martinez said. "We know she was alive until nine thirty-seven."

"Unless it wasn't her on the phone," Tatum said.

Martinez nodded, conceding the possibility.

"Well," the medical examiner said, "she didn't die after ten thirty."

"And she didn't die here, either," Martinez said. "There's no blood on the ground."

The detachment came over Zoe, as it always did. As far as her brain was concerned, the body on the floor wasn't a dead woman. It was a collection of clues and indications. A footprint left by the killer. This was how her brain coped, and she knew it well by now. She also knew it was a temporary reprieve, that the body in the alley would haunt her later.

But that was later.

She crouched by the woman, looking at her intently.

"This doesn't look like the work of the same killer," Tatum said.

"Really?" Zoe glanced at the sides of the woman's neck. "Why not?"

"Well, she isn't embalmed, her throat is cut, she isn't posed, and we found her almost immediately after she disappeared . . . nothing is similar."

"She was tied," Zoe said, indicating the woman's wrists, which were scraped and bloody. "And I think she might have been strangled as well." She pointed at a bruise on the side of the neck.

"This looks all wrong for our killer."

"I definitely agree that this isn't what he wanted."

"But you think it's the same guy?" Tatum sounded very skeptical.

"I think it's too soon to tell," Zoe said.

"Why did he slash her throat?"

Zoe chewed her lip. That was a very good question. Everything else could be explained by the fact that the victim had contacted the police. The killer had panicked, killed the woman, and put her in the trunk, fleeing the crime scene. Realizing there were roadblocks everywhere, he had driven up to the alley and dumped the body.

But why slash her throat? It wasn't his MO; he always strangled the victims.

"I don't know," she finally admitted.

"I think it's a different guy, Zoe."

"Well," she said, irritated, "you have a right to your own opinion, Agent Gray."

Tatum sighed and stood up.

Zoe blocked the interaction with Tatum from her mind. The man was needlessly contrary and wasn't helping. She focused on the body. Around her, others were trying to figure out what had happened, tracing forensic evidence, perhaps finding a breadcrumb that would lead to the killer. Their job was to look at the past. Her job was to study the past, sure—then look at the present and the future.

What was the killer going through right now? What would his next move be?

This had not gone as he had planned. The body was not posed, probably not even embalmed. As far as this killer was concerned, the killing was not the point. It was the time after the killing that mattered. That was what he fantasized about.

And he hadn't gotten it. His fantasy had not been fulfilled this time. His need was still there. Perhaps even worse than before.

Serial killers usually had a learning curve. The killer had a fantasy. He killed, trying to fulfill the fantasy, but it didn't work as well as he hoped it would. It didn't match the fantasy. So he would think of ways to improve his actions so that the next murder would work out better. Killed again. Improved his methods even more. Killed again.

This was something people rarely understood about serial killers. Most people assumed killers had a constant signature. But often, the killer changed his methods and signatures to accommodate the elaborate fantasies in his mind.

This killer obviously adapted. His techniques became more refined with each murder. How would he adapt this time?

They'd nearly caught him. He was scared. He would need time to regroup, to understand what had happened and what had gone wrong. He knew the big screwup was leaving the phone with his victim, so they could be sure that wouldn't happen again. But that wouldn't be enough. Next time he grabbed someone, he'd kill her faster, not give her time to contact anyone. And he might change his target as well. He knew they thought he was targeting prostitutes. So he would search for a different victim—still vulnerable but not a working girl.

"Hey," Martinez said, crouching by her side. "Are you okay?"

"He's going to strike again," Zoe said. "And he'll adapt. We won't be able to find him through his future victims anymore. We'll have to find him by tracing the breadcrumbs he left in his past crimes. His past mistakes."

CHAPTER 39

He gazed at the shower's porcelain floor, watching the foamy water, pink with blood, swirling into the drain. There was something mesmerizing about it—the translucent white, pink, and red bubbles crowding the dark hole, sliding inside one after the other. A sob emerged from his throat, uncontrollable.

It had all gone so wrong.

He had thought that by the end of this evening, they would be together. Served him right for trusting a woman before the treatment. He should have finished her last night as soon as he had her. Instead, he'd decided to wait, and this was what happened.

He was alone.

Finally, the water running down his body became colorless, transparent. He switched the water off, stepped out of the shower, and grabbed his towel.

The shirt and pants he had worn, soaked in that woman's blood, were in a tied trash bag on the floor. He considered burning it, but that sounded like a hassle. Would anyone really go through a tied trash bag? He resolved to dump it in a public trash bin once he went out. Removing the evidence from his house was good enough.

He still found it difficult to believe the cop at the roadblock had let him drive through with his clothes looking like that.

He plodded to his room slowly. He could almost feel the oppressive emptiness of the apartment. No one but him in the bedroom. If he sat down to drink a beer, he would do so alone. No one to talk to about his day, to hear how he had evaded the police, slipped right through their fingers.

He put on a pair of jeans and a plaid button-down shirt and took a look in the mirror. His reflection stared back at him. He looked closely at his face and neck, made sure there was no speck of blood he had missed. There wasn't.

That bitch. And the cops had been looking for her; he was sure of it. They knew he had taken her. How?

Because they knew what he was looking for. Girls on the streets. Whores. Next time he stopped by a street corner, there might be a police stakeout waiting just for him. He felt a shiver of fear. And he wanted to talk to someone. Wanted a sympathetic ear, someone who would listen to his terror. There was no one.

A visit to the fridge earned him a cold can of beer. He walked over to his apartment's balcony and watched the view from above. It was hardly a luxurious home, but the view wasn't half-bad, considering the rent. Chicago's buildings blocked the view of Lake Michigan, but he didn't care about that. You couldn't really see the lake at night, only a black shape. It was much better to look at the windows, some of them alight even at this late hour. The city never really went to sleep. And somewhere in it, there was someone for him.

CHAPTER 40

Zoe's eyes were wide open, staring at the motel ceiling. The paint peeled at several points, and a diagonal crack zigzagged across almost the entire ceiling. The light had a dusty glass cover in which two distinct dead flies could be spotted. But her brain hardly registered all that. It was too busy processing the image of a dead woman, her neck bloody, her eyes vacant. And the detachment was gone, as she had known it would be.

Once she had a moment of quiet, a second to process, it always hit her. Her brain, wired to try to imagine everything, began working in high gear. What would the parents of this victim feel when they heard about it? How would her partner feel or children, if she had any? And, of course, how had *she* felt when it had happened? Scared? In pain? Violated?

During Zoe's fifteen minutes of fame, after helping catch one of the most infamous serial killers of the twenty-first century, she'd heard people talking about how clever she was. Her credentials would often be touted—PhD and JD from Harvard, top of her class, and so on and so forth. But they didn't get it. What made her so damn good was her vivid imagination. When she tried to, she could get into the killer's mind, imagine what he felt, what he saw. It was a double-edged sword because she'd also see things from the victim's point of view. And she'd see them clearly.

Tied by her wrists somewhere, trying desperately to tell the cops where she was, her mouth gagged. She'd been taken almost twenty-four hours earlier. Had she been tied that entire time? Probably. That meant her throat was parched; she was weak from thirst, hunger, and fear. Her jaw would ache from whatever had been shoved into her mouth to gag her, her shoulders throbbing in pain. And mix all that with the knowledge that death could be moments away, and then the killer came for her—

A knock on the door startled her. She was breathing hard, her palms sweaty. She took a moment to steady her breath and got off the bed. She padded over to the door.

"Yeah?" she said. She didn't ask who it was. Who else would knock on her motel door at two in the morning?

"Did I wake you up?" Tatum's voice sounded muffled from the other side.

"No, I was still awake."

"Can you open the door? I come bearing gifts."

Zoe considered this. She wore a wide, long shirt that covered her up to midthigh and a pair of underwear. She could go and put on a pair of jeans, maybe a bra, but it sounded like the worst sort of idea, and the glimpse of a dead young woman put the notions of modesty in a certain perspective.

She opened the door. Tatum stood outside, wearing jeans and a T-shirt, holding a 7-Eleven bag in his hand. His eyes widened slowly.

"Uh, sorry," he said. "I just thought neither of us had anything to eat for dinner, and I figured—"

"Come in," Zoe said, opening the door a bit wider. He slid in, and she caught a whiff of soapy lavender from him. He had showered before coming. She was relieved. She didn't want the smell of the crime scene in her room.

He sat on the small couch in the room's corner, putting the bag on the glass table. "I brought two meals. You can pick whichever you like.

There's a . . ." He pulled out the first box from the bag and read the label. "Buffalo chicken roller . . . and there's, uh . . . something else . . . with cheese, I guess. And two hotdogs, with some toppings I selected randomly."

"You know how to spoil a girl," Zoe said dryly, sitting on the other side of the couch, readjusting the shirt to cover as much as possible. "I'll take the something-else-with-cheese."

"And also"—Tatum pulled two bottles of Honker's Ale out of the bag—"something to drink. Because I think otherwise there's no way we can force this food down our throats." He pulled a set of keys from his pocket and used one of them to remove the cap from a bottle. He then handed it to Zoe.

Zoe took a bite from her something-else-with-cheese. It was stale and soggy and tasted like morning breath. She put it down and took the beer bottle. "Beer has caloric value," she said. "I think it can be considered a meal."

Tatum chewed the buffalo chicken roller, his face far from a warm endorsement. "This is terrible."

"Here. Allow me," Zoe said, holding out her hand. He gave her the roller, and she thrust it in the bag. Then she took the entire thing and dumped it in the trash. She bent by her suitcase on the floor and rummaged inside, locating the Snickers bars. It occurred to her that in this pose, dressed as she was, she was giving Tatum quite a view. She quickly straightened and turned toward him. He stared at the wall with fascination, his cheeks slightly red.

"Here," she said, handing one over. "I always pack a bunch of Snickers bars when I travel."

"Wise woman," he said, tearing the wrapper.

She unwrapped her own bar and took a bite. The peanuty crunchiness and the sweetness of the chocolate began tangoing in her mouth, and she shut her eyes, breathing deeply through her nose. She had tried yoga, meditation, running, and swimming. So far, nothing cleansed the soul better than a Snickers bar. It was the ultimate therapy. It was cheap, and it could be carried in her bag. She drank a swig of beer. The tastes meshed well together. She was enjoying this dinner of Snickers à la Honker's.

"Yum," Tatum said in a muffled voice, chewing happily.

Zoe smiled, her body relaxing. She was only half looking at Tatum, enjoying the first moment of serenity that evening.

"So, about today . . ." Tatum said.

"What about today?" Zoe asked, taking another swig from her beer bottle. She had finished half her Snickers bar, and her brain was mostly consumed by the complex process of dividing the Snickers bar bites evenly throughout the beer. She didn't want to drink the final third of the bottle with no chocolate to accompany it. Bad planning of chocolate division was how things went downhill.

"You practically bit my head off when I said I don't agree with you."

"I just said you're entitled to your own opinion. Aren't you?"

"Yeah, I mean, your tone was—"

"Look, I'm sorry I hurt your sensitive feelings. There was another dead woman in that alley, and every moment we dawdle increases the danger of another killing. This is what I'm focusing on right now."

"Me too. You know, I'm part of the BAU just like you. I'm not just a pretty face in a suit. I have good instincts and experience."

"You're not wearing a suit," Zoe remarked.

"I was speaking figuratively," he said, his eyes flicking downward, as if to stress the fact that compared to her, he was in very formal clothing.

She wasn't sure what he wanted—an apology? She wasn't about to apologize for doing her job. She decided to do the next best thing: change the subject. "Are you unhappy with your new position in the BAU?" she asked, her voice soft, placating.

He eyed her, frowning. He crumpled the empty Snickers wrapper, his beer bottle still half-full. Amateur. "I don't know," he said and sipped from the bottle. "It's not what I wanted. And I loved LA. But so far it hasn't been boring."

"Why were you . . . *promoted*?" Zoe asked. She tried to ask delicately, but her voice rose when she said *promoted* in a way she immediately knew was offensive.

He grinned at her. "Because I was great. Why else?"

She raised her eyebrow.

He sighed. "I was working on a pedophile ring case. We were closing in on one of the main suppliers of content. When we were about to arrest him, he ran."

Zoe nodded, saying nothing.

"I caught up to him and told him to put his hands up. He reached for his shoulder bag, and I shot him."

"What was he reaching for?"

"We can't be sure, but we think he was reaching for his camera. There were some photos on it, and we think he wanted to delete them. He had no gun in his bag."

Zoe thought it over. "Wasn't the shooting justified? You thought he was reaching for his gun."

"What I was thinking is a subject of much controversy. We were alone in an alley. No one saw the shooting. Before the shooting, I'd stated more than once my thoughts about this guy."

"Which were?"

"That I thought he should get the death penalty," Tatum said, his tone dry.

"So they think you . . . what? Executed him?"

"Some people do." He shrugged. "In general, they weren't happy with how I handled the case. Too emotional. Some things weren't according to protocol. And I guess it wasn't the first time. But my chief also wanted to present this as a win to the press. There was a lot of data in that guy's home computer, and we managed to take down a lot of suppliers. So they couldn't really fire me."

"They promoted you to work in the BAU instead."

He smiled. "You keep saying that word. I don't think you know what it means."

"What word? Promoted?"

"I was just joking . . . never mind. So what about you? Do you enjoy working in the BAU?"

"It's what I always dreamed of doing," she said.

"That's nice. But doesn't really answer the question."

She blinked and looked away. "I don't really . . . enjoy a lot of things," she said. "I find them interesting. And I like being busy. But I don't skip merrily on my way to the office every day."

"Well, skipping all the way from Dale City to Quantico sounds like quite a chore."

They were silent for a second, and then Tatum said, "You're a psychologist. You could be helping people or working with kids. Why did you decide to be a forensic psychologist?"

She broke a piece from her Snickers bar and put it in her mouth, hesitating. "I'm just not . . . I'm not very good with people."

She was half expecting him to feign shock, mock her. But he said nothing, just looked at her, his eyes soft.

She wasn't sure if she was talking because of the emotional toll of the evening or because Tatum's presence reassured her somehow. She found herself saying things she had only told Andrea before. "I seem to always say the wrong thing or offend someone. When I practiced counseling—we do it in front of a class—my peers would always say I was cold, too clinical. I knew I'd never be really good at counseling. I'm too insensitive for that."

She stopped, looking at the bottle and last bite of her Snickers bar. She ate the final piece of chocolate and then drank the remainder of the bottle, not enjoying them like she'd hoped she would.

"I don't think you're insensitive," Tatum said, his voice breaking the silence. "I think you're just very focused."

She smiled weakly. "That's pretty much the same."

"No. It isn't."

She looked at him, almost as if for the first time. His smile no longer seemed self-satisfied. It was warm. The blood rushed to her face.

He cleared his throat. "Well, for what it's worth, you're good at what you do. And you help the victims' relatives and friends get closure. And prevent others from getting hurt. You're doing good."

Zoe nodded. He had a small spot of chocolate by his lips. She was overcome with the image of leaning over and kissing the chocolate off, could imagine his hand on her back, the taste of his tongue, the rough stubble scraping her lips as they kissed.

"You have some chocolate on your face," she said.

He licked it off. "Gone?"

"Yeah. Listen, I'm really tired. Thanks for dinner. See you tomorrow morning? I'll ride with you to the station."

"Sure," he said. "What time?"

"Nine?"

"You got it."

He got up, finished his beer while standing, and walked out, bidding her good night.

An overactive, vivid imagination. It was her blessing and curse. Her chest and stomach were warm, her head dizzy. She blamed the beer, knowing it wasn't that. She lay down in bed, her mind finally clear of thoughts of death.

CHAPTER 41

"Hello, Mr. Gray?" The voice on the other side of the call was collected and calm. It was the voice of a man whose entire life was in order, where nothing was unpredictable, everything was according to schedule, and each event had a reasonable explanation.

"That's right," Tatum said. Zoe and he had just entered the task force room when his phone rang. He sat down by his desk, plugging in his laptop as he held the phone between his ear and shoulder.

"This is Dr. Nassar."

Tatum took a moment to place the name. "You're Marvin's . . . my granddad's doctor."

"That's right. Your grandfather was here to see me."

"Oh, good." Tatum was pleasantly surprised.

"Not good, Mr. Gray. Not good at all."

Fear clutched at Tatum's chest. "Is he ill?"

"I am not at liberty to discuss your grandfather's medical condition, but I feel that your intervention is required for your grandfather's health. Apparently, he's not taking one of the pills I've prescribed for him."

"It makes his throat itchy."

"Instead, he's taking a pill that someone else prescribed him—"

Tatum turned his laptop on. "It wasn't prescribed to him. It was given to him by an eighty-two-year-old woman with a cocaine habit."

"His blood pressure is extremely high." Dr. Nassar's voice was morphing, becoming less calm. "This can't go on."

"Did you tell him that?"

"I told him that this would end in a stroke or a heart attack."

"So he's taking the pill now?" Tatum leaned back, trying to silence the beating of his heart.

"No, he's not."

"Why the hell not?"

"Because," Dr. Nassar said, his voice becoming unhinged, "he said it makes his throat itch."

Tatum gritted his teeth, swallowing the endless tirade of curses that threatened to spew from his mouth. "I'll talk to him."

"He will die if he doesn't take his medication."

"My grandfather isn't really worried about dying, but I'll get some sense into his head."

"In all honesty, sir, your grandfather is one of the most frustrating patients I've ever had the pleasure of—"

"Thank you for letting me know. I'll talk to him."

He hung up his phone and counted to ten. Then he counted to thirty-nine, since just counting to ten didn't do the job. He had to get the point across, but Marvin was a stubborn bastard. Tatum suspected that his grandfather thought he was made of stronger material than most and that things like high blood pressure were problems that weak people endured.

He googled the symptoms of high blood pressure and read through them. Finally, he found the key to fight Marvin's mule-like stubbornness. He dialed him.

"Tatum." Marvin sounded sleepy. "Do you know what time it is?"

"It's past nine in the morning. What are you doing asleep?"

"It was a late night." Marvin yawned.

"I just received a phone call from your doctor."

"He's a very nice man, Tatum, but very uptight. He can get really worked up over nothing."

"He's worried about your high blood pressure."

"I told him I feel fine, Tatum. Really, never better. And I stopped taking Jenna's green pills like he told me to. But really, his blue pill makes my throat itchy."

"So you feel fine?"

"Totally fine, Tatum. A bit of a hangover, and your cat attacked me again, but other than that—"

"No chest pain?"

"No, don't worry. I'm as healthy as a mule."

"No vision problems?"

"I told you, Tatum, I'm fine. There's really no—"

"No erectile dysfunction?"

There was a moment of silence. "What?" Marvin's voice sounded much sharper. This woke him up.

"Dr. Nassar said that one of the symptoms of high blood pressure is erectile dysfunction. But you're feeling fine, right?"

"I . . . what exactly did he say about the symptoms?"

"Apparently, the arteries become hard and narrow," Tatum said, reading the info on the screen, "and that limits the blood flow. So you get less flow to the penis. I mean . . . that's what it says here online. Do you want me to send you a link? There's a diagram."

There was some disgruntled muttering on the other side of the call.

"Maybe if you drink some tea with honey after you take the blue pill, your throat won't itch as much," Tatum said brightly.

"Yeah."

"It's worth a try, right?"

"You're a pain in the ass, Tatum."

"Have a nice day, Marvin. I gotta go." Grinning, Tatum hung up the phone. He checked his email and realized that Dana had forwarded a message from the morgue. The autopsy of Lily Ramos was scheduled for that morning. He glanced at his watch. It was about to start in less than an hour.

CHAPTER 42

Zoe sipped from her third cup of coffee that morning, the lingering headache in the back of her skull kept at bay with the combined efforts of caffeine and Tylenol. She had managed to fall asleep slightly after three and woke up less than five hours later. She was grumpy and tense, feeling like an overstretched rubber band, ready to snap at any moment.

"Zoe," Tatum said behind her. "I'm joining Dana to observe the autopsy. Want to come?"

"No. I have too much to process here. You'll fill me in later?"

"Sure."

He left. The task force room was empty, and it occurred to her it was the first time this had happened since she'd arrived. Zoe had gotten so used to having her own office in the BAU; she didn't realize how much she missed the silence. This was how she worked best: no people to interrupt, no distractions, just her and a mountain of evidence and theories.

She still didn't have printed pictures of the crime scene, and the squad room's printer was black and white. She was used to the high-quality printer they had at Quantico, and this irked her. She preferred surrounding herself with images of the crime scene when she worked.

She opened the email with the images from the alley and looked over them. After going through them several times, she opened a wide shot of the crime scene, displaying the entire body lying on the alley floor. She then opened a close-up of the slashed throat and positioned both images side by side. Looking at the close-up carefully, she could see a brownish-blue bruise on the neck's side. Then she looked through the previous case files, selected a few images from each of the previous crime scenes, and stood up, thinking.

Her desk was positioned in the room's corner, and she had a wall to her right, another in front of her. She tacked the images to the two walls, Susan Warner and Monique Silva in front of her, Krista Barker to her right. Satisfied, she rolled her chair backward to inspect her handiwork. *And the prize for the most morbid workspace decoration ever goes to . . . Zoe Bentley.* All she needed was a dead potted plant on her table, and everyone in the Chicago PD would think she was a lunatic.

A new email popped up in her inbox. She didn't recognize the sender, but it was from a Chicago PD email address. It was a reply to Martinez's request for the recording of the conversation from the night before. The email had the sound file attached as well as the details of the call—phone number, start time and end time of the conversation, and some technical details that meant nothing to her. She played the call.

Listening to the conversation made her sick. The adrenaline she'd felt yesterday, the desire to help this girl, the hope that they'd manage to get her out alive—those were all gone. This was a conversation with a helpless, terrified, gagged girl who was going to die horribly very soon. It went on and on, the girl's muffled cries, trying to point the detectives to the right address. Zoe wanted to yell at the recorded Martinez, "It's Huron Street, damn it. Get to Huron Street." By the time she got to the end of the call, Zoe was clenching her fists tight, anticipating and dreading the hysterical muffled screaming. She took a long breath and looked at the sound file length. Fourteen minutes and thirty-four seconds. It felt like ten hours.

Zoe picked up a pen and played the sound file a second time. As it played, she jotted down several time stamps. The first was 01:43. Mel asked Lily if she could describe the man who had taken her. A completely inane request, since the woman was gagged. But Lily responded by trying to say something. The gag swallowed her word completely, the tone frustrated, desperate. Just a jumble. Zoe played the sound bite three times. Maybe there was some sort of sound-manipulation algorithm that could extract what she had tried to say.

The second one, at 02:52, was when Martinez took charge of the call. As he spoke, Lily's heavy, labored breathing could be heard in the background. But Zoe could also hear the sound of two people talking. They sounded far away and muffled, but she was sure there were two people there. And they seemed completely oblivious to Lily's screams. Couldn't they hear her? Or were they simply ignoring her? Was one of them the killer?

Finally, she jotted down the time stamp when Lily began screaming in panic. Just before that, Martinez had actually said, "Huron," but Lily hadn't stopped him. Did they get the street name wrong? Zoe listened to this segment over and over, frowning. Prior to Lily's frightened screams, there was a slight sound, almost imperceptible. A squeak.

A door opening.

Lily had probably stopped paying attention to Martinez because she'd heard the killer coming for her. And then he'd walked in and disconnected the call.

Zoe played the sound file again, focusing on the sound bite when the two men could be heard. Zoe frowned. She had also heard them several times during the call. Completely apathetic to Lily's screaming. They sounded almost casual. She increased the volume and listened a few times more. It sounded like one man asking a question, and the other man giving a lengthy answer. She listened again to the entire file, volume high, flinching when Lily's screams echoed in the empty room. Nine minutes into the recording, one of the voices changed, while the other stayed the same. The man asking the questions was talking to a third person. Who also completely ignored Lily's screams. Because, of course, he wasn't there.

It was the sound of a talk show.

She shook her head in disgust. Stupid. Time wasted.

She focused on the monitor. The bloody throat drew her attention. She frowned, her eyes moving from the cut throat to the bruise on the side.

Finally, she dialed Tatum.

"Zoe, we're in the middle of the autopsy," he said, sounding cranky.

"I know. Sorry. Listen, do you know yet if the victim was strangled?"

"Yeah, the ME says he thinks she was strangled before her throat was cut."

"Was that the cause of death?"

"He thinks so. The victim has hemorrhages in the eyes, which often happens in cases of death by strangulation."

"Then why did he cut her throat?"

"I don't know, Zoe. Because he's crazy."

"Was the body embalmed?"

"No, definitely not."

That didn't surprise her. She doubted the killer had had time to embalm the body. "Okay, let me know what else you find."

"Right," Tatum said and hung up.

Zoe bit her lip, thinking. Could the killer have slashed the woman's throat postmortem out of rage? It didn't sound like the kind of action he'd take. What, then?

She glanced at her phone. She had an idea. She called a second number.

"Abramson Funeral Home. This is Vernon."

"Mr. Abramson, this is Zoe. I was at the funeral home the other day . . ."

"I remember. How can I help you?"

"I have a dead body, and her throat is cut. I was wondering . . . would that make embalming problematic?"

"In what way?"

"I don't know. I'm just trying to understand this wound. It was done postmortem, and—"

"Is it a cut to the common carotid artery?"

Zoe blinked. "I have no idea."

He sighed. "Is there an image you can send me?"

"Uh . . . sure. What's your email?"

He gave her his email. As she sent him the photo of the victim's throat, Scott walked into the room and waved hi. She smiled at him.

"Okay," Abramson said. "Got it. Yes, this looks like a cut to the carotid artery."

"So . . . what does that mean for the embalming process?"

"Well, I assume it was made during the embalming process," Abramson said.

"What?"

"The common carotid artery is one of the preferred places to cut when embalming to inject the embalming fluid. Though he seems to have messed it up—the drainage spurted all over the throat."

"What does that mean?"

"Like I told you before, it means you are dealing with an amateur."

"But the body isn't embalmed."

"Then he probably stopped before he was done."

"I see."

"Is there anything else?"

"No . . . thank you, Mr. Abramson. You've been very helpful."

She put down her phone, her mind trying to assemble the sequence of events.

The killer had walked in, seeing Lily trying to get the police to help her. He had disconnected the call and strangled Lily to death. Then . . . he had decided to embalm her.

Why didn't he simply get rid of the body and get another prostitute? Surely he realized how risky this was. Embalming a body took about two hours. The police, as far as he knew, were on their way . . .

This body was very important to him; that was the only explanation she could think of. He *really* wanted it embalmed.

He had begun, then stopped during the process, which he had mucked up. He had taken the body with him . . . but then discarded it in an alley when he had seen the roadblocks.

It was erratic behavior. He became erratic when he was under pressure. She made a note of that.

She returned to the first time stamp. The muffled word.

"Hey, Scott, can you come here for a sec?" she said.

He got up and walked over. "What's up?"

"Can you listen to this and tell me if you can understand what she's trying to say?"

She played the sound bite.

Scott frowned. "Can you play that one more time?"

She did. He asked again. She played it a third time. Then, when he still frowned, she played it on repeat, and they listened to the dead prostitute trying to identify her killer over and over again. One word. It seemed as if it slowly became more intelligible the more they heard it, instead of the other way around.

"You know," Scott said, "I think she might be saying *trucker*."

Zoe nodded. "I was actually about to say she said *Hummer*, like the car."

She played it again.

"Yeah, I can hear Hummer too," Scott said.

"I just thought that it sounds a bit more like trucker." Zoe smiled.

"So . . . he's either driving a Hummer or some sort of truck?"

Zoe nodded. "Thanks." She made a note.

"You think this profile will help us nail this guy?" Scott asked, glancing over her shoulder at the paper.

"I really do," Zoe said, hoping he couldn't hear the doubt in her voice.

CHAPTER 43

Harry's editor, Daniel, was occasionally a man of inspiration. A good example was his inspiration when Harry had hinted that he wasn't doing his job properly. He had responded by requesting an article from Harry titled "Nine Reasons America Loves to Hate Justin Bieber."

Harry did the only thing he could. He went looking for a story that would overcome Daniel's need for revenge—namely, what he had asked to do in the first place. He would write about the Strangling Undertaker.

But he needed a good angle. Daniel was very clear about not wanting Oprah's opinion about the murders. And Oprah probably wouldn't talk to Harry anyway after the viral article he had written two years before, "Ten Great Celebrities Who Would Make the Worst Presidents."

He decided to go to the site where the body of Monique Silva had been found. He remembered he had heard about a memorial shrine erected for her at that spot. That could be his angle—talk about the everyday citizens' reactions to the killings, instead of the murderer and the police hunt. People wanted to read about themselves.

He approached the bridge, looking at the water lilies by the shore. It was a beautiful spot, doubly so on a sunny day like this one. A young couple walked by, the man pushing a baby stroller, the woman leaning against him. Harry immediately thought of a paragraph that would star them, a couple in love, struggling to make sense of the terrible violence enacted on this spot.

The memorial shrine was on the other side of the stream. Pleased, he crossed the bridge, hoping for some tear-inducing descriptions of baby pictures, handwritten letters, and candles.

The shrine was actually a mound of rocks on which people laid flowers. Harry wondered if they had picked them in the park, when he spotted a man selling them, not far from the shrine. Harry grinned and approached the flower salesman. He was dressed in black, surrounded by several buckets in which somber roses were wilting. His face wore an expression of deep, endless grief.

"Good day, sir," the man said. "Would you like a flower to lay on the shrine for Monica Silva?"

"What a thoughtful idea," Harry said. "The poor girl, her life plucked away at such a young age."

"Terrible," the flower vendor agreed. "Just one dollar. Five dollars for a respectable bouquet."

Harry took out his wallet, thinking the man's cynicism was worth ten dollars at least. "Her name was Monique Silva, by the way," he said as he handed the bill to the vendor.

The vendor nodded distractedly as he fished one of the sorry-looking bouquets from the bucket. As he wrapped it in paper, Harry looked for his cigarettes, placed one in his mouth, and lit it. He held the pack toward the flower vendor.

"Cigarette?"

"Thank you, sir," the vendor said, plucking a cigarette. Harry gave him the lighter.

They stood in silence for a moment, each enjoying the feeling of the tobacco filling their throats and lungs. Harry watched the tendril of smoke rising from his cigarette until a gust of wind blew it away. "Would you mind if I ask you a few questions?" he asked.

Fifteen minutes later he had a spirit-lifting article about the way people were brought closer together by the tragedy. It was not Pulitzer Prize material, but it had a measure of accessibility that Harry felt made it shine. Readers of the article would be proud to be part of the Chicago community. They would, possibly, like and share the article so that their friends could see what a great city they lived in. Embedded in the article were a few tweets about the horrendous murders, by people with many followers. Maybe those people would tweet about the article, generating even more readers.

Pleased with his progress, he walked away from the flower vendor, planning the headline for the article. He would either go with a cliffhanger clickbait—"Third Victim of the Strangling Undertaker Found, and You Won't Believe What Happened Next"—or he would go with the list clickbait, "Five Courageous Ways Chicago Is Resisting the Strangling Undertaker." He would have to work on it some more. He knew better than most that the article's headline was usually make or break.

He approached the shrine, looking at it with renewed interest, wondering if he should get a photographer to take a picture of it. He was about to put his respectable bouquet on it when he spotted an envelope on the ground. It was a simple brown envelope, and the wind had knocked it off the shrine. Harry picked it up, wondering if he could open it before placing it back on the mound of rocks. He was a cynic but sometimes felt as if there were some lines he shouldn't cross. Unless he had a really good reason.

The envelope was addressed to a woman. To his surprise, the woman was not Monique Silva. But he recognized the name.

Harry had sharp instincts when it came to good stories, and as he held the envelope in his hand, he began to suspect this story was about to turn out much better than he had thought it would.

CHAPTER 44

In retrospect, Zoe was sorry she hadn't gone to the autopsy. Sure, she'd get the report later, and she believed Tatum would tell her if anything interesting came up, but this was the best link they had to the killer. Did she really have anything more important to do? She looked morosely at the sketch of the crime scene that Martinez had forwarded to her. What could she really deduce from this sketch? The killer had needed to get rid of the body before driving through the roadblocks, so he had dumped her in the alley. No elaborate posing, nothing that matched his signature. For a moment, she almost wondered if it really was the same killer. There was no shortage of men who killed prostitutes, after all.

But the postmortem cut to the carotid artery was unusual. The theory that it was a hurried, unsuccessful attempt at embalming rang true.

Fine. She looked around at her desk. Wherever she worked, she always managed to accumulate mounds of paperwork, and here was no different. Copies of the case files, reports of taxidermied animals, and printed-out transcripts of the interviews with the victims' families and friends were all jumbled together, limiting the actual space she could work in.

She decided to clear her workspace and start fresh. She piled up all the case files, put the transcripts on top of them, and shoved them into a drawer in the desk. The animal reports she would throw away. There was nothing more to be gained from them; there were copies of them in the case file, and they were very sparse in detail anyway. She grabbed them and crossed the room to the paper shredder. She fed the papers two by two into the slot, enjoying the view of the papers turned into narrow white ribbons. Shredding was great. She should do it more often.

As she shredded the last three pages, her mind focused on a new question that hadn't occurred to her before.

What had caused the killer to start practicing on animals?

It made demented sense, if he was interested in preserving his victims, but what prompted him to do that? A book he had read? A film he had watched?

The embalming process itself was not crucial to the killer. The fact that at first he had tried taxidermy proved it. He was only looking for a way to preserve the victims. The purpose was preservation.

Why?

Because he needed time with his victims without the effects of decay.

Why?

She couldn't answer this question yet. She tried to shift the question in her mind a bit. Suppose he began to obsess about killing a woman and keeping her body. Would he really make the leap in his mind and decide he had to embalm it? Embalming was a complicated process. He had to have decided there was no other way.

She thought of the cycle again. The learning curve of the killer. He kept adapting so the act would better match the fantasy in his head. In this case, there was an obvious learning curve, as she had already noted. The killer had gotten better at embalming. But what had prompted him to start embalming in the first place?

Had there been another murder? Had he killed someone before Susan Warner?

"Hey, Scott," Zoe said. "Can you help me with one more thing?"

"Sure," he said from his seat, swiveling his chair halfway to look at her. "What is it?"

"I want to check out some murder reports from a couple of years ago."

"Okay." Scott nodded. "I'll do it on my computer. I have CLEAR access there."

"Clear access? What do you mean?" She got up and walked over to him, looking over his shoulder. His desk had several pictures of two young children. She studied them for a second, noticing their resemblance to Scott.

"It's a database thing we use," Scott said. "CLEAR is an acronym for, uh . . . something . . . Law Enforcement . . . something and Reporting."

"Current Law Enforcement Access and Reporting?" Zoe suggested.

"No. That sounds dumb. No, the first word is Crime . . . no . . ."

"Custard?"

"Citizen. It's Citizen and Law Enforcement Analysis and Reporting," he breathed in relief.

"Okay. Is it any good?"

"Yeah. It's the bee's knees. What years are we talking about?"

The first animal taxidermy report was on July 2014. "Try . . . 2013 up to July 2014."

He fiddled with the digital form. After a moment, a list of names showed up onscreen. Over six hundred names.

"Just female victims," Zoe said. "And, uh . . . I think you can remove shootings."

She wasn't certain; it was definitely possible that the killer had moved from firearms to strangulation. But all his killings seemed up close and personal. Even if strangulation were a new MO for him, she was willing to bet he had previously used a knife or some other sort of weapon that would require physical contact with the victim.

"Okay," Scott said. "Fifty-three cases. The majority of Chicago killings are shootings, so that makes sense."

"Thanks, Scott," Zoe said. "I can take it from here."

"Glad I could help," he said and got up from his chair. "Tomorrow I'll try and get you CLEAR access from your own computer."

"Thanks."

"Sure. Just log off my computer when you're done. And don't read my emails."

She grinned at him, and he left. She sat down in his still-warm seat and began to check the cases one by one.

She found what she was searching for in case number twenty-three.

On April 21, 2014, Veronika Murray, a twenty-one-year-old woman, had been found dead and decomposing in an alley. There were indications of postmortem sexual intercourse, and the cause of death was strangulation. The body had been found six days after the estimated time of death, and it was clear she had been dumped there the night before. The case was still open. The killer had not been found.

She had been found a few blocks from her home, in West Pullman, where just three months later, pets began to disappear.

CHAPTER 45

Zoe's heart pounded as she sat in front of Officer Will Shepherd. He was busy writing something down, and when she tried talking, he asked her to wait. He was a plump man with a black, droopy mustache and a red nose. He kept sniffing and coughing, occasionally wiping his nose with a tissue. Zoe tapped her foot anxiously, waiting for him to finish.

"Okay," he finally said, putting the form aside and laying the pen in front of him. "How can I help you?"

"I know who the serial killer is," Zoe said in a rushed voice.

On her way to the Maynard Police Department, she'd had some time to imagine how this conversation would transpire.

In one version, the officer listened to her, writing down her testimony, then went to get an urgent search warrant for Rod Glover's home. The police found all the evidence in his room, probably matched the underwear in the shoebox to the victims, and arrested Glover.

In the second, less optimistic version, the cops didn't cooperate so well. They pointed out that it was a crime to break into Glover's home. They said the evidence she found there was inadmissible. They interrogated her in a small room for hours, intimidating her. Finally, she got them to consider that what she said was true. They investigated Glover for a few days, maybe followed him around, and finally got what they needed to get a search warrant for his home. Underwear, shoebox, arrest.

What she didn't expect was the tired, uninterested look the officer gave her.

"Who is it?" he asked.

"Our neighbor," she said. "Rod Glover."

If anything, he seemed even less interested. "How do you know?"

She laid it out carefully. She didn't want him to think she was just some airhead teen who saw her neighbor doing something weird and decided he must be a serial killer. She explained how she had researched the subject carefully. She detailed the ways that she had figured out how Glover matched the psychopath traits. She told him about Durant Pond and then quoted the interview of "Son of Sam," where he explained why he used to return to the scene of the crime. By that point, the officer seemed a bit disgusted—but interested, which was encouraging. She went on to explain how she'd poked around in Glover's home. She stressed that she had the key, so essentially she hadn't really broken into the house. She was pretty sure that wasn't how it worked, but it felt like something that would cast her in a better light. She told him about the porn. The underwear. The shoebox.

"Uh-huh," he said when she was done.

She blinked. She knew it was her word against Glover's. She hadn't taken anything from his home, but she assumed it was enough to capture the police's interest. All they needed was to search Glover's house.

"He might know I've been in his house," she said. "So he could decide to get rid of the evidence."

Officer Shepherd sighed deeply. "You shouldn't go poking around in other people's homes," he said.

She was ready for this. "These were special circumstances," she said. "I had good reasons to think he's the killer."

"Yes," Officer Shepherd said. "You saw him in Durant Pond, where many people go every day, and then he told you about an office fire, which you think was a lie, but you can't be sure. And, of course, you've read all those books, and so you got excited."

Zoe's face heated up. "There was no one in Durant Pond except me and him, and he was acting weird . . . but okay, never mind. His room—"

"Has porn and ladies' underwear," Shepherd said.

"The underwear had mud on it."

"I can think of other brown substances that might soil a pair of underwear."

Tears threatened. No. Not now. He'd never take her seriously if she began crying now. "His socks—"

"Were wet, yes. He definitely sounds like a slob. Listen, Zoe, I get that you're afraid. The entire town is afraid. But if you let us do our job—"

"I want you to do your job," she yelled, her voice breaking. She was coming apart. The tears sprang from her eyes, her voice becoming wobbly. "Just check him out! I'm telling you, he's the guy. Maybe I'm wrong, but shouldn't you at least check it out?"

He looked at her thoughtfully, as if considering what she'd told him. "Did you say Glover?" he finally asked.

"Yeah." She wiped her eyes with her sleeve.

"Hang on," he said and stood up, groaning. He went over to a file cabinet, opened the top drawer, and thumbed through it a bit, then finally pulled out a sheaf of papers. He looked through the pages, one after the other, and then back at her.

"Rod Glover?"

"That's right."

"Yeah. He's definitely not the guy."

Her heart sank. "How do you know?"

"Because he had seventy-eight people who were with him at the time that poor Clara was murdered. I was with them too."

"Seventy-eight people?" Zoe had no idea what he was talking about.

"There was a search party when Clara disappeared, kid. Rod Glover is on the list. The time of the search corresponds with the time of death. That means he has an alibi." He spoke very slowly, as if making sure she understood what he meant. "I'm telling you this so you don't keep telling people your neighbor is a serial killer. We don't need that kind of thing right now, okay?"

"M . . . maybe he just told you he was joining the search party and then—"

"Listen, honey, leave the policing to the grown-ups, okay?"

Her face flushed, her mouth twisting in humiliation. She felt like dying.

"You're Clive Bentley's kid, right?" Shepherd said.

"Y . . . yeah."

"I think it's time I take you home."

The five-minute ride in the police car was the worst ride Zoe had ever had. She kept feeling like she had to throw up but quickly realized she couldn't open the window or the door in the back of the squad car. She trembled and sobbed, hugging herself. She was cold, but she couldn't bring herself to ask Officer Shepherd to turn up the heat. Everything felt wrong. Had she been wrong to blame Glover? She had been so absolutely certain when she'd walked into the police station, but hearing Shepherd state the facts so dryly had pulled the rug out from under her feet. A series of theories and facts that fit so perfectly in her mind but made such an incomplete puzzle.

Maybe Glover told her tall tales, but she used to think it was ridiculous or funny or both. When had it become so sinister? Why had she been so quick to staple the word *psychopath* to him? So he had a shoebox with some feminine underwear and a bracelet. Maybe it was something he kept from an ex-girlfriend, something to remember her by. And porn? A lot of people had porn in their homes. Wasn't it an incredibly prosperous industry?

Was she simply obsessing about those murders so much that she had to blame someone? Was *she* the freak?

At other moments, she thought of the way Glover had looked at her just after she'd left his house. Or how weird the porn in his room seemed. Or of the other pair of underwear, the one that had mud on it. And she had a feeling that maybe she was right. Glover had somehow tricked the police into thinking he had an alibi and then killed Clara. It couldn't have been that complicated to sneak away during the search, kill her and dump the body, and come back.

Finally, Shepherd parked the car. Zoe's hopes that maybe he would just drop her off were shattered as she saw her father opening the door to their home. He crossed his arms and looked severely at the car. Shepherd had probably let him know they were coming. He had called him back from work.

The portly officer got out of the car and opened the back door. She got out, feeling the tears rise up again as the fear and humiliation hit her. Their neighbor Mrs. Ambrose peeked outside her bedroom window. By that time tomorrow, the whole town would know Zoe Bentley had been brought home in a police car.

She walked slowly to the doorway, preferring the biting cold outside to whatever waited for her inside.

"Zoe," her father said as she got to the door. "Wait for me in your room." His tone was furious; the words practically shook as he spoke them. She couldn't recall him ever being so angry at her.

She walked to her room slowly, pushing the door open, closing it behind her, throwing herself on the bed.

She cried into her pillow, letting go of everything she had managed to hold inside. It suddenly all seemed so dumb. Zoe Bentley, playing Nancy Drew games. Stupid, stupid.

Finally, she seemed to run out of tears. Her father still hadn't come for her, and she decided to look for him. Waiting was worse than the actual lecture and inevitable grounding that would follow.

She opened the door and heard Shepherd's voice. He still hadn't left. He and her father were talking in the kitchen. Walking softly, she approached the kitchen and listened.

"And her mother is sedated because she tried to kill herself," her dad was saying.

"I heard," Shepherd said. "I'm glad you two are helping them out."

"You know, Zoe used to be a good friend of Nora's, her sister."

"I didn't know that. It explains her behavior."

"Yeah, I'm really sorry."

"There's really no need to apologize so much, Clive. This is the third time this week we've gotten a bogus report for suspicious activity. People are on edge. Your daughter is just scared. Everyone is."

"Yeah."

"I hope it'll all be over soon."

"Why?" Her father sounded suddenly alert. "Do you have a suspect?"

"I can't really talk about it."

"Come on, Will. It would really help if I could tell Zoe you've arrested someone for—"

"Don't tell her that. We haven't arrested anyone. But we . . . we think we know who it was. Chase figured it out."

"Who?"

"Look, I can't give you the name, Clive. You know that."

"Will, we've known each other for a long time. You can trust me. I just need to put my daughter's mind at ease."

There was a moment of intense silence. Was Shepherd whispering the name in her father's ear? She crept as close as she could without giving her position away.

"Okay. But you can't tell anyone about this; it would screw us all. Our suspect is Manny Anderson."

Zoe held her breath. She knew Manny Anderson. He was a high school senior. He often sat in the town's library, reading by himself. Zoe had seen him several times lately when she'd borrowed books for her own research.

"Gwen and Pete's kid? No!"

"It turns out he was known to follow Beth Hartley around before he . . . before she was killed. And a student testified he heard Manny ask Clara out once. And you know the really weird thing?"

"What?" her dad whispered.

"You know how all the girls were found, right? Naked, strangled to death with a gray tie that was left around their throat?"

Zoe's eyes widened. She hadn't heard this detail until now.

"Right," her dad said.

"Pete Anderson wears gray ties to work. Every damn day. We think Manny is using his ties to kill the girls."

Gray ties. Zoe had to stop herself from barging into the kitchen, screaming. The one detail she hadn't mentioned when she had talked to Shepherd in the police station. Glover had a bunch of gray ties in his porn drawer.

How would it sound if she stepped in now? It would sound like she was using this detail to get herself off the hook. After eavesdropping on their conversation. Again, they wouldn't believe her. And she'd only make things worse for herself.

Was it just another coincidence?

Could she keep it to herself? Tell no one?

"That's . . . terrible," her dad said.

"Manny Anderson was always a weird kid. Keeps to himself. Doesn't have a lot of friends. One of those quiet types, you know?"

"Uh-huh."

"But his teacher told me he draws some really weird cartoons in his notebooks, and he plays Dungeons and Dragons with his friends almost every weekend. Never had a girlfriend . . . I don't know. It all adds up."

Zoe was suddenly furious. It added up to nothing. Weird cartoons? Dungeons and Dragons? Shepherd's reasoning was infinitely weaker than her own. Essentially, the police had done what they'd accused her of. They had searched for a suspect, and once they saw someone who more or less fit, they began tying the case to him.

They were wrong, and she was right. And they wouldn't listen to her because she was just a hysterical fourteen-year-old girl.

"But, Dad, listen." Zoe was desperate to convince him, but it was like trying to discuss things with an angry brick wall.

"No, Zoe, I don't want to hear anything more about this. Do you realize Rod could sue if he found out you're spreading these lies about him?"

"I'm not spreading lies. I just told the police what I—"

"Not to mention the fact that you broke into his house."

They had gone over this three times, and every time it came back to the fact that she had broken into Glover's house.

"I know, but he had gray ties in his—"

"Enough!"

His angry bark shocked her into silence. His face was nearly crimson, and his palms were shaking.

"Rod Glover is our neighbor," he said, his voice strained and clipped. "You can't go accusing people of horrible things without consequence. We know he has an alibi for the time Clara was killed—"

"But, Dad, we don't know he really was in the search party. Maybe he joined and then—"

"I was in the search party. I saw Rod several times."

Her entire resolve deflated. It was true, then. Rod Glover hadn't killed Clara. She had accused him for no reason.

"Breaking into our neighbor's house." He raised a finger, starting to count her misdeeds. "Going to the police, accusing him for no good reason. Going to Durant Pond on your own."

They both stared at his three raised fingers.

"Mom and I are going to a town meeting," he said. "There's going to be a discussion about the murders and the emergency measures that the community will take until the killer is behind bars. You stay here with Andrea. And tomorrow, we will talk about your punishment. At length."

She sat on her bed, staring at the floor as he left the room. She heard him and her mother saying goodbye to Andrea, and then the front door opened and closed. The lock clicked, and they were gone.

Andrea walked into the room and climbed into Zoe's bed. Zoe lay down and blinked away the looming tears. She should have let the police do their job. The killer probably *was* Manny Anderson. His romantic interest in both Clara and Beth was quite suspicious. And he had easy access to the murder weapon.

Strangled with a gray tie.

She shivered, trying to banish the images that popped into her mind.

"Zoe, are Daddy and Mommy angry at you?" Andrea asked.

"Even worse," Zoe said. "They're disappointed."

"That's not worse."

"It kinda is."

"Why are they angry?"

"Because I . . . said some things that weren't true."

Andrea's eyes widened. "You lied?"

"No. I was just wrong."

"Oh."

They lay on the bed, curling against each other. Zoe listened to Andrea's breathing, drawing strength from her sister's innocence. She could hear footsteps in the street and then the front door lock clicking. Their mother had probably forgotten her purse again. She always did.

"Mommy?" Andrea called, obviously thinking the same.

There was no response and no footsteps. Frowning, Zoe got off the bed and walked to the doorway. There was a shadowy figure in the dark hallway. Too tall to be their mother, too thin to be their father. Their eyes met.

It was Rod Glover.

CHAPTER 46

Chicago, Illinois, Thursday, July 21, 2016

Veronika Murray, the woman found dead in West Pullman two years before, had been engaged to a man named Clifford Sorenson, according to the police report. Zoe called him and asked if they could meet. Sorenson had a plumbing business in West Pullman and told her she was welcome to drop by his office.

Sorenson's Plumbing was more like a warehouse than an office. A small white sign hung above the front door with the business name on it in an uninspiring blue font. The same logo was printed on two blue vans parked in front. Zoe paid the taxi driver, a middle-aged man with a scruffy gray beard and mustache.

"You want me to wait outside?" he asked.

"It might take a while," she told him. "I can call a cab when I leave."

"Well," he said, glancing at a nearby burger joint's sign, "it's past my lunchtime, and I haven't eaten yet. I'll be around."

Zoe sighed. He was a talkative sort of guy, and she wasn't in the mood for another chat about North Korea on her way back, but she could see no way to shake him off politely. "That's great," she said. "But if you get tired of waiting, feel free to leave."

He shrugged. She got out of the cab and entered the warehouse.

The space inside was lined with long metallic shelves, all of them brimming with pipes, faucets, and tools Zoe couldn't even name. In her past, she was proud to have dealt with a clog in the sink all by herself, but anything beyond that resulted in an immediate panicked phone call to a plumber. Of all the problems that could occur in her home, she felt a plumbing problem was the worst, a crisis that would empty her bank account and turn all of her worldly possessions into a soggy mess.

Two men stood by one of the shelves, picking pipes and placing them in a large cardboard box. She approached them.

"Excuse me," she said. "I'm looking for Clifford Sorenson."

"That's me," one of them said. "You're Zoe?"

"That's right. Thank you for meeting me."

He nodded. She looked at him. He was a tall, wide-shouldered man with thinning brown hair and rough stubble on his cheeks. His eyes were red-rimmed and tired. "You said this is about Veronika?"

"I wondered if you could answer a few questions."

"Let's talk outside," he said, frowning. He turned to the other man. "You got this?"

The man nodded. "Sure, Cliff."

They stepped outside, and Clifford fished a cigarette pack from his pocket. He put one in his mouth and offered the pack to Zoe. She shook her head. He shrugged, lit his own cigarette, and inhaled. "I assumed the police were done with the case."

"It resurfaced in relation to another case that's under investigation right now."

"Yeah? At the time, they told me they were investigating a local drug addict. Is this about him?"

Zoe shook her head. The drug addict questioned during the investigation was in prison for armed robbery. "Not really."

"Uh-huh," he said, his voice tense. "Who, then?"

"We're not sure yet. Would you mind if I ask you some questions about that week?"

The police had questioned Clifford three times, and Zoe had read the transcripts. The first interview was intended mostly to establish if he was a suspect. He had an alibi for the night his fiancée had disappeared—he had gone fishing with three friends. They all verified they had been with him during that time. One of his friends had actually walked inside the house with him because he needed to use the bathroom. They'd found the house in disarray, Veronika missing.

The second interview was when the police arrested the drug dealer as a suspect. They had showed Clifford some mugshots, trying to see if he could maybe recognize the dealer. He could not, said he had never seen any of the people in the pictures as far as he remembered.

The third interview was after the police had dropped the drug dealer as a suspect and were trying to poke holes in Sorenson's alibi. Sorenson had quickly lost his cool, screaming at the cops that they were trying to frame him, and he had demanded to have an attorney present. The rest of the interview had been quite short and proved nothing.

Zoe knew that when an investigator had a suspect or goal in mind, the interview was often skewed to that purpose. There was a very clear example of this in the first interview when Clifford had mentioned that Veronika had seemed a bit on edge in the weeks before she had gone missing. A series of questions had been asked to establish if she had been on edge because of strain in her relationship with Clifford. But after asking him about that, they'd moved on. No one had raised the issue of her being on edge again. The matter had been ignored.

"I'll try to answer whatever I can," he said. "But I can't promise to remember it very well. It's been more than two years, and I've been working hard at forgetting that week."

"I understand," Zoe said, leaning against the wall. "So when was the last time you saw Veronika?"

"The morning she died," Clifford said, his voice emotionless. "Before I went to work."

"Did you talk during the day?"

"Yeah, once. She called to ask me something, I don't remember what."

According to the police report, she'd called to ask about the catering service for their upcoming wedding. Had he really forgotten, or did he simply want to avoid the topic?

"And then what happened?"

"I came back from work, and she wasn't there. She was visiting a friend. Linda."

Zoe nodded. That, too, was in the report. Linda was the main reason Clifford was not the primary suspect. She had verified that Veronika had eaten dinner with her, and by the time Veronika had left Linda's home, Cliff had been long gone for his fishing trip.

"I went fishing with three friends. I came back home sometime after midnight. The house was a mess. The table and chairs were overturned. All the closets and drawers had been opened. Veronika was missing, as well as her jewelry."

"And what did you do?"

He looked at her for a long moment. His mouth twisted. "Would you excuse me for a moment?"

Zoe blinked. "Sure."

He turned around. "Hey, Jeffrey!" he hollered.

The other man appeared in the shop's doorway. "Yeah?"

"Can you get that single-bowl Kraus sink to the van? I want us to install it today."

"Sure, Cliff."

Clifford turned back to Zoe, his face now composed. "When I saw she was missing, I called the police. Frank was with me—my friend. He came inside because he had to use the bathroom. He went looking for her in the neighborhood while I waited for the cops."

"And then what happened?"

"The police showed up. I told them what I knew. They found the body six days later. That's it, really."

Zoe nodded. "Did Veronika seem different the days before she was taken?"

"I don't think so."

"She wasn't preoccupied? Or worried?"

"I don't really remember, Miss Bentley."

"Hey, Cliff, I can't find it," Jeffrey hollered from inside. "You sure it's here?"

Clifford looked at Zoe. "I really need to get back to work—"

"Just a few more questions. It would be really helpful," she said smoothly. "Was Veronika the trusting type?"

"What do you mean?" he asked, walking inside.

She followed him to the back of the store. "Your home was trashed, but there were no signs of a break-in. Would she have opened the door to a stranger?"

"At night? I don't think so."

"What if he was dressed like a cop?"

"Are you saying a cop took her?"

"Not necessarily," Zoe said. "I'm just theorizing."

She was trying to fine-tune the killer's MO. Though it was possible that the serial killer was a law enforcement officer or working in some other official role of authority, there was another explanation. Several serial killers were known to use outfits or identities of authority figures to lure their victims. Ted Bundy was a well-known example of that. He sometimes approached women pretending to be a police officer and took them somewhere secluded.

"I don't know. Maybe. Here's the sink," he told Jeffrey. He bent and grabbed the sink, then groaned.

"I'll get it. Don't worry about it," Jeffrey said and picked up the large steel sink, carrying it outside.

Clifford straightened up, grimacing, a hand on his back. He walked slowly back to the front of the store. Zoe kept following him.

"Would she open the door if someone was hurt or if there was a woman at the door?"

"Miss Bentley, I'm sorry. I don't know."

"Did you tell anyone you were going fishing that day?"

He looked at her, raising an eyebrow. "Why?"

"The killer knew when to strike."

"It was probably just bad luck, Miss Bentley. I go fishing a lot. Twice, sometimes three times every week. Hell, I went four times with my brother last week. Of course, these days I tend to go fishing even more since I have no one at home . . ." His gaze became vacant. "I'm sorry. I really have to get back to work."

Zoe nodded. "Thank you for your time," she said.

He'd already turned away, checking something on one of the shelves. "Sure," he said.

She left the store, disappointed. Outside, the day was bright, and she squinted, protecting her eyes from the glare with her palm. Jeffrey was loading the sink into one of the vans. The sink made a loud clang as he finally lowered it into the back of the van. He slammed the door and turned around.

"Hey," he said when he noticed her. "Are you a cop?"

"I'm working with the police," she answered, walking closer. He seemed slightly younger than Clifford, his hair thick and brown. He was tall, his shoulders wide.

"Listen, I don't know what you told Cliff, but I hope you didn't get him all worked up. Veronika's death has been really tough for him. He acted like a zombie for more than a year after it had happened. He's seemed better only in the last couple of months."

"I'm sorry," Zoe said. "Did you work for him when she died?"

"Yeah, he was a mess. Hardly left home."

"Do you remember if Veronika was preoccupied or worried before she disappeared?"

"She was mostly just happy. They were about to get married."

"Right."

"He and Veronika were trying to have a child," Jeffrey said. "He would have made a great father."

Zoe nodded.

"Do you think you're going to catch her killer?"

"I don't know," Zoe said. "I hope so."

CHAPTER 47

It was early afternoon, and Zoe, Tatum, and Martinez were sitting in the meeting room. Zoe had just filled them in about Veronika Murray. The three of them sat in silence after she finished talking.

Finally, Martinez broke the silence. He cleared his throat. "Are you sure it's the same killer?"

"No way I can be sure." Zoe shrugged. "Like in the other cases, the killer was careful, used a condom, and didn't leave any DNA behind. Maybe there's some other forensic data you can use to match the cases. I'd talk to your technicians."

Martinez nodded. "I'll do that."

"The circumstantial evidence is quite indicative," she added. "Veronika died three months before the pets started disappearing, and in the same neighborhood. The body was found six days later with indications of postmortem sexual intercourse. Assuming it's the same guy, I'd say the decay forced him to dump the body, after which he decided he had to find a way to overcome this problem."

"And then, while experimenting on animals, he figured out embalming was a good solution," Tatum said. He seemed intrigued. "That sounds like a very likely scenario."

"I agree," Martinez said. "I'll have someone look into this immediately."

Zoe followed Martinez and Tatum back to the task force room. Zoe sat by her computer and was just about to start writing a detailed report for Mancuso when her desk phone rang. It took her a moment to realize it was her own phone. She picked it up.

"Hello?"

"Dr. Bentley? This is Officer Tucker from the front desk. There's a guy here to see you."

"To see me? Are you sure?"

"Yeah, he was very specific."

"Okay, I'll be right down."

Curious, she walked down the stairs to the front desk. There were a bunch of civilians waiting around, but she could see no one familiar. She approached the officer at the front desk. "Hi, I'm Zoe Bentley. You just called—"

"Zoe Bentley? Dr. Zoe Bentley?" A man got up and approached her, grinning. He had rich black hair and very dark eyebrows that immediately drew attention to his eyes. He had a small smile that made him look as if he were in on a joke no one else knew about. He scanned her, top to bottom, in a way she found offensive. "I'm thrilled to finally meet you. I'm a huge fan."

"I didn't know I had any fans," she said coldly. His manner irritated her.

"Oh, you do. At least one. I've read all about your involvement with the Jovan Stokes case as well as some interesting earlier cases. And now you're part of the BAU—that's incredible."

"I'm sorry, sir. You are . . . ?"

"Harry."

"Harry what?"

He muttered something that sounded like "Barrer," then quickly said, "I think I have something that's intended for you."

He rummaged in his briefcase for a few seconds and then drew out three brown envelopes. He handed them to her, and she plucked them from his hand and looked at them.

Her blood ran cold.

There was no address this time, only her name, but the handwriting was unmistakable. The three envelopes matched the stack of envelopes she had in her apartment in Dale City, one of which she had received only a week before.

"Who gave you these?" she asked weakly.

He looked at her carefully. "No one gave me these. I found them."

"Where?"

"One at Foster Beach. The second in Humboldt Park, and I bet you can guess where I found the third."

She swallowed and said nothing.

"No? It was at Ohio Street Beach."

The three places where the bodies had been left. "Were they just . . . discarded there? I mean—"

"They were placed on shrines," Harry said. "The ones people made for the dead girls. I took some photos. I can send them to you. They're not so good. I'm terrible with a camera."

"I see."

"Aren't you going to open them?" he asked.

She raised her eyes sharply. He looked at her innocently. "No," she said. She then saw all three envelopes were unsealed.

"You've opened them," she said.

"Well, I wasn't about to walk into a police station with an envelope that might contain explosives. Or anthrax," he pointed out. "I wanted to make sure it was safe."

"Sure."

"You'll be happy to learn there's no anthrax inside them. I'm not sure what anthrax looks like, frankly, but I'm pretty sure it doesn't look like that."

"Thank you," she said, feeling sick.

"I should probably let the cops here take my fingerprints," he said. "For when they dust these, right?"

She didn't say anything. She stood there frozen, dizzy.

"You should have them take your fingerprints as well."

"They won't find any fingerprints," she said, her voice a thousand miles away.

"You've received envelopes like these before?"

"What?"

"You seem to know what's inside, and you already know they won't find any fingerprints. I take it you've received envelopes like these before."

She tried to focus. "Who are you, exactly?"

"I'm Harry." He smiled, two lines of bright-white teeth showing.

"Harry, you just happened to find these three envelopes?"

"No," he said. "I just happened to find one of them. But then I went and looked for the other two."

The reality sank in. "You're a reporter," she said.

"That's right." He beamed. "So . . . what can you tell me about these envelopes?"

"Absolutely nothing."

"Okay. I guess my story won't have your response. It'll just mention the three envelopes containing—"

"You can't go public with this. It would hurt the investigation."

"Dr. Bentley, it's not your job or my job to decide. I publish what captures the interest of the public. Well, frankly, I publish what captures the interest of my editor and me, and then—"

She turned toward the front desk. "Get some officers in here, and detain this man for questioning."

"If I don't call my editor in ten minutes," Harry said calmly, "he'll publish what I gave him so far."

"You're bluffing."

"Dr. Bentley, you're the forensic psychologist here. Look at my face, and tell me that again."

There was silence, the officer in the front desk watching them both, phone in hand.

"What do you want?" she finally asked.

"I want a story," he said.

"You can't write about these envelopes."

"Give me something I can write about. Something that no one else knows."

She bit her lip. "I need some time."

"Absolutely," the man said. "I trust you, Zoe—"

"Don't call me that."

"Okay, then." He offered her his hand. "I trust you, Dr. Bentley. You have twenty-four hours."

He turned around and left.

Knees buckling, she got herself to the elevator, not entirely sure she could manage the stairs at that moment. It seemed to take her years to get to her desk, the envelopes dragging her hand down.

Could it be?

It felt impossible. But so many things suddenly aligned. The strangling. The bodies' proximity to water. The posing, different but somehow the same.

She sat down by her table and upturned the three envelopes.

Three gray ties landed on the table in a twisting pile.

CHAPTER 48

Maynard, Massachusetts, Monday, December 15, 1997

Time trickled slowly, a rushing noise in Zoe's ears. Behind her, Andrea called out again. "Mommy?" Glover's eyes held hers. Not the childish, funny neighbor, the goofy man who enthusiastically talked with her about Buffy and Angel. Cold, hard eyes, capable of anything. He tensed. She could see him bracing as the world around her transformed into one long tunnel, Glover on the edge, only darkness between them. He started toward her, a sharp movement that jolted her out of her dreamlike freeze.

She screamed, slammed the door shut, turned the key in the door's lock.

There was a loud thumping noise, the door shuddering. Glover had run into the door. Zoe looked around frantically. Her desk was large and wooden. She dashed to it and began dragging it, inch by inch, Andrea watching her from the bed, her eyes wide.

"Zoe," Glover said from the other side. "I just want to talk. I think you may have misunderstood something."

She pulled the desk, whimpering, until she could wedge her body between it and the wall. Then she began leaning against it, pushing herself and the desk away from the wall. She breathed hurriedly, short, fearful gulps of air, her body trembling as she strained against the desk.

"Were you in my bedroom this morning, Zoe? I'm not angry; I just think we should chat about this." He knocked on the door, politely at first, then thumped it angrily, the loud noise making Andrea burst into frightened tears. The doorknob twisted over and over.

She remembered that a few months ago, her mother had taken her room key, telling her she didn't want locked doors in the house. It had taken a lot of begging to get the key back, with Zoe claiming she didn't want Andrea to barge into her room while she undressed. Now, with the door shuddering as Glover thumped on it, she thanked God her mom had returned the key.

"Just open the door, Zoe. I'd hate for this to ruin our friendship."

"We . . . have . . . no . . . friendship," she said through gritted teeth as she pushed the desk. It was halfway across the room now. So heavy. She recalled her dad dragging it across the floor effortlessly. She hadn't realized how strong he was.

"Zoe! Open the door right now! Or I'll call your parents and tell them how you're behaving."

"Call them!" she yelled, her voice breaking, and gave the desk another push. The corner now touched the door.

There was silence, except for Andrea's sobbing. "We'll be okay, Ray-Ray," she said, her voice shaking uncontrollably.

There was a crash, and the door shuddered even more than before. He was trying to break down the door. Panicking, she gave the desk a heave. She managed to push it against the door, holding it tight. She leaned against the desk, hoping her own weight would help. Her heart thundered in her ears.

There was a series of loud thumps. He was kicking the door. To her relief, it seemed to hold. She heard him cursing.

"Zoe, if you open the door right now, things will go much easier on you."

"Like they were for Clara?" she asked. "And Jackie? And Beth?"

"It was terrible, what happened to those girls," he said beyond the door. "I hope the police find the killer soon."

"They will!" she screamed. "I told them everything. They said they'll check you out."

He laughed. A high-pitched, unbalanced laugh. "Did you? Because I don't see the police here. No, they are after the real killer, right? That Manny Anderson kid."

Andrea began to cry loudly.

"Is that your sister, Zoe? Open the door, and I promise you nothing will happen to her. But if you don't . . ."

Zoe left her position by the desk and leaped on the bed, wrapping her hands around Andrea.

"Don't worry, Ray-Ray. He can't hurt us," she whispered, hugging her sister tight.

"I would never kill anyone," Glover said behind the door. "What made you think I would do such a thing? Those magazines? It's just adult stuff. I bet your dad has some of his own."

Zoe covered Andrea's ears, gritting her teeth furiously. "What convinced me were the souvenirs you kept. And the gray ties."

There was silence. "Gray ties?" Glover finally said.

"I know what you did with them, Glover! I have a phone in here. I'm calling the cops right now."

He laughed again. "No, you don't. I've been to your room, remember?"

Her skin crawled when she recalled it was true. She had invited him to her room once to show him the track trophy she'd won at school.

Footsteps getting further away, the front door opening and slamming. She rushed to the window, made sure it was locked. Would he try to break it and enter the room from there? She didn't think so; someone would hear the glass pane breaking. He wouldn't risk it.

She hoped.

"I'm scared," Andrea whimpered.

"Shhhh, I'm here, Ray-Ray. You have nothing to be scared about."

They waited in silence. After what felt like hours, she considered leaving the room to call the police. She got up, was about to shove the desk away, when a thought occurred to her. She reached out and turned the key in the lock.

Almost instantly the doorknob twisted, and the door juddered against the desk. Shrieking, she locked the door again. He hadn't left at all. He'd almost tricked her. Almost.

There was another laugh from behind the door. Not even a laugh. A giggle. A demented, tortured giggle. "Zoe, open the door. Can't stay in there forever, Zoe."

She couldn't, but she didn't need to. Just until Mom and Dad came home. How much longer . . . ?

"Zoe," he said. His voice changed. Softer. Angrier. The voice of a killer. "If I need to break this door, you'll regret it, Zoe."

Shaking, she looked around for a weapon—any weapon. She saw none. She used to have a baseball bat in the room when she was ten, but she'd gotten rid of it when she stopped playing. Stupid. So stupid.

"You know what I do to women who make me angry, Zoe," he said, and there was another giggle. "You might like it."

Andrea sobbed, eyes shut tight. Zoe hurried to her side, covered her ears again.

"Beth liked it. She moaned when I shoved myself inside her. She acted like she hated it, but I could feel how much she loved it. She loved it, Zoe."

She wished she had four hands. She wanted to cover her own ears as well as her sister's.

"Do you think you would like it, Zoe? When I rip your shirt and your pants? When I give you what you want, bitch? Would you moan like Beth did?"

She was crying as well, sobs of fear and horror, her hands plugging Andrea's ears tightly, hoping she wasn't hearing any of it.

"Do you think little Ray-Ray would like it?"

"You stay away from her!" Zoe shrieked, tears of fear and anger in her eyes.

The same giggle. "Oh. You wouldn't like that, would you? Maybe I should start with her. Open this damn door, or I start with her, Zoe."

She got off the bed and flung open the window. The freezing cold outside chilled her bones.

"Help us!" she cried desperately. "Help! Police! The killer is here. Help!"

The thumping on the door began again. "Open this damn door, you whore! You bitch! Open the door. Open it. Open it!"

"Help us!"

The light switched on in Mrs. Ambrose's bedroom.

"Please help."

The door juddered again.

Mrs. Ambrose moved slowly to the window. A woman who had all the time in the world, shambling over to check what the noise was all about. She peered outside, saw Zoe screaming. Her eyes widened.

"Call the police!" Zoe shouted.

Mrs. Ambrose hurried away. The woman picked up the phone in her bedroom. She dialed quickly and began to talk animatedly on the phone, glancing back toward her window constantly.

If they hurried, they could catch Glover in the act.

The house had gone suddenly silent. Glover wasn't trying to cajole his way inside or threaten her or break down the door. He was gone.

Almost six months had passed since the night Glover had nearly broken into her room. It was early morning, and the summer sunlight shone through Zoe's window. She gazed at the wall, holding one shoe in her hand. She had been in the process of putting it on when she'd become lost in thoughts and memory, her bare foot forgotten.

The nightmares were slowly fading. Only two, maybe three nights a week she'd wake up screaming, which was almost normal. Definitely better than the weeks that had followed that night, when she couldn't sleep for more than four hours straight.

No more murders had transpired in Maynard during that time. And Glover was gone.

He had disappeared that very night. Her dad and the cops had come knocking on his door, but no one had answered. The bedroom had been mostly cleared. He'd left a few magazines in the drawer, but no gray ties, no shoebox.

No one believed he was the killer.

They believed he had come into the house that day, that he had yelled at Zoe. But the police assumed it was because he was embarrassed she had seen his porn collection. That she misunderstood his intentions, that he just wanted to talk. She'd even overheard one of the cops say, as he left their house, "That crazy girl scared the poor guy away." Her mother had begged her to stop telling people that Glover was the killer. Especially now that they knew who the killer really was.

Manny Anderson had been arrested, suspected of the murders. The police had found a picture of Beth in his home and other "suggestive evidence." What could this suggestive evidence be? His Dungeons and Dragons collection? He and his parents maintained his innocence while his face was plastered on the front page of all the local newspapers alongside the portraits of the three dead young women.

And then he had managed to hang himself with a bedsheet in his cell. Case closed. The Maynard serial killer was gone. People could sleep again. Zoe had cried for hours when she heard about it. She cried for herself as much as for him. With his death, the chance to prove his innocence and shine the suspicion on Glover was gone. Rod Glover had raped and killed three young women and had gotten away with it. She didn't know how he had managed to get his alibi to stick, but he had.

She kept thinking that if she'd been older, if she had had a shred of authority, Glover would be in jail. Manny Anderson would still be alive.

She turned her eyes to glare at her bookshelf, brimming with books about serial murders, psychopathy, forensic psychology. She didn't bother hiding them anymore.

She sighed and put on the other shoe. It was time to face another day.

Her mother was in the kitchen making breakfast. The smell and the sizzle of the bacon and the eggs in the pan made Zoe's mouth water.

"Good morning," her mom said. "I was just about to check up on you. It's late. You need to be outside in five minutes."

"Okay." Zoe yawned. Five minutes was plenty of time. Eat bacon and eggs, brush teeth, wash face, comb hair . . . yeah, she could definitely make it in five minutes.

"There's a letter for you," her mom said, her tone slightly disapproving.

Zoe had started to correspond with a freelance private investigator and profiler a month before. She suspected he mostly enjoyed the adoring letters of a young teenager. She was milking him for every bit of knowledge that he had.

"Thanks, Mom," Zoe said and approached the small stack of envelopes. Mostly things for her parents, bills and similar stuff. One brown envelope, addressed to Zoe Bentley. She opened the envelope and shoved her hand inside to pull out the contents.

She frowned. There was no paper inside. Only a smooth strip of cloth. She pulled it out and stared at it, feeling her insides grow cold.

It was a gray tie.

CHAPTER 49

Chicago, Illinois, Thursday, July 21, 2016

Zoe bit her lip and opened the drawer in the desk. The three ties were discarded inside, on top of the envelopes, as foreboding as three snakes. She would give them to Martinez tomorrow; she just needed to present the case in a convincing manner. If she went to him now and told him that the murderer hounding Chicago might be a man she had accused of being a serial killer when she was fourteen, he'd assume she was crazy. He would probably remove her from the case. Maybe Tatum as well.

She had to do her research carefully before talking to him. Find all the corresponding evidence. The important thing was not to present this as the guy she had been obsessed with as a teenager but as a dangerous man, one who'd killed many times before.

Had Glover really sent her those ties? She tried to think of alternative explanations. Could it be the reporter himself? But how would he have known about the former envelopes? And though she was not a forensic document examiner, the handwriting on the three new envelopes seemed very similar to the handwriting on the envelopes she had at home. Was it possible that the same person had sent her all the envelopes, but it wasn't Glover? No. There was no way anyone else would know about the ties and their significance.

The envelopes had come from Glover; she was convinced of that.

She was less convinced regarding her gut instinct, that he was the killer that the newspapers called the Strangling Undertaker. She tried to force herself to be objective about this. Did Glover really fit the profile of the embalming serial killer?

There was at least one distinct change in his behavior: the fixation upon dead women. Rod Glover's targets were very much alive. They were alive when he raped them, and once he had killed them, they no longer interested him. Could this have changed? She could feel the gnawing of doubt in her mind.

She set that contradiction aside and examined the rest of the evidence. She could see many links between the murders in Maynard and the current murders in Chicago, but what had he done between then and now?

Years before, when Zoe had begun working with the FBI, she'd gained access to the bureau's Violent Criminal Apprehension Program. She'd immediately begun using ViCAP to search for more murders that fit Glover's MO and signature. She learned that the word *tie* was very problematic when searching for crimes since it brought up thousands of reports where victims had been tied. Searching for *gray tie* resulted in nothing relevant, but that meant nothing. The person who submitted the crime report to ViCAP might have simply neglected to mention the tie color. Or maybe Glover had switched colors. It took her months, but she finally concluded that if Glover had murdered anyone, the murder was not in ViCAP. She was disappointed to find that more than 90 percent of murders and rapes in the United States were not submitted to ViCAP at all. People were busy, it was a cumbersome procedure, and using it wasn't required in most places.

That morning, Scott had helped her get access to the CLEAR system from her own computer. She was now going over all the murders involving rape or strangulation since 2002. She would have preferred to go all the way back to 1998, when Glover had disappeared from Maynard, but the database didn't go that far back.

She was sleep deprived and rattled to the core, her usual detachment gone. Reading report after report of women being raped and murdered was overwhelming. After about forty reports, she felt a lump in her throat, and her fingers were shaking. She went for a walk in the hallway, breathing deeply, trying to relax. Then she sat down and sighed. She decided to play some music, feeling the need to have a background distraction for this soul-wrenching task. Desperate for cheerfulness, she plugged in her earbuds and played the album *One of the Boys*, by Katy Perry. The dissonance was too much to bear, and she turned the music off after "I Kissed a Girl." Murder reports weren't meant to be accompanied by pop music.

She found what she was searching for when she got to 2008. Two murder cases, seven months apart, of women whose bodies had been found naked and strangled. Shirley Wattenberg had been found in Little Calumet River under the bridge on Woodlawn West Avenue. The item used to strangle her was missing, and Zoe suspected it might have been washed away into the lake. The second victim, Pamela Vance, had been found in Saganashkee Slough. This one had had a tie around her neck. Both cases were still open.

"Hey, want a ride?"

A voice behind her made her jump. She turned around, looking up at Tatum's smiling face. He stood with briefcase in hand, on his way out. She checked the time: 9:00 p.m. The room was completely deserted. She hadn't even noticed the people around her leaving.

"No, thanks," Zoe said. "I'm, uh . . . I'll take a taxi when I'm done. I really just want to get that report to Mancuso this evening."

He shrugged. "Suit yourself."

He left, and she turned back to her computer. She kept looking up to 2016 and found no other cases. This didn't discourage her at all. The claim that serial killers never stopped, that they *had* to keep on killing, was nothing but a myth. Serial killers often stopped for months and years, fulfilling their needs with self-relief. Sometimes they didn't stop but hid the bodies well or killed in faraway places. There was nothing strange about the long pause between the two murders in 2008 and the five murders that began in 2014.

She read through the case reports slowly. Though the item used to strangle Shirley Wattenberg had been missing, the marks on her throat indicated a wide, smooth, flexible noose. One of the detectives on the case had theorized that it was a belt, though there were no markings that indicated a belt buckle. This definitely seemed to fit Zoe's theory that a tie had been used. The crime scene photos showed a naked body of a woman lying on her stomach, partially in the water. This was identical to the way the bodies had been found in Maynard, back in 1997.

Pamela Vance's photo looked similar. The autopsy report detailed several indications that the victim had struggled violently before dying. There were several overlapping markings of ligature, and the ME concluded that the first attempt to strangle the victim had been unsuccessful due to her struggling. The murderer had had to try again, and the noose had shifted a bit, resulting in the overlapping bruises. There were injuries due to sexual assault both antemortem and postmortem.

The victim had died of strangulation as she was being raped. And he had kept on going.

Zoe leaned back, feeling sick. Was this it? The moment that Glover had changed? It definitely fit.

Was it enough?

She imagined herself presenting the case to Tatum and Martinez. Three murders in 1997 in Maynard, the suspect never convicted because he had killed himself while incarcerated. Two murders in 2008 matching the MO and the signature of the Maynard serial killer. And five murders between 2014 and 2016 with clear links in the MO and the signature to the murders in 2008. And the gray ties. She tried to figure out a way to bring up the gray ties sent to her. How would she explain Glover's obsession with her?

She'd have to tell them about that night. About what she had seen in his home. And she had to make them see she had been right then and that she was right now.

A fear she hadn't felt for many years crept in. The fear that they wouldn't listen.

She needed more. And then it occurred to her. If it really was Glover, he had to have known Susan Warner somehow. Perhaps he'd been her neighbor or someone she'd dated. He had to have known she was alone, that no one would barge in as he embalmed her in her home. And if that was the case, maybe Daniella Ortiz knew him.

Daniella seemed subdued somehow when she opened the door. Her happy rainbow outfit gone, she wore a black pair of yoga pants and a pink shirt that said LIVE SLOW, DIE WHENEVER. Her eyes seemed a bit puffy.

"I'm sorry for the late hour," Zoe said.

"No, please, come in. I'm happy to have a bit of company."

Zoe entered the apartment. "Everything okay?"

"Oh, just a rough couple of days." Daniella sniffed. "They happen to everyone, right?"

"Sure."

"Can I get you any coffee?"

Remembering the condensed caffeine monstrosity from last time, Zoe said, "No, uh . . . maybe tea?"

"Sure." Daniella stomped to the kitchen. Zoe sat down, looking around her. The pictures bombarded her already-frayed brain, and she shut her eyes, taking a deep breath. She was still reeling from the implications of the envelopes the reporter had found, and memories from the past kept emerging. People and places she hadn't thought of in years were swimming in her mind.

"Here," Daniella said. She handed Zoe a cup of tea. She had one for herself as well. This time she didn't get a chair for herself, sitting next to Zoe on the couch. Zoe didn't mind. There was plenty of room for both of them, and she wasn't there to question Daniella, just to show her a picture.

She sipped from her tea, which turned out to be thick with sugar. Grimacing, she put the teacup on the table and fished the printed image from her pocket.

"Do you recognize this man?" she asked, handing Daniella the page. It was a print of the only picture she had of Rod Glover. She had acquired it when she was fifteen, from the office he had worked at. They had a picture of him from a Thanksgiving party. He looked happy and slightly drunk. Not the face of a killer. But then, most killers didn't have a particularly violent face.

Daniella took the picture and stared at it for a long time. "No," she finally said.

"Look carefully. Are you sure you've never seen him before? Maybe Susan knew him somehow?"

"If she did, I don't think she told me. He doesn't look familiar. I'm sorry."

Disappointed, Zoe took the printed image from her. "Do you think Ryan might recognize him?"

Daniella shrugged. "He might. He's not here, though."

"Do you know when he'll be back?"

"He never tells me, and if I ask, I'm nagging, right?"

Zoe nodded in kinship. "Do you have a pen?" she asked.

"Sure." Daniella went to the kitchen. The kitchen was the place where pens were in the Ortiz household. She returned a moment later, handing the pen to Zoe.

Zoe wrote her phone number on the paper. "Can you show Ryan this picture when he gets back?" she asked. "If he's seen this man, just give me a call, okay? Or if you recall seeing him."

Daniella nodded. "Sure," she said. "We'll call."

"Thanks." Zoe got up. "And, uh . . . I hope you have a nice evening."

Daniella nodded, staring down. Zoe followed her eyes to the bare floor. There was nothing there. Only loneliness.

It was as if she were dragging heavy chains behind her as she walked up the motel stairs, lifting one foot after the other, each step heavy and tired. During the past years, whenever she would get an envelope, she'd feel as if Glover were reaching out and pulling her back. For him, she was still a fourteen-year-old girl who could be intimidated and terrorized with little to no consequence. Sometimes years would pass between the envelopes. She'd start relaxing her guard. And then another envelope would arrive in the mail. Always with a gray tie inside.

Now it was worse. He was somewhere in this city. He was killing young women. And he was laughing at her, taunting her, so sure she couldn't find him.

She gritted her teeth and clenched her fists. That twisted, psycho bastard. She'd find him. She would get him arrested. He would die in prison.

She reached her room, unlocked the door, and stumbled inside. She lay on her bed, too drained to brush her teeth or shower. Too worked up to fall asleep. Stuck in her own looping thoughts.

Finally, she pulled out her phone and called Andrea.

"Zoe?" her sleepy sister said over the phone.

"Hey, Ray-Ray."

"What time is it?"

"Almost midnight, I think."

"Okay . . ." A pause. "Are you drunk?"

"No," Zoe said sadly. "Though that's not such a bad idea."

"What's going on, Zoe?"

"I don't know. I think I just needed to hear your voice."

"Okay. It sounds better in the morning."

"Ray-Ray, do you remember Rod Glover?"

There was a moment of silence. "Do I remember the serial killer who nearly murdered us both?" Andrea finally asked. "It sounds familiar."

Andrea didn't remember what Glover had said that night. But she was the only one who'd really believed everything Zoe had said. As a child, she'd quickly gotten over the terrible night they'd spent locked in Zoe's room with Glover screaming on the other side of the door. She'd had her big sister to protect her; she'd known nothing would happen to her.

"I think he may be in Chicago."

"Did you see him?" Andrea asked, her voice sharp. She was now wide awake.

"No, but . . . I have reason to suspect it."

"Is he killing again?"

"I think so."

Silence. Finally, Andrea asked, "Did you tell the cops?"

"I'll do it tomorrow."

"Okay. Do you want me to fly over?"

"To Chicago?" Zoe asked in surprise. "No, there's no need."

"Could be a nice vacation," Andrea said.

"No . . . it's okay. But thanks."

"All right. Be careful, okay?"

"Yeah. Thanks for talking to me."

"Good night, Zoe."

"Night, Ray-Ray." She hung up, staring at the ceiling. She hoped she would fall asleep soon.

CHAPTER 50

Chicago, Illinois, Friday, July 22, 2016

"You want to grab some breakfast before going to the station?" Tatum asked. They were on their way from the motel to the police department. Zoe gazed outside the passenger's side window. She'd been acting subdued all morning. Tatum wasn't entirely surprised. He wasn't sure when she had gone to sleep the night before, but it had looked like she'd been planning a late night. She probably hadn't slept much.

He had to hand it to her: she worked harder than most agents he had partnered with. And she got results too. The link to Veronika Murray's murder was a big win for the investigation, and it had earned both of them a measure of respect. Martinez was now actively involving them both in the investigation, his suspicions of the FBI's nefarious plans laid to rest.

"Hey," he said. "Did you hear what I said?"

They were sitting at a traffic light on Thirty-Seventh Street. Traffic was thick, rows and rows of people on their way to work, participating in mankind's dumbest dance—rush hour. More than a hundred years before, the German engineer Rudolf Diesel had invented something amazing called the combustion engine—a manmade engine that could propel a wheeled vehicle down a paved road at an incredible speed. And right now, millions of such vehicles were crowding the streets of

Chicago, driving at a speed that would embarrass a kid with a tricycle. Poor Rudolf must be turning in his grave. Whatever the German word for *grave* was. Probably *graven*, spoken in an angry, curt tone.

He shook his head, derailing his moronic train of thought. "Zoe," he said aloud for the third time. "Breakfast, please?"

She jolted and stared at him in confusion. He was getting worried.

"Yeah," she mumbled. "Sure."

"Excellent." He smiled. There was a diner just past the next traffic light, a place called Wilma's. It had a badly drawn imitation of Wilma Flintstone for a sign. Tatum parked the car, got out, and entered the restaurant. Zoe followed a step behind him, silent and withdrawn.

The Flintstones theme pretty much ended with the sign outside. The decor inside was pink walls, a black-and-white checkered floor, and peach-colored seats. Tatum hoped the food would be better than the owner's skill at interior design.

They sat down, and a waitress approached them with a cheery smile.

"Hi," she squawked. "What can I get you?"

Tatum winced at the high-pitched tone. It really was too early for this helium-inhaling bubble of cheerfulness.

"Do you have cheese omelets?"

"Of course. It's one of the best—"

"That's great," he said hurriedly. "Get me that and some strong coffee."

"And what will you be having?" the waitress asked, her supersonic voice aimed at Zoe.

Zoe gazed at the wall. It almost looked as if she didn't hear the waitress, but that wasn't humanly possible.

"Excuse me? Miss? What will you have? We have pancakes, banana bread, waffles . . ."

She was about to recite the entire menu. Tatum's cranium would not be able to withstand it. "She'll have bacon and eggs," he said. "Make the bacon extra crispy and the eggs sunny-side up. And strong coffee for her as well."

"Okay." The waitress turned around. Tatum would not have been surprised if she'd hopped to the kitchen to deliver the order. But she just walked. Like a normal person with a normal voice.

"She's like an extreme version of Alvin and the Chipmunks," he said in a low voice.

Zoe looked at him, though she seemed to be actually looking through him. And through the wall behind him.

"What's going on, Zoe?" he asked.

"I'm just . . . preoccupied," she said.

"I can see that," he said dryly. "Preoccupied with what?"

"This case," she said. She bit her lip again. By now he knew she bit her lip when thinking, when she wasn't sure of something. He decided to give her some time to organize her thoughts.

The waitress came over with two mugs of coffee and put them on the table, emitting a batlike, high-pitched "Here you go." Tatum drank from his cup, the coffee banishing the tiredness from his brain and the droopiness from his eyes. Blessed coffee. He had been told by several people that he drank too much coffee, that it wasn't good for him. As far as he was concerned, those people were just jealous and cranky because they didn't drink enough coffee.

Wilma's apparently had some pretty fast cooks in the kitchen, because their orders were on the table just five minutes later. Tatum took a bite from his cheese omelet, happy to find it was good. Zoe ate as well, slicing large pieces of egg and shoving them into her mouth distractedly.

"Okay, something's wrong," he said, feeling concerned.

"What?" Zoe asked.

"The way you eat—usually you treat your food like it's a miracle sent by God to your plate. Right now, you're swallowing it like it's some sort of chore. Talk to me."

"There were two murders in 2008 here in Chicago," she said.

"Okay, go on, but lower your voice, please."

"Both murdered women were found submerged in water, strangled. The murderer was never caught."

"Uh-huh."

"I think it's the same guy."

Tatum frowned. "Why?"

"The locations were public and had large bodies of water involved."

"That's far from enough."

"There was . . . I think . . ."

He leaned forward to hear her better.

"When I was a . . . young girl, there was a serial killer in my home-town. In Massachusetts."

"Okay."

"No one was ever convicted. They caught someone, he hanged himself in his cell, and the killings stopped. The Maynard serial killer—that's what they called him—also had a thing with leaving bodies next to bodies of water."

"So you think the same need propelled those killers?"

"No," Zoe said. "I think it was the same guy."

There was a moment of silence.

"Zoe," Tatum said. "This sounds . . ." He searched for the right word.

"No, listen. The thing is, I had this neighbor who—"

"It sounds tenuous," he said. "You're looking for connections in places that aren't there."

He knew what would come next. She'd explode. She'd yell at him or storm out or become cold and furious.

To his surprise, her shoulders drooped. "Okay," she said, her voice small. "Forget it."

"Hang on," he said. "Let's talk about this. Maybe I don't see the whole picture. Or maybe you've got something there, and we need to talk it out."

"No," she said. "It doesn't matter."

It doesn't matter?

"Zoe—"

"Let's pay and go," she said. Her plate was half-full. "It's getting late."

CHAPTER 51

Zoe trudged behind Tatum to the task force room, dispirited. As soon as she had begun to lay out the reasons why she suspected the killer was Glover, she had realized how dumb it sounded. It was like being a teenager again, trying to convince her mother and the cops. What she knew in her gut to be right came out as a string of dubious connections and half-assed theories once spoken aloud. Because essentially, it all came down to what she *felt*. When she had decided to break into Glover's house, it was mostly because she had felt his behavior was strange and suspicious; she hadn't had any tangible proof. Even after she knew what was in his room, it was still mostly the feeling that the items she found were mementos from victims. And now she felt Glover was telling her, via their one-sided creepy conversation, that he was the killer in Chicago as well.

But once those feelings were spoken aloud, it was easy to see how she sounded even more questionable than Dr. Bernstein. A fragment of a memory filled her mind, of her standing in the police station in Maynard, doing her best to hold it together, as the officer had told her, "I can think of other brown substances that might soil a pair of underwear."

Never again. She had to build a stronger case this time.

As she passed by the meeting room on their way down the hall, she saw Martinez inside through the half-open door. Peeking in, she saw the entire team sitting around the table.

"Zoe," Martinez called, noticing her. "Get in here. It's a quick status meeting."

She called Tatum back and walked into the room, sitting down. Tatum followed her, closing the door behind him.

"Okay," Martinez said. "As I was saying, we now have the full autopsy report of Lily Ramos as well as a detailed report of the findings from the crime scene. We have very little to go on. Cause of death is strangulation, and the cut on the throat was performed postmortem. The cut was to the"—Martinez glanced at the paper in his hand—"common carotid artery, and we've found that embalmers use this as an entry point for embalming fluid. There were traces of what seems to be embalming fluid near the cut . . . we've sent those for testing to verify. The body didn't have the postmortem sexual intercourse signs that we've found so far."

Zoe tried to concentrate. That all indicated, as she had previously assumed, that the killer had tried to hurriedly embalm the victim, even skipping his sexual abuse of the body. She was satisfied, knowing they had prevented Lily's body from being defiled that way.

Martinez glanced at his paper again. "There were scratches on the victim's back, which have been attributed to her being dragged into the alley. Also, both of her heels were bruised."

"Why?" Dana asked.

"I don't know."

"If she was dragged out of a vehicle's trunk, that could cause it," Tatum said.

Everyone looked at him.

"When people grab bodies, they mostly do so by grabbing under the armpits," he said. "If the killer got her out of the trunk that way, assuming no one helped him, both her feet would hit the ground forcefully. She was barefoot, so it would cause a bruise."

Martinez nodded slowly. "That sounds like a probable explanation," he said. "Mangled wrists, as you all saw in the crime scene pictures. The victim was probably handcuffed, and she struggled against them. No results from the toxicology tests yet. That's about it for the autopsy." He looked around the room. "Questions?"

A second of silence followed.

"All right. Let's talk about the crime scene. Some cigarette butts, a candy wrapper, and a piece of string found at the crime scene, all sent for testing. There were multiple tire marks from vehicles driving in reverse to the opening of the alley, at least two of them recent. The rain was unfortunate, but we still have some decent photos, and we're trying to match them. Also, once we have a suspect, this will be useful as evidence. Both vehicles have wide tires and are probably vans of some sort. We're trying to match the tire marks to the vehicles parked nearby, to eliminate them. There was also a smudged footprint—not really useful for the investigation, but again, might be useful for court. Right. Now . . . security cam footage. Tommy?"

Tommy cleared his throat. His eyes were red rimmed. "We've procured some footage from nearby establishments. Nothing in the immediate vicinity of the alley. I'm going over the footage, but without any indication of what I'm looking for, it's like looking for . . ." He seemed to be searching for a fitting analogy.

"A needle in a haystack?" Scott suggested.

"No. If I had a haystack and a needle inside, I'd eventually find it. You just have to be methodical. This is more like finding hay in a haystack . . . except this hay I'm looking for is a bit different, but I don't know what's different about it."

His brain was probably half-dead from staring at security cam footage for hours.

Martinez coughed. "An apt description. Right . . . we're doing a door-to-door investigation of the entire segment of Huron Street where we suspect Lily Ramos was held. Dana?"

Dana nodded. "The relevant stretch of Huron Street is one point one miles long, and the search is conducted by me and three additional patrol officers. So far, no one has seen anything that pertains to the case. We'll double back on doors where no one opened, and hopefully we might eventually find the place where Lily was kept. Though it's like looking for hay in a haystack."

Martinez raised an eyebrow. "See that, Tommy? You've coined a new phrase. I hope you're pleased with yourself. Okay. Dr. Bentley, any progress with the profile?"

The question jolted her. Ever since the reporter had handed her the three envelopes, any attempt at profiling the killer had been forgotten. What was the use of creating a profile when she was almost certain she knew who the murderer was? She just had to tie the case together better. For now, she frowned, trying to remember her last notes.

"The fact that he decided to practice his preservation techniques on animals, and that he kept at it for a long time, indicates a methodical person. When he decides to pursue his fantasy, he doesn't improvise. He plans ahead and then executes the plan patiently and carefully. This stems from the leading attribute of his personality . . ." She bit her lip.

"Which is?" Martinez prompted her after a second.

"An obsession with control. We can see it in everything he does. His victims are tied up. He preserves them in a way that enables him to pose them however he wants. He chooses high-risk, weak victims and takes them to a location where he has absolute control over them. Even his strangulation method has absolute control. A noose tightened by twisting it from behind, probably while his victims are tied. No messy blood, no physical contact with the victim, no chance for the victim to cry out . . . total control."

The room was silent.

"I believe this is a man who had little to no control over his life as a child. When we finally catch him, we'll find he had an abusive parent and an unstable childhood. He's making up for it now."

Zoe became silent, thinking over her own words. She'd pegged him completely.

"All right," Martinez said. "Now, as most of you know, Dr. Bentley linked those murders to the murder of Veronika Murray in 2014. Dana is in charge of investigating that case with the new facts we have, once she's done with the door to door. Scott is still in charge of the Susan Warner case, trying to establish suspects from her acquaintances. Tommy is on the security feeds, and Mel is checking the missing prostitutes—"

"What missing prostitutes?" Tatum asked.

"Vice informed us of two missing prostitutes since yesterday," Martinez said. "Tiffany Styles and Amber Dew. We're trying to establish if they're really missing. If they are, they might have been our killer's latest victims. Amber Dew was seen entering a dark Ford Focus, and we've alerted dispatch about it."

Zoe cleared her throat. "I think it's unlikely that was him. He'd almost certainly target a different group now that he knows we're on to his interest in prostitutes—"

"He doesn't necessarily know that," Martinez said. "He might simply think he should watch out for mobile phones in the future. We can't ignore those leads."

"You're stretched too thin as it is. Don't underestimate this man's intelligence. We're talking about a man who learned how to embalm on his own and is even improvising and refining the technique—"

"Thank you, Dr. Bentley. I understand what you're saying, but I don't think we can overlook these cases. Mel, you have your assignment.

Anyone who is finished with his task or just bored can help out Tommy since we have . . . how many video hours of security camera feeds in the nearby streets, Tommy?"

"A bazillion."

"There you go. A bazillion hours of security camera feeds. And I have a meeting with the captain and the chief because it's Friday, another week has passed, and the killer is still out there. See? I get all the real fun."

CHAPTER 52

Harry glanced at the time. It was half past five, and he really had given Zoe Bentley fair warning. He had the article ready; all he had to do was think of a good clickbait headline. "FBI Profiler Gets Chilling Messages at Crime Scenes" or maybe "Three Mysterious Envelopes Left for FBI Profiler, and You Won't Believe What's in Them." With an article like this, the headlines practically wrote themselves. Just publish, watch as the endless online readers flocked to read his article, and enjoy the songs of praise from his editor.

Except . . . some part of him wanted more. It was that nagging, enthusiastic part that had made him take the journalist's path in the first place. It wasn't the search for the truth—Harry had never cared much about the truth—but it was the search for a *good story*. Mysterious envelopes left for a profiler wasn't a story. It wasn't even a scene. It had no context, no beginning, no end. It would get people to read it, maybe click an ad or two, but after reading, they'd move on and forget.

He wanted to write something that would make people talk.

He sighed, trying to ignore that naive part of him. Better take what he could get. A bird in the hand was worth two in the bush.

Unless it crapped on your fingers and pecked you. Some birds carried salmonella too. And those two in the bush were awesome birds. They had the prettiest feathers.

He took out his phone and sent Zoe Bentley a text message. His phone began ringing a minute later.

"Hello," he answered, trying not to sound smug.

"You can't publish that story," Zoe said. She sounded hollow. Weary.

"Give me something better to publish," he said. "Right now."

There was a moment of silence. "What if I give you a damn good story . . . a story no one could possibly have? But you have to promise not to publish it until I tell you."

"That . . . depends," he said, his curiosity flaring. "I want to hear the story, and I want a deadline. I can't wait forever for your permission."

"Okay," she agreed. "There's a place not far from the police station called Wilma's. Do you know it?"

"Sure."

"Can you be there in twenty minutes?"

"Give me half an hour," he said. "Traffic."

"See you there."

It took him only twenty-five minutes, and Zoe was already waiting for him, her face a mask of anxiety and exhaustion. He pulled up the opposite chair and sat down. She nursed a mug of coffee. The way she looked, he wasn't sure coffee was a good idea. He smiled. She didn't smile back.

They sat in silence for a bit.

"I'll start," he suggested. "You were about to tell me an amazing story no one else has."

She nodded, staring at him. "You can't publish it until I—"

"Until you tell me," he said. "But we have to agree on a final date. And I sure as hell don't want this story to get out before—"

"It won't."

The waitress approached him. "What can I get you?"

"Just coffee, thanks," he said.

"Do you want cappuccino, pumpkin latte, or—"

255

"Just good old regular coffee."

She walked away.

"Okay, let's hear it," he said.

Zoe's eyes glazed, as if focusing on a distant memory. "Back in 1997, there was a serial killer in Maynard, Massachusetts. He raped and killed three young women. A suspect was arrested and killed himself while incarcerated."

Harry nodded, writing in his notebook. The notebook was mostly for show. He was recording the entire conversation. But writing also helped him concentrate. He penned down *1997—Maynard, killings*.

"Massachusetts," he muttered, recalling the articles he had read about Zoe. "That's where you grew up, right?"

"Maynard was my hometown."

His focus sharpened considerably. "Okay," he said. "How old were you when that took place?"

"Fourteen."

"Right. Go ahead."

"I believe the man who killed those three women back then is the serial killer currently murdering in Chicago."

"The Strangling Undertaker?" he asked in surprise.

She twisted her lips in displeasure. "I detest that nickname. He is not an undertaker. Just a killer, letting his fantasies and urges take control."

"A monster." Harry nodded.

"No." She leaned forward. "Not a monster. Much worse. A human. One of us. I've researched you, Harry Barry."

Harry winced as she said his full name.

"You like articles that shock and tantalize. More than half your stories are about sex scandals."

"It's not what *I* like. It's what my readers like."

"Sure. In any case, you write those tabloid articles . . . but your writing isn't cheap. You do your research. You don't fall to clichés, and you give your stories an interesting angle. You take pride in your work."

"Thank you," he said warily.

"The Chicago serial killer is not a monster. He isn't the bogeyman. He's a very dark person with warped sexual ideas and an obsession with death."

"Why do you think he's the same killer as the one in Maynard?" Harry asked.

She narrowed her eyes, and Harry folded his arms. The tension built between them. He wasn't worried. He held all the cards here. She'd give him the story he was looking for.

"Here's your coffee," the waitress said, putting down the cup in front of him.

"Thanks."

"Do you want anything else? We have—"

"No, thank you," Harry said. "I have everything I need. Thank you."

The waitress nodded and left. He sipped from his cup, looking at Zoe. Her face was distant. Some of the worry faded from her posture, she sat straighter. Harry found that concerning.

He cleared his throat, putting the cup on the table. "You were about to explain—"

"Look up what I told you," she interrupted him. "Start doing your research. I'll give you the rest of the story in a few days. I promise."

"You'll give me the story now, or I go live with what I have."

"Go ahead. I'll deny everything. And you'll have a dumb story no one cares about. Like so many others you've written."

He stared at her. Her eyes met his, piercing, unrelenting. Eyes that could see right through him. And for a moment he became convinced she had read his thoughts, fears, and hopes. That was why she had relaxed. She had watched his behavior, his body language, the way he talked to her and to the waitress, and somehow, she knew he wouldn't publish the story. "But your investigation will—"

"Like you told me yesterday, it's not my job to decide what would hurt the investigation. Nor is it yours. You have a taste of the real story. You'll get the rest in a few days."

She took out her purse, took out a bill, and slapped it on the table. "The coffee's on me," she said, got up, and left.

He looked after her, then at the bill on the table. It was a twenty-dollar bill, when all they'd had were two cups of coffee. He shook his head in amusement. People loved their dramatic exits. He picked up the bill and thumbed his wallet for a crumpled ten-dollar bill, which he laid on the table instead. His mouth stretched in a Cheshire Cat grin. There was a story here. A big story. And hidden inside it was an even bigger story.

The real story wasn't about the Chicago serial killer or the Maynard serial killer at all. The real story was about Dr. Zoe Bentley.

CHAPTER 53

As she sat in the cab, something alerted Zoe, made her tense up, but she couldn't put her finger on it. It was as if something buried deep inside her brain were emitting faint warning signs, but she didn't know what it was warning her about or trying to alert her to. She glanced at the cab driver, concerned, but he was the nicest cab driver she'd ridden with since she'd arrived in Chicago. He was polite, and the only conversation he made was asking for her destination. Was it something about his body language? Something that years as a forensic psychologist had etched into her subconscious? No. That wasn't it.

She almost felt as if she were being followed. Her mind considered the reporter, Harry Barry. He could have tailed her after their meeting. Would he stoop to following her around?

Of course he would.

She glanced at the rearview mirror, trying to catch a glimpse of his smug face in the cars behind, but he wasn't there.

She was just sleep deprived. Of course she felt anxious; she was running on fumes.

"There we are," the driver said.

"Wait here," Zoe said. "I'll only be ten minutes."

He nodded, and she became convinced that whatever had triggered her alert signals, it wasn't him. She got out and marched into Sorenson's Plumbing.

The only man in the store was Clifford Sorenson's employee, Jeffrey. He frowned when he saw her.

"Good day, miss," he said.

"Hello. Is Clifford here?"

"He'll be back in a moment. Is this about Veronika?"

"Well . . . yes."

Jeffrey nodded. "He's been upset ever since you last came here. I hoped you'd leave him alone."

"I'm sorry. I won't be long."

"Do you think you'll catch the guy?"

"I don't know. We might have some leads."

"Okay."

Clifford walked into the office from the back room. "Oh," he said. "It's you."

"Yeah," Zoe said apologetically. "I just wanted to ask you one question."

"Sure."

She took out a printout of her Rod Glover image. "Have you ever seen this man?"

Clifford looked closely at the picture, frowning. "No, I don't think so."

"Are you sure? Maybe around the time of Veronika's death?"

"Do you think he's the killer?"

"I don't know yet. I'm following some leads."

"I see a lot of people. I doubt I would have remembered him even if I did meet him two years ago."

Zoe nodded. She wasn't surprised. He handed her the paper. She took it, and as she had done with Daniella before, she wrote her phone number on the page and placed it on the office desk. "I'll leave it here. Call me if you happen to remember anything."

"Sure."

She had turned to leave when Clifford said, "Miss Bentley."

"Yeah?"

"I, uh . . . wanted to tell you something. You asked me before if Veronika was tense before her disappearance."

"That's right," Zoe said.

"She was. I think she was afraid. She . . . she was angry that I kept going fishing, leaving her alone in the evenings."

"Did she tell you that?"

"Not in so many words. But once, when she was really agitated, she said some apples really don't fall far from the tree."

Zoe blinked. "What did she—"

"My father left when I was just a baby. It was a jab at the fact that I kept leaving. I . . . if I hadn't gone fishing that night . . ."

"You can't blame yourself," Zoe said mechanically. "You couldn't stay by her side at all times."

Clifford nodded, and Zoe knew her words didn't matter. If he hadn't gone fishing that night, Veronika might have lived. She doubted he could really shake off the knowledge of that.

CHAPTER 54

Zoe looked out the cab's passenger window, glimpsing the water of Saganashkee Slough between the trees. The murky water of the pond was calm, reflecting the dark-blue sky. The sun was setting slowly, and the tree shadows were lengthening. Zoe cursed herself for not getting there sooner, but Harry had caught her on the phone just as she had been about to leave.

Then again, she wasn't there for any specific reason. As always, she found herself drawn to the scene of the crime, as if standing where the killer had stood would somehow give her an insight into his frame of mind. It hardly ever did. Her plan had been to walk around the crime scenes of both 2008 murder victims. First, Saganashkee Slough, where Pamela Vance had been found. Next she'd go to Little Calumet River, Shirley Wattenberg's crime scene. Seeing the sun set made her realize she wouldn't have time to see both. She'd go to Little Calumet River tomorrow.

She glanced at the map she had printed earlier and then at the Google Maps app on her phone. As far as she could tell, she was just about where the body had been found.

"Can you stop here, please?" she said.

"Here?" The cab driver sounded surprised.

"Yeah."

He muttered something and nudged the steering wheel, parking the car on the side of the road.

"Thanks," she said, rummaging in her shoulder bag for her purse.

"Uh . . . do you want me to wait?"

She didn't want the driver looking over her shoulder as she walked the shore, trying to think. "No, thank you."

"But how will you leave?"

She could see his point. It wasn't as if she could just flag a taxi down out here. The whole problem had started with her decision to ride with Tatum instead of renting her own car. Now she was stuck, dependent on the goodwill of cab drivers.

"Yeah, thanks," she said. "Just wait for me here."

"How long will you be?"

She checked the darkening sky. "Half an hour, tops."

He nodded, content. She gave him the credit card, but he waved it away. "Pay me at the end of the day."

She thanked him and got out of the cab. She glanced carefully both ways. The road was nearly empty, a single car passing them by. She crossed the road and walked down the grassy shore. Facing the water, she tried to imagine the murder of Pamela Vance, eight years earlier. Her kayak had been found near her body. Had Glover known she'd be kayaking there, or had he noticed her from the road, deciding to seize the opportunity? He might have befriended her, maybe even joined her for a kayaking trip. Did the kayak have one seat or two? The case file hadn't mentioned this. She made a mental note to check the crime scene pictures again when she returned to the office.

The shore was in plain sight of the road, and it was the same for a long stretch to the west. But to the east, the shoreline got further from the road, the foliage blocking the line of sight. Glover wouldn't have raped and strangled her with the road in plain view; that much was certain. She turned to her left and began to pace the shore, the foliage between her and the road thickening until she could hardly see the gray asphalt through the leaves and branches. The shoreline was tricky to navigate, the ground dotted with bushes and trees. It was hard to spot some of the obstacles in the shadowy gloom, and she nearly tripped on a thick root.

She looked out onto the water again. The air was calm, and there was hardly any wind, the water nearly a straight plateau. The sun was getting lower, the blue shades of the pond water getting darker, nearly black. It was time to leave. She resolved to ride back to the motel and talk to Tatum about the envelopes. The thought filled her with trepidation. She hadn't mentioned the envelopes to anyone in years. But it definitely wasn't something she could keep to herself anymore.

She turned around and froze. A man walked toward her, his face intent on the ground as he stepped around a small bush. He paced slowly. Was it because of the growing darkness?

No. He was trying to make no noise.

He was only ten yards from her, the grass and the muddy shore masking his steps. He raised his face from the ground, and their eyes met.

Twenty years older, putting him in his midforties, the once thin, lanky man now had a sagging belly; his face was a bit fatter as well. He was vastly different from the memory ingrained in her mind, a teenager's memory of a killer. But his eyes were the same. Those childish, mocking eyes, hiding a mind brimming with violence. It was Rod Glover.

Her feet were already moving, her reflexes faster than her mind. Glover blocked her way back—she could only go forward, farther away from the road. Leaping over a low bush, she dashed as fast as her weary muscles could take her, the surge of adrenaline rushing into her brain, masking the fatigue, a single message pounding over and over. *Go. Go. Go.*

He ran behind her, a heavy man, his steps thudding much harder than hers. She was in good shape. He didn't seem to be. She glanced backward, saw he was farther back, and dove left into the tree line, toward the road.

It was the reasonable course. The right course. The road meant safety. If she could get to the road, get back to the cab waiting for her, she'd be safe.

She underestimated how thick the foliage would be. Six feet into the foliage, she ran into a bush, veered left, nearly collided into a tree, veered again, tripped on something, stumbled. Disoriented, she got up and turned around, and he was upon her, hitting her in the face with a blunt object.

She floundered back gasping, half-blind, spots swimming in her field of vision, darkness surrounding her. It took her several seconds to figure out she was lying on the ground, staring at the dark sky. Something cold and metallic pressed against her neck. Her left ear rang, a constant high-pitched sound.

"Scream and I'll cut your throat, bitch," a voice rasped in her ear.

She breathed heavily, something sticky trickling on her forehead. Blood? What happened?

He had hit her with something, she remembered.

A viselike grip grabbed her under her armpits, pulling her up. She began struggling, and the blade pressed harder against her skin. She bit back a whimper of pain as it broke her skin. Glover had cut the side of her neck, the knife tearing into muscle. More blood trickled on her shoulder and chest, soaking into her shirt.

"Let's try again," he whispered in her ear, his voice vicious, hungry. "Stand up."

He pulled, and she complied, standing up on wobbly legs, nausea overwhelming her, nearly making her gag. The blade never left her throat, Glover's other hand grabbing her arm, twisting it behind her back.

"Move," he rasped, pointing her toward the water, away from the trees. Away from the road.

She stumbled forward, walking slowly, buying time, trying to think through her clouded mind, through the pain shooting up her neck and forehead. Glover wanted to get her away from the road, away from her cab and possible witnesses, where no one would see her, no one would hear her scream. Once he got her far enough from the road, her fate would follow the fate of his other victims. The thought was chilling, and she shivered involuntary. Even that small motion made Glover tense, and he pushed the blade against her.

"Please," she said through gritted teeth. "I—"

"Quiet," he whispered. "I've heard your voice enough for a lifetime. Now walk."

Three more small steps, Glover pushing her onward. She nearly lost her balance, her head spinning and pounding. Glover pulled her up by her arm, twisting it further. A small scream emerged from her, and the blade flashed, cutting deep through her shoulder this time.

"Three strikes and you're out," he said.

"What do you want?" she whispered.

"I want you to move," he said and shoved again.

Step after step, he pushed her out of the shadows of the trees. She couldn't let him take her, had to fight. It was better to die now, throat cut, than to let him get her far enough away to do whatever he wanted. And yet her muscles refused to obey, her heart and head pounding together as she walked another step. And another. And another.

He began talking, his tone mocking. "Fancy meeting you again, Zoe, after so many years. We have so much to talk about, so much catching up to do, right? How is your sister? And your parents?"

As she nearly stumbled again, the cogs in her brain spun, analyzing him, assessing him. His confidence was building. He was getting cocky. Perhaps getting away from safety was the way to beat him. Cocky, strong men often made mistakes. He remembered her as a small, weak fourteen-year-old girl. But twenty years had passed. She'd grown;

she'd learned. All she had to do was lean on his self-confidence, wait for one little slip.

"Didn't see me following you, bitch? I've been on your tail all day. An FBI agent would have noticed. But you aren't an agent, are you, *Dr.* Bentley?"

She didn't answer, kept walking, her mind sharpening. *That* was what had triggered the warning bells in her brain earlier. He had been following her cab.

"Got my envelopes? I left them for you as soon as I found out you were in town. I thought it would be a nice way of saying hello to an old friend."

"You could've just called."

He laughed, a strained, twisting laugh, familiar and chilling at once. He then shoved her forcefully onward.

The ringing in her ears faded away. Her stumbles were more for show now than actual missteps, the weakness in her limbs an act. She took in a deep breath, inhaling the clear evening air, waiting for that blade to move an inch away, for that hand to let go, for anything to change.

He leaned close to her ear, his hot breath on her cheek. "It wasn't here, you know, where I took her. It was a bit farther."

"Who, Pamela?" she asked.

"Don't play dumb, bitch. You were never dumb. I still remember her whimpering under me. Struggling. She was strong, Zoe. She worked out. It didn't help her. Not one bit."

"Are you taking me to the same place?" she asked. *Buy time. More time.*

"No need," he said, his voice lower, hungrier. "Here is far enough. Get down."

"What?"

"On your knees."

"Glover, you're making a—"

"Now, damn it!"

Slowly and carefully she got down on her knees, her body tensing up. There was no more time. She had to act now.

The blade disappeared from her neck. She began to twist, her fist clenching, preparing to smash into his flabby, fat stomach.

And then something looped around her neck and tightened hard. The effect was instantaneous, her next breath of air out of reach. Something made strange sounds. It was her; she was wheezing, coughing, trying to get some air into her system. Her sight dimmed as her fingernails clutched at the thing around her neck, trying to pull it free, desperate for that one thing: air.

She didn't see her life flashing in front of her eyes. Instead, she saw the pictures she had looked through when she'd managed to get the case files from the Maynard Police Department. Of Beth and Clara and Jackie, their naked bodies submerged in water, a tie wrapped around their throats. This was what had happened to them.

Blood pounded in her ears, and beyond it, she could hear the heavy breathing of the man behind her, his fingers already pawing at her zipper, trying to pull her pants down, his throat making angry growls. She knew that if she could only focus, she might get out of this alive. She was sharp; he was consumed by lust. But she had no air, and all she wanted was to breathe. Her mouth opened and closed now, gasping desperately, trying to inhale. She tried grabbing the hand on her pants, the only part of him within reach, but she could do nothing. Everything faded, her fingers slack, hands dropping.

And the noose loosened. She could take a small, impossibly tiny breath. The world swam into focus. His fingers were in her pants, scraping her left thigh. He laughed to himself, the same high-pitched, maddened giggle that she had heard all those years ago. He was giving her air on purpose. He wanted her alive for this.

Too self-confident. Too cocky.

She threw her head back as far as she could. She had hoped to hit him in the stomach, but instead she heard a crunch and a roar of pain. He had crouched behind her to get her pants off, and she had just smashed his nose. The noose loosened completely as he stumbled back, and she drew in a wheezing breath, already moving. She leaped forward, not really able to stand yet but strong enough to crawl away and roll onto her back, see what Glover was doing.

He stood above her, blood streaming down his face, rage in his eyes, his mouth twisted in an animal snarl. He lunged at her, roaring, and she lifted one knee, kicked as hard as she could, hitting him . . . somewhere. Chest, stomach, she couldn't really tell. It didn't stop him. He was on her, flexing his fingers into a fist and punching her, pain bursting as his fist hit her cheek.

Her hand clutched at something hard—a rock; she swung up, the rock hitting him in his face, his broken nose. He fell back, howling. This time she wouldn't crawl away. She pushed herself forward onto him, swinging her free hand, fingernails raking at his bloody face, searching for his eyes.

He screamed and shook her off. She rolled and felt a hot, sharp pain in her hip. Her hand flew down to the searing flesh, feeling blood pulsing between her fingers. Something had cut her.

The knife. He had dropped the knife when he'd choked her, and she'd just rolled onto the blade.

Her eyes searched frantically on the ground, noticing a glint. There.

She leaped at it, her fingers tightening in a hard grip around the knife's handle. Glover turned his eyes on her, looking more like a beast than a man.

Almost like an actual monster.

Her hand tensed. The hand clutching the knife was on the ground, hidden in the grass. She hoped he couldn't see it beyond the blood and the rage. She feigned weakness, stumbling, letting out a cry of pain that was hardly fake. She followed his eyes, knew how he'd move, where he'd strike. All she had to do was push her hand forward.

He lunged, and she thrust the knife, not realizing how weak she was, how dizzy. Instead of plunging it into his stomach like she had intended, she slashed his thigh.

He roared in pain, but there was something else there. Her mind processed the sound, years of training kicking into focus. Fear.

Her reflexes told her to turn and run again. She had the knife now; his leg was hurt. She had the advantage. She could get away.

Instead, she forced herself to get up, her body screaming in agony. Her slashed shoulder was numb with pain. She stood straight, holding the knife in front of her, and grimaced, her fingers tightening on the handle. Their eyes locked, and her grimace widened. Not a smile. The face of an animal baring its teeth.

Glover hesitated, then turned and ran.

She almost laughed as she lunged after him, but her adrenaline began to fade. Her head throbbed painfully, her shoulder burned, her neck prickled where he had cut her, and she realized she was still wheezing. Her throat still hurt. She could hardly walk, couldn't even chase Glover, limping as fast as he could on his one good leg. She forced herself to remain standing. He glanced back, and whatever he saw made him keep running. She hid her weakness well.

Once he was out of sight, her knees buckled, her fingers dropping the knife, and she fell to the ground. A sob that was also a groan emerged from her throat.

She half crawled, half limped back. A hundred feet from the shore, she stumbled again and lay down in the grass, thinking she'd just close her eyes and rest for a second.

CHAPTER 55

Tatum counted his steps as he paced the waiting room in the hospital. *One . . . two . . . three . . .* he reached thirteen. Last time he had done it in twelve, and the time before it had been fifteen because someone had gotten in his way.

He wasn't sure how many times he'd paced the same path, though. He had lost count of that. A hundred? Two hundred? A thousand?

The linoleum floor was scratched in numerous places. He guessed he wasn't the only one who had paced it back and forth over the years. This room had already seen more anxiety and worry than most rooms saw in a lifetime. If the waiting room were to meet a classroom in a bar, it would say, "You think *you* know what apprehension is? Let me tell you . . ."

He lost his train of thought, the comical spiral of associations that usually swam through his mind fading into nothingness.

He had seen one glimpse of Zoe before a nurse had shoved him out of the emergency room. Her neck and torso had been drenched in blood, her face bruised and pale. Just that one glimpse had sent his heart into a flurry. The nurse had promised they'd let him know what her situation was as soon as possible.

And yet he had paced this room over and over, and no one had called him.

Martinez had been with him for about ten minutes before leaving. He said he'd come back later. He wanted to get the taxi driver's statement and to see what the forensic technician had recovered from the crime scene.

The small, intense woman had seemed so helpless on that table. Unable to shout at him or contradict him in any way. His fists clenched, the desire to punch something overwhelming. Back in LA, he'd had a punching bag at home and would use it to relieve his work stress almost every evening. But he hadn't had the time to hang one in his new apartment. How he missed that punching bag right now.

Not knowing what had happened was terrible. He had seen that with people over the years, begging him for a shred of information, asking a flood of questions that could easily be summarized into one word—*why?* What had she been doing in the Saganashkee Slough? Who had attacked her? Where was her attacker now?

Why?

She had seemed so subdued and worried earlier. At the time, he had thought it was only tiredness. But now he wasn't sure.

He sat down and tried to empty his mind of the questions. He wasn't much for praying, but whenever someone close to him was in danger, he found himself trying to cut deals with God. That was why he had stopped smoking three years before, when his partner had been shot—he had promised God he would if his partner lived through it. That was also why he hadn't sold his brand-new Toyota Camry and given the money to the church: God hadn't helped his mother overcome her kidney failure.

And now it was time to cut another deal with God. He tried to think what he could give God in return for Zoe's life.

God, if Zoe—

"Tatum Gray?"

He whirled, looking intently at the nurse approaching him. Was there a comforting look in her eye? Worry? Motherly affection?

No. Just calm. He didn't know what that meant.

"She's in recovery, and she'll be fine," the nurse said.

Tatum let out a shuddering breath. "Can I see her?"

"Are you related?"

"No," Tatum said, and as an afterthought, he pulled out his badge and flipped it. "FBI. She has some crucial information we need as soon as possible."

The nurse pursed her lips. She wasn't buying it. "Fine," she finally said, her voice a tad colder. "You'll be able to see her for a few minutes. I'll come and get you once she's ready."

Tatum nodded, full of relief.

The nurse left, and Tatum sat down on an empty chair, pressing his palms together. He let out a long breath. And another one.

There was a rustle as someone sat by his side and offered him a paper cup.

"Here," Martinez said. "Coffee."

Tatum gratefully took the warm cup. "Thanks. The nurse just told me Zoe's fine."

"Oh, good," Martinez said, relief in his voice.

"What did the cab driver say?"

"She asked him to take her to Saganashkee Slough, told him where to stop," Martinez said. "Got out, told him she'd be back in half an hour, and went for a stroll on the shore. A few minutes later, a car stopped ahead of him, and a man stepped out of it."

"Did he say what the man looked like?"

"Very vague description. They're working with him in the station right now. He actually tried not to look too hard; he figured Zoe was there to meet the guy for a fling."

Tatum nodded. Of course.

"Anyway, he waited there. After a while he saw the man coming back. Limping. The cab driver called to him, but the man didn't answer.

Got in his car and drove off. The driver got worried, went to look for Zoe, and found her unconscious a few hundred yards from the road. Which is when he called the ambulance and the police."

"Did he give a description of the car?"

"A white Toyota Prius," Martinez said. "Didn't see the license plate number."

"Anything from the crime scene?"

"We found the knife and some blood. There was a trail of blood to where the guy's car was parked, so looks like Zoe cut him as well."

Tatum nodded.

"Listen, Agent . . . I've asked you this before. Why did she go there?"

"I don't know," Tatum said tiredly. "I swear I don't."

"She didn't talk to you about it before?"

"No."

"Didn't mention the Saganashkee Slough?"

"No."

"Tatum Gray?" The nurse approached him again. "Please follow me."

Tatum got up, and Martinez followed suit.

"I'm sorry," the nurse said to Martinez. "Only—"

He flipped his badge. "Chicago PD," he said. "I need to speak to—"

The nurse rolled her eyes. "Fine. Follow me."

She led them down a small hallway and into a small white room. Zoe was lying on a hospital bed, looking groggy. Tatum's fingers clenched as he took in the bandage on her neck, the black eye and purple bruise on her forehead.

"Agent Gray," she said, her voice sluggish. "Lieutenant Martinez . . ."

For a second, Tatum thought she was going to say thanks for visiting her. Or reassure them that she was okay.

"Rod Glover," she said. "That's his name."

He blinked. It took his brain a moment to process it.

"That's the name of the man who attacked you?" Martinez asked, his voice sharp.

"Yes. He followed me from the station."

Her voice was raspy, as if it was hard for her to talk. There were bruises alongside her neck, where the bandage didn't hide them. She had been strangled.

"Who is Rod Glover?" Martinez asked.

"He's a serial killer. I think he's the man who is embalming those women."

"How do you know him?"

She remained silent for a moment, her eyes shutting slowly. "He killed three women in Maynard. Long ago."

"In 1997," Tatum said, feeling sick.

"That's right."

Martinez looked at him. "So you *did* know?"

"I . . ." Tatum hesitated. He wasn't sure what he knew. "I think she tried to tell me about it."

"Why did you go to Saganashkee Slough?" Martinez asked.

"Because I wanted to see where Pamela Vance had been killed."

"Who is Pamela Vance?" Martinez and Tatum asked, almost in sync.

"Another victim." She was clearly losing focus, her eyelids fluttering.

"Okay." The nurse barged in. "That's enough. You can talk to her again tomorrow morning."

Tatum shuffled out of the room, dragging his feet as if they were attached to cartloads of rocks. She had told him about Glover, and he had brushed it off. He had discounted her one time too many, and she had gone to check it out by herself. And it had nearly gotten her killed. His fault.

"Agent Gray," Martinez said behind him, his voice sharp, cold.

He stopped and turned around. "Yeah?"

"You said you knew nothing about this."

"I didn't know . . . she started telling me about it. A serial killer who murdered three young women in the town where she grew up. And I wouldn't listen."

"And she didn't tell us," Martinez said. "And she got hurt."

"Yes."

"Tell me what you do know."

Tatum told him what he remembered of his discussion with Zoe, back at the restaurant. It wasn't much.

"Okay," Martinez said. "I'll come back tomorrow to question her more thoroughly. And as of right now, you two are no longer part of this case."

"What?" Tatum asked in shock. "But we—"

"You're running an investigation on your own. Like I thought you would. Dr. Bentley endangered herself, and it was partly because you didn't share all the information earlier."

"Hang on—"

"We're done here, Agent. We'll talk again tomorrow."

CHAPTER 56

Quantico, Virginia, Monday, July 25, 2016

Zoe couldn't remember Mancuso ever looking as furious as she did when they walked into her office on Monday morning. The unit chief breathed steadily, inhaling through her nose and exhaling slowly, while looking at them both, saying nothing. Zoe was almost sure Mancuso was silently counting, and she wondered up to what number.

They both sat in front of Mancuso's desk. Tatum sat on the right-hand chair of the condemned, his face a mask of atonement mixed with defiance, a neat trick. Zoe sat to his left, wincing as the stitches in her hip flared in pain. She had a slight concussion and stitches on her neck as well, the wound on her shoulder glued. She also had a huge black eye. Whenever she made a sudden movement, everything would start hurting at once. Last night, just before their flight back from Chicago, a woman had approached her in the airport and handed her a flyer: a shelter for abused women. She had also given Tatum a dirty look, probably assuming he was Zoe's spouse.

"Okay," Mancuso said, her voice controlled and measured. "I just read through the extensive reports you both sent me, as well as the very short, angry email I received from Lieutenant Martinez and the one-line email I got from the Chicago chief of police."

Zoe lowered her eyes, staring at her palms. Her report was a long, dry account of all the ways she'd messed up. Not sharing her suspicions with the police or her partner. Not informing them about the three envelopes left at the crime scenes. Going to check up on a crime scene on her own. Not noticing the tail. Those were the reasons that Glover had managed to disappear completely.

"The Chicago police and the FBI agreed not to say anything to the press about the debacle, because tensions in the populace regarding this killer are high, and we want to give an *impression* of competence."

Tatum cleared his throat, looking as if he were about to say something, but Mancuso raised an eyebrow, projecting infinite menace. He said nothing.

"Of course, both the lieutenant in charge and I are interested in knowing why you withheld crucial information about the case. Neither of your reports explains the reasoning behind this decision."

Zoe squirmed uncomfortably. "I—"

"The tip seemed far fetched at first," Tatum said, his voice even. "Dr. Bentley began telling me about it, but I convinced her that her theory held no merit. In retrospect, I should have involved the Chicago PD."

"Hang on," Zoe said. "That's not—"

"Damn right you should have!" Mancuso thumped her desk, the fish behind her fleeing in horror, desperate to find shelter. "I told you, Agent Gray: this cowboy act of yours won't work in this unit."

Zoe tried to interrupt. "Chief, it was me who—"

"Sorry, Chief," Tatum said, his voice loud enough to drown out Zoe. "I think it's best if I'm removed from this case."

"There *is* no damn case!" she nearly shouted. "The Chicago PD does not want our help anymore. Lieutenant Martinez was very clear about that."

"But we've made so much progress," Zoe blurted. "We can—"

"*You* can remain at home for your sick leave, instead of showing up here," Mancuso said, her dark eyes focusing on Zoe. "After this meeting, I want you to get straight home. If I see you here before next week, I'll fire you."

Zoe's eyes narrowed. The threat was supposed to scare her into submission, but instead, it just made her angry. "Chief, Rod Glover is—"

"I don't want to hear it right now," Mancuso said. She sat down wearily, spent. "Get out of here, both of you."

Tatum stood up and left.

Zoe hesitated, then said, "Agent Gray didn't—"

"I'm not blind, Zoe," Mancuso said, her voice low. "I know what just happened here, and I know what Gray did and didn't do. Now get out."

She left, closing the door behind her. She ran after Tatum, her stitches screaming in protest as she did so. "Tatum."

He turned around and smiled weakly at her. "Well, that wasn't so bad."

"Why did you tell her it was your fault?" Zoe asked, furious. "I'm the one who went to the crime scene alone, and I'm the one who didn't tell Martinez anything. It was my fault."

"Yeah, it was," Tatum said, folding his hands. "So what?"

Zoe stared at him. She had actually expected him to argue a bit. Still, it really was her fault. "You're already known as a problematic agent. What if—"

"I'm a problematic agent with some nice commendations in his file," he said. "You're a civilian consultant, taking a position many think should be given to an agent. Who do you think has a better chance of being fired?"

"Mancuso wouldn't—"

"Mancuso is under a huge amount of pressure," Tatum said. "I don't know what she would or wouldn't do. Anyway, you tried to tell me. I should have listened. Though, damn it, I wish you'd tried harder."

"Yeah," Zoe said. Her head was beginning to hurt. Her shoulders slumped. "I think I'll go home."

"Do you need a ride?"

"No, thanks. I'll just get a cab."

An invisible weight dragged Zoe down as she walked into her apartment. She closed the door behind her and then simply gazed at it for several seconds, her mind blank. She wasn't sure what she planned to do for the rest of the day or even for the next ten minutes. In fact, the last seventy-two hours had been mostly made up of small actions, one following the next. It had been easy, since most of the time she'd had doctors or nurses to tell her where to go, when to eat, and when to sleep. Later, it was Tatum who had gently guided her to the airport and the plane. And that morning, she'd gone back to work because . . . what else was there to do?

But Mancuso had made things clear. She didn't want Zoe in the office that week. Zoe didn't know if it was really because she had sick leave or because Mancuso hoped people would forget about the Chicago debacle. Was Tatum right? Would Mancuso really fire her? There would be a certain closure to it. Rod Glover was the one who'd made Zoe turn to forensic psychology, and he would be the one to terminate her short-lived career at it. It made her sick to think how much control the twisted bastard had over her life.

Come to think of it, it literally made her sick. She stumbled to the bathroom and threw up what little food she had in her stomach. Then, seeing as she was already in the bathroom, she figured she might as well shower. She had showered when she'd gotten home in the middle of the night, then again in the morning before work, but another shower wouldn't hurt.

She took off her clothes, discarding them in the corner of the room, and turned on the water, setting the temperature to something just below boiling lava. The current felt good as it washed over her back and neck, though it stung as it hit her cut shoulder. She grabbed the soap and began a thorough cleansing of her body.

After a minute, she realized she was scrubbing the same areas over and over again. Her lower stomach, her upper left thigh.

She could still feel Glover's fingers pawing there, struggling with her zipper, his palm sliding for a second into her pants, scraping her thigh. She took a deep breath, trying to calm her rushing pulse. She was a psychologist, and she knew the symptoms as they hit her. Just a brief moment of anxiety. There was no need to lose her cool over this. She put the soap away. Shampooed her hair, wincing as her hand brushed against the bruise on her forehead. Then, after washing her hair, she stared at the tiles in the shower, taking deep breaths.

When Andrea swung the bathroom door open half an hour later, Zoe was still in the shower, sitting on the floor sobbing, the water running. Andrea rushed to her side, turned off the water. Then she wavered helplessly, finally getting Zoe's towel.

"Come on," she said, helping Zoe get up. She wrapped Zoe in the towel and began rubbing it against her.

"I can dry myself," Zoe spat angrily. Andrea took a step back and waited.

"Would you mind waiting outside?" Zoe asked. It irked her that her sister had that worried look on her face.

"Tell you what," Andrea said. "Why don't you go lie down while I make some lunch?"

"Fine."

She wiped her feet on the shower rug, then walked to her bedroom, closing the door behind her. She was furious at herself, letting Andrea find her like that. She finished toweling her body and then lay on the bed, dragging the blanket over her. She'd get dressed in a minute.

The bed slowly warmed up, and there was a comforting feeling to it. Bedsheets from her apartment in Boston, a place that felt like home. Not like this apartment, in which she had barely spent any time. She had been happy in Boston. Well, maybe not happy exactly, but content. Why had she moved here? She knew no one here, most of the people she worked with resented her, and Andrea hated Dale City, no matter what she claimed. Maybe they could just go back to Boston. She could try to open a private clinic or work in a school.

The bedroom door opened.

"Where do you keep your eggs?" Andrea asked.

"In the fridge."

"There are no eggs there."

"I guess I'm out of eggs, then."

Andrea sighed and closed the door.

Zoe shut her eyes. She could probably just sleep. She hadn't slept during the flight, had had only two or three hours of sleep before going to work. Wasn't that what she was supposed to do? Rest?

Instead she got up, rummaged in her closet, and found a long-sleeved shirt and a pair of sweatpants. The shirt had once been white, but Zoe hadn't been careful when she'd washed it with a red dress, and now it was a washed-out pink. A pair of underwear, no bra, because the hell with that. Then she put on the pants and the shirt and padded out. Andrea was in the kitchen, chopping vegetables for a small salad, an omelet frying on the gas stove.

"I thought I was out of eggs," Zoe muttered.

"You are. I borrowed four eggs from your neighbor. She's really nice."

"I'm not even sure what she looks like," Zoe said, sitting down. "I think I only met her twice."

"Yeah, well . . ." Andrea said. She took the frying pan off the gas and distributed the omelet onto two plates. She handed one to Zoe and put the other across the table for herself.

"Thanks," Zoe said. It looked amazing. Andrea had fried the omelet with basil and sprinkled some cheddar in it. She put a dollop of cream cheese next to it, as well as a nice portion of the salad.

"You should buy olive oil," Andrea said. "It would really improve the salad."

Zoe cut a piece of omelet and speared it on the fork. She added some cream cheese and ate it, closing her eyes and breathing through her nose. The hot egg and the cool cheese rolled across her tongue, feeling sublime.

"Hahtishsho good," she said, her mouth full.

"When did you last eat a normal meal?" Andrea asked.

She'd hardly eaten anything for breakfast and had had something tasteless in the airport, and before that, it had been two days of hospital food. "A long time ago."

"Next time you feel like crying in the shower, maybe grab a bite first," Andrea suggested.

Zoe teared up.

"I'm sorry," Andrea blurted. "I was just kidding. You can cry. Oh, damn it, just ignore me and my stupid mouth."

Zoe ate another bite of the omelet quickly, the taste mixing with the tears in her throat. She stabbed some vegetables, and they followed the omelet. Slowly, she got control back. Andrea was focusing on her plate, saying nothing. Zoe cleared her throat.

"There's soda in the fridge," she said. "Would you mind getting it for me?"

Her body ached, and she knew asking Andrea for help would calm her sister down. Win-win. Andrea bounded off her chair and hurried to get Zoe the soda.

She drank gratefully, then had another bite from the omelet. Life was beginning to look up. The hopelessness from earlier was gone—or at least much faded. Thank God for food.

"If you want to talk about what happened in Chicago, you know you can tell me," Andrea said.

Her sister had picked her up from the airport and had nearly fainted when she'd seen the shape Zoe was in. Zoe had shaken her head when she'd asked her what had happened and had said she couldn't talk about it. It was true, though not because it was confidential. Simply because it had been too raw to talk about.

But now, after resting a bit, she thought it might help to talk to Andrea about it. The envelopes Glover had sent her all these years, his recent victims, their encounter, his fingers on her body as she clutched at her throat, desperate for air . . .

But Andrea had her own memories. Talking about it might help Zoe, but she had no idea what it would do to Andrea.

"Thanks," she said. "It's fine . . . I was just in the wrong place at the wrong time. I promise you that it won't happen again."

"Okay," Andrea said, looking unconvinced.

They ate the rest of the meal. Andrea talked most of the time about troubles at work. Her shift manager was apparently a bitch and hated Andrea. Zoe wondered how bitches who hated Andrea always seemed to pop up wherever Andrea went. It was almost as if Andrea had something to do with it.

Finally, Zoe pushed away the plate. "That was an amazing meal."

"I have a special dessert for you." Andrea grinned.

"Oh, thanks. I think I'm full."

"Really?" Andrea looked at her in mock disappointment. "I guess I'll have to finish up the Snickers ice cream all by myself."

Zoe felt a surge of love for her sister. "You know what," she said. "I might be able to stuff another bite down."

CHAPTER 57

Tatum sat in his car, frozen by indecision. He knew he should probably go home, but he wasn't sure it was habitable yet. He had arrived the night before, taken one look at the living room and bedroom, and left, locking the door behind him. He had slept in his car, which was totally fine by him. People underestimated the joy of car camping. The throbbing neck, the freezing cold around four a.m., waking up when the homeless guy knocked on your window . . . good times, good times.

He had called Marvin in the morning and yelled at him for several minutes, the old man listening patiently to his enraged grandson. His grandfather had apparently slept at a friend's house and was in a cheerful mood. Finally, when Tatum had run out of words and rage, Marvin had promised to send someone to clean the place up. After seeing the ungodly things that had been done to his couch, Tatum was pretty sure they would need a flamethrower and an exorcist to really get the job done. Come to think of it, an exorcist with a flamethrower would make an awesome movie. They'd call it *Burn, Demon, Burn.* The exorcist would be played by Dominic Purcell; that was nonnegotiable.

He sighed, focusing. The real reason he wasn't home was that he was worried. He had spent a whole week with Zoe, and though the psychologist could be incredibly frustrating, he'd developed a taste for her company. And there had been something . . . *off* about her ever since the incident. He scrolled through his contacts, located her name, and called her.

She answered after three rings.

"Hello?"

"Zoe, it's Tatum."

"Yeah, I know. I have you in my contact list."

"Right. Uh . . . I wanted to ask how you are."

"I'm fine."

"How's your hip? Are the stitches—"

"I'm fine, Tatum. Thank you for calling."

"Wait." He drummed on the steering wheel in frustration. "Listen, I was hoping I could drop by."

"Why?"

"To see that you're okay."

"I just told you I'm okay."

"Look . . . it would let me sleep easier at night, okay?"

There was a moment of silence. "Fine," she said. "I live in the Dale Forest Apartments. It's in—"

"I know where that is," Tatum said, glancing at the sign out the car's window that said **DALE FOREST APARTMENTS**. "I'm nearby. I can be there in five minutes."

"Okay," she said. She gave him her apartment number and hung up.

He patiently waited four minutes. There really was no need for Zoe to know he had already found her address. Then he got out of the car and went over to her apartment.

A young black-haired woman with mesmerizing green eyes opened the door for him.

"Well, hello," she said, smiling, one eyebrow raised. "You must be Tatum."

Her resemblance to Zoe was strong. "And you're Andrea," he said.

"Come in," she said, giving him another top-to-bottom look. Tatum felt very objectified. He was more than a pretty face, damn it.

He walked inside, taking in the small living room. Zoe sat on one of the couches, a brown folder open in her lap. She looked at its contents, frowning, and raised her eyes to meet his as he walked inside. He felt a pang in his heart as he saw her black eye, the purple bruise on her forehead, the black stitches on her neck. Her eyes were bloodshot and tired. Tatum considered himself progressive—"go, girl power" and all that—but seeing her in that state made him want to take her in his arms and hug her. And then annihilate the man who had done this.

The sharp look she gave him clarified that if he tried to hug her, she would bite his face off. He cleared his throat.

"Hey, glad to see you're"—he searched for a happy word—"sitting."

As if to aggravate him, she stood up, wincing as she did so. "Happy you could stop by," she said. "Do you want anything to drink?"

"Uh . . ."

"I'll get you a cup of coffee," Andrea said.

Zoe turned to her sister. "Andrea, I can—"

"You need to sit or lie down," Andrea said, in the same stubborn tone he had been hearing from Zoe all week. It made him smile.

"What?" Zoe asked.

"Nothing," he said innocently.

She sat back down and set the folder on the coffee table, next to a stack of similar folders and some scattered papers.

"What's that?" he asked. "I thought you weren't supposed to be working."

"Well, since we're no longer assigned to the Chicago case, this isn't work," Zoe said. "I guess it's a hobby."

He sat down on the other couch and picked up one of the folders and flipped it open. It was a case file, all the paperwork photocopied. The papers were yellow with age, and the printed crime scene photos had a grainy quality. There was a wide shot of a nude female body, lying in what looked like a pond. The victim's name was Jackie Teller.

"Is this one of Rod Glover's victims?" he asked, scanning the details.

"That depends on who you ask," Zoe said. "It's one of the three Maynard serial killer victims from 1997. If you ask the police, they'll either say it's unresolved or claim a teenager named Manny Anderson killed her. Which is easy to say, because he's dead."

Tatum nodded and checked out the rest of the files. He glanced at Zoe. "You got copies of the Chicago murders?"

"Yeah."

Andrea walked into the living room as Tatum was reading another of the Maynard case files. She handed him a cup of coffee.

"Okay," she said. "I'm going. I have a shift tonight. I'll come back once I'm off."

Zoe glanced at her. "You don't need to—"

"I'm sleeping here. You might need me. This is not a discussion," Andrea said. "Bye, Tatum. It was nice meeting you."

She closed the door loudly behind her.

Tatum put down the folder and looked at the papers scattered on the table. They were handwritten; some looked aged, some fresh. He leaned forward to get one of them. Zoe nearly leaped at the pages, slapping her hand down onto them.

"That's private," she said.

"Is it?" Tatum asked calmly. He suspected he knew what these were. "I saw you writing down notes when you were doing the profile for the Chicago killer. That page over there looks suspiciously like those notes."

"I composed the profile into a report," she said sharply.

"You did." He nodded. "But this is the raw material."

"So?"

"I want to see it," he said.

"No."

He sighed. "Zoe, we were tracking this guy together. The only reason everything went to shit is that you didn't tell me everything."

Her mouth tightened into a line so thin it was nearly two dimensional.

"Listen," he said, his voice softening. "I admit I didn't really have a lot of faith in your . . . profession. But watching you work this past week opened my eyes. You're the real thing. You can read a crime scene in a way I would never be able to."

Her face softened, her eyes widening.

"But even you can make mistakes," he said. "Can you please share your notes with me? We can talk them over. I promise you I won't tell anyone about these notes, okay?"

She hesitated for a moment, then took her hand off the pages. "This is the Chicago serial killer." She pointed at three pages. "And those"—she pointed at the rest of the pages, some of them yellowed or crumpled—"are the notes for the profile I wrote for Rod Glover. Over the years."

He thumbed through the old pages until he reached the one that seemed most ancient. It was written on a page ripped from a spiral notebook. Her handwriting was more circular on that page, and there were doodles of cats on the bottom.

He scanned it. Some sentences were underlined several times, like *Lied about fire and about meeting Sarah Michelle Gellar.* She had circled the words *Durant Pond* several times. And one of the bottom lines was *Gray Ties!!!!!*

"That's what I wrote when I was fourteen," Zoe said. She looked uncomfortable, like a person whose secret poems were being read by someone else for the first time. "I keep it mostly . . . for sentimental value."

"Remembering the good ole innocent days when you chased serial killers?"

"This was a mistake. Give that back—"

"Sorry," he said hurriedly. "I didn't mean to be sarcastic. I'm sorry."

She was letting him in, allowing him to read what was tantamount to a journal. This was no time for idiotic jokes. He began reading the other pages, confusion sinking in.

"I don't get it," he said. "You wrote these for Rod Glover. Some are more than ten years old. But I see you mentioning envelopes with ties, so how is that—"

She stood up abruptly and walked off. "Wait here," she said, not looking back. He heard her walking into another room and then something like a drawer being opened. She returned, holding a stack of brown envelopes. She dropped them on the table. Two slid onto the floor, and he picked them up. He opened one of them and looked inside.

A gray tie.

He checked two more. All had gray ties in them. Some of the envelopes seemed very old; some were newer. They had all been sent by mail, one to Maynard, several to Harvard, then to two different addresses in Boston. The top one, one of the two that had fallen to the floor, was addressed to the Dale Forest Apartments. All had Zoe's name on them.

"There are eleven envelopes here," Tatum said, dumbfounded.

"He sent fourteen," she said, her voice firm, challenging. "I gave the first one to the cops at Maynard. They did nothing with it. When I started working for the FBI, I gave one to the agent in charge. She nearly stopped working with me because she thought I was obsessed with some teenage memory. I burned the third one. Then I began collecting them. I tried several times to check them for fingerprints and DNA. There was nothing."

"And every envelope has a gray tie?" he asked.

"Yes," she said sharply. Then she added quietly, "Some had drawings as well. Of me, being violated. Glover is a pretty decent artist. I, uh . . . threw them away."

Tatum struggled with the sudden impulse to hug her again.

"You can't tell Mancuso about this," she said. Her voice was cold, toneless, but there was desperation underneath. "I stopped reporting them because no one took me seriously."

He knew Zoe well enough to realize there was nothing she hated more than people not taking her seriously.

"Okay," he said slowly. "So . . . Rod Glover seems to be obsessed with you. Why?"

"The very short version is that I suspected him, broke into his house, found the stash of mementos he had, and reported him to the police," Zoe said.

"I would be happy to hear the long version in a few minutes, but if that's the case, why didn't they arrest him?"

"They didn't believe me," she said, her mouth twisting in anger. "They thought I was just hysterical about his porn stash. And they had a suspect. And Glover had a tight alibi for the last murder."

"How tight?"

"Very. He was part of the search party that went looking for the third victim at the exact time she had been killed. My dad saw him there several times. Other people as well. I talked to several of them."

"And how do you explain it?"

"I don't know." Zoe shrugged helplessly. "Maybe there was another murderer. Maybe he sneaked away from the search party, killed her, and came back. If the police had looked into it, they would have figured it out."

"All right," Tatum said. "Now I want the full story, not the one-line abstract. How do you know Rod Glover, and what exactly happened in Chicago?"

She told him everything, and he listened in disbelief as she described how, as a fourteen-year-old girl, she had gotten herself involved with this serial killer. It was almost surreal . . . yet it made sense with this woman. She outlined what had happened just before the attack in Chicago. He nodded.

"Okay," Tatum said. "One more question: Why do you think Rod Glover is the person who killed and embalmed those women in Chicago?"

"What?" She looked at him in shock.

"I mean, I get the superficial reasons. He left those ties at the body-dumping locations. He followed you. He tried to rape and kill you. But there's nothing to connect the embalming to Rod Glover. The signatures in the last killings are very different—"

"Serial killers change their signature all the time."

"Come on! Sure, they change it a bit, try new things, but nothing so radical."

"All the killings had something to do with water—"

"No, they didn't," Tatum said. "Glover's victims were *in* the water. The Chicago killer posed the victims *near* water. And Veronika Murray, the earliest victim of the embalming serial killer, wasn't close to water when they found her."

"Maybe I was wrong about her. She hadn't been embalmed."

"You weren't wrong. This killer doesn't care about water. He picked those locations because they were abandoned at night and because they fit the poses he gave the bodies."

"I'm right," she said. "Rod Glover is the killer of all these women."

"Look at your initial profile." Tatum tapped the paper violently with his finger. "Remember this? Methodic? Obsession for control? Does this really fit your Maynard serial killer, who simply grabbed women who were wandering around in a remote location, raped them brutally, killed them, and left them in the same location?"

She stared at him angrily, and he looked back at her, challenging. Neither averted their gazes.

"Here's what I think," he finally said. "Rod Glover probably did kill those two women back in 2008. Hell, he admitted to killing one of them, with no prompting from you, right? But other than that, he's messing with your head. He went to all those sites to leave those envelopes for you after seeing you in the news. He decided to follow you around, maybe hoping to get you in some alley. And to his delight, you went straight to one of his favorite locations, where he had already killed Pamela Vance. This guy who is killing women and embalming them . . . I think he's someone else."

"You're wrong," Zoe said.

"Why?"

"Because my gut says you are," she said sharply. "Yeah, sure. I'm good at what I do. But it's not all experience and deduction. It has a lot to do with instincts, and my instincts say it was Glover."

"And I'm telling you that your instincts can't be trusted when it comes to that psycho. He's got an obsession with you—there's no doubt about it. But you know what, Zoe? You're just as obsessed about him."

"Go to hell."

He looked at her, saying nothing. There was nothing but fury in her eyes, the anger underscored by the blue bruise that circled one of them.

Finally, he sighed. "It's late," he said. "Get some rest, okay?"

She hardly moved as he got up to leave. He opened the front door and took a final look at her. Then he walked out and closed the door behind him.

CHAPTER 58

The idea popped into his mind as he was driving past another corner. A row of dead, empty eyes followed his car as he slowed down, voices calling out to him, offering unattractive short pastimes for little money. He no longer saw the potential in any of those women. He now knew them for what they were: conniving, lying bitches, ready to stab him in the back as soon as he looked away.

His foot pressed the gas pedal, and he drove away, gritting his teeth in anger. They didn't deserve his treatment, his eternal offer, his affection.

He needed something else.

He parked his car near a club. A line of teenagers stood outside, waiting to be let in. He stared at the young girls. Was this what he needed? Had his problem been the women's age? After all, these young girls were still innocent. Some had probably never been with a man before. He gripped the wheel tightly, looking at one of the girls. No visible tattoos, barely any makeup compared to her friends, her skin smooth.

He had already begun concocting a plan. He would wait outside until they left the club and follow her from afar. Either he'd get an opportunity to grab her tonight, or he'd find out where she lived.

And if not her, there were others. Thousands and thousands of innocent young girls who were only looking for a grown man to—

Her friend pointed straight at him, and she turned to look. Their eyes locked, and after a second, he gave her a bashful smile.

She flipped him the finger, her face twisted in contempt. Panicking, he quickly hit the gas pedal, lurching into the traffic. A car honked at him and swerved to avoid collision. His heart thrummed in his chest.

Innocent. Right. Damn whores.

Maybe there wasn't such a thing as real love. Maybe he had been wrong. Woman after woman, they had all disappointed him. Perhaps he should just take them for one night or two, silence them, and enjoy their company before the smell became a problem.

The idea was attractive, but he fought it. He was better than this. He wasn't one of those sad, empty people, swiping left and right on their dating apps, looking for a one-night release.

He was searching for something real. Something that would fill the void, dispel the loneliness.

It was then that it came to him. He was thinking about it all wrong. He was looking for a woman to be his companion for years to come. But a woman couldn't really be enough. After watching all these happy couples on television and in real life, he should have figured it out long before.

A woman was just another lonely soul, like him. Two lonely people couldn't fill the void for each other. Such a relationship was bound to end in disappointment.

What he really needed was a family.

CHAPTER 59

It was just after ten when Tatum got back to his apartment. He took a deep breath, prayed to the saint of lost apartments, and opened the door.

The living room was almost its former self. One of the couches had a weird new stain, the TV had a three-inch crack in its top-left corner, and two potted plants were mysteriously missing. But other than that, the place was nice and neat, and the unholy horrors Tatum had seen the night before were mostly gone. The fish, the only model citizen in the house, swam in its aquarium, looking pleased. There was a strange item decorating the aquarium floor, and when Tatum came closer, he saw it was a beer bottle. The fish didn't seem to mind, so Tatum left it there.

He checked out his bedroom. The bedsheets were missing, and Tatum hoped someone had burned them. There was a sealed bag, and he could barely discern the shape of his brown shoes inside. He took the bag to the kitchen and threw it into the trash. Freckle sat on the kitchen table, a look of deep disdain in his eyes. Tatum made sure he had food and water. He tried to pet the cat, who morphed from calm feline into crazed scratch monster in less than a nanosecond. Tatum withdrew his newly bleeding hand.

"Asshole," he said.

Freckle hissed at him and lay down, content to plot his evil plans undisturbed.

Tatum walked over to Marvin's bedroom and knocked on the door.

"Hey, Marvin?" he said.

His grandfather opened the door and grinned. "Welcome back," he said.

"Thanks for cleaning up the place," Tatum said.

"I didn't clean it up. Are you insane? Did you see how it looked? I hired a nice woman to do it."

"Well . . . that's almost as thoughtful, so thanks."

"Sure, sure. You want some tea?"

Tatum nodded and followed his grandfather to the kitchen. Marvin stopped at the doorway, looking at Freckle, who stared back, narrowing his eyes.

"Get out, Freckle," Tatum snapped, still annoyed about his scratched hand.

The cat stood up, stretched, bounced off the table, and walked out of the kitchen slowly, radiating contempt.

"There's something very wrong about that cat," Marvin said, getting two mugs from the cupboard.

"True," Tatum said. "I noticed the fish was fine."

"Yeah." Marvin nodded. "I think it's happy in its new home. So how was Chicago?"

"Not so good. I kinda messed things up."

"That's some nasty killer they have there. I read about it in the paper. Is he the one you were investigating?"

"That's the one."

"I also read that they sent a cute woman with you."

"Did the paper say she was cute?"

"No, but there was a picture of you two at one of the crime scenes, and I determined with my own two eyes that she's cute. Was she any good?"

Tatum shot the old man a look and realized to his relief that it was an innocent question. Marvin was referring to her profiling abilities. "She's . . . incredible, really."

"Then why didn't you catch the guy?"

"We got distracted," Tatum said. "There was another serial killer . . . or maybe he's the same guy. We're not sure yet."

"Is there a serial killer convention in Chicago?"

"Sounds like it, huh?" Tatum sat at the kitchen table.

Marvin put a steaming mug on the table in front of him, then sat on the other side, drinking from his own mug. "So," he said, "are you going to catch the guy?"

"The police will probably catch him," Tatum said distractedly, frowning. He was thinking over the story Zoe had told him about the Maynard serial killings.

"There's a place called Maynard," he said.

"Sounds like some kind of sauce."

"No, it's a town. In Massachusetts."

"Never heard of it."

"Not surprising. It's a small town."

"Like Wickenburg?" Marvin asked. There was distaste in his tone

"Yeah, I guess. Maybe just a bit larger. I thought you liked Wickenburg."

"Bah. At first it seemed wonderful. A peaceful, small town, a place where everyone knows everyone and people say hello to each other in the street. Sounds ideal, huh?"

"I don't know about ideal, but it sounds nice, I guess."

"The thing you have to understand, Tatum, is that when everyone in town knows each other, everyone also has an opinion about each other. And those opinions stick and sometimes spread. You get into one small argument with your neighbor, everyone knows about it. If your kid gets into a fight in school, it's suddenly everyone's business. And these things don't go away—they accumulate. I was Marvin Gray when I got there, and by the time I left, I was Marvin Shouted-at-the-Town-Meeting-That-One-Time-and-Always-Argues-with-the-School-Principal Gray."

"That's a long name," Tatum said. "Was Dad such a problematic kid that you had to argue with the principal?"

"He was a teenager. Occasionally, he was a bit stubborn. And he could never keep his mouth shut." Marvin grinned, like he always did when talking about Tatum's dad. "He was a good kid. But everyone formed their opinions about him. Never gave him a real chance when he grew up."

"Guilty until proven innocent, huh?" Tatum said slowly, sipping his tea.

"That's right."

Tatum stared at the mug in his hand. "I might have to go away for a day or two," he said. "This time, don't trash the house, please."

CHAPTER 60

Maynard, Massachusetts, Wednesday, July 27, 2016

Nathan Price, the Maynard chief of police, was a gray-haired man with a weathered, ruddy face. He was wide shouldered and lean, an outline of muscles visible underneath the uniform. He inspected Tatum with an alertness and suspicion that could only come from dozens of years of political struggles. Tatum leaned comfortably in a chair designed to be anything but hospitable and smiled disarmingly. He was tired. The night flight from Washington to Boston had hardly left him any sleep time, but that was the earliest flight he'd been able to get. Mancuso wanted him back next week, and he had little time to waste.

"How can I help you, Agent Gray?" Chief Price asked.

"I'm interested in a few murders that took place in Maynard some time ago," Tatum said.

Chief Price nodded. "I assume you're talking about Beth Hartley, Jackie Teller, and Clara Smith."

Tatum raised an eyebrow. "How did you know?"

"This is a peaceful town, Agent Gray. We don't have that many murders, and I doubt you came to talk to me about the Mill Pond murder back in 1953."

Tatum nodded. "You're right, of course. I wanted to ask you a few questions about the so-called Maynard serial killer. I understand you were the officer in charge of the case back then?"

"That's right," Chief Price said. "But we were all deeply involved. As you can imagine, we left no stone unturned when trying to find the killer."

Until you had a suspect. Tatum nodded cordially. "Of course. The murderer was never brought to trial—is that correct?"

"That's correct. Our primary suspect had been arrested a few days after killing Clara Smith and committed suicide while incarcerated."

"And the killings stopped," Tatum said, noticing how easily the chief had said the suspect had killed Clara Smith.

"Well, naturally."

"Can I ask you a few questions about specific details of the case?" Tatum asked, retrieving the three case files he had in his briefcase.

The chief's eyes widened in surprise as he saw Tatum opening the top case file. The picture of Clara Smith's body was on top.

"I . . . of course. I'm not sure if I'll remember. It's been almost twenty years—"

"Well, it was the only murder case you ever investigated," Tatum said. "Surely you remember most of it."

"Probably, yes."

"Okay. So during your main suspect's interrogation, it turned out he was in the library the day Clara Smith was killed."

"Yes," Chief Price said. "I remember."

"Now the estimated time of death as determined by the medical examiner was . . . between six and seven p.m. Manny Anderson was in the library until four."

Chief Price held his hand out, and Tatum gave him the file. The chief scanned it and said, "Yes, that's right."

"But Clara Smith had been missing since two, when she didn't come home from school."

"We don't know she was missing," Chief Price said. "She just didn't return home. She could have gone to a friend's house."

"Her mother called all her friends, and no one knew where she was, right? That's why you organized a search party."

The chief's eyes narrowed. "You talked to a few people about this case," he said.

"I have," Tatum said. "On the phone. But I wanted to see you in person."

"What we think happened," the chief said testily, "is that Clara had a boyfriend her mother didn't know about. She went to see him after school. On her way back home, she was grabbed by force or coerced by Manny Anderson. He took her into a secluded spot where he raped and finally strangled her to death."

"But you never found this supposed boyfriend," Tatum said.

"No."

"So you can't be sure what Clara was doing between the time she left school and the estimated time of death."

"We can't," the chief said. He had shifted to single syllables, a sure sign Tatum was getting on his nerves.

"Okay," Tatum said. "Just one more question and then I'll let you go back to your work. I noticed the medical examiner's report, with the time of death, was dated two days after the murder took place."

"Uh-huh."

"But in the Beth Hartley and Jackie Teller murders, it was dated merely hours after the murder. Is there a reason for the delay?"

"I can't really say," the chief said. "Maybe she was just busy—"

"At a time like this? When all of you 'left no stone unturned'?"

"What does it matter what time she did the paperwork?"

"I agree." Tatum nodded, grinning. "It's just paperwork, right?"

"Right. We had a murder investigation on our hands. Everyone was stressed—"

"Desperate to find a suspect," Tatum said.

The chief twisted his mouth in clear distaste. "Desperate to find a *killer*, Agent Gray."

"That too," Tatum said, standing up. "Thank you for your time, Chief Price."

The chief glowered and stayed silent as Tatum nodded at him and left the office.

CHAPTER 61

Zoe had to admit that her home office had begun to look like the rooms of some of her subjects. Every image from the four crime scenes in Chicago was hanging on the wall, as well as images from the 2008 killings. She had a map of Maynard and a map of Chicago, both marked with the locations of the murders. Various articles from her Maynard serial killer scrapbook spotted the wall as well. She had purchased two whiteboards and filled them with all of the victims, both from Maynard and from Chicago, listing their names, ages, professions, and times and locations of disappearance. She stopped herself before she began tying bits of strings between things that seemed connected.

It was, perhaps, a good time to find a real hobby.

The room had a single bed, for when Andrea decided she wanted to crash at her apartment. Zoe had nodded off on it the night before. She had woken up in the morning surrounded by crime scene photos and case files. After orienting herself, she returned to work, trying to connect the dots, fill in the missing time between 1997 and 2016.

At times she could feel her resolve weakening. She considered grabbing a book or watching something dumb on TV. But then she'd recall Tatum's face when he said he thought she was wrong. It intermingled with memories of her parents telling her she should leave Rod Glover alone and of the cop telling her to leave the detective work to the grown-ups. If any of them had listened to her, Glover would have been incarcerated a long time ago. Lives would have been spared. Tatum should have known better. But all he saw when he looked at her was a civilian taking the place of a real agent.

Knowing she was locking herself into one train of thought, she'd occasionally try to stop thinking of the Chicago serial killer as Rod Glover. She'd try and call him *the killer* in her mind. *When the killer grabbed Krista* or *the killer needed a steady supply of embalming fluid.* But pretty quickly she'd find her thoughts dragged back to *Glover grabbed Krista* and *Glover needed a supply of embalming fluid.*

Her stomach and left thigh chafed. She'd scrubbed them raw in the shower, and they were now inflamed and tender to the touch. But at least she didn't feel as if Glover's fingers were on her anymore. His face still hounded her, the predatory look in his eyes as he approached her by the lake. The voice in her ear as he held the knife to her throat. *On your knees.* These would suddenly flicker into her mind, and she'd lose her train of thought, stand staring at the plethora of evidence, chills running down her spine. And then she'd start over.

She had to do this right.

CHAPTER 62

He could see them through the window, bathed in the soft yellow glow of their kitchen's light. The two children were young; he could just see the tops of their heads through the glass pane, their bodies hidden by the house's wall. One of them, the little girl, bounced excitedly as she talked to her mother.

The mother was a lovely thing to look at, her beauty barely marred after two childbirths. He could already imagine her after his treatment, eternally adoring, with everlasting motherly affection. She was a good mother even now, as her children were scurrying around. Making them dinner as she listened to her daughter's tales of her day.

No father.

He didn't know the whole story, but he knew enough. There was only the mother. He'd been watching them from his car two nights in a row, and he hadn't seen the face of a new boyfriend in sight. The woman was still alone, just like she had been a month before. He could do the treatment in their own house.

He could hardly wait. He considered entering at that very moment but realized he was in the wrong car. All his gear was in the van. He was alternating between his two vehicles in case someone noticed the strange car parked in the street every night. Neighbors could have prying eyes.

No, not tonight. But soon, very soon.

He envisioned their lovely future. Christmas evenings together. For the first time ever, he would have a reason to buy a tree, decorate it, buy the children gifts. When he'd wake up in the morning, they would sit with him around the table as he ate. He could put them to sleep, read them a bedtime story. He would never be like his parents. He would be a good father.

And he wouldn't have to suffer through the pain of watching his kids grow up, become strangers, leave his home to raise families of their own. No, these kids would stay with him and love him forever. Alongside their mother.

One woman, a boy, and a girl. A family, ready to be his.

Forever.

CHAPTER 63

Maynard's Summer Street was quite charming, countless trees casting their shade on the narrow road. Large yards dotted the street, most of them trimmed with care. Tatum got out of his rental and stood in the sun for several moments, enjoying the tranquility that the place offered. Finally, feeling he had dawdled enough, he went up the driveway of the house he had parked near. It was a white house with an orange tiled roof, two windows, and a door in the middle. It was the kind of house Tatum used to draw as a child. It was easy, really. A blue pencil to color the top of the page—that was the sky—then a green pencil to color in grass at the bottom of the page. A square in the middle of the grass and a triangle on top. Two squares for windows and a rectangular door. Add flowers according to your mood and the colors at your disposal. Oh, and a yellow quarter of a circle on the top left part of the page. That was the sun. This house was almost as symmetrical as Tatum's drawings, though a bit larger, and some small trees decorated the grass.

He knocked on the door. A few minutes later, an old, gray-haired woman with pearl earrings and a kind smile opened the door.

"Yes?" she said.

"Dr. Foster?" Tatum asked.

"That's right."

He flipped his badge. "I'm Agent Gray from the Federal Bureau of Investigation. Would you mind if I asked you a few questions?"

"Oh." Her eyes widened. This woman, he decided, had never seen an FBI agent outside her television set before. "What about? Is everything all right?"

"Yes, just a follow-up on an old case."

"Okay. Do you want lemonade? I just made some."

Drinking lemonade was something that would definitely diminish his intimidation factor. But he didn't feel like intimidating this nice lady, anyway. And lemonade sounded wonderful.

"I'd love some," he said, smiling.

She led him to a back porch, where two plastic chairs stood by a small table. He sat down in one of the chairs while she went inside. He glanced at the time. He had a few hours before his return flight. He was cutting things close. Living on the edge.

Dr. Foster came out a moment later with a pitcher of lemonade and two glasses.

"Cookies?" she asked as she set the jar on the plastic table.

The line had to be drawn somewhere. "No, thank you."

She sat down and poured the lemonade. "How can I help you?"

"I'm following up on the murder of Clara Smith," he said.

"Oh," she said. "That was a long time ago. She was killed by a very disturbed teenager."

"Really?" Tatum sipped from his glass. "I thought no one was ever convicted."

"Only because he killed himself," Foster said. "It's a well-known fact that it was him."

Tatum nearly winced at the word *fact*. If all the people around you said the same thing over and over, it could easily turn from suspicion to fact.

"I wanted to ask you about your time-of-death estimation," he said, pulling out the case file and verifying it was the right one.

"I hope I'll be able to answer. It's been quite a long time."

"Of course. You estimated that Clara Smith died between . . . six and seven p.m."

"If you say so."

"But Chief Price told me that your initial estimation had pegged it as a bit earlier," Tatum said, the lie slipping easily. He smiled and took another sip of the cool lemonade.

"Well, yes. I remember that. I initially thought it had been earlier, but I became convinced I was wrong. It was tricky to estimate. The body had been left in the water on a snowy day. It cooled very quickly."

"Completely understandable." Tatum nodded, his suspicion verified. "So do you remember what your initial assessment was?"

She frowned. "I don't know. Somewhere around noon, I think. Maybe around two p.m."

"But that couldn't be right," Tatum said. "Because Manny Anderson was in the library between one and four p.m. He couldn't have killed her then."

"Well, as I said, I quickly saw I was wrong."

"Not so quickly, Dr. Foster," Tatum said. "It took you two days." He showed her the report.

There was a flicker of something in her eyes. Suspicion, shrewdness. The transformation was uncanny and disappeared as fast as it had appeared.

"I . . . can't really remember. It was a long time ago."

Tatum emptied his glass. "This is really good lemonade," he said. "I have an interesting *fact* for you. During your estimated time of death, a search party was looking for Clara. People were worried after she disappeared, and it was organized quickly. And Clara's real killer was in that search party. But because of your estimation, he had an ironclad alibi."

The color drained from Dr. Foster's face.

"Manny Anderson never killed anyone," Tatum said. "But he was under heavy suspicion. When people are scared, they just want someone to blame. Chief Price—he wasn't chief then, of course—told you that you were wrong, that the time of death couldn't possibly be right. Maybe it took him two days to convince you. Maybe it just took him two days to verify that Manny had no alibi for that evening. Either way, you changed your estimation so Manny could be prosecuted."

"It . . . it was hard to be sure. It was so cold outside . . ."

"Of course," Tatum said.

"And the killings stopped. It had to be the Anderson kid."

Tatum sighed. He almost told her about the killings in Chicago in 2008. The grief Manny Anderson's parents had gone through, losing their only son and then trying for years to prove he was innocent. But he remained silent. His job was to catch killers. Not to upset seventy-year-old women who made good lemonade. She'd made a mistake, but she had been scared and desperate, just like the rest of the town.

"Did you change your time-of-death estimate from two to sometime between six and seven?" he asked.

"Yes," she said weakly.

"And did you know about Manny's alibi at the time?"

"Yes, but—"

"Thank you, Dr. Foster."

CHAPTER 64

Zoe was startled by a firm knock on the door. Andrea coming to check up on her, probably. Her sister didn't hide her concern over Zoe's frame of mind. The only thing that reassured Andrea was that Zoe's sick leave was almost up. Once she was back in the office, Zoe had told Andrea, she would probably stop obsessing about this case she was no longer assigned to. She was far from sure this would actually turn out to be true. She muted the radio and went to the front door. Looking through the peephole, she sighed, then opened the door.

Tatum stood in the doorway. He held a bag in his hand. Zoe felt as if they'd been there before.

"Hi," she said. She didn't intend for her voice to convey any sort of warmness, but to her surprise, it came out as an actual happy-to-see-you voice. Perhaps it was because of the time she spent cooped up alone with her research. It was nice to see another human being who wasn't her worried sister.

"I brought some food," he said. "Not from the 7-Eleven this time."

"Okay," Zoe said. "What is it?"

"Hummus." Tatum grinned.

"What?"

"They opened this Middle Eastern place in Woodbridge. And they make deliveries to Dale City. *And* they include two pitas with each meal."

"You didn't strike me as the Middle Eastern food type of guy," Zoe said, moving aside to let him enter.

"There was a great Middle Eastern place near where I lived in LA," Tatum said, walking inside. He glanced at the coffee table in the living room, and Zoe spotted a flicker of relief on his face. The coffee table was empty, no research files scattered about. What would he say if he walked into her home office right now?

"Come on," she said, leading him to the kitchen. His timing was perfect; she had been about to make something for herself. He put the bag on the table, taking out several small boxes and a plastic container with the pasty beige hummus. Zoe grabbed a bottle of Coke from the fridge and poured two glasses. Then she set the table. The pitas' aroma made her stomach rumble in anticipation, and she flinched, praying Tatum didn't hear it. If he did, his face didn't betray anything.

They sat down, and Zoe put a dollop of the hummus on her plate. She tore off a piece of the pita, dipping it in the hummus thoroughly, and put it in her mouth. It was warm, and the taste—so different from what she was used to—was wholesome and delicious. She closed her eyes and took a deep breath, then allowed herself a small smile.

"Good, huh?" Tatum said. He ate a big piece of pita and sipped from his Coke.

"It's great." She nodded. "You say they deliver to Dale City?"

"Yeah. It really improved the way I feel about living here, I gotta admit."

Zoe prepared herself another piece of pita and hummus. This, at least, was something they could talk about without arguing.

"So," Tatum said. "Guess where I was for the past two days?"

"You weren't here?"

"No."

"Where?"

"You don't want to guess?"

"Not particularly."

"I was in Maynard," Tatum said, sounding like a magician who just announced there was a rabbit in the previously empty hat. It was a tone of voice that anticipated shock or applause.

"Really," Zoe said dryly. She wasn't about to give him any satisfaction, though she was curious.

"The officer who used to be the lead detective on the serial killer case is now the chief of police," Tatum said.

"Uh-huh."

"Yeah. Anyway, you know that alibi that Rod Glover had for the Clara Smith murder? I managed to break it."

This time, Zoe could not help letting the surprise widen her eyes. "How?" she demanded. How could he so easily have done what she'd failed to do for years? Had he located a witness who saw Glover leaving the search party? Perhaps there was a man whose body was similar to Glover's and in the darkness—

"You were focusing on the wrong profile," Tatum said. "You should have been profiling the investigators."

"What do you mean?" Her palms were shaking. She quickly hid them under the table.

"The police were desperate to implicate Manny Anderson," Tatum said. "He had an alibi for Clara's time of death, so they convinced the ME to rethink her estimated time of death."

"And it provided Glover with his alibi," Zoe said, numb with shock.

"That's right."

How could she have missed it? She always looked at every angle, searched for every crack, went through every—

"You couldn't have figured it out," Tatum said softly. "Not when you were fourteen."

He was right. At fourteen, she would never have even considered the possibility that the cops might mess with the evidence to implicate someone. The thought would have been completely alien to her. Though they angered her and she often thought of them as incompetents, it would never have occurred to her, at fourteen, that they might actually hurt their own investigation that way. It would be years before she would learn anything was possible.

But when thinking of the Maynard killings, she was always fourteen years old. Always picking at the same ideas, deepening the grooves the thoughts left in her mind.

"I should have picked up on that," she said, frustrated. "You have no idea how many times I've turned the facts of this case over in my head. It should have been obvious."

"If you could have been detached, it would have," Tatum said. "But you weren't. This is your childhood, Zoe. The killer nearly got you too. He keeps sending you these envelopes, messing with your mind, scaring you—"

"I'm not scared."

"Aren't you? Stalked by this guy for years? What do you really feel when you get an envelope from him? Can you really say it doesn't drag you back all those years?"

She was silent.

"And when these same envelopes came up during our investigation, how did you feel? Were you Zoe the forensic psychologist or Zoe the fourteen-year-old high school student?"

"I was—" She started to answer, then stopped. Thinking back to that moment. Taking the envelopes from the reporter. Feeling the dread sinking in her gut.

Tatum looked at her, his eyes sad and warm, and she wanted to slap him for his understanding. She wanted him to mock her and berate her and tell her she had been wrong. She turned away.

"Damn it," she muttered, her voice choked.

"In case I wasn't clear," Tatum said, "I think you profiled Glover brilliantly all those years ago. And I believe you were brilliant in this case as well. You just made a small mistake."

"Small?" Zoe almost snorted.

"Do you want to give it another try? With what we know now? And without Rod Glover interfering?" Tatum asked. "I mean . . . I know you're resting, but—"

"Come on," Zoe said, standing up. She went to her office room and turned around. She watched Tatum's eyes shift around as he entered the office and took in the new decor.

"Holy crap," he muttered.

Zoe approached the wall and snapped off one of the taped articles. "Help me take these down," she said, removing another one. "I want to clear my mind for this."

CHAPTER 65

Zoe's home office made Tatum feel like he was walking around inside the psychologist's brain, and it was a mess. He helped her remove all the items related to the Maynard serial killer and to the 2008 Chicago killings. Now they were left with five dead women, three of them embalmed. Zoe began reorganizing the images according to a pattern she somehow deemed helpful, while Tatum went to the kitchen to make some coffee. He made the pot extra strong, knowing this was going to be a long night.

He returned with the pot and two mugs and poured each of them some coffee. He handed one of the steaming mugs to Zoe, who thanked him distractedly, staring at the whiteboard. Tatum followed her eyes and cataloged the five faces on it. He had personally seen the bodies of two of the victims—Krista Barker, who had been left on the beach, and Lily Ramos, whom they had managed to contact before she died. Seeing their pictures alongside the three other women tugged at Tatum's emotions. This killer roamed Chicago freely, killing at whim, neither the FBI nor the police managing to stop him. He turned to Zoe, waiting for her to speak. When she didn't, he sighed.

"Okay, listen," he said. "This won't work like that."

"What won't work?" Zoe asked, glancing at him.

"You're locked in your own head. You never try and talk it out."

"Yes, I do. I talk to you all the time."

"*Only* when you know what you want to say," Tatum pointed out. "Then, you're more than happy to lecture me and tell me about your amazing conclusions. But if you're unsure, you just keep working by yourself."

She opened her mouth, her eyes narrowing, then closed it. Tatum folded his arms and waited.

"Fine," she finally spat. "What do you want?"

"Well, you say what you're thinking about, then I contribute my own thoughts on the matter. Maybe I have a different idea. Then, instead of shooting me down, try going along with what I say, even if it's dumb. I call it *brainstorming*."

"Don't patronize me. I know what brainstorming is."

Tatum grinned.

"All right, you start," Zoe challenged him.

"You've been spending the past few days assuming the killer was Glover, but I think we both agree now that it's likely there is another killer out there, right?"

"Yes."

"I think we should start by looking at our existing possible suspects, narrow the pool down. Maybe one of them meets the narrow profile you created."

"I don't think that's the way to—"

Tatum raised an eyebrow. "Don't shoot it down yet," he said. "Roll with me."

"Okay, okay," Zoe grumbled. "So we're looking at people who knew Susan Warner, right? We have an ex-boyfriend, a handicapped uncle, some friends from college . . ." A thought occurred to her. "It could, for example, be Daniella's boyfriend, right? What was his name? Ryan."

Tatum smiled, enjoying the new spark in her eye. "There you go. Does he fit the profile?"

"He's the right age; he has a van. She mentioned that he disappears without telling her where, which might mean he has another place to stay . . . he works as an auto mechanic, which displays a lot of the characteristics we're looking for. He was in Susan's apartment. He is a very likely suspect." She was clearly getting excited.

"That's great." Tatum grinned. "Except he has an alibi."

"What alibi?"

"He was in Venice as an exchange student when all those animals got embalmed and taxidermied."

"Oh, right," Zoe said, slumping, and then she glared at Tatum. "You've already thought of all that."

"Maybe." He looked at her innocently. "Still, it's worth considering other possible suspects, right?"

"I . . . it's not a bad idea."

He laughed, feeling a surge of warmth for the irate psychologist. "What are your thoughts? Want to share?"

Her lips moved a bit, no sound emerging, as if she were trying this new concept of conversation and failing at it. Finally, some words emerged. "The killings are all motivated by his fantasy, right? All four recent killings. We can see an arc of improvement in his implementation, though we don't know what the purpose is yet."

"Right," Tatum agreed. "It looks like he's creating and playing with human dolls."

"Right." She became silent again.

Did she think they were done brainstorming? "What *is* his fantasy, then?" he asked.

"It looks like some sort of power play, except he already had them tied up . . . and he can't have sex with them once he embalms them, and that seems like a loss of power, right?"

"I suppose it is," Tatum said slowly.

"So something else motivates him here. What is it?"

"Maybe he gets turned on by their immobile state and masturbates to it."

"No, that's not it. It doesn't fit," Zoe said impatiently and bit her lip.

Tatum cleared his throat. When this didn't elicit a reaction, he said, "Brainstorming, remember?"

Zoe looked at him and rolled her eyes. "Okay. Let's suppose he is turned on by their immobile state. Why is the flexibility so important? Why does he dress them up in clothes, put jewelry on them? Why not use some other, less complex method of preservation, like freezing them?"

"Okay, maybe he's posing them like a certain image or a situation in his mind," Tatum said.

"Like what?" Zoe asked. She sounded curious. Good sign.

"I don't know. What is he saying in those scenes?"

"What scenes?"

"The last two crime scenes? They're like . . . fragments of a story, right? When you played with dolls as a child, you used to sit Barbie on her chair and put some teacups on the doll table, and voilà, she was having a tea party."

"I never had dolls."

Tatum raised an eyebrow. "Seriously?"

"I suppose I had some, but I've never played with them. I gave them all to Andrea. Did you play with dolls?"

"Well . . . not dolls, but you know. I had a bunch of Playmobil figures, and I'd act out all sorts of stories. For example, they would fight and shoot each other. Then I'd remove their hair and change it around—"

"Why?"

"Because it's pretty much the only detachable thing."

"That's very strange."

"Not as strange as a Playmobil figure without the hair. Their heads are hollow, and they look really freaky, and at a certain point you lose all the hair pieces, so you just have a bunch of lobotomized figures—"

"This isn't helpful," Zoe interjected sharply.

"*Anyway*, the point I was making is that when you pose those dolls, you're acting out your own story, right? So what's the story here?"

They looked at the pictures. Monique Silva standing on the bridge, hands on the rail, staring at the stream. Krista Barker sitting on the beach, face buried in her hands.

"They're sad," Zoe said.

"Yeah, Krista is posed like she's crying."

"Why are they sad?"

"Maybe the killer posed them like that because they're sad they're dead," Tatum suggested.

"No . . ." Zoe said, shaking her head. "They were missing for a while. You're right; there's a whole story here. If they were just sad they're dead, he'd drop them off as soon as he embalmed them. But he spent a long time with them, and in the end, he dropped them, posing them as if they're sad."

"Yeah."

"They're sad," Zoe said ponderously, "because he dropped them off."

"What do you mean?"

"There was a ring on Krista Barker's finger," Zoe said. "An engagement ring."

"Well . . . it was a ring."

"It was an engagement ring. Susan Warner was found wearing an evening dress, as if she were out on a big date. And then, when he leaves them, they're sad."

"Hang on—"

"He's having a relationship with them," Zoe said. Her eyes focused on Tatum, sparkling. "That's what this is all about. He is embalming these women so he can have a relationship with them."

"What, like a sexual relationship?"

"Like a full relationship, Tatum. This isn't about sex. I mean, he has necrophiliac tendencies, sure. But it's about having someone with him, in his home. This is all about loneliness."

"Okay," Tatum said. Her enthusiasm was not infectious, and he felt mostly disturbed. "So what does this mean?"

"Well, the killer would be someone who never had a long, successful relationship," Zoe said. "He's witnessed other people in love and wants the same. But he can't manage it himself—"

"Why?"

"Well, I would imagine his obsession with total control makes a relationship almost impossible. He's also erratic, and it's possible that if the woman is alive, he can't sexually function."

"Okay, so he grabs a woman, strangles her to death . . . why embalm her?"

"Because he wants a lasting relationship."

"That's crazy logic, but fine. And then what? He puts her in his bed? Does he carry her to the dining room table in the morning? Put her in front of the TV with him? Hold her hand?"

Zoe nodded slowly. "Pretty much, yes."

"Okay," Tatum said. He began to feel it. "And then he dumps them . . . why?"

"Because it doesn't work out."

"Come on. Are they having issues?"

"No. But he stops feeling *it*, whatever it is. He gets lonely again. Her presence stops reassuring him. The playacting becomes . . . empty."

A shiver ran up Tatum's spine. "So he looks for another one. That's pretty deranged thinking, Zoe."

She shrugged.

"So how do we use this?" Tatum asked.

"I don't know yet. We know how the story ends, right? The killer presumably breaks up with the woman, leaves her somewhere, poses her as if she's heartbroken."

"Corniest serial killer ever."

"Sure. How does the story begin?"

"Well, he finds a prostitute—"

"That's not the beginning. That's like . . . preparation. He doesn't have full control yet, right? The story starts when he finishes embalming the body."

"Okay. So I guess he takes her home—"

"I'm going to stop you right there, but it's not because I don't appreciate your opinion, okay?" Zoe said, trying to smile encouragingly.

Tatum burst out laughing. "I'm glad to see you don't want to hurt my feelings."

"I just have a . . . knack. I can imagine these things. He finishes embalming her. Now, embalming is a messy business, so I assume he's taken off most of her clothes first. Remember Lily's body? There was blood all over her neck, but her shirt was mostly clean."

"Okay, so he cleans them up and dresses them. He didn't clean Lily up."

"No, he didn't have time, and he was panicking. He wasn't thinking straight. But with the other victims, I think you're right. He cleans them up, dresses them . . ." She stopped, staring at the pictures.

"What is it?"

"He doesn't dress them in their own clothing. He doesn't want to be in a relationship with a prostitute. He would dress them up in new clothing."

"Okay, I guess that makes sense," Tatum said. "So he bought the clothing beforehand . . ."

"Their clothing fits, Tatum. All of them."

"So?"

"How did he know what to buy?"

"They're all thin girls. I mean, he probably—"

"But Krista Barker was much taller than Monique Silva. And Lily wasn't as thin as them. And these aren't cheap one-size-fits-all clothes. With Susan Warner there was no issue—he had her entire wardrobe at his disposal, since he killed her at home. But the prostitutes only had what they were wearing."

"You're saying he took them shopping," Tatum said slowly.

Zoe nodded. "Before he killed them, when they still thought he was a client. He probably told them he wanted to dress them up nicely for their night. And then he took them somewhere—"

"A shopping mall."

"Probably."

"All right." Tatum smiled. He sat down at her laptop and opened the browser.

"What are you doing?"

"We know where he picked up Lily, right? At the corner of Clark and Grand, at River North." He opened up Google Maps and found it.

"Yeah."

"And we know he took Lily to Huron Street, somewhere . . . here." Tatum pointed at a segment of Huron Street on the map. "He would have taken Lily somewhere in the route between those two locations, right? Either that or a place near where he killed her."

"You can't be sure," Zoe said. "He may have a shop he prefers. Somewhere that's halfway across Chicago."

"That's true. But I can guess, right? If it's halfway across Chicago, we have nothing. But if it's on this route . . . we have a finite number of malls."

"It's still a large number," Zoe said, but Tatum could hear she was excited by the idea. "But if you're right, he'd probably pick somewhere close to where he killed her."

"Why?"

"Well, I assume that's where he embalms his victims. He'd be tense and would prefer a place he knew well. Somewhere he had visited several times before. Somewhere he'd feel he has more control."

"You think he always went to the same mall?"

"I think it's probable, yeah."

"All right." Tatum grinned. "Then let's make a list."

"And then what?"

"And then we fly back to Chicago and check out security cam feeds in those malls for the evening Lily was taken. Maybe we can spot her and the Corny Serial Killer."

"What? You can't be serious."

Tatum shrugged, already writing down addresses. "You're still on sick leave. I'm on vacation until next week. Do you have anywhere better to be?"

CHAPTER 66

Chicago, Illinois, Friday, July 29, 2016

Zoe was never much for shopping, and it occurred to her that perhaps Andrea would have been a better fit for this investigation. Andrea could walk in and out of clothing shops all day for *fun*. This was their fifth clothing shop, and Zoe felt like she was in the tenth circle of clothing hell.

It didn't help that their investigation was incredibly threadbare and groundless. In one of the stores they had visited, the security footage had already been destroyed, and in another, the manager refused to hand it over, demanding a search warrant. Even if the Corny Serial Killer, as Tatum began calling him, had gone to one of the stores on their list, they might miss him.

Tatum was arguing with another store manager, who was also refusing to show them the security footage, while Zoe walked around the store, feeling despondent. This store was one of the larger ones, catering to men, women, and children. It was lit by dozens of spotlights, illuminating rows upon rows of skirts, pants, shirts, dresses . . . Zoe tried to picture the Corny Serial Killer entering this shop and choosing something. It was an impossible sequence of events. He probably let the prostitute choose, while he waited alongside the other impatient husbands and boyfriends. Then again, it wasn't likely he'd give the prostitute such a large measure of control. Maybe she had gotten it all wrong. Maybe he hadn't gone shopping with—

Her eye caught one of the mannequins. It was wearing the shirt Lily had been wearing when they'd found her.

She walked slowly toward the mannequin, almost as if she was afraid to spook the thing away. It was a realistic-looking mannequin, one of the most lifelike mannequins Zoe had ever seen, sculpted and painted to look like a stunningly proportioned woman, frozen in time, a vacant plastic stare looking directly at Zoe. The plastic face gave Zoe an eerie feeling. She knew there was a term to describe this phenomenon— the uncanny valley. The more closely something artificial resembled a human, the more alien it seemed.

It also seemed like the artificial twin of the embalmed dead bodies of Krista Barker and Monique Silva, the killer's own mannequins.

Suddenly she could picture a much more likely sequence for the killer's clothing shopping. He'd approach the mannequin, which already resembled his dream woman—a woman who would never argue, never leave, who could be posed. And he'd tell the nearest clerk that he wanted what the mannequin was wearing, in a size that fit the prostitute with him.

Most of the shops had simple, nondescript dolls, hardly looking like a human figure. But the mannequins in this shop had hair; they were colored right; they had beautiful large eyes. Perfect for their killer.

They'd easily fuel his fantasies. Did he have a mannequin like that at home? One he used for practice? Zoe was convinced he did, or used to.

"Zoe." Tatum touched her arm. "Come on. Maybe we'll get lucky in the next—"

"Hang on," Zoe said. She approached the manager, a severe-looking woman who eyed them both with annoyance.

"Excuse me," Zoe said. "We're looking for a—"

"Your partner told me. The Strangling Undertaker, right? Look, I don't remember any weirdos walking around here, and if you want the security footage—"

"Okay," Zoe said. "I get it. But I have a different question. The man we're looking for is probably in his early thirties—"

"We have lots of those."

"And he'd probably be obsessed with your mannequins. He'd always buy what the mannequins were wearing and—"

"Oh, *that* guy."

Zoe blinked at the woman. She could feel Tatum tense by her side.

"Sure, he comes by every once in a while. He freaks the girls out. He stands by the mannequins for ten, sometimes twenty minutes, just looking at them. He touched them a few times but stopped once I threatened to call security."

"Does he come here with women?" Zoe asked.

"I think so. He came in with a girl not long ago. Bought her some clothes."

"Just what the mannequins were wearing, right?"

The manager shrugged. "I don't know. Maybe."

"When was the last time he came by?" Tatum asked.

"Just yesterday."

"Did he have a woman with him?" Zoe asked urgently.

"No. He came alone. He was here around three in the afternoon, I think. Just staring at the mannequins, like always."

"But he didn't buy anything?"

"I don't think so."

"Ma'am, we have to see the security footage," Tatum said.

"I already told you—"

"That man is the serial killer," Zoe said. "And he comes here a lot, you said. He might decide to pick up one of your girls next time."

The manager's eyes flickered in fear. Yeah, Zoe knew the feeling.

"Once he picks a girl, he won't let go," Zoe said, her voice lowering. "He'll stalk her, get her when she's alone. He strangles his victims to death using a noose. He violates their bodies once they're dead. He keeps them as—"

"Okay," the manager said, her voice croaking. There were tears in her eyes. She was shaking. "Will this help you catch him?"

"It would be invaluable," Tatum said.

"And you'll let us know? Once you get him?"

Fear had taken root, Zoe knew. This woman wouldn't be able to sleep tonight. She wouldn't leave the store alone in the evening. She might quit this job altogether, look for a different one. Zoe searched her conscience and decided there was no reason to feel guilty. The woman had forced her hand.

"We'll let you know," she said.

"And . . . what if he comes to the store?"

"Call the police, and try to keep him from leaving," Zoe said. "You tell the dispatcher to call Lieutenant Samuel Martinez and tell him the Strangling Undertaker is in your shop."

"O-okay."

"The security footage?" Tatum asked. His voice was soft.

"Right. Please follow me."

CHAPTER 67

Tatum sat in front of the console. The clothing store's security guard had stepped aside, letting him sit in his chair. It was a comfortable chair, and on any other day, Tatum would have felt an urge to swivel in it and see how many full spins he could do with one push. But now his heart beat fast, the thrill of the chase taking over his thoughts.

There were several screens in the console. Five showed the shop's interior, and one was positioned outside, streaming the people who went in and out of the store. The guard showed him how to display recorded footages and how to switch between the various cameras. It was needlessly complicated, but Tatum slowly got the hang of it.

The store manager stood by him, breathing heavily. Zoe had spooked the woman out of her wits. It had definitely worked, but he was certain they could have managed to persuade her without it. This woman would be looking over her shoulder for months now. Tatum promised himself he'd let her know as soon as they had the Corny Serial Killer behind bars.

He fast-forwarded the video. The time read *7/28, 14:47:32*. He fast-forwarded a whole hour, occasionally glancing at the manager.

"See him?" he asked.

She shook her head. "Try this camera." She pointed at one of the live monitors. "It's closer to one of the mannequins he likes."

He switched to the correct feed, inserted the time *7/28, 14:30:00*, and began to fast-forward again.

When the time stamp read *15:07:06*, the manager said sharply, "There."

He paused the video. She pointed at a person standing at the corner of the frame. His face could barely be seen.

"Are you sure that's him?"

"Yes. See how he stands in front of the mannequin? Fast-forward—you'll see that he doesn't move."

Tatum fast-forwarded and saw that the manager was right. The man didn't shift at all for more than six minutes. Then he stepped away, disappearing from the frame.

"Did you see that?" Tatum told Zoe.

"Yes," she said in a hushed tone and put a hand on his shoulder. They shared a thrilling moment. They had just seen the invisible killer they had been chasing for two weeks.

"Can we see where he walked to?" Tatum asked the security guy.

"It looks like he just went toward the entrance," he answered. "There are no cameras beyond that point up to the entrance."

"He came from the same direction," Tatum said, rewinding and watching the man appearing and stopping in front of the mannequin.

Zoe cleared her throat. "He walked into the shop, went straight to the mannequin, looked at her for several minutes, then went outside."

"Okay," Tatum said. "Let's check out the footage of the entrance."

The man had appeared in the footage at the time stamp of 15:06:42. Tatum switched to the entrance and set the time to 15:04:00. He let it play in normal speed.

"There he is," Zoe said as the man appeared. He was looking at the ground, and they couldn't see his face clearly. Tatum rewound the footage a bit.

"Look," he said, breathing hard. "We can see the car."

The footage showed about a dozen cars from the parking lot. The man shut the door of one and stepped outside. Tatum rewound a bit more, and the monitor displayed the car parking before the man came out.

"It's hard to read the license plate," Zoe said.

"I know someone who can get the plate from this footage easily," Tatum said, grinning. "We got the bastard."

He fast-forwarded. The man disappeared into the store. Seven minutes later he went out, but instead of going to his car, he turned right and disappeared from view.

"Maybe he needed to buy some milk," Tatum muttered as he fast-forwarded the video. At 15:32:11, the car drove away. He paused and rewound a bit. They could now see the man returning, and he had a bag in his hand.

"Yeah, he went grocery shopping," Tatum said. "I guess he ran out of food."

"That's not a bag from the supermarket," the manager said. "It's from the toy store next door."

"Toy store?" Tatum frowned. "So . . . what, this guy has a child?"

"I hope so," Zoe said in a tense voice.

"Hope so? Why?"

"Because if not, he might have decided he needs more than a woman in his life. He might have decided he needs kids."

CHAPTER 68

He rang the doorbell. After a minute, the door opened a crack two inches wide, exposing the living room beyond. Toys were scattered on the floor. He pursed his lips. Kids required discipline. When he became their father, there wouldn't be any toys on the floor; that much was certain.

"Yes?" A woman peered at him from beyond the crack. "Oh, hello."

"Hi, miss." He smiled at her. "I heard you need assistance again."

"Really? I didn't call. Everything is fine."

"That's strange." He frowned, glancing at the clipboard in his hand. "It has your name and address here."

"It must be a mis—"

"Mommy," a high-pitched voice called from behind her.

"Just a minute, sweetie," she said, glancing backward, and then smiled at him. "I'm sure it's a mistake."

"Oh, okay. Uh . . . would you mind just writing on the form here that you didn't call and signing it? My boss can be a real hard-ass."

"Of course," she said. "Hang on."

She closed the door, and he could hear her removing the chain bolt. Then the door opened wide.

And he lunged inside.

CHAPTER 69

Zoe shut the passenger door, trying to focus. The video footage from the store kept running through her mind. Something in the man's stance or the small glimpse she'd had of part of his face seemed familiar, though it had been really hard to get a good look. The video quality was low, the man's face almost constantly hidden. Still, something nagged at her, as if he were a word at the tip of her tongue.

She shook her head and looked at the small ramshackle house. It was a tiny structure, the walls all white clapboard, the color peeling to reveal the gray material underneath. Both front windows were murky with dust. The grass in front of the house was speckled with brown dirt and covered with dry leaves. It bordered the street, but there was no fence to distinguish where the street ended and the front yard, if there was one, began. The houses around it weren't much better.

Tatum's friend, someone from the field office in LA, had managed to extract the license plate number from the footage they had sent him. The car, according to the DMV, was registered to Bertha Alston, and this was her home. There was a small garage behind the house, its size almost the same. Its door was closed, and it was impossible to see if a car was inside.

"Wait here," Tatum said.

"Uh . . . no."

"It could be dangerous."

"That's why I'm hanging around with an FBI agent. So I'll be safe."

He rolled his eyes. "You're a very annoying woman." He began to move forward.

Zoe followed two steps behind. He signaled her to stand against the wall, and she obediently did, feeling her heart pound. Tatum leaned against the wall on the other side of the door and then knocked.

They waited. After a few seconds, he knocked again. There was no sound from within.

"FBI. Open up," Tatum called.

The sound of a faraway airplane and the buzzing of the traffic were the only things Zoe could hear over her pounding heart.

She carefully glanced at the window. The drape was down, blocking the view into the house entirely. She wasn't sure she could have seen beyond the dust in any case.

Tatum thumped the door again, this time with his fist.

"She's not there!" a withered, croaky voice shouted at them from the house next door. Zoe glanced over to the speaker. A wizened walnut wearing humongous spectacles stared at them with interest. She raised one shriveled hand, thin as a broomstick, and straightened her binocular-sized glasses.

"Who's not here?" Tatum asked.

"Well . . . who are you looking for?"

"We're looking for Bertha."

"Bertha's dead. Died a few months ago."

"Then we're looking for whoever lives in this house," Zoe said. "Is it her son?"

"Well, no one lives there anymore. I think her sons are trying to sell the place."

"Do you know where they are, ma'am?"

"Well, that depends. Who are you?"

Tatum flipped his badge. "FBI, ma'am."

She seemed far from impressed. "Well, what do you want with Bertha's sons?"

"We just want to talk to them, ma'am."

She nodded thoughtfully but said nothing.

"Can you tell us where we can reach them?"

"Well, I don't really know."

Tatum sighed.

"Are they in trouble?" the crone asked, straightening her glasses again.

"We just want to talk to them," Tatum said again.

"Well, I always knew they'd get in trouble. You don't get to grow up like Bertha's kids did and turn out fine." The hag cackled as if this were the best joke she had ever told. Maybe it was.

The woman's speech pattern—starting every sentence with the word *well*—was getting on Zoe's nerves. "What do you mean? Was she abusive?"

"Well, I don't know what you call abusive, but she sure walloped her sons a lot. Her daughter even worse, I think. And she'd scream at them and throw things at them . . . and that was when she was sober. She got *real* nasty when she was drunk."

"Ma'am," Tatum said, "we really need to—"

"Nasty how?" Zoe asked. She felt as if this wrinkled, gnarled hag might hold all the answers. And she seemed to be happy to share.

"Well, she was damn crazy when she was drunk. Said she could hear the devil speaking to her, or sometimes it was her ex-husband. She sprayed one of her boys with hairspray once, tried to light him up with a match. It was out in the street too. I called the police."

She said the word *police* strangely, pausing after saying *po* for a whole second, then half screaming *lis*. Zoe began to suspect Bertha wasn't the only crazy person who had lived in the neighborhood.

"And, well, of course, there was the thing with her daughter. Surely you know about that."

Her tone was gleeful, as if she knew they didn't and was dying to tell them, but they had to ask.

"What about her daughter?" Zoe asked.

"Well, I thought everyone knew 'bout that. Her daughter died when she was thirteen. It turned out she had lung cancer, probably because Bertha kept smoking in the house. The crazy thing was, when her daughter died, Bertha didn't tell anyone about it. Just left her there for more than a week. She said the girl was resting. Later we all found out Bertha made her sons keep their dead sister company. She locked them inside, told them their sister was finally behaving like a good little girl. And that they had to pray she'd get better. They were all locked in with that rotting body for over a week. In the damn summer."

Zoe glanced at Tatum, and he looked back at her, his eyes full of horror. *There it was.*

"There was a terrible smell coming from there. I had to call the po . . . lis. They barged in, found the daughter covered in maggots, the boys half-sick, vomit all over the place, Bertha drunk and unconscious. Yeah . . ." She became silent. "Thought everybody knew about that," she finally said.

"What happened to the sons?" Zoe asked.

"Well, they're both still around."

"What are their names?"

"Well . . ." The neighbor stared for a moment. "I'll be damned. Can't remember. One of them changed his last name; he hated his mother so much. The other kept the name. I'll remember in a second . . ." She licked her gums and smacked them. "Nope. Nothing."

"Do you know where we can find them?"

"Well, one of them owns a business. Some sort of handyman. An electrician, I think. Yeah, definitely an electrician."

Zoe's brain cells sparked, a flurry of ideas emerging all at once. Her heart raced. Lily hadn't been saying "Hummer" or "trucker."

"I think he's a plumber," she said.

"Well, I think you're right," the old neighbor agreed loudly. "A plumber, not an electrician. His name is—"

"Clifford Sorenson."

"Yes. But when he was a young boy, his mom used to call him Cliff."

CHAPTER 70

Tatum's fingers tightened on the steering wheel, squeezing it angrily as the traffic moved at a snail's pace.

"It all fits," he told Zoe, his voice sharp and tense. "Sorenson believes the perfect woman is a dead woman. That's what he learned from his psycho mother. His dead sister was the only one who didn't make his mom angry. And she kept them inside for a week, holding the body's hand, combing her hair, God knows what else. I mean, *of course* he turned out crazy."

"So he kills his fiancée," Zoe said.

"Right. Body decays—he has to get rid of it, or the neighbors will complain. He dumps it but becomes obsessed with the idea of having a dead spouse."

"He could have known Susan Warner because he fixed the pipes at her home," Zoe said. She stared ahead, biting her lip. "Remember what her friend said? That the apartment's sewage kept overflowing? She must have needed a plumber multiple times. Plenty of time to look around, see that she lived alone."

"You met the man. Does he look like the person in the security footage?"

"It could be him. It was really hard to get a good look at his face in the video. But he did look familiar. Maybe his body language or his stance."

"Fits your profile nicely too. Early thirties, works with his hands . . . does he own a van in addition to his mom's car?"

"Yeah. There were two vans when I stopped by. His employee was loading a sink on one. It had *Sorenson's Plumbing* painted on it, which explains how Lily knew he was a plumber . . ." She slowed down, frowning.

"What is it?" Tatum asked.

"He doesn't fit the profile so neatly. I saw him try to lift a steel sink and hurt his back. How did he carry those bodies so far away with a weak back? Monique Silva was practically in the middle of the park."

"Maybe that's why his back was so sensitive. From the exertion."

"Yeah, but . . . Clifford Sorenson functioned well with women. He was engaged. They were trying to start a family—this wasn't a man who couldn't have a relationship. This wasn't a lonely man. It doesn't fit at all."

"Okay, but listen," Tatum said slowly, trying to find a way to disagree without saying that maybe she was wrong. "Maybe you were, uh . . ." *The hell with it.* "Wrong. I mean, you couldn't have known about this crazy story with his mother. Maybe he just has a thing for dead women, and after some time with his fiancée, he decided—"

"The other brother," Zoe interrupted. She clearly hadn't listened to a word he'd said.

"Yeah? Sure, there's another one, but Clifford Sorenson is a plumber, and you said—"

"What if the other brother is a plumber too? Clifford has an employee named Jeffrey who seemed to be really close to him. And he called him Cliff. That woman said his mother used to call him Cliff when he was a boy, so his brother probably calls him the same. Jeffrey was strong. He picked up the steel sink easily. He would be able to carry a woman's body if he needed to."

"So if you're right, this guy Jeffrey was the one who went to fix the sewage problems in Susan Warner's apartment."

"Yes. And Jeffrey killed Clifford's fiancée. That would explain how Clifford had such a tight alibi. Because he really was innocent. It also makes sense that his brother would wait for a day he knew Clifford would be gone. A day when Clifford went fishing with his friends."

"Damn. We should call Martinez," Tatum said.

"We still have nothing," Zoe said quickly. "This is completely circumstantial. It's probably not even enough for a warrant. And we aren't supposed to be here."

She was right. They were building an intricate castle on a fluffy, thin cloud. "Then what do you suggest?"

"Let's look around. Maybe we can spot some blood on one of the vans. Maybe if we look through their windows, we can see a container of formaldehyde. I don't know . . . anything that would give us a shred of actual evidence. Enough to show Martinez."

Tatum grimaced. There he was again. Going forward with no backup, without consulting his superior. This time he'd be kicked out of the bureau for sure.

CHAPTER 71

The woman and her two children were dealt with, for now, bound and gagged. He had been surprised to find out how easily a mother could be controlled. All he had to do was threaten to cut the throat of her little girl, and she willingly let him tie her up. After that, tying the frightened children took a matter of minutes.

He stared at the three of them, trying to make up his mind. The little girl was nice; he could imagine himself as her dad, playing with her and her dolls, dressing her up in frilly pink dresses. He smiled at the thought of their shared life together. Him, a father—who would have thought? He'd be a good father; he'd never follow his mother's example. He would spend time every day with his child, never yell at her or hit her. But the boy? A toddler. A line of snot ran from his nose, his eyes red and teary from crying. To be entirely honest, he didn't want two children. He wanted only one. Embalming both of them would be a hassle, and he'd have to carry them back to his home, not to mention the endless chore of moving them from one spot to the next once they began their life together.

No, he had no use for the boy.

He yanked the child up. Where had he put his knife? He glanced around. There, on the counter. He dragged the boy over to the counter, the little runt screaming hysterically into the rag in his mouth. He grabbed the knife and put it against the kid's throat. The mother emitted muffled screams as well, her eyes wide, shaking her head.

"I don't need him," he said simply, pressing the blade harder.

He paused and pulled the blade back.

He had never embalmed a child before. He might screw things up. It was safe to assume their veins were smaller; he might botch the girl. Having a backup would be useful. He could learn to love the boy, sure. If he had to.

He inspected the child's throat. Hardly nicked it at all. Good. He dragged the boy back, dumped him by his sister.

It was time to prepare the embalming table.

It was just like the time with Susan. The best place to do it all was the bathroom, where the shower supplied both running water and a drain. He didn't want blood all over the floor; it would be messy to step in. He had a folding table in the van that would fit well enough. It wasn't the table in his workshop, but he couldn't have it all.

It was a lot of effort, carrying the table, the containers with the embalming fluid, the embalming machine. Then he grabbed the bag with the toys he had bought the day before. It was purely sentimental, really, but he wanted to give his child a new toy to play with once they were done. Last time he had been there, he had noticed that most of their toys were used and broken.

He'd be a good father.

CHAPTER 72

Only one van was in front of Sorenson's Plumbing when they parked next to the small warehouse. One of the plumbers was gone. Zoe got out of the car, slamming the door behind her, and marched toward the remaining van. She heard Tatum run after her, felt his hand grab her wrist.

"What?" she snapped.

He looked at her with concern. "We have no warrant or permission to be here. Just . . . be cool."

"Right," she muttered, feeling anything but cool.

They approached the van together at a measured pace. Once they reached it, Tatum slid against the van, trying the door handle. The door didn't budge. Locked. Zoe circled the van, glancing inside it, trying to see its interior. The rear windows of the van were darkened; it was impossible to see anything through them. Tatum joined her at the van's rear, glancing at it.

"No blood, no formaldehyde, not even a serial killer club membership card."

Zoe nodded glumly. "Let's go inside."

"And do what?"

"Well . . . I've been here before. I can just say I came to ask a few more questions."

Tatum looked at her unhappily, and she shrugged. Did they have any other choice? Calling Martinez right now would get them nothing except a one-way ticket out of Chicago.

She walked into the shop, her eyes scanning the interior quickly. Clifford Sorenson sat behind his desk, reading a newspaper. As Tatum joined her, Clifford put down the newspaper and looked at them both.

"Hello," he said. "You're the one from the FBI, right?"

Zoe swallowed. "That's right," she said. "This is Agent Gray, my partner."

Clifford nodded at Tatum. "How can I help you?" he asked, his tone of voice slightly chilly.

"Just a few follow-up questions," Zoe said. "Do you have a minute?"

"Sure," Clifford said, folding his hands. He didn't ask them to sit down or offer them coffee. They were not wanted here.

"I prefer that no one overhears our talk," Zoe said, treading carefully. "Are we alone here, or is your brother here?"

"Just you, me, and your partner," Clifford answered. "My brother went to a client's house."

Zoe nodded, feeling an inkling of satisfaction. They really were brothers. "Okay. I wanted to verify the timeline before you discovered your fiancée was missing. You went on a fishing trip with your friends, right?"

"That's right."

"Just your friends? No one else?"

"No, just my friends."

"The reason I'm asking this is that sometimes people remember things differently, especially after a long time. Didn't your brother join you on your fishing trips?"

"Sometimes he did. Not that time. And I remember that day perfectly. It was the worst day of my life."

Was it? Was it really worse than being locked up with your dead sister in your own house?

"Do you remember why he didn't join you on the trip?"

Clifford's eyes narrowed. "I get the idea that this isn't just a follow-up, Agent. Are you trying to pin this murder on me again? I think I should call my lawyer."

"Was Susan Warner a customer of yours?" Zoe asked desperately.

"Now I'm definitely calling my lawyer."

"We're not accusing you of your fiancée's murder, sir," Tatum said in a low voice. "But we do have a likely suspect. And it would help if you answered our questions."

"Really?" Clifford said. "Because it sounds like those questions are about me."

Her insides churned as she stared at the man's hardening features. How sure was she that his brother was the murderer and not him? Because if she was wrong and told him what they knew, he could give up his brother's location, and then, once they were gone, he could disappear. The prudent thing to do was to talk to Martinez. Try to convince him they had a good enough case here. Get a search warrant, maybe someone to watch both brothers.

The only problem was that she couldn't shake the hunch that Jeffrey was prowling for a victim. Maybe had even found one. They could have only hours until another woman was dead. Or minutes.

But this was all it was. A hunch. For all she knew, Clifford was the murderer. Or maybe both of the brothers. Or they could both be innocent. Would she really endanger the case by showing their cards?

She glanced at Tatum worriedly. His eyes were calm, and he gave her a gentle nod. He trusted her.

She turned to Clifford Sorenson. "Sir, we have reason to believe your brother is the man who killed your fiancée."

His eyes widened. He picked up the desk phone and began to dial. "I'm calling my lawyer," he said. "And then I'm calling my brother to make sure he talks to my lawyer too. You bastards—"

"Think back," Zoe said hurriedly. "Did Jeffrey usually miss your fishing trips? You said you went fishing with him several times two weeks ago. But on that night, he didn't join you, did he? And where was he during the week that your fiancée was missing, before her body was found?" She could see that he'd stopped dialing, that his hand trembled. "Did you see him at all? I'm betting you didn't. Where do you think he was? What was more important than supporting his brother and helping in the search?"

Sorenson looked ill, and she knew the possibility had occurred to him that his brother had been with his fiancée's body.

"Remember what you said? Veronika told you *some* apples didn't fall far from the tree. She wasn't referring to your father and you. She was talking about your brother and your mother. We know about your history, Mr. Sorenson. We know about your mother's illness. What if Jeffrey began saying strange things to Veronika? What if his irrational behavior was scaring her? That would explain why she was so tense, why she didn't want to be left alone. Did Jeffrey have a key to your home? Was he stable after what happened with your sister? Or maybe he got into trouble. Did he ever date anyone? Ever meet any of his girlfriends? Can you really be sure it wasn't your brother, Mr. Sorenson?"

It was a shotgun blast of guesses and hunches, and his face showed that some, or even most, hit their mark. He slowly put the phone back in its cradle. Zoe knew that the shock would fade, that in a minute or two he would start rationalizing, finding answers to all her questions. She had to keep striking now, while the metal was hot.

"A woman named Susan Warner died a few months ago," she said. "You might have read about it in the paper. We have reason to believe her death was linked to Veronika's. And we suspect she may have been your client, that your brother went to her home several times. Can you look it up? Maybe we're completely mistaken. Maybe this was all just a huge misunderstanding."

Clifford turned to his laptop and began tapping, his keystrokes mechanical, his expression dazed. Finally, he leaned back and said in a defeated, toneless voice, "Susan Warner was our client. Jeffrey went to her home three times."

Zoe's mind whirred. There were so many questions she wanted to ask this man. But one question took priority over all the rest.

"Where is your brother now?" she asked.

"I . . . I don't know. He didn't tell me."

"You said he went to see a client."

"That's what I assumed. He didn't tell me."

"We need a list of all the clients your brother's handled in the past three months," Tatum said.

"Could be hundreds of names."

"Let's check, okay?"

Clifford's fighting spirit had been shattered. He showed them how to read the Excel sheet on the laptop. Tatum sat by the computer and began to go over the list. Zoe was about to argue but then saw he was clearly much more proficient than her when it came to manipulating the data. For a burly FBI field agent, he had impressive computer skills.

There were ninety-three names on the list.

"He'll be attacking her in her home," Zoe said. "That means he'll probably target a single woman."

Tatum removed the men, leaving forty-one names.

"Do you think he's targeting a woman with children?" Tatum asked.

"Probably," Zoe said. "But we can't really tell if the client is a single mother from this list."

"Laura Summer," Clifford said. "She wanted a discount because she's a single mom."

Zoe glanced at the name. "He visited her twice," she said. "I think that's her."

"We need to make sure," Tatum said.

Zoe dialed the number on the file, and as she listened to the phone ring, she said, "Email this list to Martinez. We'll call him on the way and explain."

Tatum nodded. As he worked on it, he asked Clifford, "Does Jeffrey have a phone with him?"

"Uh . . . yeah. Sure."

"We'll need the phone number."

Clifford nodded and grabbed a piece of paper.

Zoe waited, tapping her foot anxiously. Laura didn't answer her phone.

"No answer," she said.

Tatum pressed send and stood up, grabbing the piece of paper with Jeffrey's number on it. "Let's go."

CHAPTER 73

The blue van Zoe had first seen by Sorenson's Plumbing was parked in front of Laura Summer's home, instantly dispelling Zoe's hope that Jeffrey Alston was really fixing someone's drain. Tatum switched off the engine and checked his gun.

Zoe had called Martinez on the way and explained in very general terms what they had learned. Martinez sounded livid but was professional enough to realize that his top priority had to be taking the serial killer off the street. He'd handle the rogue FBI personnel later. Police squads were on their way.

"I'll take the back door in case he tries to bolt when they get here," Tatum said. "You wait in the car. Watch the front door. Let me know if he leaves through it. And welcome the cavalry when it gets here."

Zoe nodded. She was useless here, of course. She was untrained. She'd stay in the car.

Tatum drew a small gun from an ankle holster and handed it over to Zoe. "That's a Glock 43. It has seven bullets. Use it only if there's no other option."

She nodded numbly, taking the metal object from his hand. It was cold and surprisingly light. She held it pointed away from them both, terrified.

Tatum opened the driver's door and got out.

"Don't be a hero," Zoe said.

He smiled at her, more a grimace than a real smile, and shut the door.

Zoe watched him creeping alongside the house to the back. He was smooth, alert, and fast. Every movement was calculated to avoid the line of sight from the windows. She found herself fascinated with her partner's skill as he edged his way, crouched, gun in his hand. As she spent days with Tatum and his silly jokes and antics, it was easy to forget he was also highly trained for hostile situations such as this one.

He disappeared behind the corner of the wall, and she was left alone. Almost instantly, she could taste bile in her mouth. Her throat constricted, and she breathed heavily, staring at the house. What was going on in there? Were Laura and her children dead already? Was Jeffrey pumping embalming fluid through Laura's throat right now?

The hand holding the gun trembled. Scared it might accidentally fire, she placed it on the seat next to her, still warm from Tatum's body heat. He had only left half a minute ago. It felt like hours. It felt like weeks.

She glanced at the road. How long until the cops showed up?

She thought of Lily Ramos, screaming through her gag, praying for the cops to show up before she died.

She clenched her fists and waited.

CHAPTER 74

Laura Summer's backyard was strewn with children's toys, a rusty tricycle, dry leaves from the neighbor's tree. Moving silently in that mess was slow work. Halfway into the yard, Tatum stepped on a twig, hidden under the layer of leaves, and the sudden snap sounded to him like a gunshot, piercing the air. He froze, glancing at the back door, waiting.

It didn't budge.

His target was the wall by the door, but a large window looking out to the yard prevented him from sidling up to it. Instead, he crouched low, moving slowly, hopefully out of sight, knowing well that if someone decided to walk to the window and look outside, he would be completely visible.

Perhaps the prudent thing to do would have been to position himself farther away, gun trained on the door, and wait for the approaching backup. But his mind was on Laura Summer and her two children.

He prayed they were still alive.

The door was still three steps away, but the windowsill was behind him, meaning he could stand up. He did so and glanced through the glass pane. From his new vantage point he could see the children.

They were alive.

Tied in the corner of the room, gags in their mouths, faces wet with tears, but undoubtedly alive, and Tatum let out a long breath of relief. Now he just had to—

A muffled scream drew his attention. Something crashed inside the house, and he saw the children crying harder, looking at something beyond his vantage point. Their mother, of course, and by the sound of it, she was struggling for her life.

Reflex took control as he rushed across the remaining distance to the door, took a step back, and kicked it open, swiveling his Glock to take a bead on the struggling two figures.

The man, whom Tatum pegged as Jeffrey Alston, held a woman whose mouth was taped shut. Her hands were twisted behind her back. She faced Tatum, and Jeffrey stood behind her, his body almost entirely hidden. His eyes widened as he saw what was going on, and he reflexively lowered his head, taking cover behind his human shield.

Laura's face was purple, her eyes bulging, a nylon rope around her neck. She was thinner than Jeffrey, and his body was partly exposed. Almost good enough to take a shot.

But Laura buckled and moved, the lack of air driving her to struggle desperately, and it was a difficult shot. If he missed, he would hit Laura.

Both men were frozen in place, but Jeffrey reacted first, lunging sideways, grabbing a knife from the counter. He held the knife to the woman's throat.

"Drop it!" he roared.

Laura's eyes stared at the ceiling as she convulsed. She was seconds away from death.

Tatum aimed the gun desperately at Jeffrey's protruding body. "Take that thing off her throat, or I shoot."

"Drop the gun, or I kill her."

"If she chokes to death, I'll kill you, you bastard. Take that thing off."

Apparently understanding he was losing his leverage, Jeffrey twisted something behind the woman's neck, and the noose loosened. The woman let out a wheeze, trying to draw breath through her gagged mouth. Her nostrils widened and narrowed as she snorted air into her lungs.

"Drop the damn gun, or I cut her throat."

The knife nicked Laura's throat below the rope, and blood dripped down its blade. Tatum hesitated, knowing that there was no right answer to this desperate situation. But the police were on their way. He could try to buy some time.

He lowered the gun, heart beating fast, trying to take in his surroundings. The two children were bundled in the corner, their eyes wide. They were shrieking incomprehensibly, rags taped to their mouths as well. A small coffee table lay on the floor. Laura must have kicked it as Jeffrey was strangling her. That was the crash Tatum had heard before.

"Put the gun on the floor."

Tatum very slowly crouched and put the Glock on the floor, his eyes not moving from Jeffrey and the knife on Laura's throat.

"Kick it over."

Tatum hesitated, calculating. If Jeffrey had the gun, nothing would stop him from shooting Tatum and then finishing off Laura and her children.

"Do it!"

Tatum gave the gun a small kick, and it spun on the floor. It stopped midway between them. Jeffrey stared at him, his eyes furious.

"Don't do anything you might regret," Tatum said. "If you kill that woman, you'll spend the rest of your life behind bars."

He hoped that Jeffrey wouldn't figure out what was going on. The man didn't know that Tatum was with the FBI or that the police now knew who he was. All Jeffrey knew for sure was that an armed man had barged into the house to try to help Laura.

"You could still walk away," Tatum continued softly. "No one was harmed here, right? No one needs to know."

"Shut up. Go sit over there." Jeffrey motioned with his head to the corner where the kids were crying.

Tatum nodded and began to move, his first step taking him closer to Jeffrey and Laura.

"Stay away!" Jeffrey's voice was hysterical. "I will cut her—do you hear me? I will cut her throat."

Blood was still trickling from Laura's throat, and Tatum froze. Nodding very slowly and raising his hands, he walked sideways alongside the wall until he reached the crying children.

"Sit down. On the floor."

"Okay." Tatum sat, crouching slowly.

"Sit. On your ass."

Where were the damned police? Tatum sat down and watched Jeffrey, who seemed to be frozen by indecision.

"Just walk away—"

"Be quiet! All of you, be quiet."

Tatum closed his mouth, but the kids were sobbing uncontrollably. Their crying seemed to be making Jeffrey even angrier. He looked at them, then at the gun on the floor. He took a step toward the gun.

Sitting as he was, Tatum could never make a lunge for the gun and get to it in time. Jeffrey would reach the gun, but he would have to remove the knife from Laura's throat and crouch to pick the gun up. That would be the only moment that Tatum would be able to act. He tensed, preparing himself for an impossible lunge.

Then the front door opened slowly. And to Tatum's horror and disbelief, Zoe stood framed in the doorway, raising her empty hands high above her head.

CHAPTER 75

Zoe had seen fragments of the struggle in the house through the window and realized that they had just run out of time. She was out of the car, running to the front door, when she saw Tatum lowering the gun. He had no choice, she knew. He probably planned to stall, hoping for the police to arrive. And perhaps it was the best course of action . . . but Zoe wasn't sure.

Jeffrey Alston was erratic under pressure. He didn't think clearly. He might decide to shoot Tatum, Laura, and the kids, then make a run for it. He might cut Laura's throat just to remove her from the picture. He might even kill Laura by accident.

She forced herself to calm down, to think. She'd spent the last two weeks profiling this man. She knew what made him tick, what he wanted, what he yearned for.

She formed a plan.

She was relieved to find the front door unlocked. When it opened, Jeffrey turned his eyes to her, then back at Tatum, who sat frozen on the floor, then back at her.

"I'm unarmed," she quickly said, stepping into the house, keeping her hands held up. "I'm closing the door."

She had to make him feel in control. Had to make him calm down. Right now, he was unpredictable, dangerous, a ticking bomb. She carefully lowered her right hand and pushed the door closed.

"I'll cut her," Jeffrey warned, his eyes shifting back and forth. "Put down your gun."

"I don't have a gun."

"Like hell you don't. You're both police detectives." His eyes flickered to Tatum, who seemed to shift slightly. "Don't move."

"I'm not a police detective," Zoe said. "I'm a psychologist."

He snorted. "Like hell you are."

What he wanted was control. It was always about control and loneliness with him. Especially when it came to women. That was the fuel to his fantasies, and those fantasies dictated his actions. He dreamed about a dead woman, her body never decaying, keeping him company. That's what spurred him to kill over and over. She had to maneuver herself into his fantasy to take control from him.

"I'm unarmed," she said again. "I'll show you."

Slowly, she unbuttoned the top button of her blouse, then the second.

"You should let the woman go," she said. "You don't want to go to jail."

"I'm going to jail anyway. Maybe I should cut her throat just for the hell of it, huh?"

"If you kill her, you won't be able to take her with you. The cops are on their way. You won't have time to get her to your car." She unbuttoned the bottom button and opened the blouse, letting it drop to the floor. She looked at his eyes, searching for excitement, but there was none. She didn't interest him. She was talking, opinionated, alive. He preferred them dead and silent.

"You won't even have five minutes of fun with her," she said, unzipping her skirt, pulling it down slowly and very carefully. He remained standing, watching her as if he were watching a piece of furniture.

This was a man whose imagination ran rampant. She had to give his imagination something to work with.

"I have a better idea for you," she said.

"Stop talking."

"Take me instead. I won't struggle. You won't need to carry me to get me to your car. I'll go willingly." She straightened. She stood in her bra and underwear in front of him, and she knew it was enough for him to believe she was unarmed, that she could stop.

She didn't stop. Instead, she reached for the clasp of her bra.

"That man over there," she said, motioning with her head at Tatum, "has a pair of handcuffs. He can handcuff my hands behind my back to make sure I won't try anything."

She made a small movement toward Tatum, and Jeffrey's hand tightened around the knife; his teeth clenched. She stopped.

"When you get me somewhere safe, you can put that strap around my neck and tighten it."

She removed her left bra strap. Shivers ran up her arms, but she wasn't sure if it was the cold or pure fear. The right strap followed.

"Once I stop struggling, you'll be able to have some fun with me. Not just once. Maybe even twice. It's been so long, hasn't it?"

His eyes flickered, his mouth slightly open. The hand holding the knife was still rigid against Laura's neck. She shrugged the bra off, hearing it rustle as it hit the floor.

"And then you can do what you need to do for this to last. For us to last. That's what you really want, isn't it? Someone to lie against you at night? To sit by your side when you eat breakfast in the morning?"

She took a step toward Tatum. And another.

"Someone to love you unconditionally? Can you really do better than me? Is *she* better than me?"

The knife hand wavered.

"Can you see it, Jeffrey? This mouth, frozen forever, my skin cold, my arms and legs posed however you want them to? Can you picture it in your mind?"

Another step—and another. Always facing him, her eyes locked with him, her movements slow and calculated. She hoped fervently that

Jeffrey would keep still. And that the Glock tucked into the waistband of her underwear behind her back wouldn't tumble down to the floor.

"Every day together. Dressing me. Caressing me. Kissing me. There will finally be someone in your life. Someone who'll never leave."

She took another step, and the gun shifted, lowering slightly. Her heart skipped a beat, but it didn't fall; the underwear band held. She took another step. And another.

"The rest of them were mistakes. I am the real deal."

She reached Tatum and the kids.

Jeffrey swallowed. "You!" he barked at Tatum. "Handcuff her hands. *Slowly.*"

Zoe waited, hearing Tatum move behind her. She felt the cold touch of one of the handcuffs tightening around her left wrist. Then she felt the shift of the gun in her underwear. The second cuff tightened around her right wrist.

She took one step forward, carefully hiding Tatum with her body.

"Finally we'll both have someone to love. Come on, Jeffrey. Let's leave before the cops get here."

There was a slight nod, the blade lowering. She took another step forward.

And then she dove to the floor.

There were three consecutive blasts as she hit the hard floor tiles with her shoulder, her cuffed hands unable to stop her fall. There was a jolt of pain, and she felt the coppery taste of blood in her mouth. She had bitten her tongue.

She felt someone grab her hands, and there was a click. The pressure of the cuffs was removed from her right hand, and she pulled it out, turning around.

Tatum handed her the key, and she tried to unlock the second cuff. It was hard. Her fingers were trembling.

Sirens screamed close by, and she wanted to sob. Instead, she finally unlocked the cuff, removed it, got up, and hurried to the woman, removing the gag from her mouth in one fast rip. The woman took in a wheezing breath and a sob.

"My children," she said.

"They're fine," Zoe said. "Don't worry. They're fine." She inspected Laura's throat. It was bleeding, but it was a shallow scratch, no more.

Tatum was crouching by Jeffrey's body. For a moment Zoe was about to shout at him angrily. They had to untie the family. Then she saw that Jeffrey was coughing blood. He was still alive. Tatum tore the killer's shirt open. He found a bit of cloth and shoved it against Jeffrey's bleeding belly.

Zoe blinked and looked at Tatum. He focused on Jeffrey, not looking at her. "You should get dressed. Half the Chicago PD is about to barge in."

"I can't," Zoe said, her voice tight, covering her chest with one arm. "You just turned my blouse into a bandage."

Tatum blinked at the shirt pressed against the blood. "Oh. Sorry." He cleared his throat. "It was a nice blouse."

CHAPTER 76

Quantico, Virginia, Monday, August 1, 2016

Zoe frowned, tapping her capped pen on her desk as she read her notes from Clifford Sorenson's interview for the third time. It was a shoddy job, and she was disappointed with herself. The interview had transpired only two days after Jeffrey had been arrested. Clifford was still in shock, the truth acidic and destructive. His own brother had killed his fiancée. Had kept her body in his home and molested it over and over while Clifford had been looking for her. Then he had used Clifford's business to find other victims. Used the van Clifford had provided to assist him in those murders.

He had been unfocused during the interview. Zoe wasn't sure if he had been drunk, stoned, or just overwhelmed. Her own questions had been basic, shallow.

She'd had an amazing opportunity here. Two men, sharing the same childhood. One had grown up to be a functioning member of society, with his own business and a meaningful relationship with a woman. The other, a serial killer. This could answer so many conundrums and questions about serial killers.

But Jeffrey was refusing to talk at the moment, and the only reason Clifford had talked to her was because he was still struggling to get a grip on reality.

This was about to slip from her fingers. She'd have to talk to Mancuso, get her to approve an extended trip back to Chicago. Or maybe they could transfer Jeffrey closer and interview Clifford on the phone? Would she be able to promise Jeffrey something in return for his cooperation? He seemed to have no interest in fame, unlike many other serial killers. What would make him talk?

She sighed, put her pen down, and leaned back. It probably wasn't a good time to ask Mancuso for anything, really.

There was a knock on the door to her office.

"Yeah?" she said.

The door opened, and Tatum stood in the doorway. "Hey," he said, smiling. "How are you feeling?"

"I'm fine," she said, her fingers brushing against her hip. Two of the stitches had popped during her charge into Laura Summer's home, and she'd had to get the wound resutured immediately after. They would remove the stitches in a few days, but Zoe insisted she was already healthy enough to go to work.

"Glad to hear it. I'm on my way to Mancuso. She said she wants to talk to me."

Zoe nodded grimly. "I just came back from there. She's . . . not happy. We had a long talk."

"But she didn't fire you, right?"

"Not yet." A grudging smile made it through to her mouth.

His grin widened. "Excellent. Well, I'll go see where she's shipping me. I heard there's good fishing near the field office in Alaska."

"Good luck," Zoe said, worried. She looked forward to working with Tatum, but she knew Mancuso might have to get rid of him to protect herself. She regretted not saying something about Tatum earlier. She could have told Mancuso it was all her doing, that Tatum had wanted to do things by the book this time. She doubted the chief would have believed her, but still . . .

"Thanks." He winked. "I'll drop by on my way out."

He closed the door, and Zoe stared at it, her heart heavy. She resolved to talk to Mancuso later. Perhaps she could still take the fall for Tatum.

Her phone rang, dancing on her desk. The ringtone was Rihanna's "Where Have You Been," Andrea's assigned ringtone. She picked up the mobile, answered the call.

"Hey," she said, feeling distracted.

"Did you see the story they published about you?" Andrea half asked, half shrieked.

"Mancuso mentioned it," Zoe said, turning the phone's volume down. "I haven't had a chance to read it yet."

"Holy crap, Zoe. You know I just searched your name online, and this story is quoted everywhere."

"Don't get excited. It'll die off very quickly."

"Two of my friends called me to ask if Zoe Bentley is really my sister," Andrea said. "They wanted autographs."

"That's idiotic," Zoe said. She began skimming her Sorenson interview again as Andrea droned on.

"I mean, you're famous, sis. Like, national news famous. It's crazy. A guy stopped me on the street today and wanted to know if you were my sister. Asked to take my picture."

"Yeah, right." Zoe laughed.

"Hey. You can shun your fame all you want, but I am cashing in. From now on, you can call me Andrea My-Sister-Is-Zoe-Can-I-Have-Free-Stuff Bentley."

"You coming over tonight?" Zoe asked.

"Nah. Got a late shift. But I'll probably drop by tomorrow."

"Okay. I'm not making anything fancy."

"That's fine. I'll cook dinner and drink your booze."

"Bye, Andrea."

"Bye."

She disconnected the phone and began reading the interview again, her mind elsewhere. She wondered how bad it was going for Tatum.

CHAPTER 77

Tatum sat comfortably in the chair of the condemned while Mancuso read a multipage report on her desk, pointedly ignoring him. Her lips were tight, and she flipped the pages sharply and angrily, as if the paper were hurling insults at her. Tatum suspected her rage had less to do with the report she was reading and more to do with him. Was he about to be transferred to another city again? Or kicked out of the bureau altogether? He couldn't rule it out. He glanced at the aquarium behind the chief, wondering if the fish could sense their owner's moods. All the fish were currently flocking in the farthest corner from the chief. Not a good omen.

He decided to prepare a complex facial expression. He knew a perfect recipe for angry managers. One-third atonement, one-third humbleness, and the rest divided in equal measures between good humor and sympathy. Serve cold, with a little lime and some apologies, not necessarily heartfelt.

Finally, Mancuso looked up at him.

"So," she said.

"Chief—"

"Shut up and listen."

Good. Probably for the best, since he had no follow-up.

"I talked to Martinez this morning. At length. You're goddamn lucky, Agent Gray. First of all, you're lucky that Jeffrey Alston survived and was placed under arrest. Second, you're lucky that Laura Summer gave a very long account of how you and Zoe saved her life and the life of her children and that you did the only thing you could do. Third, you're lucky because of this article." She rummaged in her drawer, pulled out a newspaper, and slammed it on the table. It was the *Chicago Daily Gazette.* The headline on the front page read, "Strangling Undertaker Arrested."

"It's a four-page article," Mancuso said.

"Oh." Tatum allowed himself a small grin. "So it says nice things about me?"

"Well," Mancuso said, "let's read the part about you together."

She scanned the article, flipping a page, and finally nodded. "There we go. 'Second to the scene was Agent Gray from the FBI.'"

Tatum waited. Mancuso folded the paper.

"That was it?" Tatum asked, shocked.

"Yes. It's one of the longest articles about the arrest. You can thank H. Barry for his glowing praise."

"It's a four-page article. That's all he wrote about me?"

"Not exactly. I rephrased a bit." Mancuso reopened the paper and turned it around so Tatum could see it. She pointed at the correct line. He read it.

"Second to the scene was Agent Dray . . . Agent *Dray*?" Tatum grabbed the paper and shook it, as if the typo would be corrected if jolted sufficiently.

"Reporter H. Barry received long interviews from Lieutenant Martinez, the Chicago chief of police, and me," Mancuso said. "And all of us wanted to . . . minimize the involvement of the FBI."

"There are"—he scanned the article—"two pages about Zoe here. And he got her name right."

"Yeah, but you'll notice he mentions her as a consultant and doesn't say who she worked for, so you see, everything turned out well."

Tatum put the paper on the desk, shrugging. "I don't get it. This is good press. Why would you want to minimize—"

"I don't *need* an article praising us," Mancuso said sharply. "Sure, it would have been nice, but next time a serial killer hits, do you think the police would call us? This business is full of inflated egos that bruise easily. I want this unit to have a solid reputation for *consulting*. We don't swoop in and take control, we don't conduct our own investigation under the police's nose, and we don't arrest the killer ourselves, nearly killing him in the process."

"Okay." Tatum raised his hands in surrender. "I don't care. I have no ego at all."

"Right," Mancuso said, grabbing the paper and shoving it into her drawer. She closed it silently this time.

"What happens with me now?"

"You go to your allocated desk, which I assume you have never even seen, and you compose some reports. I might want you to look at some cases later, give me your opinion."

Tatum chewed this over. "You're not transferring me?"

"Agent Gray, I'm not blind. I saw the work you did on this case. And while I don't approve of some of the methods you and Dr. Bentley employed, I think you could be a fantastic agent with the right guidance."

"And by 'right guidance,' you mean—"

"You do exactly as I say."

"Awesome."

"And quite frankly, you two make a good team. I was thinking of creating a small field task force for cases such as the last one. And you and Bentley . . . well. We'll see."

"Okay." Tatum felt unsettled by the progression of this meeting.

Mancuso read something on her desk and then raised her eyes. "Why are you still here?"

"Uh, right. I'll be off, then." He stood up and approached the door.

"Agent Gray."

He paused and looked back at her.

"There *won't* be a third chance."

CHAPTER 78

Zoe's apartment was silent as she fried some chopped carrots and peas in a wok. She enjoyed the quiet. She hadn't had much time for herself lately. Even when she had been alone these past weeks, she was always thinking about the case, turning it in her mind frantically, trying to piece together the puzzle. The stillness of her thoughts was soothing. She chopped the ginger and added it to the wok, the sharp smell filling the kitchen. Zoe breathed it in.

She was relieved Tatum was still assigned to the BAU. He was unclear about his current role in the unit, but it was fine. The thought of occasionally meeting him for lunch or running into him in the hallways made her feel warm and happy.

She stirred the vegetables a bit more and then tipped the wok's contents onto a plate, then emptied a bowl of rice into the wok, letting it fry and get a bit crunchy. As she stirred, she glanced at the newspaper lying beside the plate on the counter.

The front page had a picture of Jeffrey Alston handcuffed to his hospital bed, and next to it was a photo of her above one of Martinez. She shook her head in irritation and picked up the plate. She added the fried vegetables into the rice and stirred it all. Then she used a spoon to create a small hole in the middle of her fried rice. She cracked two eggs inside the hole and began scrambling them. Her phone rang again. The screen read *Harry Barry*.

She answered. "You have some nerve calling me after writing this ridiculous article."

"You don't like it? You're a hero."

"Half of it is completely taken out of context. Some claims are almost lies—"

"Embellishments, really."

"And you only told part of the story." She stirred the scrambled egg into the rice and the vegetables, her movements sharp and angry, resulting in some rice and carrot refugees on the floor.

"I write whatever is interesting to my readers."

"Yeah? Tatum was there too. Did you know that? Do you even know who he is?"

"Yeah, yeah. Listen, people don't care about FBI agents. They have FBI agents up the wazoo. People care about everyday heroes. Now, a profiler who has caught two serial killers, after encountering one when she was young—that's a real hero."

Zoe added soy and stirred. "Bullshit. And my job title is forensic psychologist."

"I prefer to keep it simple. Is this a good time to talk about my book deal?"

"What book deal?" She took the wok off the stove, imagining how it would feel to bash Harry's face with it.

"I've received a book deal to write about Zoe Bentley. Now, I have a few good stories about you, but I'd really be interested in some more."

"Go to hell."

"I'd like to point out that I didn't mention some things you probably preferred were left in the dark."

"Like what?"

"Like your theory that the serial killer in Chicago was the Maynard serial killer. Or like the fact that for some reason you were wearing nothing but your underwear when Jeffrey Alston was shot."

Zoe gritted her teeth.

"You can cowrite this book with me. You'll have final say on everything we put in. Or I can write a book about a profiler who shows her boobs to distract killers. It's really your—"

She hung up, seething. Trying to calm down, she transferred the rice from the wok to her plate. She poured herself a glass of red wine. Then she walked to the living room and sat down on the couch with the plate and the wine. She turned on the stereo. Beyoncé's album *I Am . . . Sasha Fierce* was in it. She skipped "If I Were a Boy," going straight to "Halo." As the claps began to accompany the music, she rocked her body in pleasure, taking a sip from the red wine. Beyoncé got her; that was for sure. She scooped some rice and put it in her mouth, closing her eyes. The leftover wine colored the taste of the ginger and rice as Beyoncé sang only for her.

Someone rang the doorbell. Annoyed, she put down the plate and the glass on the table and walked to the door.

She glanced through the peephole. A man in a courier uniform.

"Yeah?"

"Letter for you, ma'am."

She opened the door and glanced at the brown envelope in his hand, her heart sinking. She signed for it.

"Do you know who sent it?"

"No. I just got it from the central—"

"Yeah." She had tried to follow this path before, always ending in a dead end.

She closed the door and looked at the envelope. Maybe this time, she'd show it to Tatum. Maybe they could investigate it together. The thought made her smile, the envelope suddenly a lot less threatening. She tore it open. A gray tie, of course.

There was something else inside. A square laminated piece of paper. She pulled it out in trepidation.

Dread and horror crawled up her spine as she stared at the picture.

A guy stopped me on the street today and wanted to know if you were my sister. Asked to take my picture.

Andrea's face smiled at her from the printed selfie, her upper arm hugged by a grinning Rod Glover.

ACKNOWLEDGMENTS

This, like all my other books, would never have been written without the support of my wife, Liora. When I interrupt a conversation about our children's education by asking her if she thinks an embalmed body would be flexible enough to pose, she does not flinch or search for a good divorce lawyer. Instead, she brainstorms with me. We create a better story together. *Then* we resume talking about our children's education. This book, specifically, was plotted during our vacation, and she spent much of it talking about serial killers.

Christine Mancuso provided invaluable comments that helped shape this novel to be sharper and more engaging. She keeps telling me to let the readers feel as if they're really experiencing the events of the book from the characters' eyes, and she always points out the sections where I fail to do just that. One day, I'll learn.

Elayne Morgan wrestled with and edited this book's first draft, with its endless grammar mistakes and plot holes, and came out winning.

Thanks to Jessica Tribble for giving this book its chance and for her awesome editorial notes. Zoe's past was a mess before her notes. It is still a mess, but it's a mess by design, not by accident.

Bryon Quertermous, my developmental editor, made this book much better by singling out the story's weaknesses and clobbering them with his editor's pen. The book's ending was a sad caterpillar when

Bryon first approached it, and it turned into a bloody, violent butterfly by the time he was done.

Stephanie Chou received the final draft and demonstrated that "final" is a relative term, her sharp editor's eye correcting numerous mistakes and inconsistencies.

Thanks to Sarah Hershman, my agent, for believing in my book, for pushing it forward, and for giving it this magnificent chance.

Thanks to Richard Stockford, the retired chief of the Bangor Police Department, who answered all of my questions with the patience and diligence of a saint.

Robert K. Ressler wrote the book *Whoever Fights Monsters*, which is mentioned in this book. It was instrumental to my knowledge, and to this novel, more than anything else I found in my research.

Thanks to all of the authors in Author's Corner for being there every step of the way, giving me endless, much-needed advice, cheering me on, and helping me when I needed them the most.

Thanks to my parents for both their invaluable advice and their endless support.

ABOUT THE AUTHOR

Mike Omer has been a journalist, a game developer, and the CEO of Loadingames, but he can currently be found penning the next in his series of thrillers featuring forensic psychologist Zoe Bentley. Omer loves to write about two things: real people who could be the perpetrators or victims of crimes—and funny stuff. He mixes these two loves quite passionately into his often-macabre, suspenseful mysteries. Omer is married to a woman who diligently forces him to live his dream, and he is father to an angel, a pixie, and a gremlin. He has two voracious hounds that wag their tails quite menacingly at anyone who dares approach his home. Learn more by emailing him at mike@strangerealm.com.